Betty & Veronica®

SENIOR YEAR

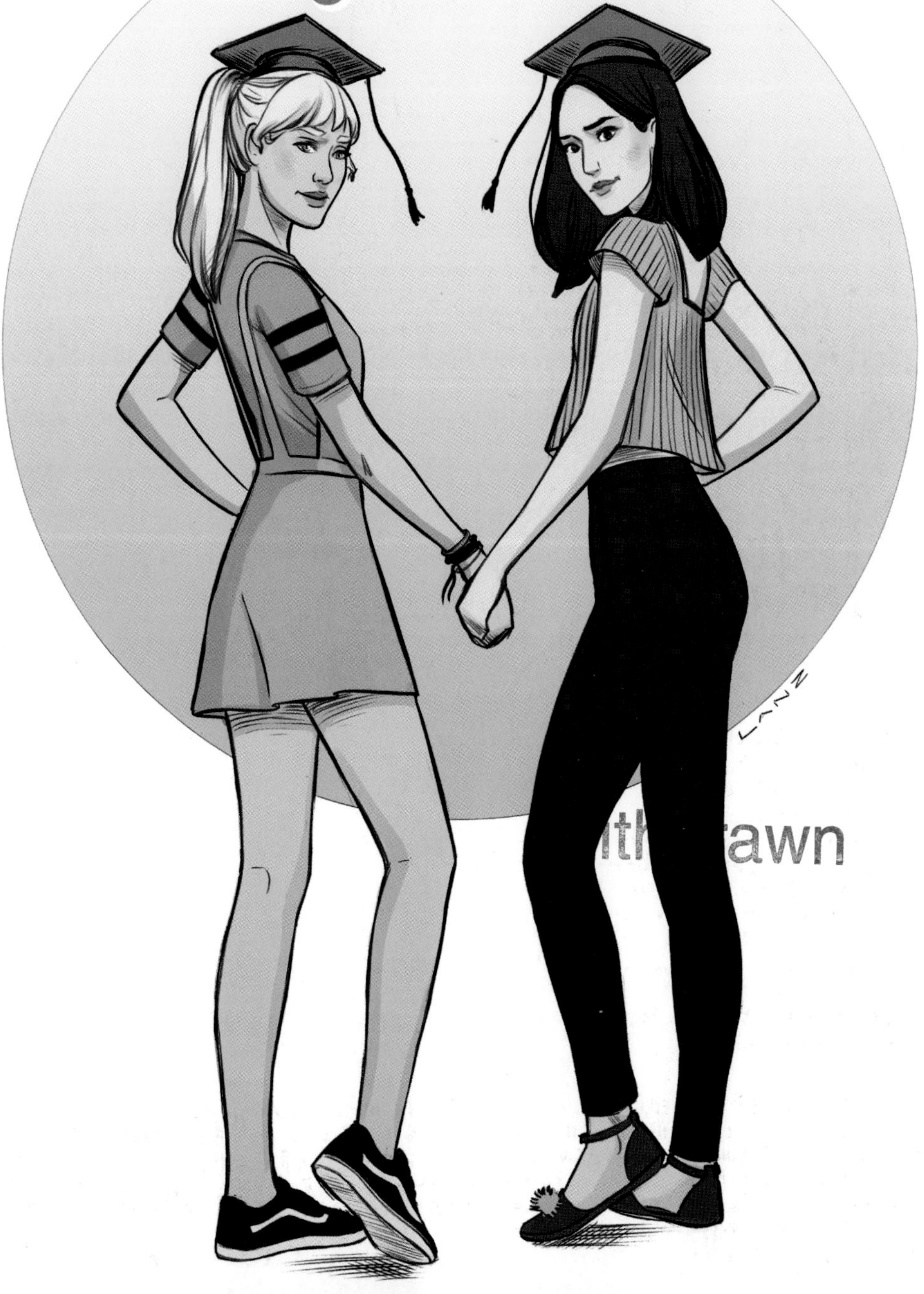
LANZ

STORY BY
JAMIE LEE ROTANTE

ART BY
SANDRA LANZ

LETTERING BY
JACK MORELLI

COLORS BY
KELLY FITZPATRICK

EDITORS
**ALEX SEGURA
& VINCENT LOVALLO**
ASSISTANT EDITOR
STEPHEN OSWALD

GRAPHIC DESIGN BY
KARI McLACHLAN

EDITOR-IN-CHIEF
VICTOR GORELICK

PUBLISHER
JON GOLDWATER

Betty & Veronica
SENIOR YEAR

Betty and Veronica have been through a lot in their over seven decades of existence. The perennial-teenagers have survived a zombie apocalypse, developed their futures in alternate timelines where they both marry the same red-headed, freckle-faced love, hunted werewolves, became immortal creatures of the night and even started their very own all-girl biker gang (that might be one of my favorite scenarios, but what can I say? I'm a little biased).

But there's one thing they haven't experienced... their senior year of high school. I know, pretty crazy, right? We've seen Betty and Veronica as children, we've seen them as freshmen in high school, and we've seen them as adults—but we've never taken a close look at the two of them on the verge of leaving the hallowed halls of Riverdale High School.

The transition from high school to college is arguably one of the most challenging times in any teenager's life. You're juggling homework, college applications, and extra-curricular activities while also trying to savor every moment with your friends. Being on the cusp of adulthood brings with it so many challenges and questions—what do you want to be when you grow up? What does the future have in store for you? Who are you and who

do you want to be? So much pressure is placed on teens' shoulders and it's important to recognize that and shine a light on what teenagers all over the world go through, especially at this crucial time in their lives.

But, first and foremost, this is a book about Betty and Veronica. Every teen worries that college and adulthood might drive a wedge between themselves and their friends, but that's not always the case. And not all friendships are perfect; they go through rough patches, difficult situations and sometimes people get in the way—but the best friendships will always be defined by how strong each person is after going through those hardships.

And if Betty and Veronica can still be friends after fighting over the same boy for 75 years, battling zombies, witches, werewolves, vampires and biker gangs—I think it's safe to say that college won't be an obstacle. And I, for one, am looking forward to seeing what the future has in store for the BFFs.

JAMIE LEE ROTANTE
Writer

01

STORY BY
JAMIE LEE ROTANTE

ART BY
SANDRA LANZ

LETTERING BY
JACK MORELLI

COLORS BY
KELLY FITZPATRICK

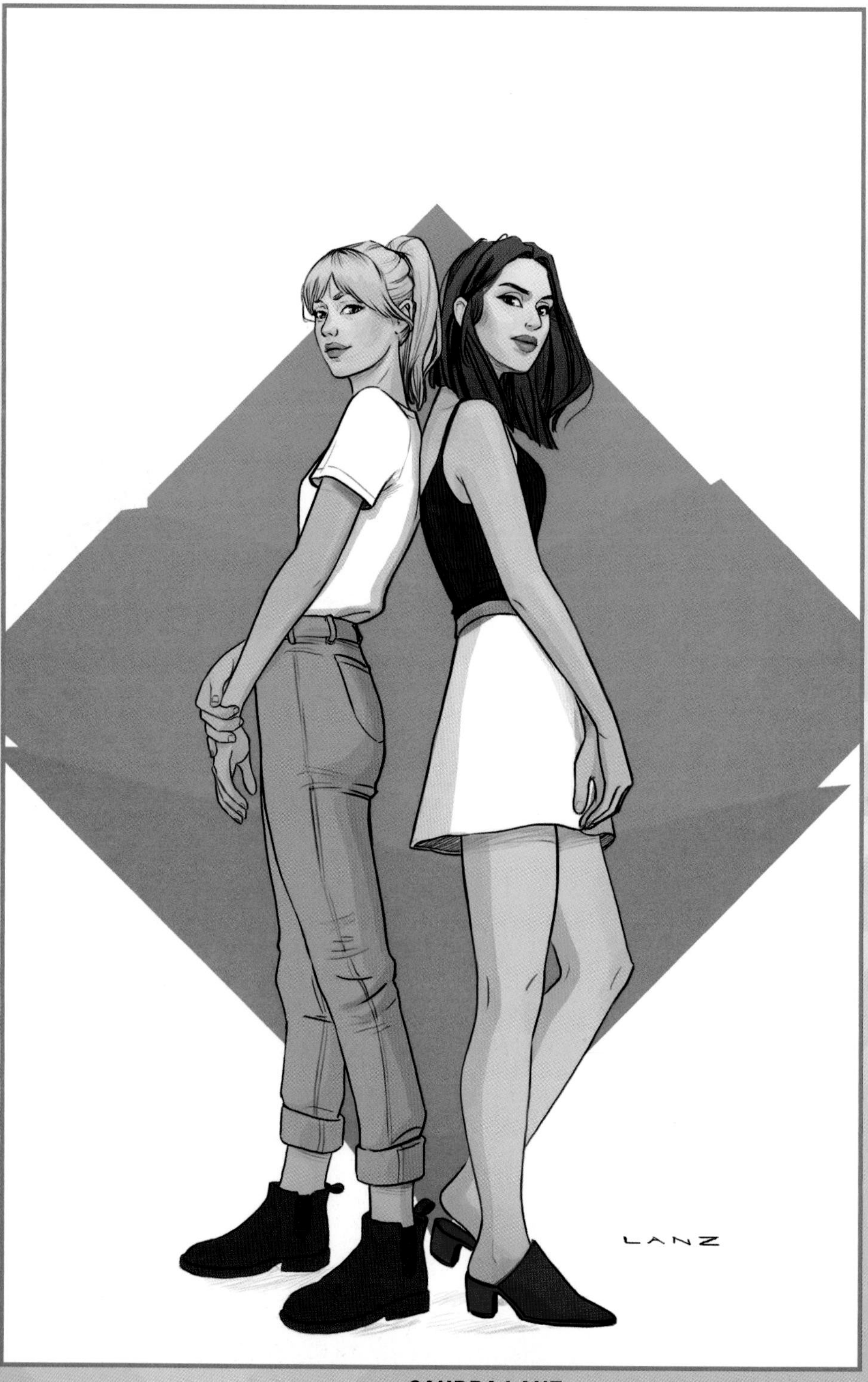
LANZ

COVER ART: **SANDRA LANZ**

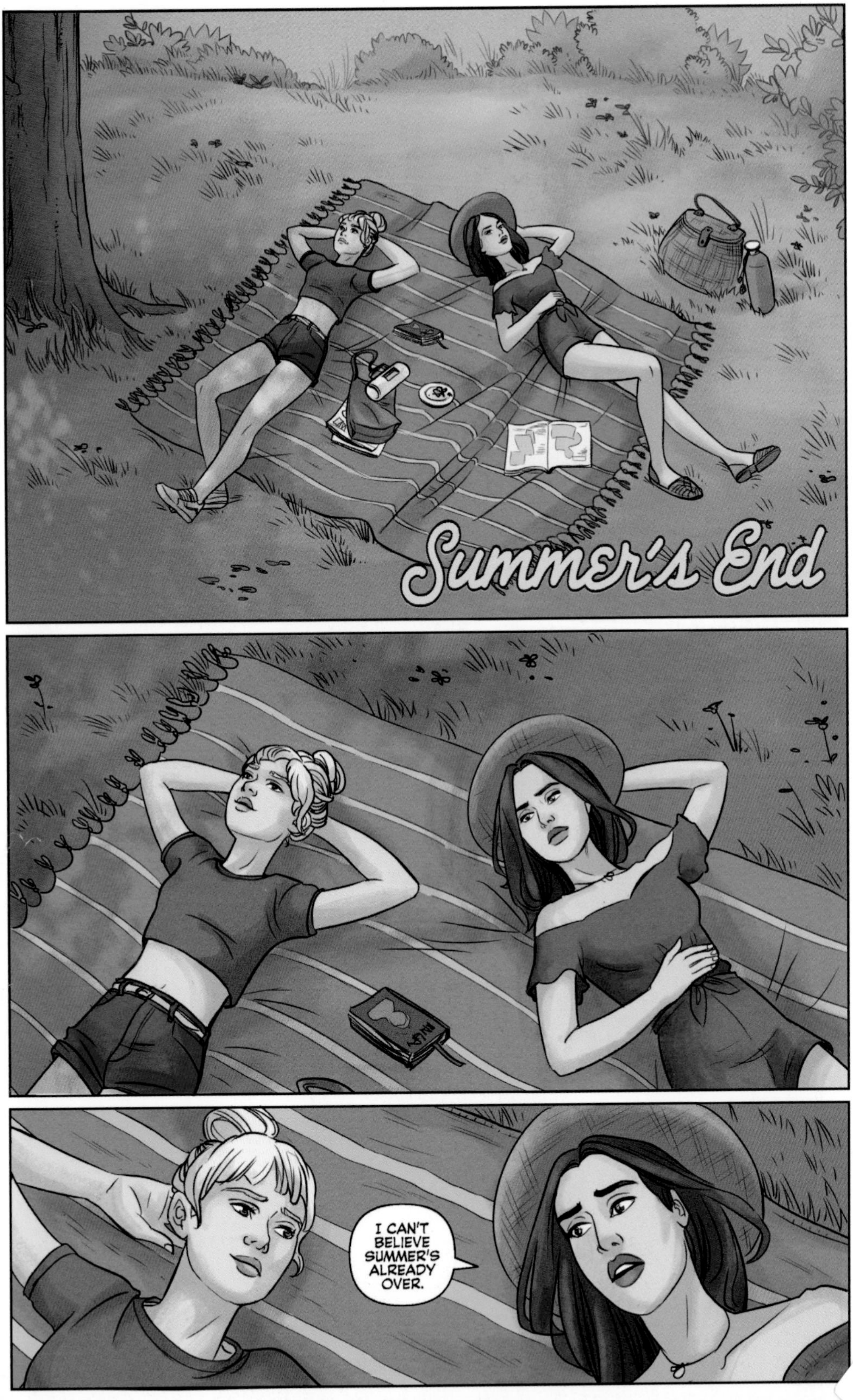
Summer's End
I CAN'T BELIEVE SUMMER'S ALREADY OVER.

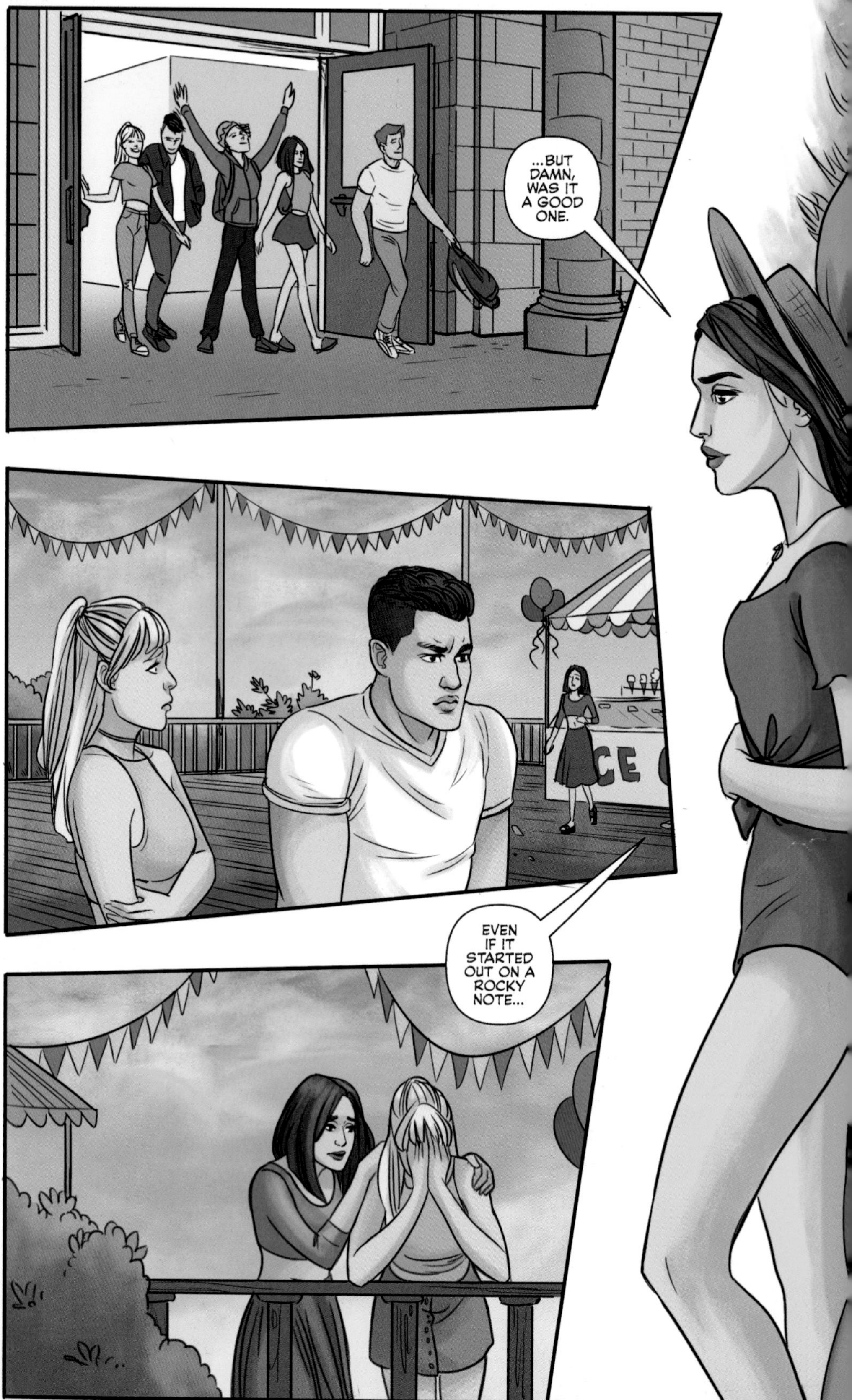
...BUT DAMN, WAS IT A GOOD ONE.
EVEN IF IT STARTED OUT ON A ROCKY NOTE...
CE

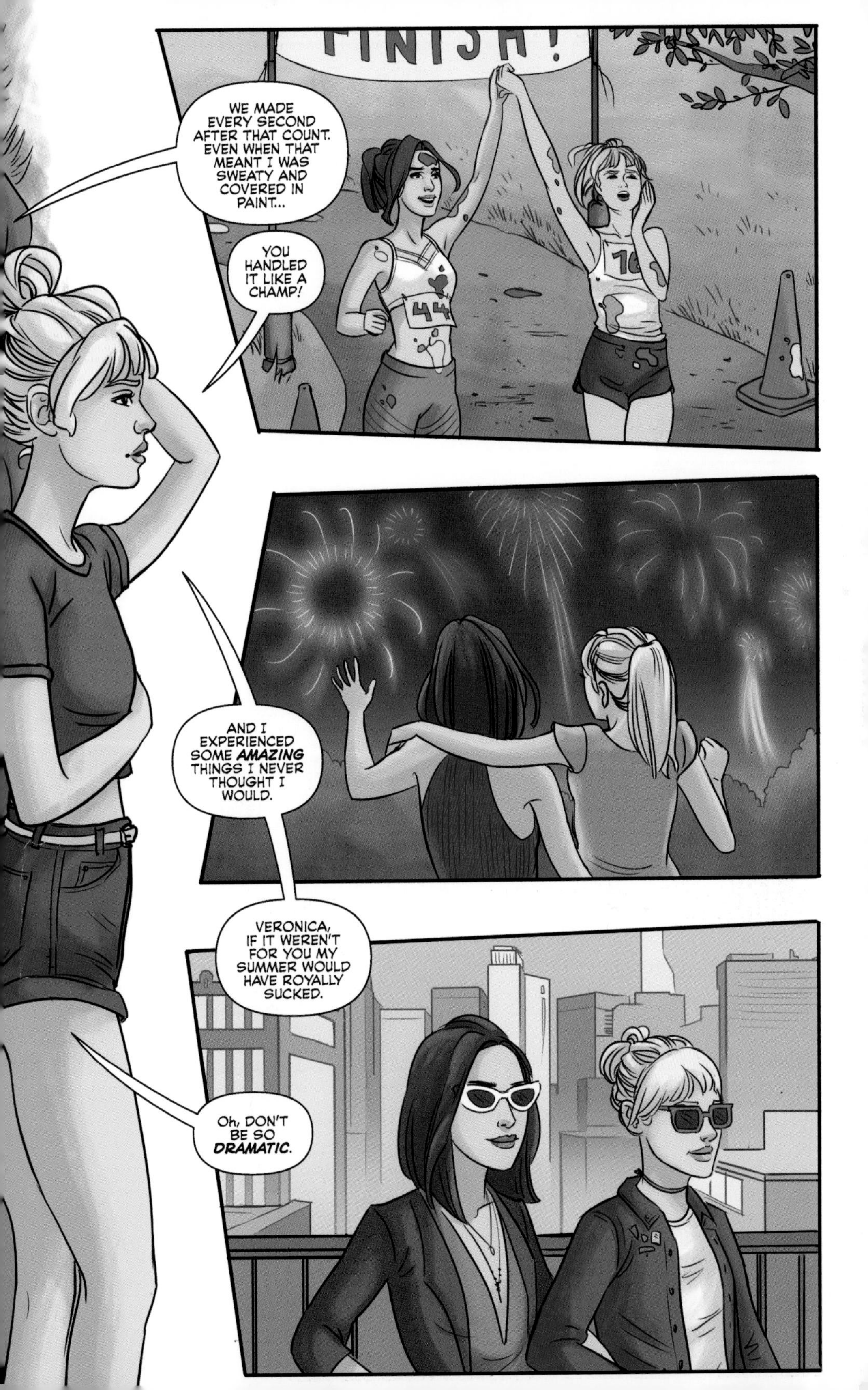
FINISH!
WE MADE EVERY SECOND AFTER THAT COUNT. EVEN WHEN THAT MEANT I WAS SWEATY AND COVERED IN PAINT...
YOU HANDLED IT LIKE A CHAMP!
44
76
AND I EXPERIENCED SOME AMAZING THINGS I NEVER THOUGHT I WOULD.
VERONICA, IF IT WEREN'T FOR YOU MY SUMMER WOULD HAVE ROYALLY SUCKED.
Oh, DON'T BE SO DRAMATIC.

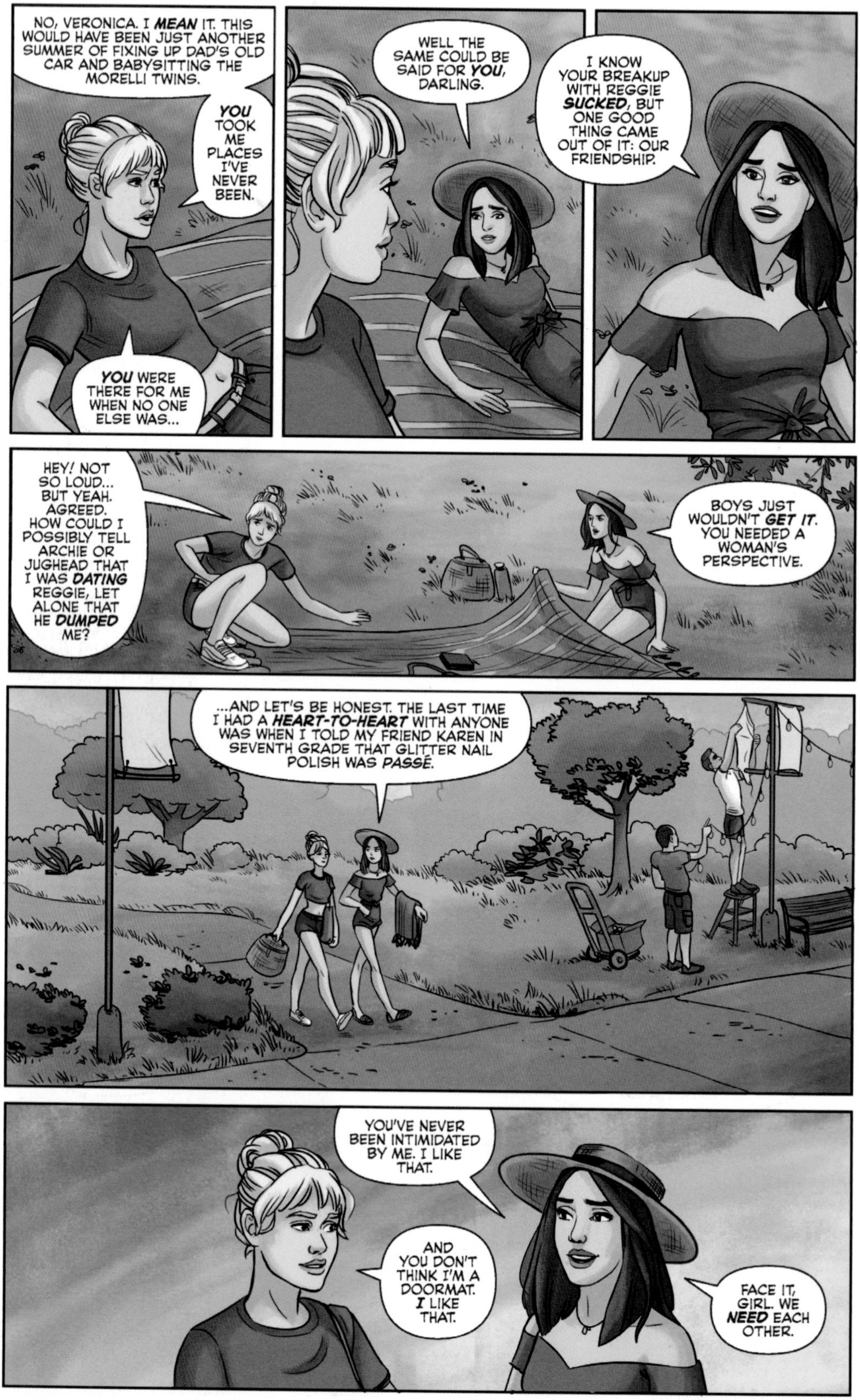
NO, VERONICA. I MEAN IT. THIS WOULD HAVE BEEN JUST ANOTHER SUMMER OF FIXING UP DAD'S OLD CAR AND BABYSITTING THE MORELLI TWINS.
YOU TOOK ME PLACES I'VE NEVER BEEN.
YOU WERE THERE FOR ME WHEN NO ONE ELSE WAS...
WELL THE SAME COULD BE SAID FOR YOU, DARLING.
I KNOW YOUR BREAKUP WITH REGGIE SUCKED, BUT ONE GOOD THING CAME OUT OF IT: OUR FRIENDSHIP.
HEY! NOT SO LOUD... BUT YEAH. AGREED. HOW COULD I POSSIBLY TELL ARCHIE OR JUGHEAD THAT I WAS DATING REGGIE, LET ALONE THAT HE DUMPED ME?
BOYS JUST WOULDN'T GET IT. YOU NEEDED A WOMAN'S PERSPECTIVE.
...AND LET'S BE HONEST. THE LAST TIME I HAD A HEART-TO-HEART WITH ANYONE WAS WHEN I TOLD MY FRIEND KAREN IN SEVENTH GRADE THAT GLITTER NAIL POLISH WAS PASSÉ.
YOU'VE NEVER BEEN INTIMIDATED BY ME. I LIKE THAT.
AND YOU DON'T THINK I'M A DOORMAT. I LIKE THAT.
FACE IT, GIRL. WE NEED EACH OTHER.

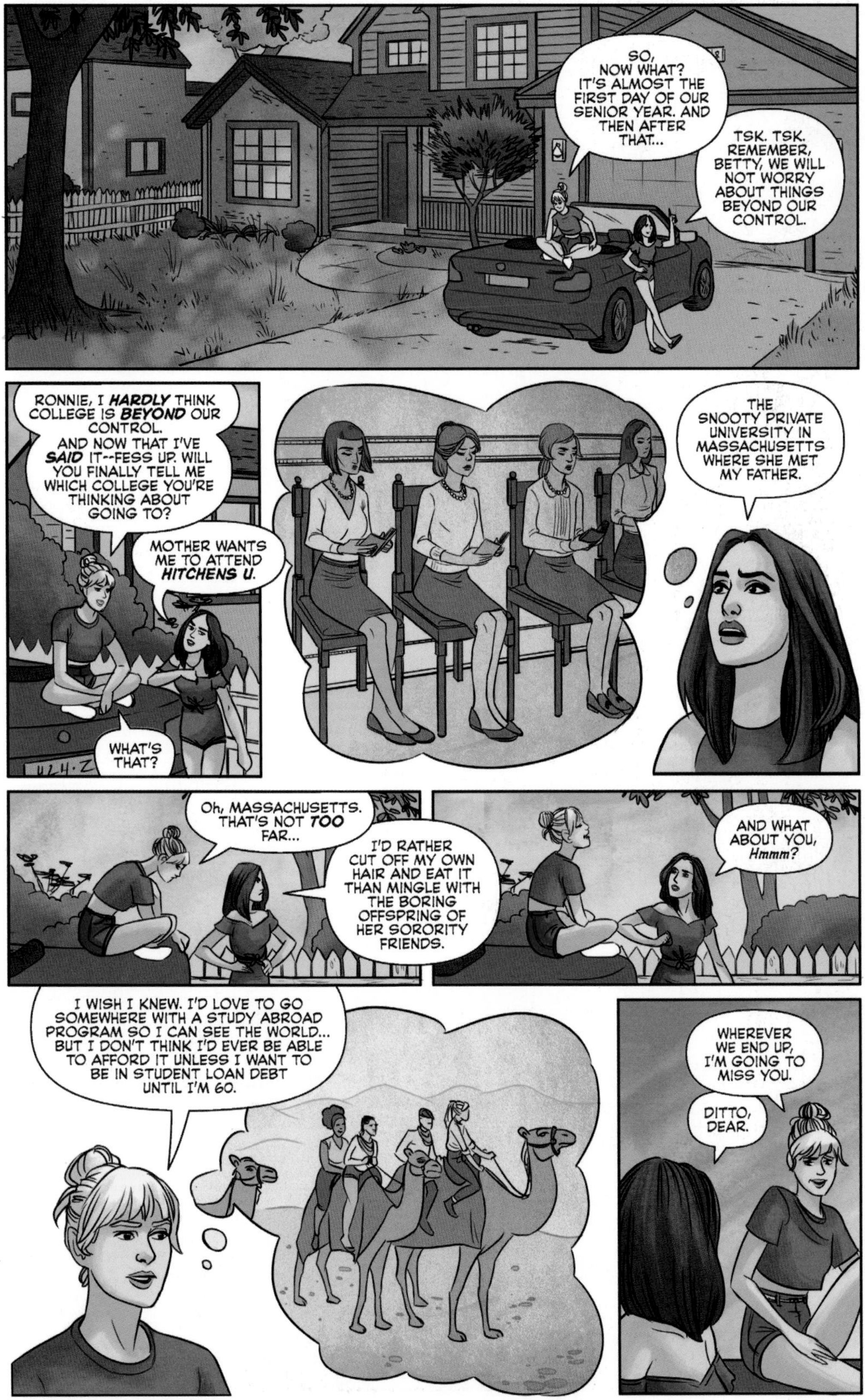
SO, NOW WHAT? IT'S ALMOST THE FIRST DAY OF OUR SENIOR YEAR. AND THEN AFTER THAT...
TSK. TSK. REMEMBER, BETTY, WE WILL NOT WORRY ABOUT THINGS BEYOND OUR CONTROL.
RONNIE, I HARDLY THINK COLLEGE IS BEYOND OUR CONTROL. AND NOW THAT I'VE SAID IT--FESS UP. WILL YOU FINALLY TELL ME WHICH COLLEGE YOU'RE THINKING ABOUT GOING TO?
MOTHER WANTS ME TO ATTEND HITCHENS U.
WHAT'S THAT?
THE SNOOTY PRIVATE UNIVERSITY IN MASSACHUSETTS WHERE SHE MET MY FATHER.
Oh, MASSACHUSETTS. THAT'S NOT TOO FAR...
I'D RATHER CUT OFF MY OWN HAIR AND EAT IT THAN MINGLE WITH THE BORING OFFSPRING OF HER SORORITY FRIENDS.
AND WHAT ABOUT YOU, Hmmm?
I WISH I KNEW. I'D LOVE TO GO SOMEWHERE WITH A STUDY ABROAD PROGRAM SO I CAN SEE THE WORLD... BUT I DON'T THINK I'D EVER BE ABLE TO AFFORD IT UNLESS I WANT TO BE IN STUDENT LOAN DEBT UNTIL I'M 60.
WHEREVER WE END UP, I'M GOING TO MISS YOU.
DITTO, DEAR.

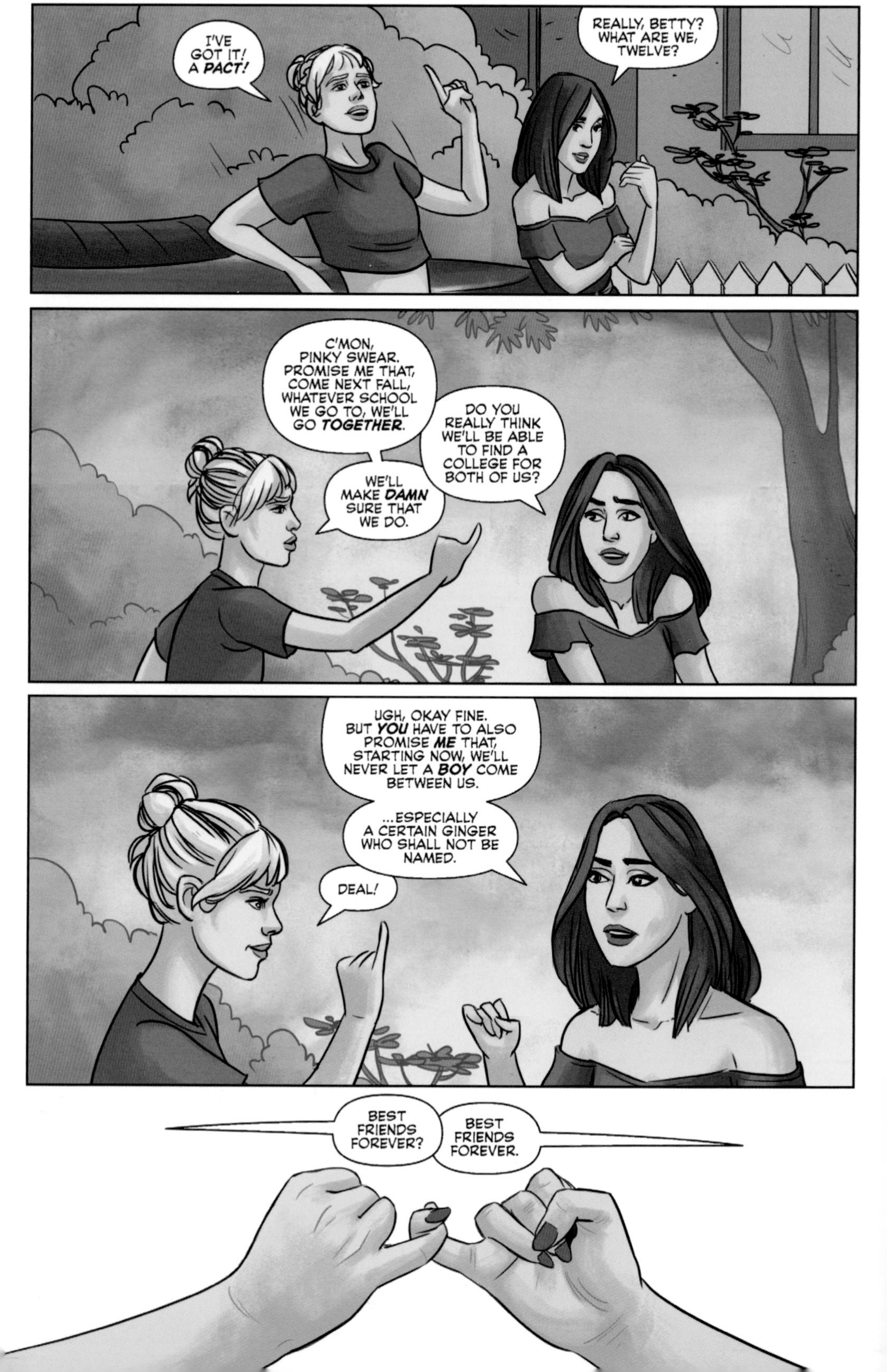
I'VE GOT IT! A PACT!
REALLY, BETTY? WHAT ARE WE, TWELVE?
C'MON, PINKY SWEAR. PROMISE ME THAT, COME NEXT FALL, WHATEVER SCHOOL WE GO TO, WE'LL GO TOGETHER.
DO YOU REALLY THINK WE'LL BE ABLE TO FIND A COLLEGE FOR BOTH OF US?
WE'LL MAKE DAMN SURE THAT WE DO.
UGH, OKAY FINE. BUT YOU HAVE TO ALSO PROMISE ME THAT, STARTING NOW, WE'LL NEVER LET A BOY COME BETWEEN US.
...ESPECIALLY A CERTAIN GINGER WHO SHALL NOT BE NAMED.
DEAL!
BEST FRIENDS FOREVER?
BEST FRIENDS FOREVER.

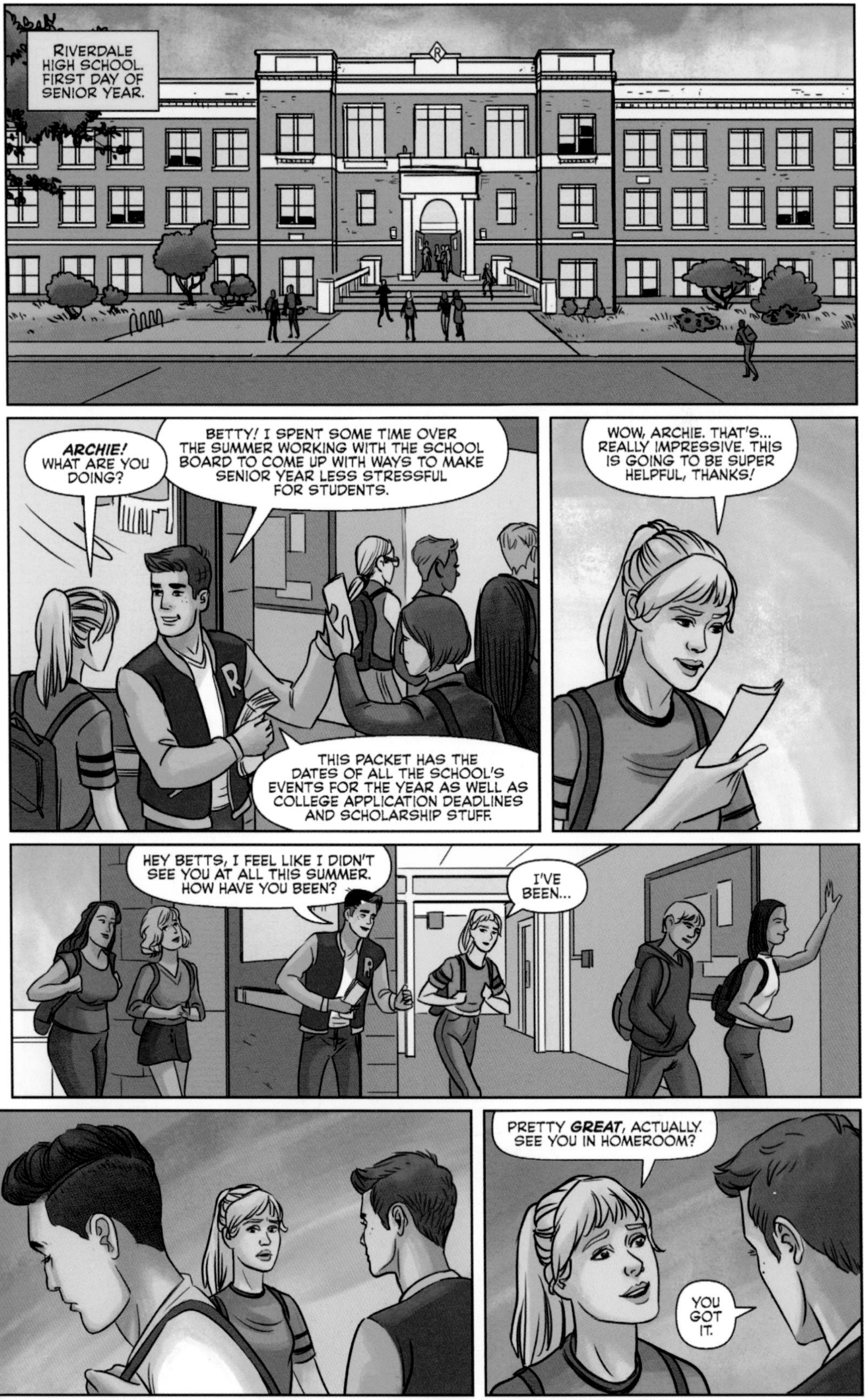
RIVERDALE HIGH SCHOOL. FIRST DAY OF SENIOR YEAR.
ARCHIE! WHAT ARE YOU DOING?
BETTY! I SPENT SOME TIME OVER THE SUMMER WORKING WITH THE SCHOOL BOARD TO COME UP WITH WAYS TO MAKE SENIOR YEAR LESS STRESSFUL FOR STUDENTS.
THIS PACKET HAS THE DATES OF ALL THE SCHOOL'S EVENTS FOR THE YEAR AS WELL AS COLLEGE APPLICATION DEADLINES AND SCHOLARSHIP STUFF.
WOW, ARCHIE. THAT'S... REALLY IMPRESSIVE. THIS IS GOING TO BE SUPER HELPFUL, THANKS!
HEY BETTS, I FEEL LIKE I DIDN'T SEE YOU AT ALL THIS SUMMER. HOW HAVE YOU BEEN?
I'VE BEEN...
PRETTY GREAT, ACTUALLY. SEE YOU IN HOMEROOM?
YOU GOT IT.

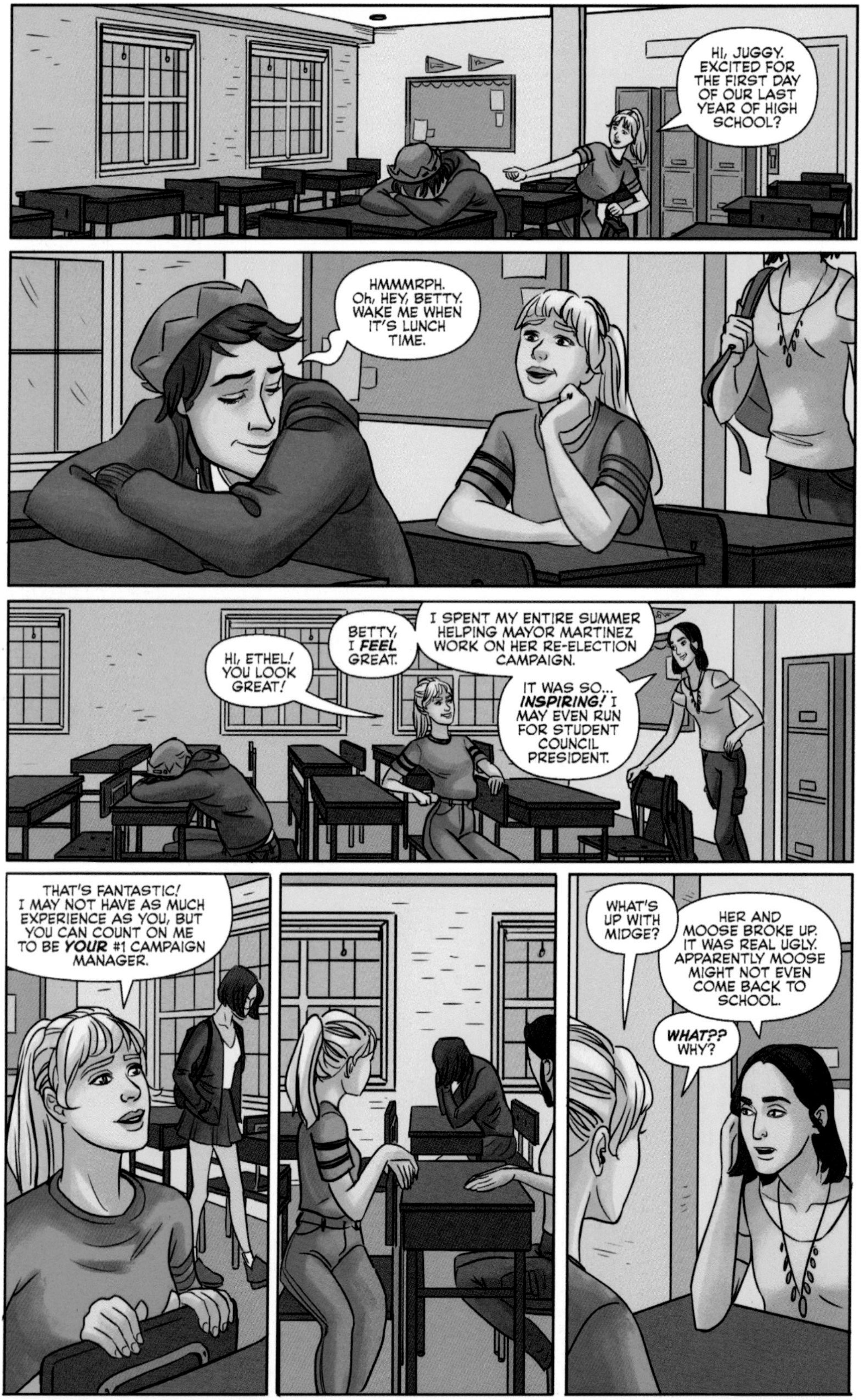
HI, JUGGY. EXCITED FOR THE FIRST DAY OF OUR LAST YEAR OF HIGH SCHOOL?
HMMMRPH. Oh, HEY, BETTY. WAKE ME WHEN IT'S LUNCH TIME.
HI, ETHEL! YOU LOOK GREAT!
BETTY, I FEEL GREAT.
I SPENT MY ENTIRE SUMMER HELPING MAYOR MARTINEZ WORK ON HER RE-ELECTION CAMPAIGN.
IT WAS SO... INSPIRING! I MAY EVEN RUN FOR STUDENT COUNCIL PRESIDENT.
THAT'S FANTASTIC! I MAY NOT HAVE AS MUCH EXPERIENCE AS YOU, BUT YOU CAN COUNT ON ME TO BE YOUR #1 CAMPAIGN MANAGER.
WHAT'S UP WITH MIDGE?
HER AND MOOSE BROKE UP. IT WAS REAL UGLY. APPARENTLY MOOSE MIGHT NOT EVEN COME BACK TO SCHOOL.
WHAT?? WHY?

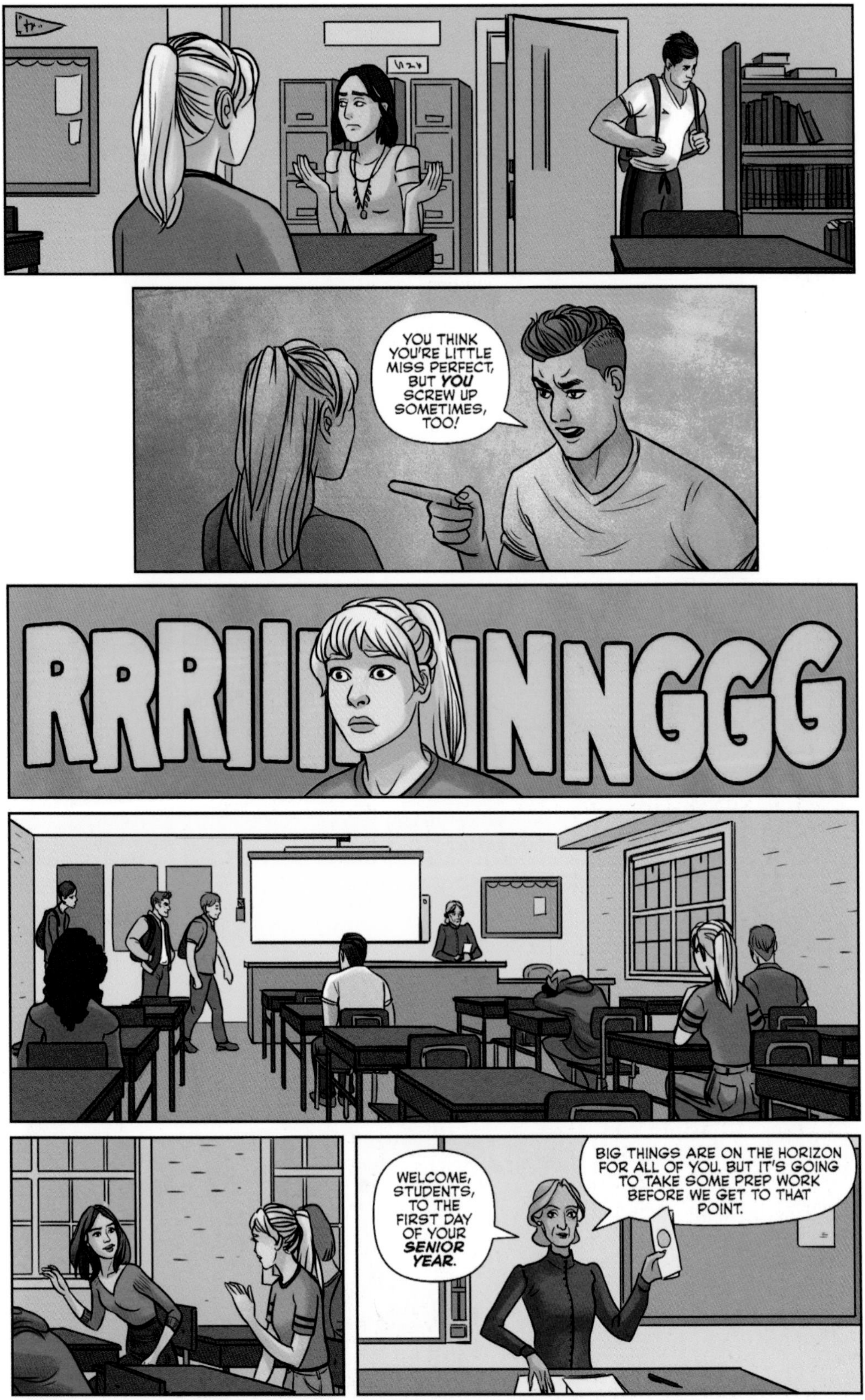
YOU THINK YOU'RE LITTLE MISS PERFECT, BUT *YOU* SCREW UP SOMETIMES, TOO!
RRRIIIIINNGGG
WELCOME, STUDENTS, TO THE FIRST DAY OF YOUR ***SENIOR YEAR***.
BIG THINGS ARE ON THE HORIZON FOR ALL OF YOU. BUT IT'S GOING TO TAKE SOME PREP WORK BEFORE WE GET TO THAT POINT.

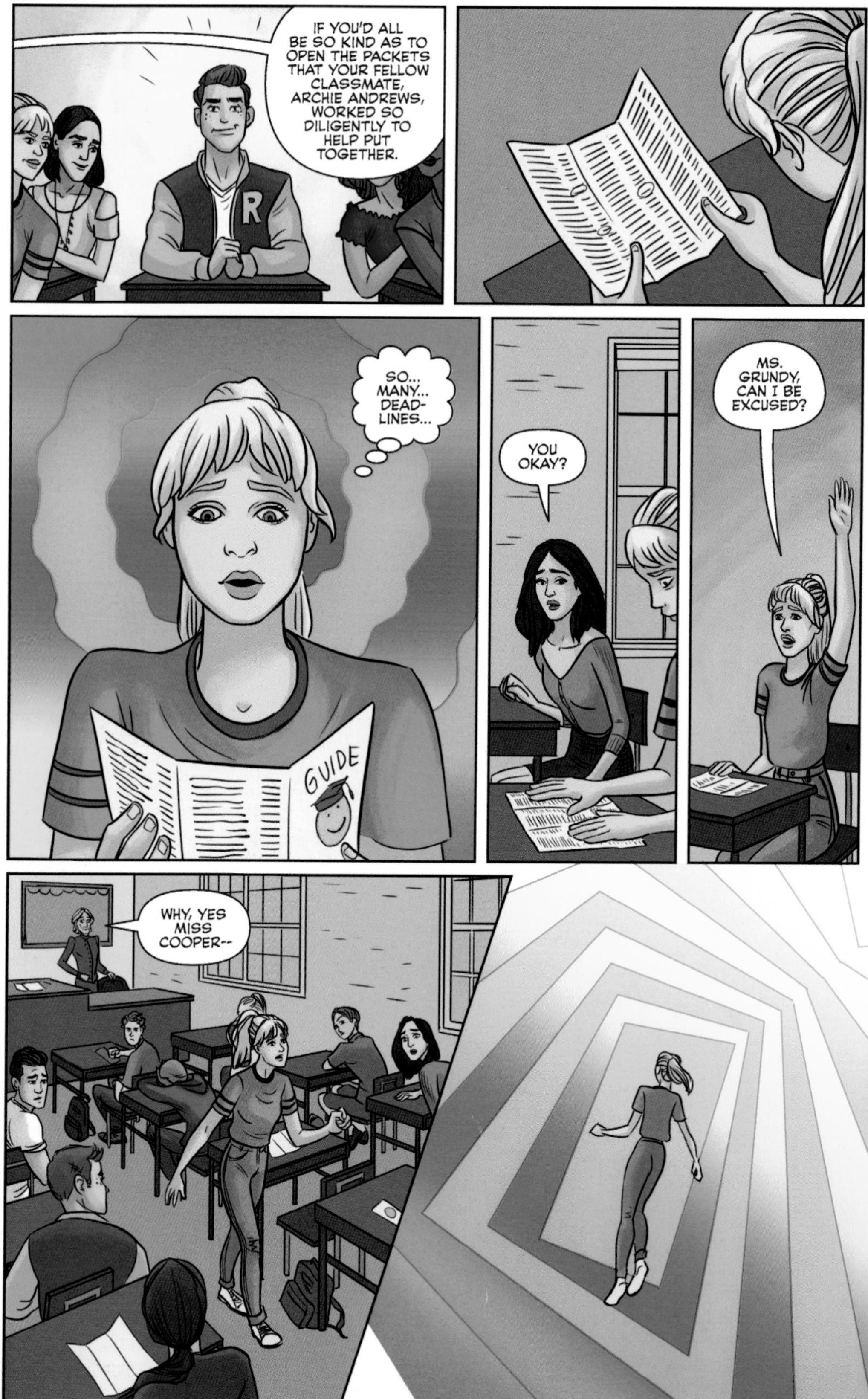
IF YOU'D ALL BE SO KIND AS TO OPEN THE PACKETS THAT YOUR FELLOW CLASSMATE, ARCHIE ANDREWS, WORKED SO DILIGENTLY TO HELP PUT TOGETHER.
SO... MANY... DEAD-LINES...
GUIDE
YOU OKAY?
MS. GRUNDY, CAN I BE EXCUSED?
WHY, YES MISS COOPER--

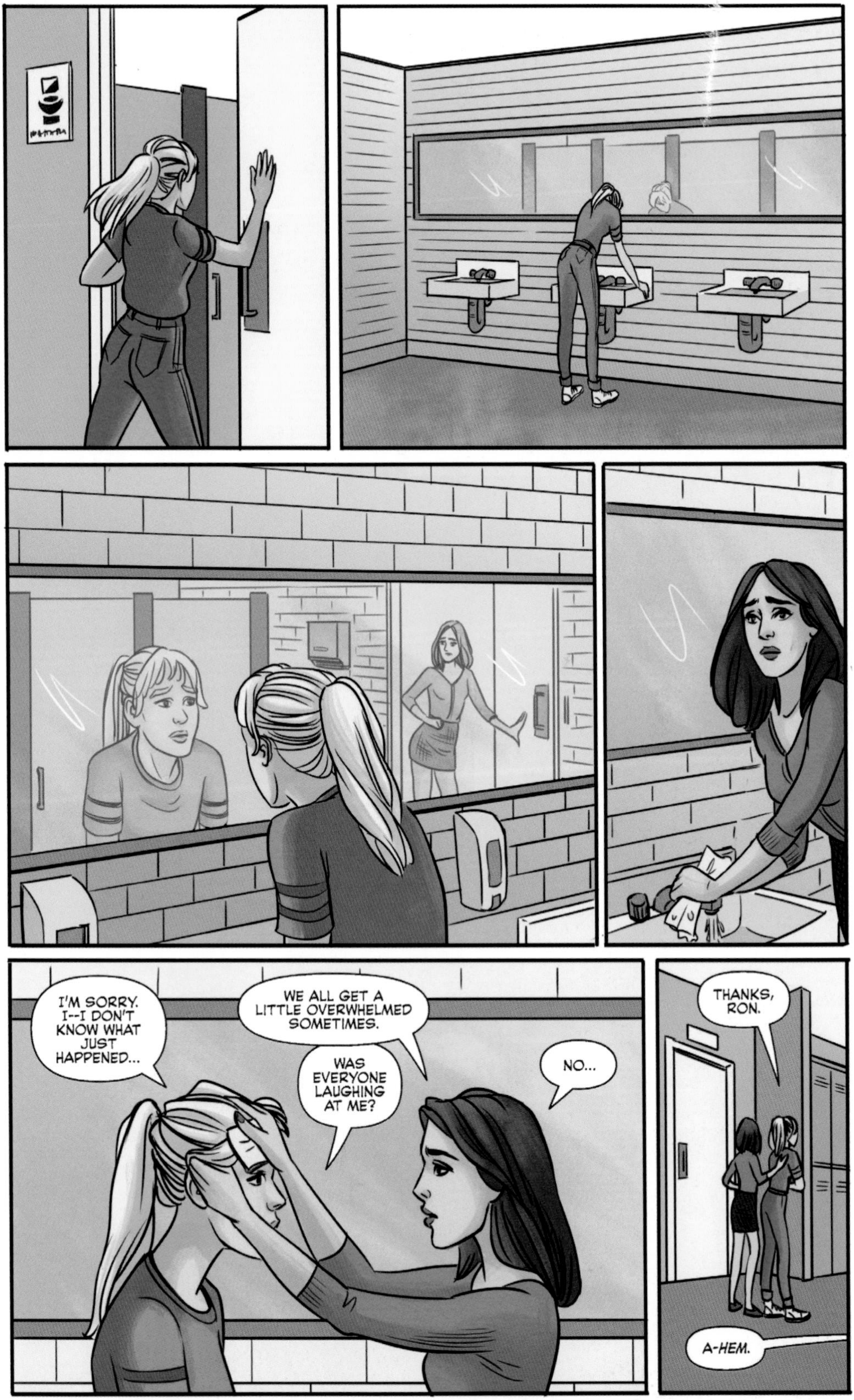

I'M SORRY. I--I DON'T KNOW WHAT JUST HAPPENED...
WE ALL GET A LITTLE OVERWHELMED SOMETIMES.
WAS EVERYONE LAUGHING AT ME?
NO...
THANKS, RON.
A-HEM.

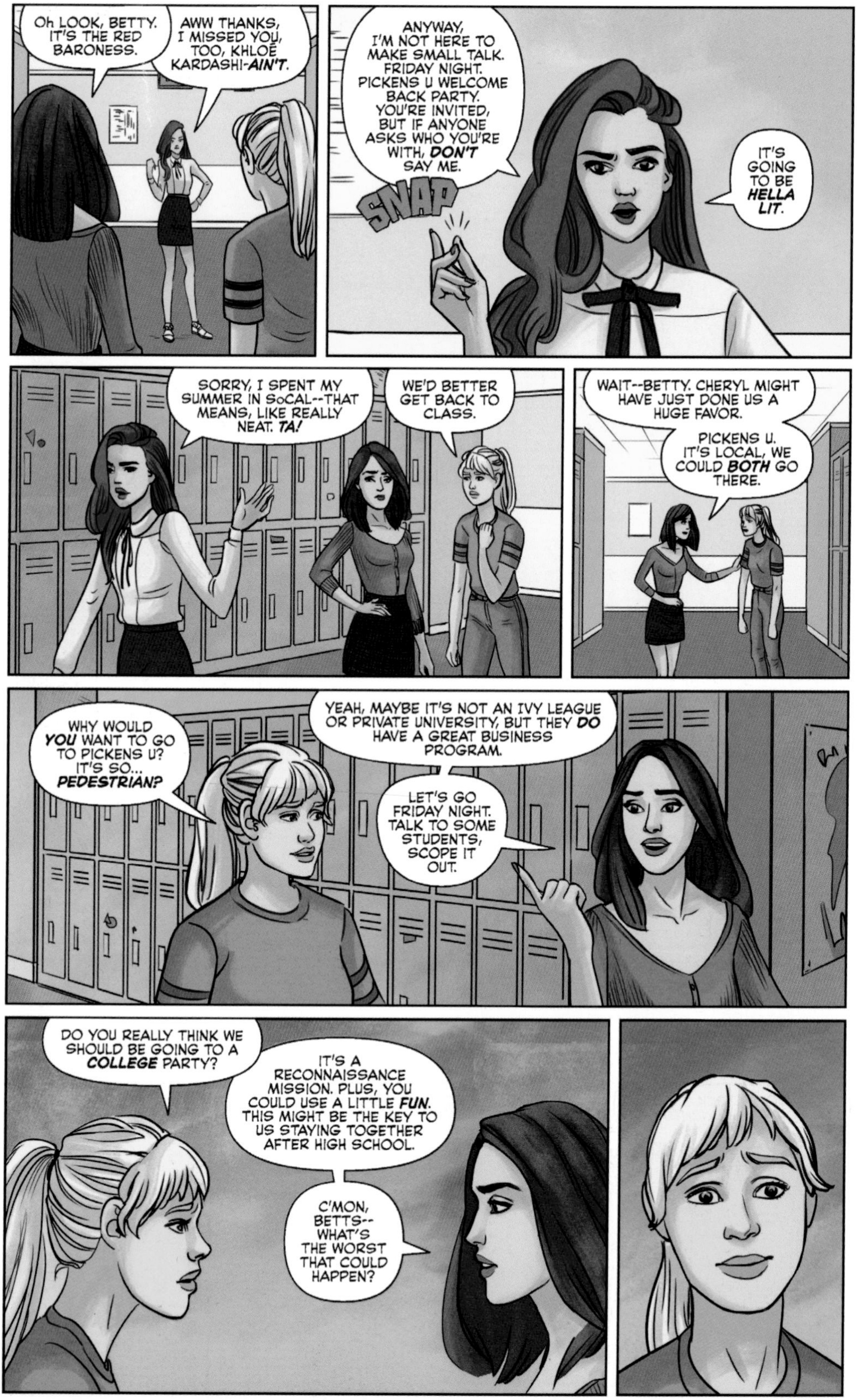

Oh LOOK, BETTY. IT'S THE RED BARONESS.
AWW THANKS, I MISSED YOU, TOO, KHLOÉ KARDASHI-**AIN'T**.
ANYWAY, I'M NOT HERE TO MAKE SMALL TALK. FRIDAY NIGHT. PICKENS U WELCOME BACK PARTY. YOU'RE INVITED, BUT IF ANYONE ASKS WHO YOU'RE WITH, **DON'T** SAY ME.
SNAP
IT'S GOING TO BE **HELLA LIT**.
SORRY, I SPENT MY SUMMER IN SoCAL--THAT MEANS, LIKE REALLY NEAT. **TA!**
WE'D BETTER GET BACK TO CLASS.
WAIT--BETTY. CHERYL MIGHT HAVE JUST DONE US A HUGE FAVOR.
PICKENS U. IT'S LOCAL, WE COULD **BOTH** GO THERE.
WHY WOULD **YOU** WANT TO GO TO PICKENS U? IT'S SO... **PEDESTRIAN?**
YEAH, MAYBE IT'S NOT AN IVY LEAGUE OR PRIVATE UNIVERSITY, BUT THEY **DO** HAVE A GREAT BUSINESS PROGRAM.
LET'S GO FRIDAY NIGHT. TALK TO SOME STUDENTS, SCOPE IT OUT.
DO YOU REALLY THINK WE SHOULD BE GOING TO A **COLLEGE** PARTY?
IT'S A RECONNAISSANCE MISSION. PLUS, YOU COULD USE A LITTLE **FUN**. THIS MIGHT BE THE KEY TO US STAYING TOGETHER AFTER HIGH SCHOOL.
C'MON, BETTS--WHAT'S THE WORST THAT COULD HAPPEN?

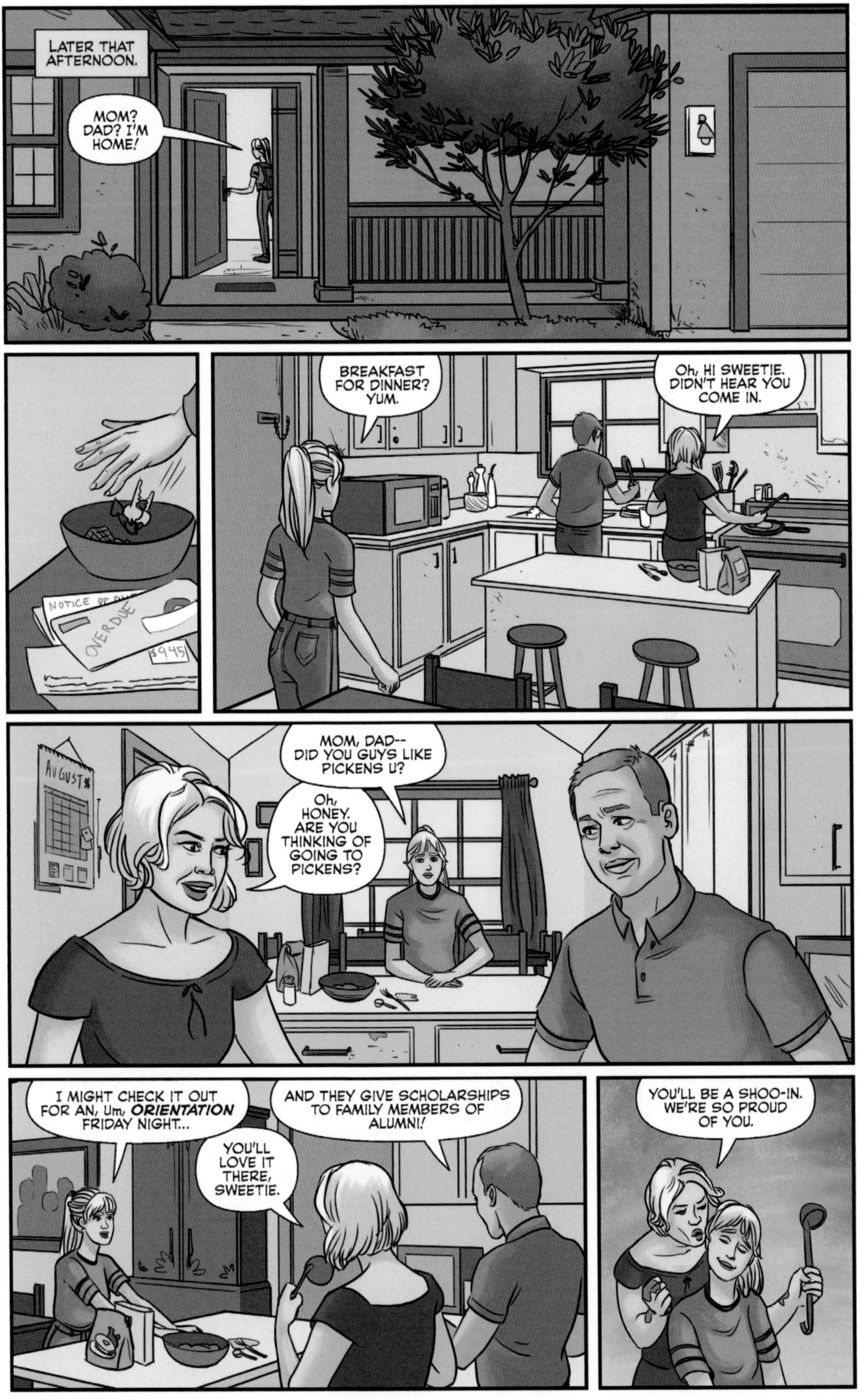
LATER THAT AFTERNOON.
MOM? DAD? I'M HOME!
OVERDUE
$945
BREAKFAST FOR DINNER? YUM.
Oh, HI SWEETIE. DIDN'T HEAR YOU COME IN.
AUGUST
MOM, DAD-- DID YOU GUYS LIKE PICKENS U?
Oh, HONEY. ARE YOU THINKING OF GOING TO PICKENS?
I MIGHT CHECK IT OUT FOR AN, Um, ORIENTATION FRIDAY NIGHT...
YOU'LL LOVE IT THERE, SWEETIE.
AND THEY GIVE SCHOLARSHIPS TO FAMILY MEMBERS OF ALUMNI!
YOU'LL BE A SHOO-IN. WE'RE SO PROUD OF YOU.

MEANWHILE. LODGE MANOR.

HELLO, MOTHER.

HELLO, SWEETHEART. HOW WAS YOUR FIRST DAY?

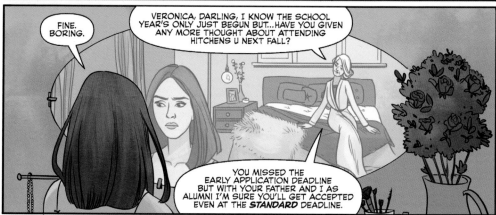

FINE. BORING.

VERONICA, DARLING, I KNOW THE SCHOOL YEAR'S ONLY JUST BEGUN BUT...HAVE YOU GIVEN ANY MORE THOUGHT ABOUT ATTENDING HITCHENS U NEXT FALL?

YOU MISSED THE EARLY APPLICATION DEADLINE BUT WITH YOUR FATHER AND I AS ALUMNI I'M SURE YOU'LL GET ACCEPTED EVEN AT THE **STANDARD** DEADLINE.

MOM, I TOLD YOU, I NEED SOME TIME. I'M ALSO GOING TO CHECK OUT PICKENS FRIDAY NIGHT.

PICKENS? **REALLY?**

Hrm. ALL RIGHT, VERONICA. WELL DO LET US KNOW WHEN YOU FINALLY MAKE YOUR DECISION.

Hitchens University

Dear Ms. Veronica Lodge,

With sincere regret, I must report that the committee Admissions has completed its selection of the class ente in the upcoming Fall and has not been able to offer you

We reviewed your features. Ther programs and to accept.

We encour you every s

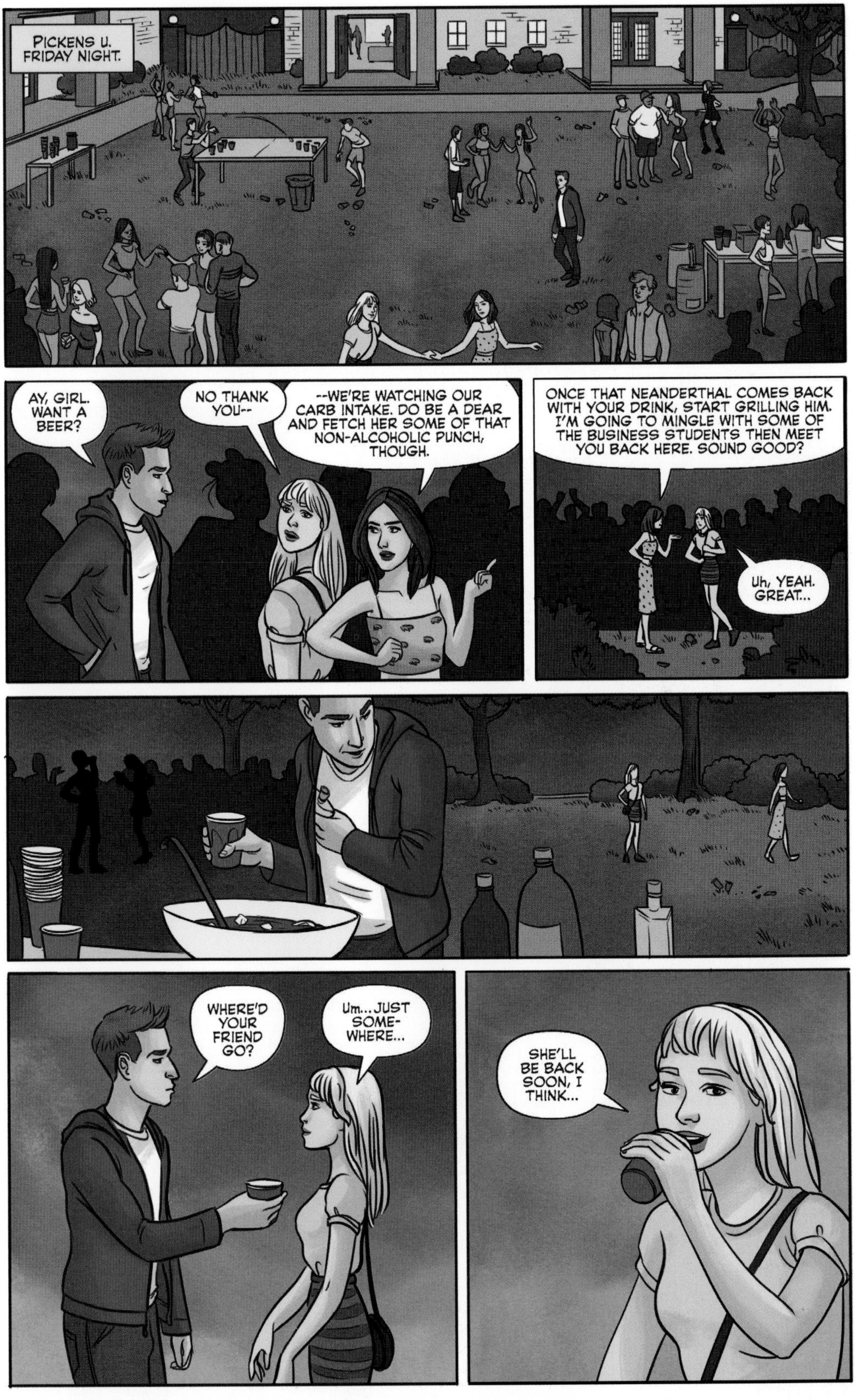
Pickens U. Friday night.
Ay, girl. Want a beer?
No thank you--
--We're watching our carb intake. Do be a dear and fetch her some of that non-alcoholic punch, though.
Once that Neanderthal comes back with your drink, start grilling him. I'm going to mingle with some of the business students then meet you back here. Sound good?
Uh, yeah. Great...
Where'd your friend go?
Um... just some-where...
She'll be back soon, I think...

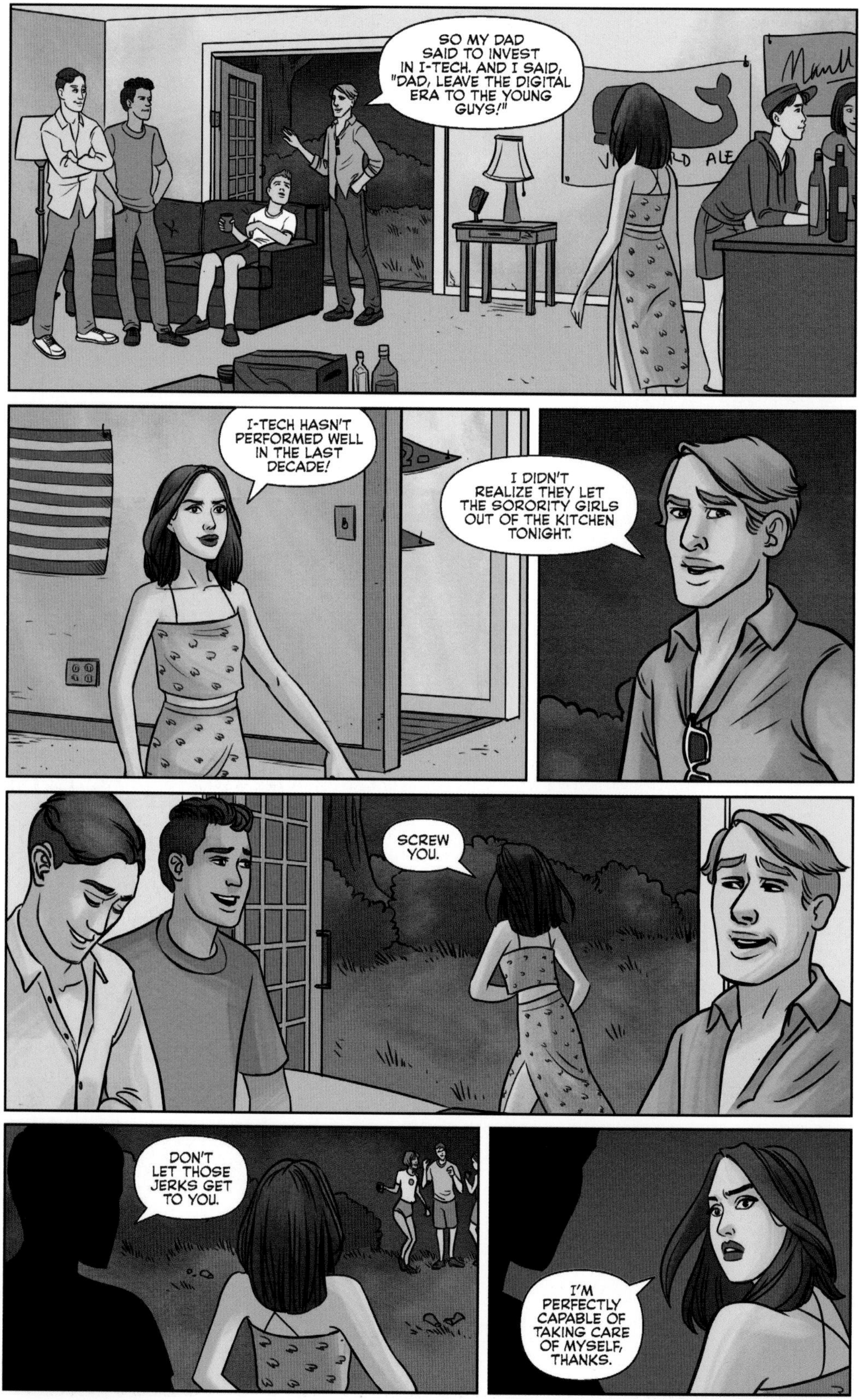
SO MY DAD SAID TO INVEST IN I-TECH. AND I SAID, "DAD, LEAVE THE DIGITAL ERA TO THE YOUNG GUYS!"
I-TECH HASN'T PERFORMED WELL IN THE LAST DECADE!
I DIDN'T REALIZE THEY LET THE SORORITY GIRLS OUT OF THE KITCHEN TONIGHT.
SCREW YOU.
DON'T LET THOSE JERKS GET TO YOU.
I'M PERFECTLY CAPABLE OF TAKING CARE OF MYSELF, THANKS.

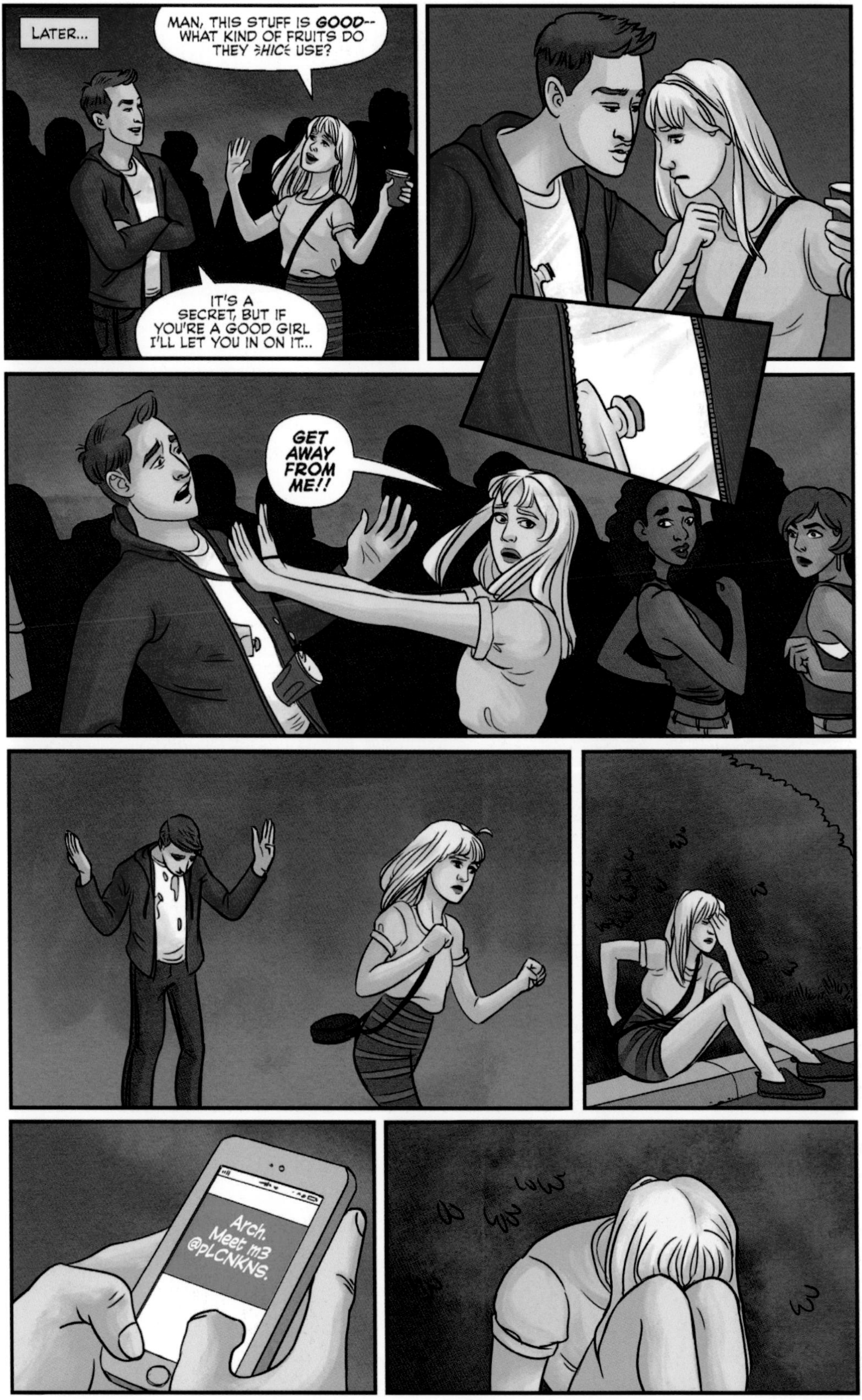
LATER...
MAN, THIS STUFF IS GOOD-- WHAT KIND OF FRUITS DO THEY *HIC* USE?
IT'S A SECRET, BUT IF YOU'RE A GOOD GIRL I'LL LET YOU IN ON IT...
GET AWAY FROM ME!!
Arch. Meet m3 @pLCNKNS.

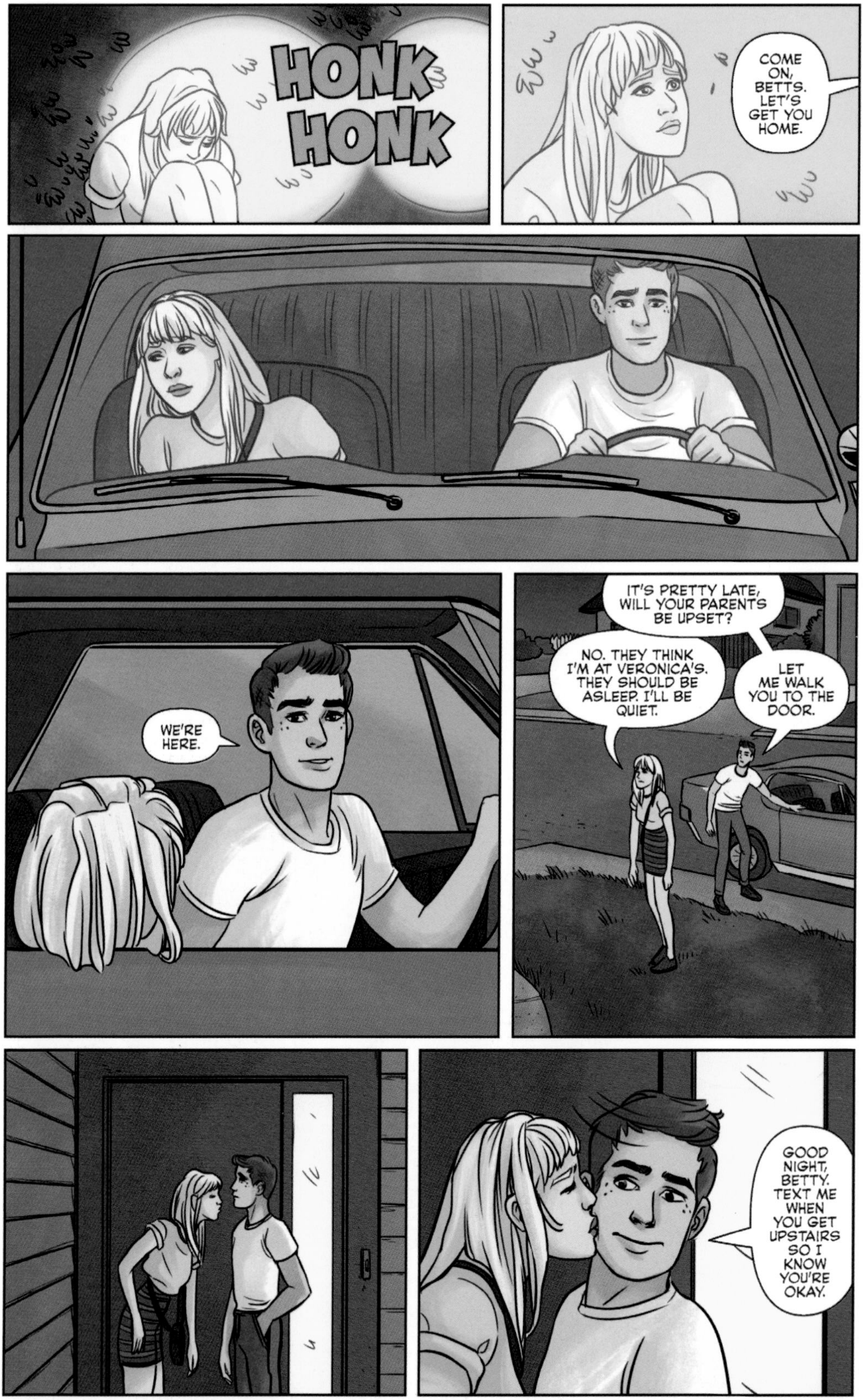
HONK
HONK
COME ON, BETTS. LET'S GET YOU HOME.
WE'RE HERE.
IT'S PRETTY LATE, WILL YOUR PARENTS BE UPSET?
NO. THEY THINK I'M AT VERONICA'S. THEY SHOULD BE ASLEEP. I'LL BE QUIET.
LET ME WALK YOU TO THE DOOR.
GOOD NIGHT, BETTY. TEXT ME WHEN YOU GET UPSTAIRS SO I KNOW YOU'RE OKAY.

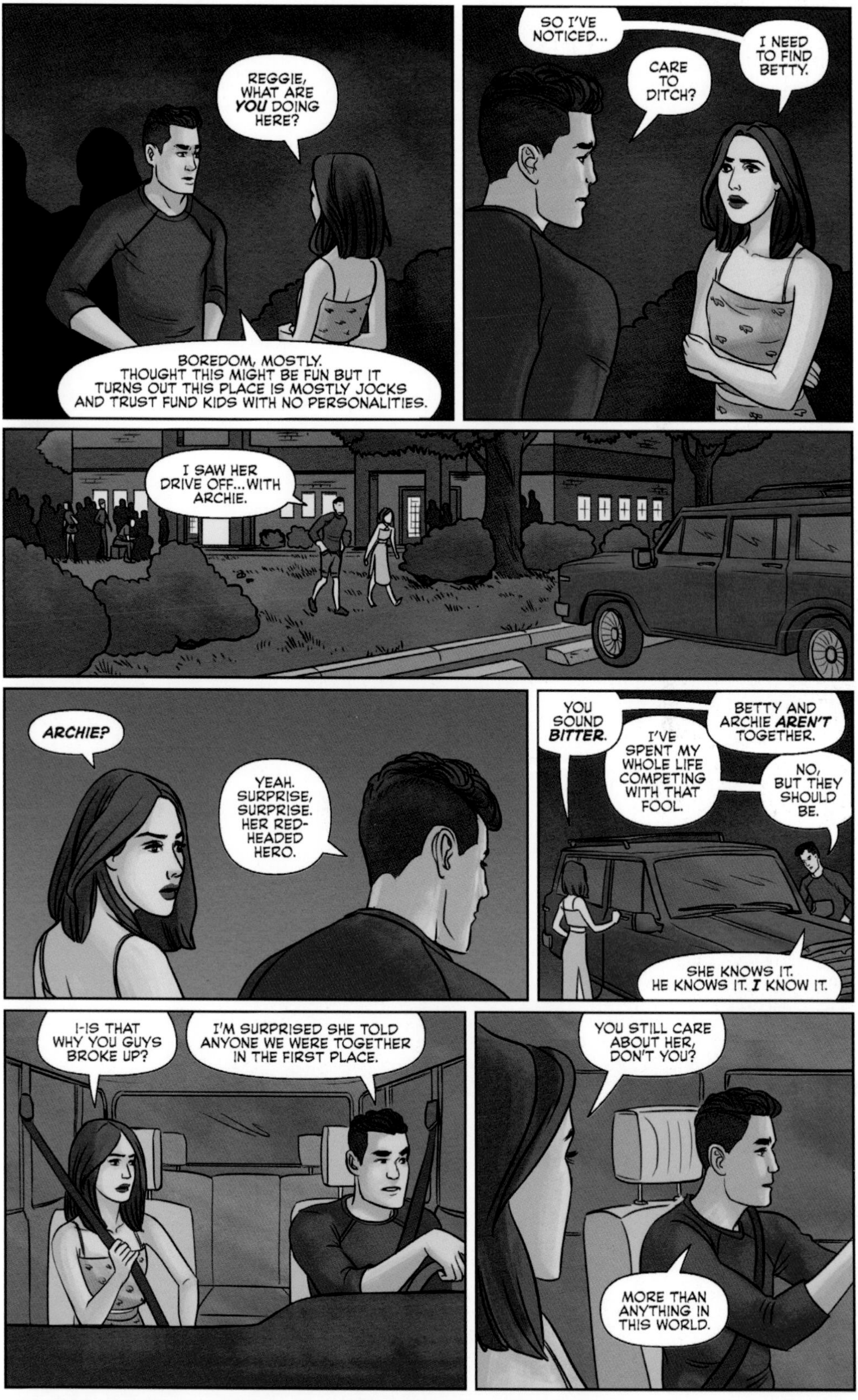
REGGIE, WHAT ARE YOU DOING HERE?
BOREDOM, MOSTLY. THOUGHT THIS MIGHT BE FUN BUT IT TURNS OUT THIS PLACE IS MOSTLY JOCKS AND TRUST FUND KIDS WITH NO PERSONALITIES.
SO I'VE NOTICED...
CARE TO DITCH?
I NEED TO FIND BETTY.
I SAW HER DRIVE OFF...WITH ARCHIE.
ARCHIE?
YEAH. SURPRISE, SURPRISE. HER RED-HEADED HERO.
YOU SOUND BITTER.
I'VE SPENT MY WHOLE LIFE COMPETING WITH THAT FOOL.
BETTY AND ARCHIE AREN'T TOGETHER.
NO, BUT THEY SHOULD BE.
SHE KNOWS IT. HE KNOWS IT. I KNOW IT.
I-IS THAT WHY YOU GUYS BROKE UP?
I'M SURPRISED SHE TOLD ANYONE WE WERE TOGETHER IN THE FIRST PLACE.
YOU STILL CARE ABOUT HER, DON'T YOU?
MORE THAN ANYTHING IN THIS WORLD.

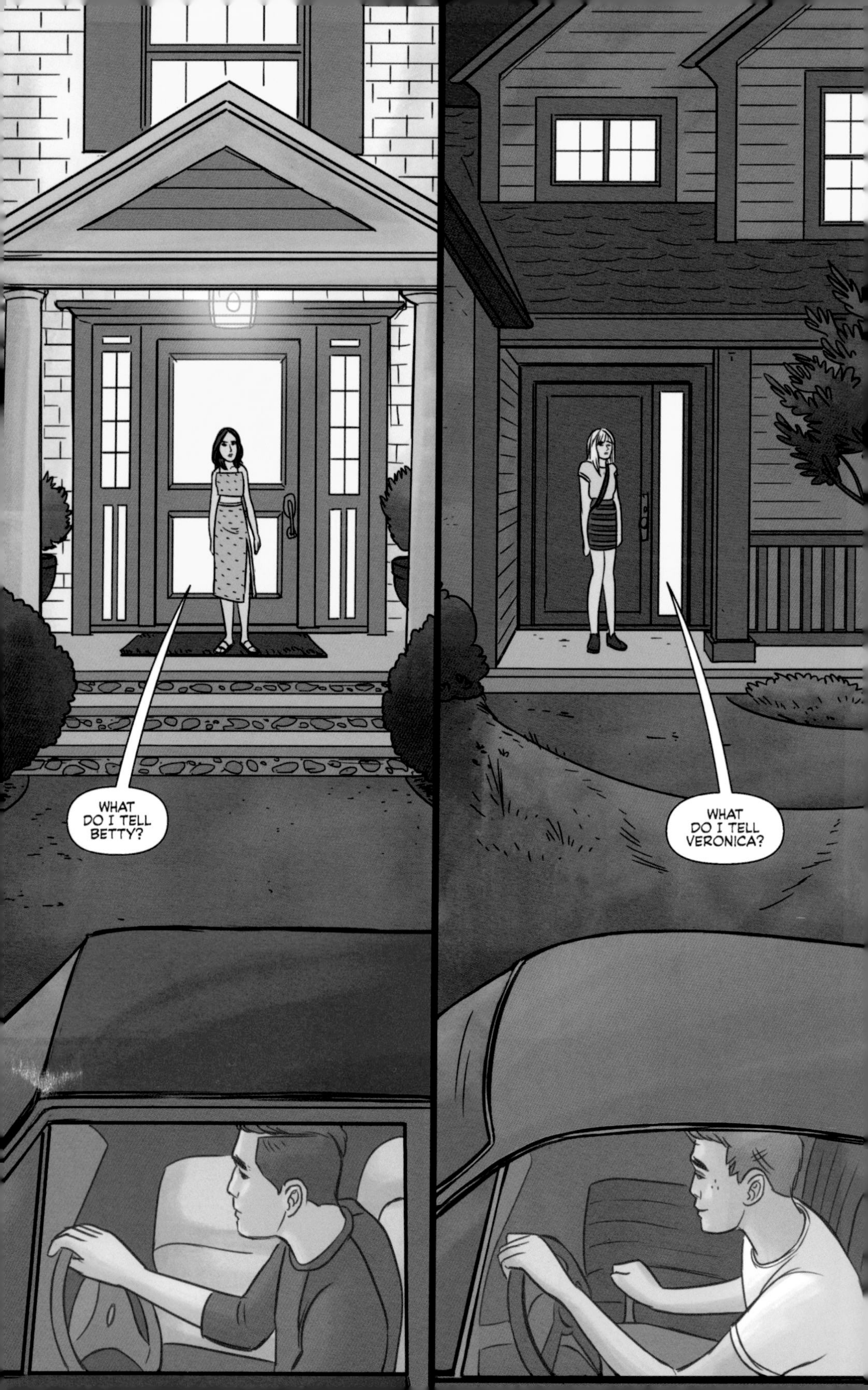
WHAT DO I TELL BETTY?
WHAT DO I TELL VERONICA?

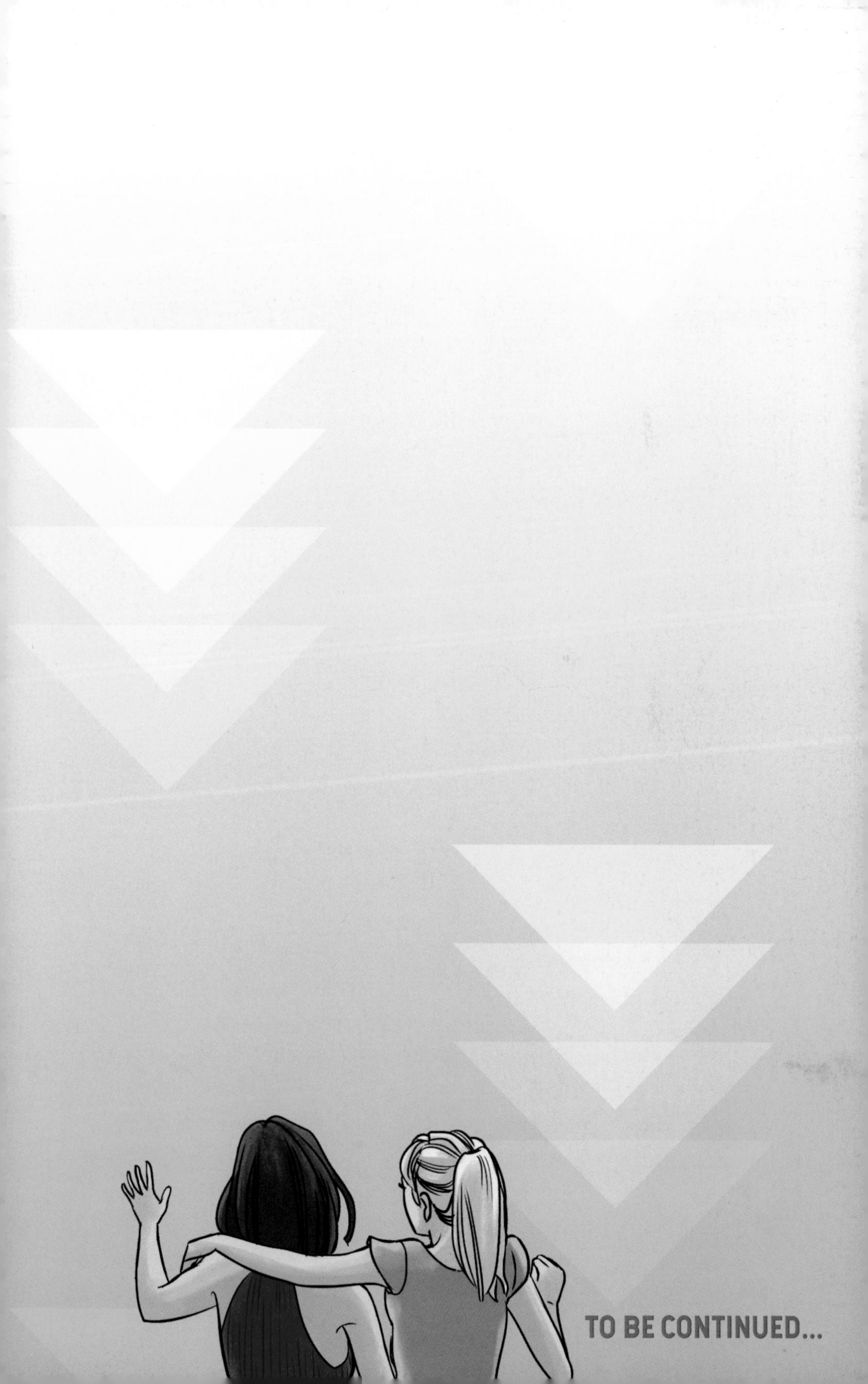
TO BE CONTINUED...

02

STORY BY
JAMIE LEE ROTANTE

LETTERING BY
JACK MORELLI

ART BY
SANDRA LANZ

COLORS BY
KELLY FITZPATRICK

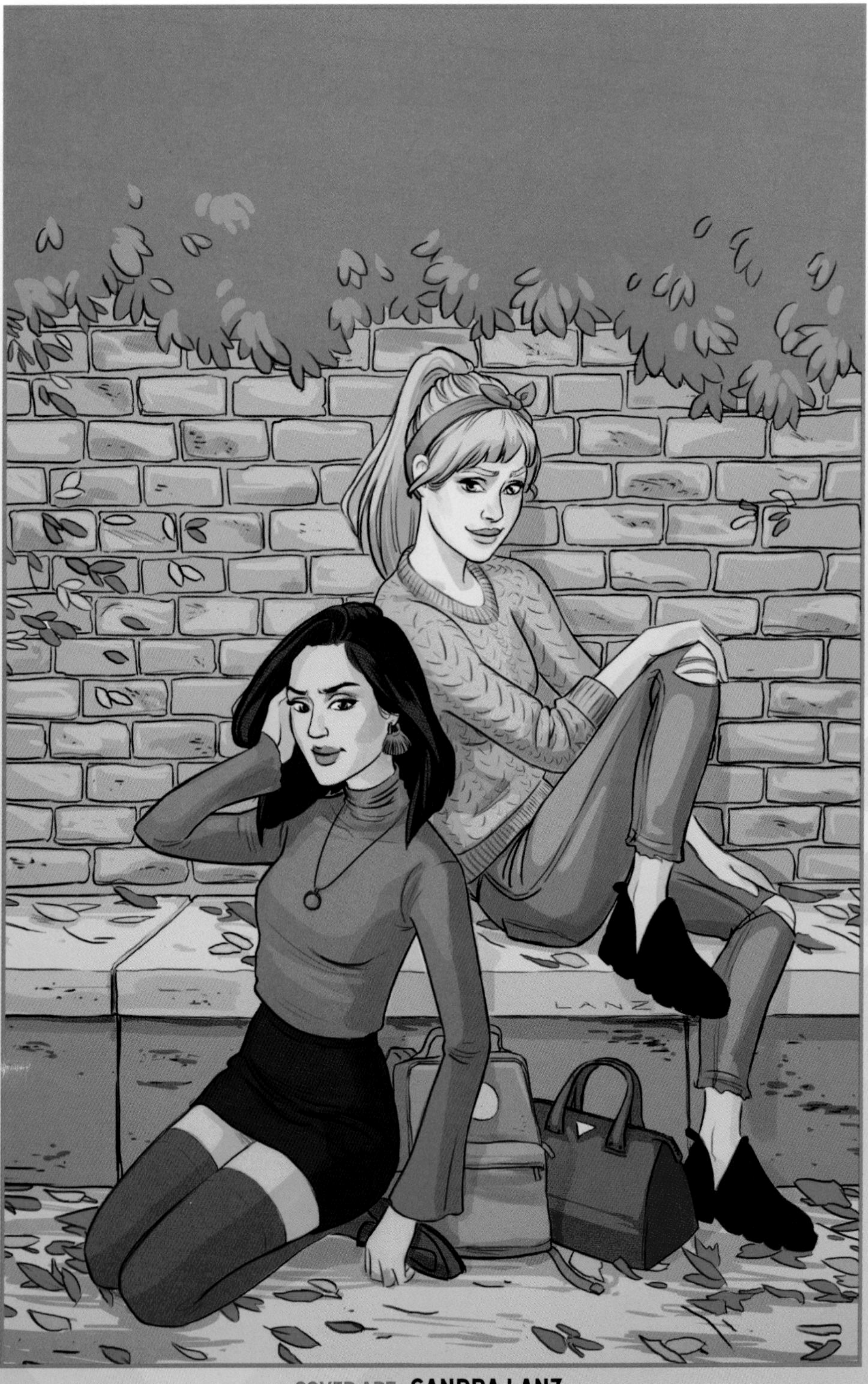
LANZ

COVER ART: **SANDRA LANZ**

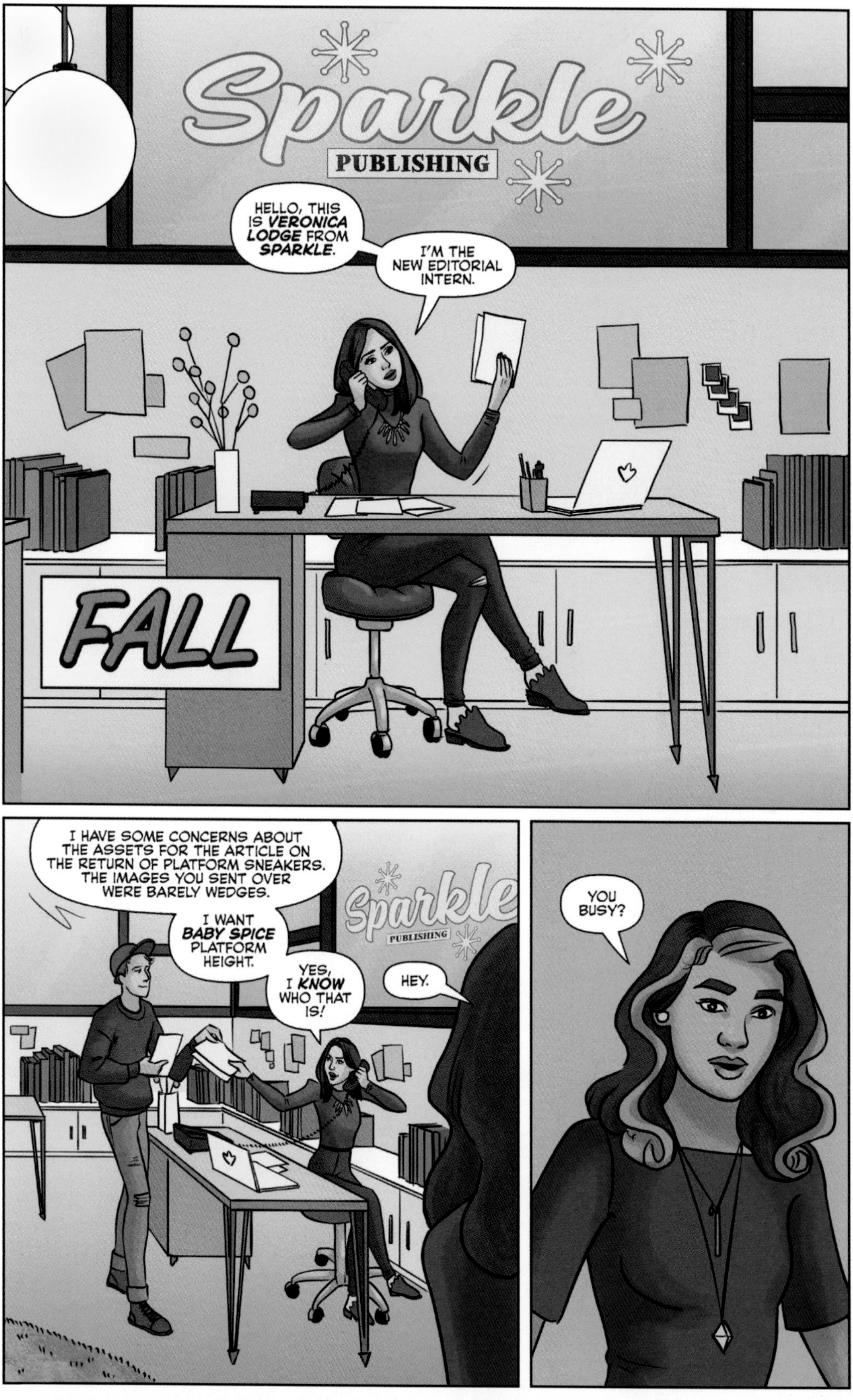
Sparkle
PUBLISHING
HELLO, THIS IS VERONICA LODGE FROM SPARKLE.
I'M THE NEW EDITORIAL INTERN.
FALL
I HAVE SOME CONCERNS ABOUT THE ASSETS FOR THE ARTICLE ON THE RETURN OF PLATFORM SNEAKERS. THE IMAGES YOU SENT OVER WERE BARELY WEDGES.
Sparkle
PUBLISHING
I WANT BABY SPICE PLATFORM HEIGHT.
YES, I KNOW WHO THAT IS!
HEY.
YOU BUSY?

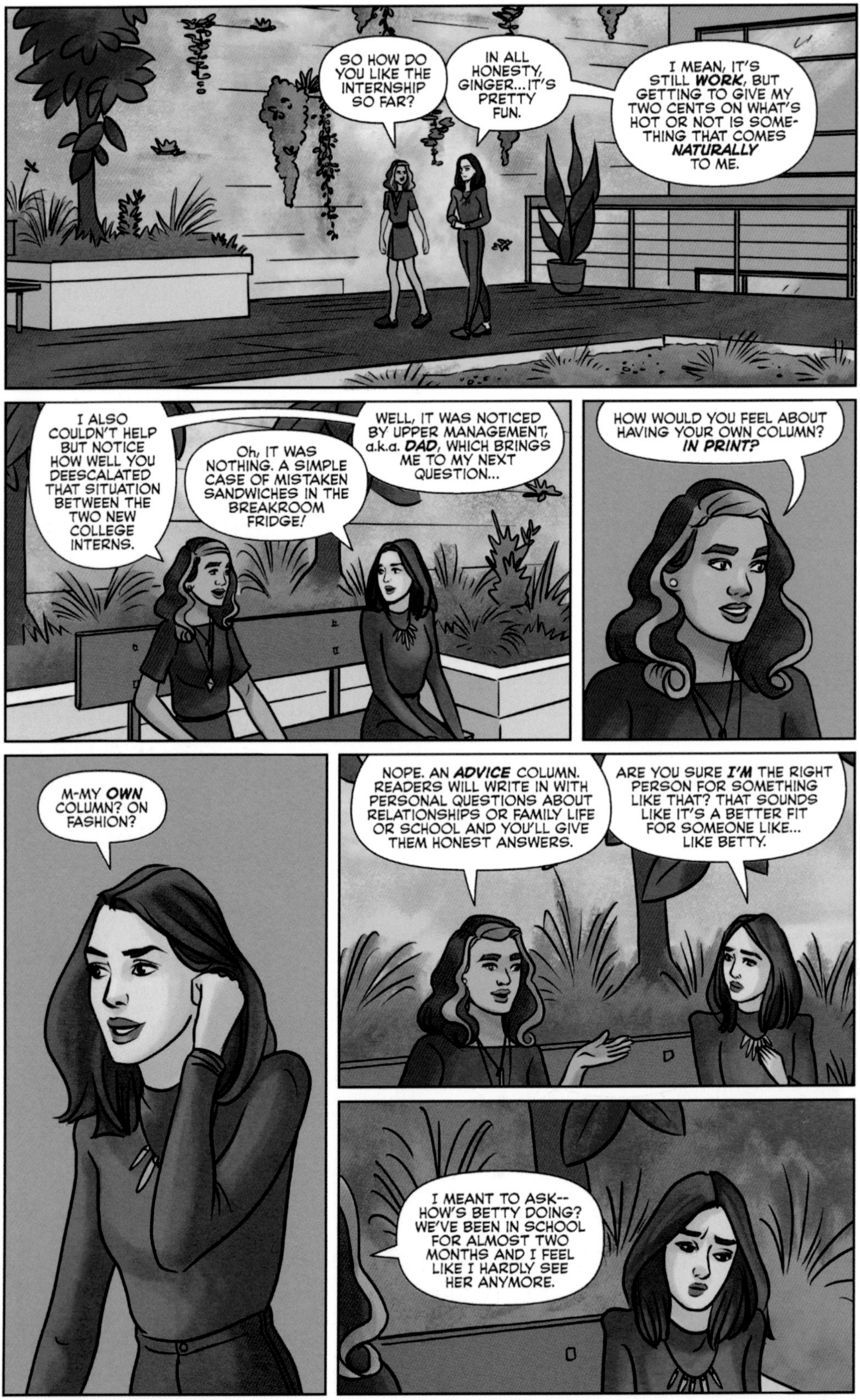
SO HOW DO YOU LIKE THE INTERNSHIP SO FAR?
IN ALL HONESTY, GINGER... IT'S PRETTY FUN.
I MEAN, IT'S STILL WORK, BUT GETTING TO GIVE MY TWO CENTS ON WHAT'S HOT OR NOT IS SOMETHING THAT COMES NATURALLY TO ME.
I ALSO COULDN'T HELP BUT NOTICE HOW WELL YOU DEESCALATED THAT SITUATION BETWEEN THE TWO NEW COLLEGE INTERNS.
Oh, IT WAS NOTHING. A SIMPLE CASE OF MISTAKEN SANDWICHES IN THE BREAKROOM FRIDGE!
WELL, IT WAS NOTICED BY UPPER MANAGEMENT, a.k.a. DAD, WHICH BRINGS ME TO MY NEXT QUESTION...
HOW WOULD YOU FEEL ABOUT HAVING YOUR OWN COLUMN? IN PRINT?
M-MY OWN COLUMN? ON FASHION?
NOPE. AN ADVICE COLUMN. READERS WILL WRITE IN WITH PERSONAL QUESTIONS ABOUT RELATIONSHIPS OR FAMILY LIFE OR SCHOOL AND YOU'LL GIVE THEM HONEST ANSWERS.
ARE YOU SURE I'M THE RIGHT PERSON FOR SOMETHING LIKE THAT? THAT SOUNDS LIKE IT'S A BETTER FIT FOR SOMEONE LIKE... LIKE BETTY.
I MEANT TO ASK-- HOW'S BETTY DOING? WE'VE BEEN IN SCHOOL FOR ALMOST TWO MONTHS AND I FEEL LIKE I HARDLY SEE HER ANYMORE.

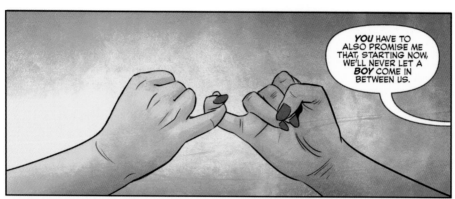

YOU HAVE TO ALSO PROMISE ME THAT, STARTING NOW, WE'LL NEVER LET A *BOY* COME IN BETWEEN US.

I SAW HER DRIVE OFF... WITH ARCHIE.

ARCHIE?

Uh, HELLO? EARTH TO VERONICA.

SHE'S FINE. JUST BUSY. WE'VE BEEN TRYING TO MEET UP, BUT OUR SCHEDULES HAVE JUST BEEN SO HECTIC.

I HEAR THAT. SO THE ADVICE COLUMN-- WHADDAYA THINK?

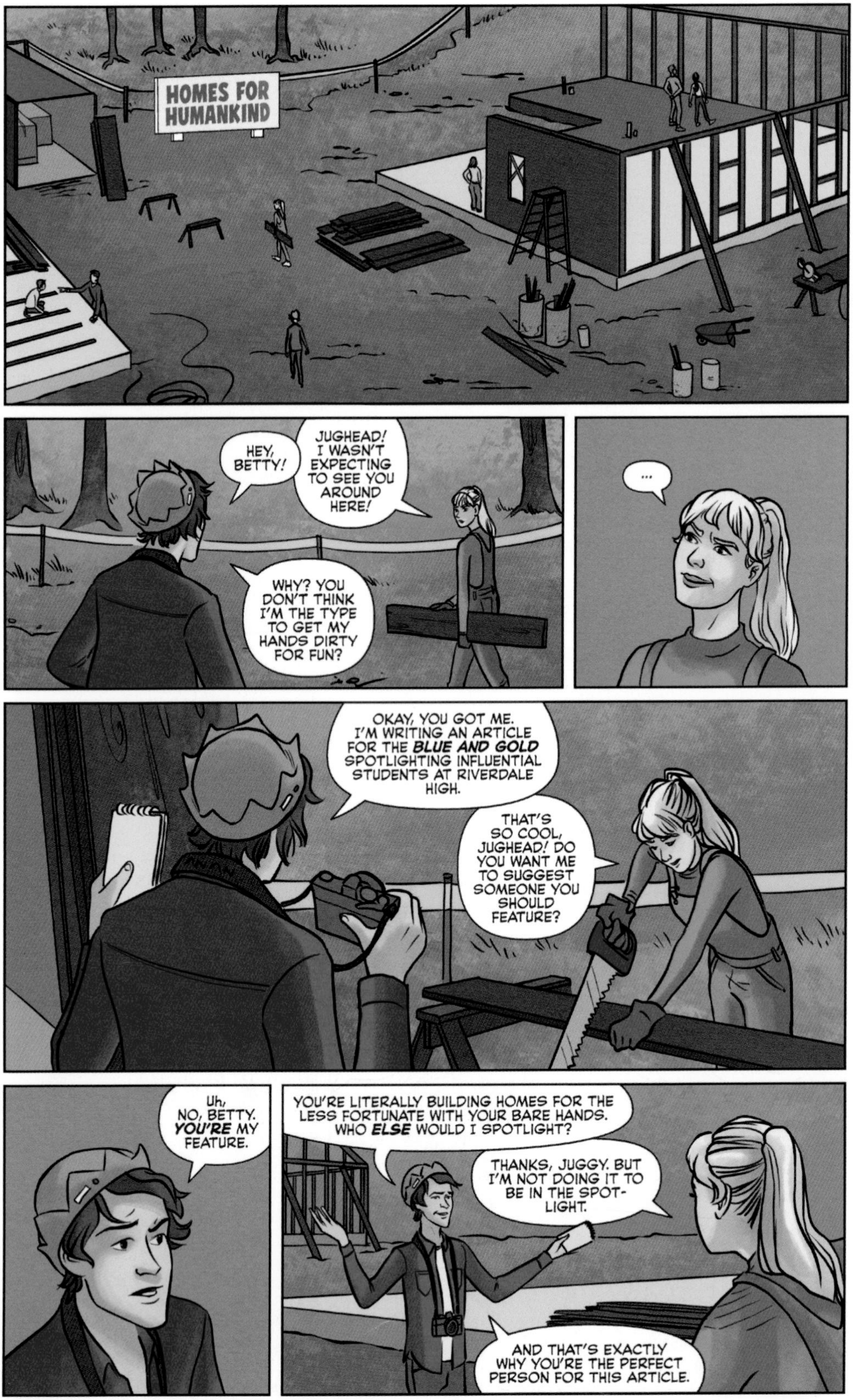
HOMES FOR HUMANKIND
HEY, BETTY!
JUGHEAD! I WASN'T EXPECTING TO SEE YOU AROUND HERE!
WHY? YOU DON'T THINK I'M THE TYPE TO GET MY HANDS DIRTY FOR FUN?
...
OKAY, YOU GOT ME. I'M WRITING AN ARTICLE FOR THE BLUE AND GOLD SPOTLIGHTING INFLUENTIAL STUDENTS AT RIVERDALE HIGH.
THAT'S SO COOL, JUGHEAD! DO YOU WANT ME TO SUGGEST SOMEONE YOU SHOULD FEATURE?
Uh, NO, BETTY. YOU'RE MY FEATURE.
YOU'RE LITERALLY BUILDING HOMES FOR THE LESS FORTUNATE WITH YOUR BARE HANDS. WHO ELSE WOULD I SPOTLIGHT?
THANKS, JUGGY. BUT I'M NOT DOING IT TO BE IN THE SPOT-LIGHT.
AND THAT'S EXACTLY WHY YOU'RE THE PERFECT PERSON FOR THIS ARTICLE.

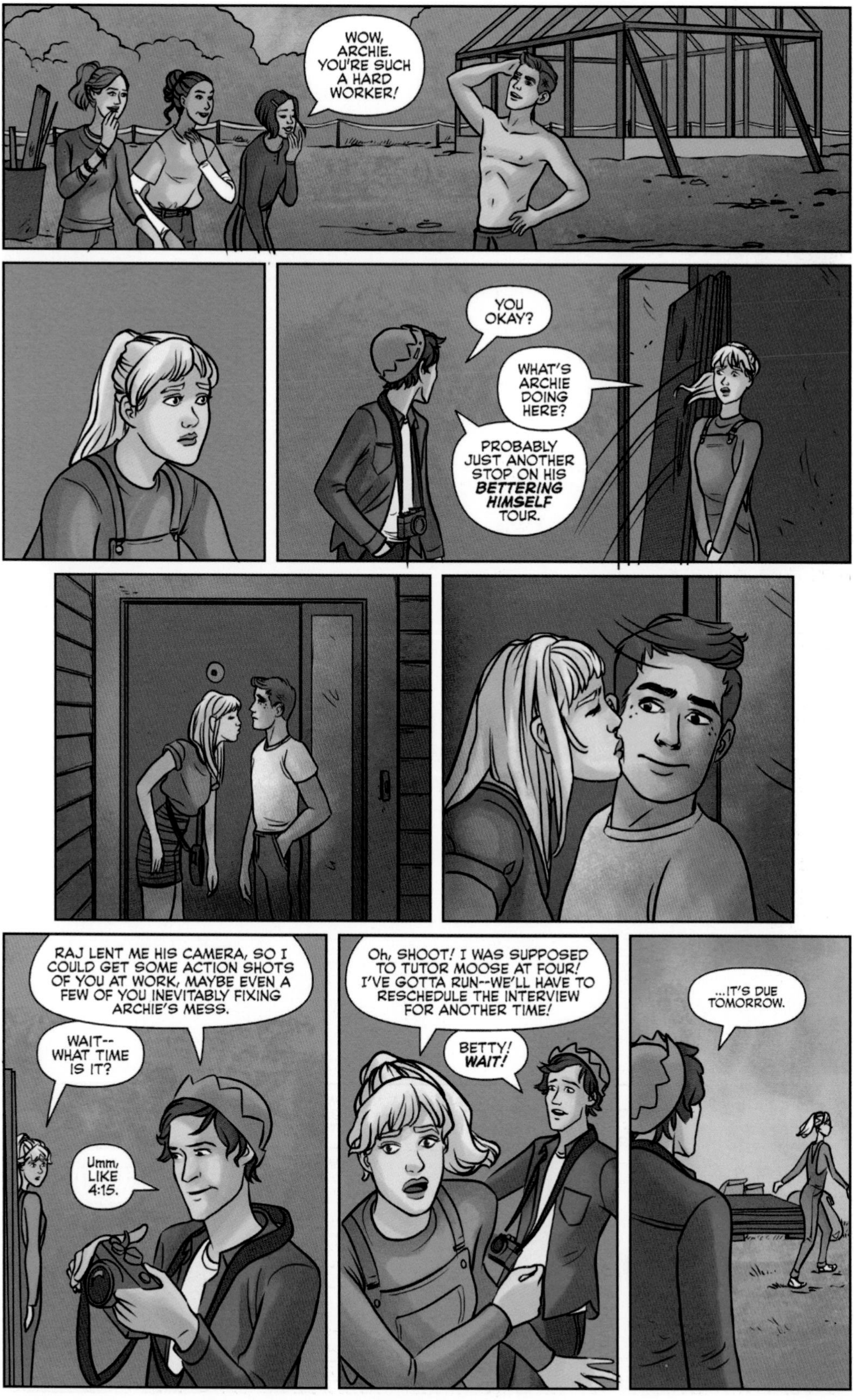
WOW, ARCHIE. YOU'RE SUCH A HARD WORKER!
YOU OKAY?
WHAT'S ARCHIE DOING HERE?
PROBABLY JUST ANOTHER STOP ON HIS *BETTERING HIMSELF* TOUR.
RAJ LENT ME HIS CAMERA, SO I COULD GET SOME ACTION SHOTS OF YOU AT WORK, MAYBE EVEN A FEW OF YOU INEVITABLY FIXING ARCHIE'S MESS.
WAIT-- WHAT TIME IS IT?
Umm, LIKE 4:15.
Oh, SHOOT! I WAS SUPPOSED TO TUTOR MOOSE AT FOUR! I'VE GOTTA RUN--WE'LL HAVE TO RESCHEDULE THE INTERVIEW FOR ANOTHER TIME!
BETTY! *WAIT!*
...IT'S DUE TOMORROW.

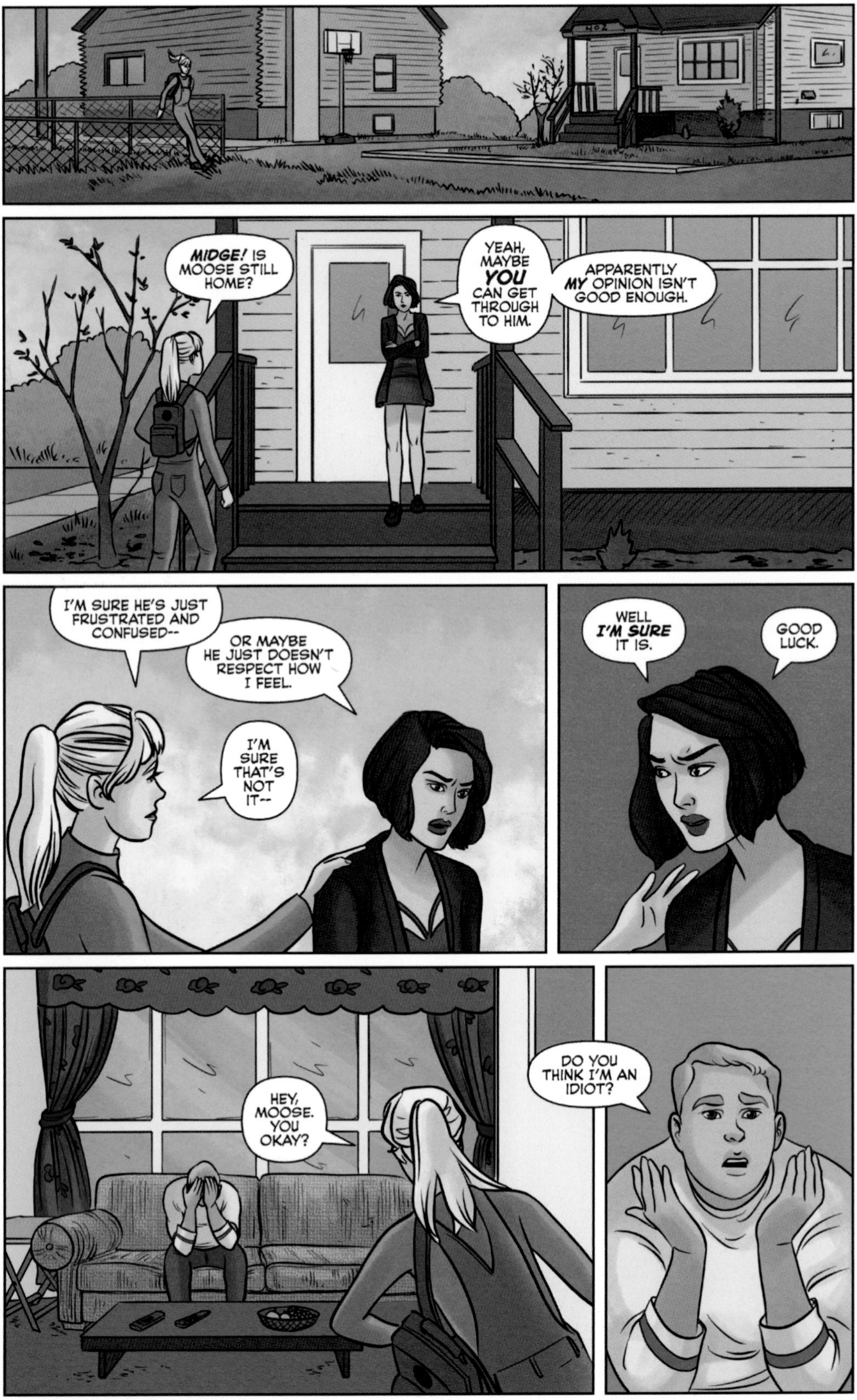

MIDGE! IS MOOSE STILL HOME?
YEAH, MAYBE YOU CAN GET THROUGH TO HIM.
APPARENTLY MY OPINION ISN'T GOOD ENOUGH.
I'M SURE HE'S JUST FRUSTRATED AND CONFUSED--
OR MAYBE HE JUST DOESN'T RESPECT HOW I FEEL.
I'M SURE THAT'S NOT IT--
WELL I'M SURE IT IS.
GOOD LUCK.
HEY, MOOSE. YOU OKAY?
DO YOU THINK I'M AN IDIOT?

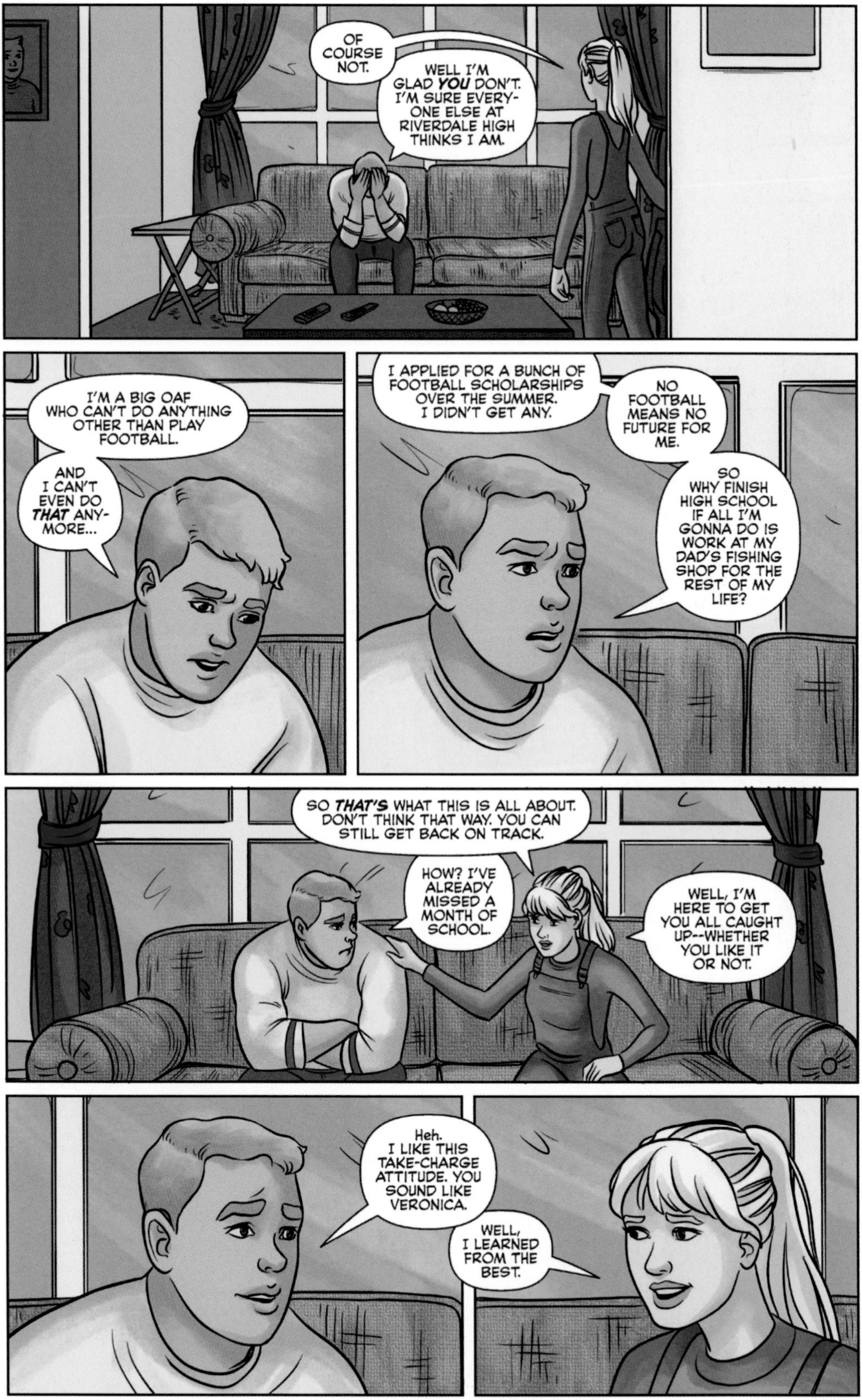
OF COURSE NOT.
WELL I'M GLAD *YOU* DON'T. I'M SURE EVERYONE ELSE AT RIVERDALE HIGH THINKS I AM.
I'M A BIG OAF WHO CAN'T DO ANYTHING OTHER THAN PLAY FOOTBALL.
AND I CAN'T EVEN DO *THAT* ANYMORE...
I APPLIED FOR A BUNCH OF FOOTBALL SCHOLARSHIPS OVER THE SUMMER. I DIDN'T GET ANY.
NO FOOTBALL MEANS NO FUTURE FOR ME.
SO WHY FINISH HIGH SCHOOL IF ALL I'M GONNA DO IS WORK AT MY DAD'S FISHING SHOP FOR THE REST OF MY LIFE?
SO *THAT'S* WHAT THIS IS ALL ABOUT. DON'T THINK THAT WAY. YOU CAN STILL GET BACK ON TRACK.
HOW? I'VE ALREADY MISSED A MONTH OF SCHOOL.
WELL, I'M HERE TO GET YOU ALL CAUGHT UP--WHETHER YOU LIKE IT OR NOT.
Heh. I LIKE THIS TAKE-CHARGE ATTITUDE. YOU SOUND LIKE VERONICA.
WELL, I LEARNED FROM THE BEST.

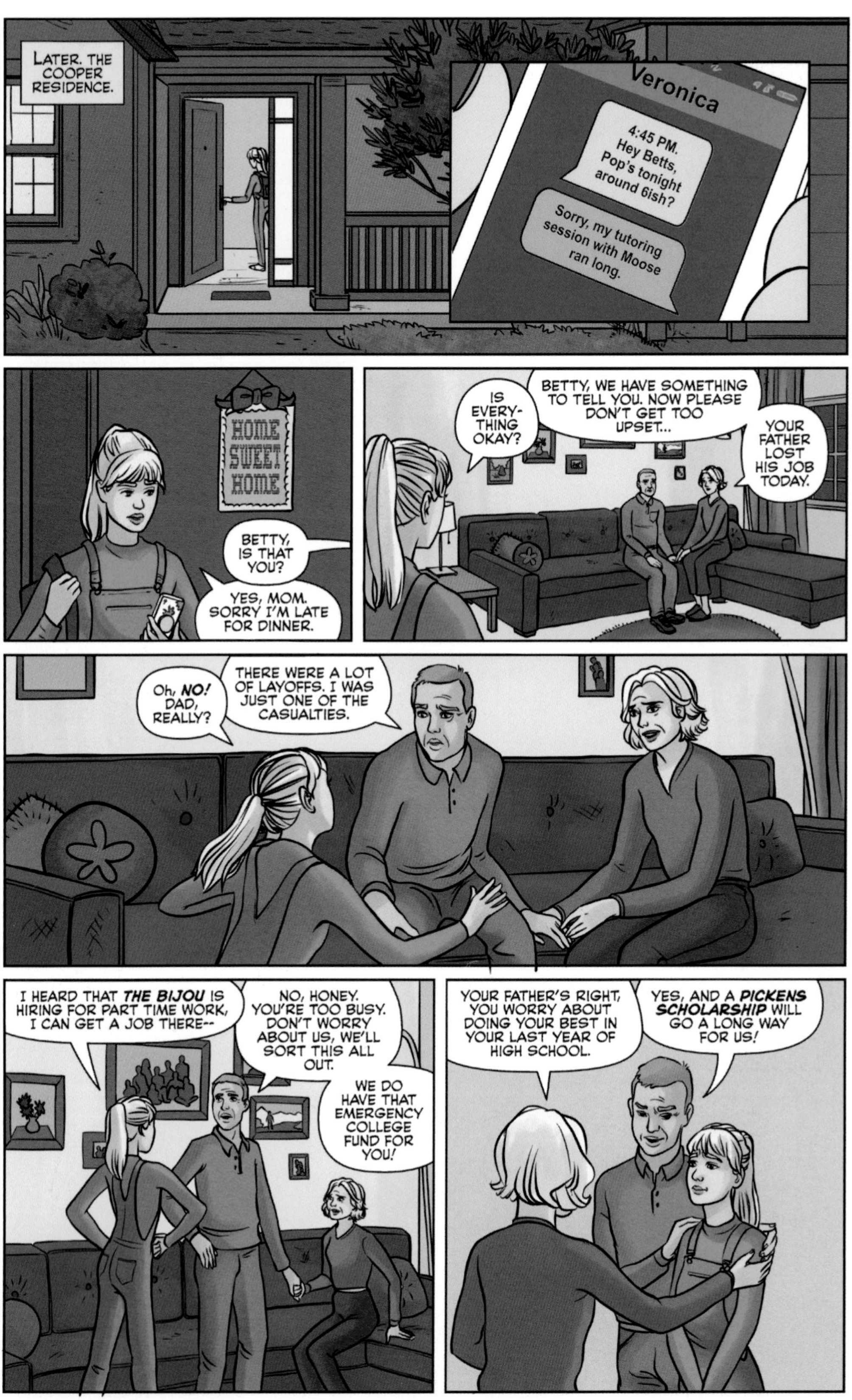
LATER. THE COOPER RESIDENCE.
Veronica
4:45 PM. Hey Betts, Pop's tonight around 6ish?
Sorry, my tutoring session with Moose ran long.
HOME SWEET HOME
BETTY, IS THAT YOU?
YES, MOM. SORRY I'M LATE FOR DINNER.
IS EVERY-THING OKAY?
BETTY, WE HAVE SOMETHING TO TELL YOU. NOW PLEASE DON'T GET TOO UPSET...
YOUR FATHER LOST HIS JOB TODAY.
Oh, NO! DAD, REALLY?
THERE WERE A LOT OF LAYOFFS. I WAS JUST ONE OF THE CASUALTIES.
I HEARD THAT THE BIJOU IS HIRING FOR PART TIME WORK, I CAN GET A JOB THERE--
NO, HONEY. YOU'RE TOO BUSY. DON'T WORRY ABOUT US, WE'LL SORT THIS ALL OUT.
WE DO HAVE THAT EMERGENCY COLLEGE FUND FOR YOU!
YOUR FATHER'S RIGHT, YOU WORRY ABOUT DOING YOUR BEST IN YOUR LAST YEAR OF HIGH SCHOOL.
YES, AND A PICKENS SCHOLARSHIP WILL GO A LONG WAY FOR US!

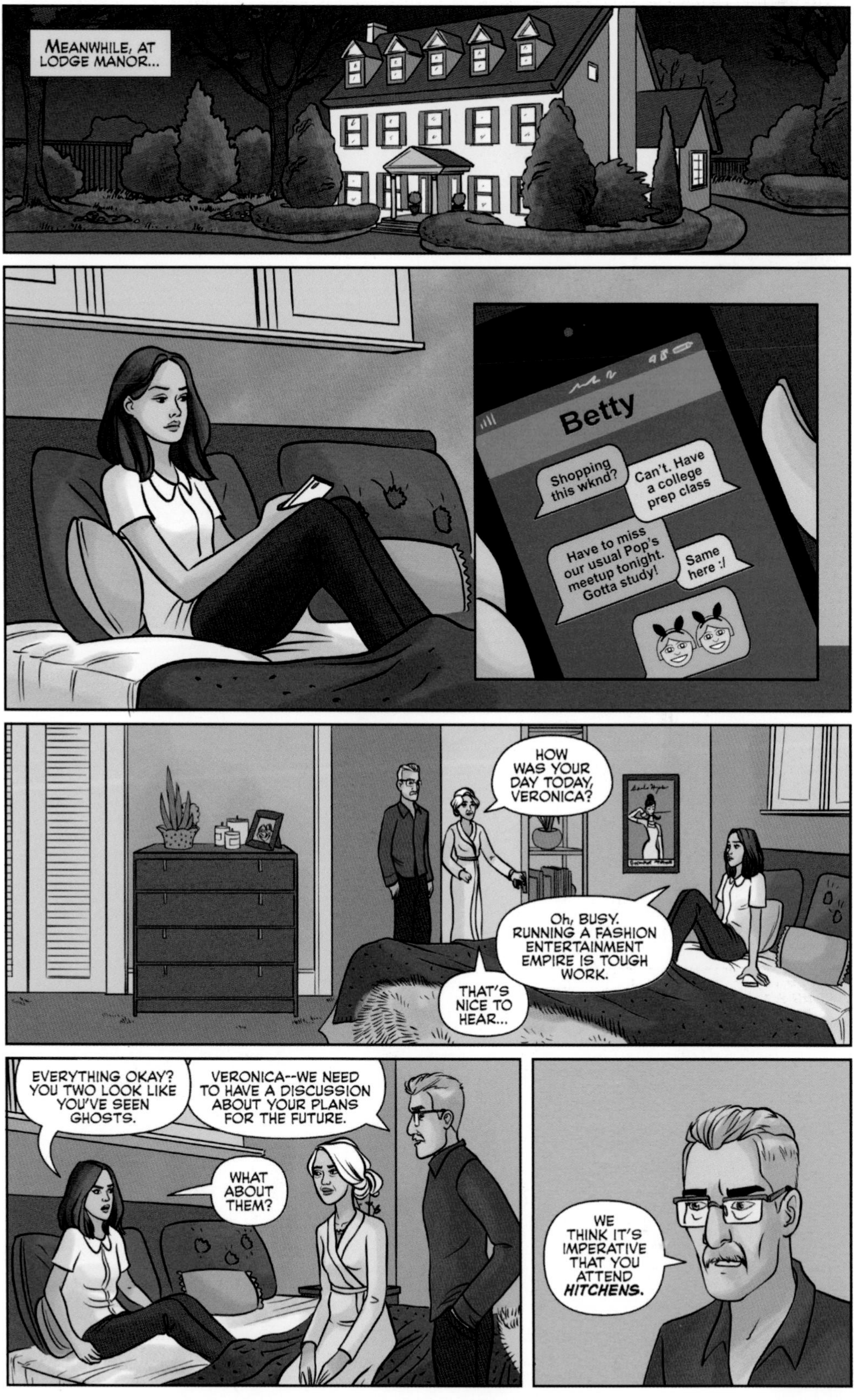
MEANWHILE, AT LODGE MANOR...
Betty
Shopping this wknd?
Can't. Have a college prep class
Have to miss our usual Pop's meetup tonight. Gotta study!
Same here :/
HOW WAS YOUR DAY TODAY, VERONICA?
Oh, BUSY. RUNNING A FASHION ENTERTAINMENT EMPIRE IS TOUGH WORK.
THAT'S NICE TO HEAR...
EVERYTHING OKAY? YOU TWO LOOK LIKE YOU'VE SEEN GHOSTS.
VERONICA--WE NEED TO HAVE A DISCUSSION ABOUT YOUR PLANS FOR THE FUTURE.
WHAT ABOUT THEM?
WE THINK IT'S IMPERATIVE THAT YOU ATTEND *HITCHENS.*

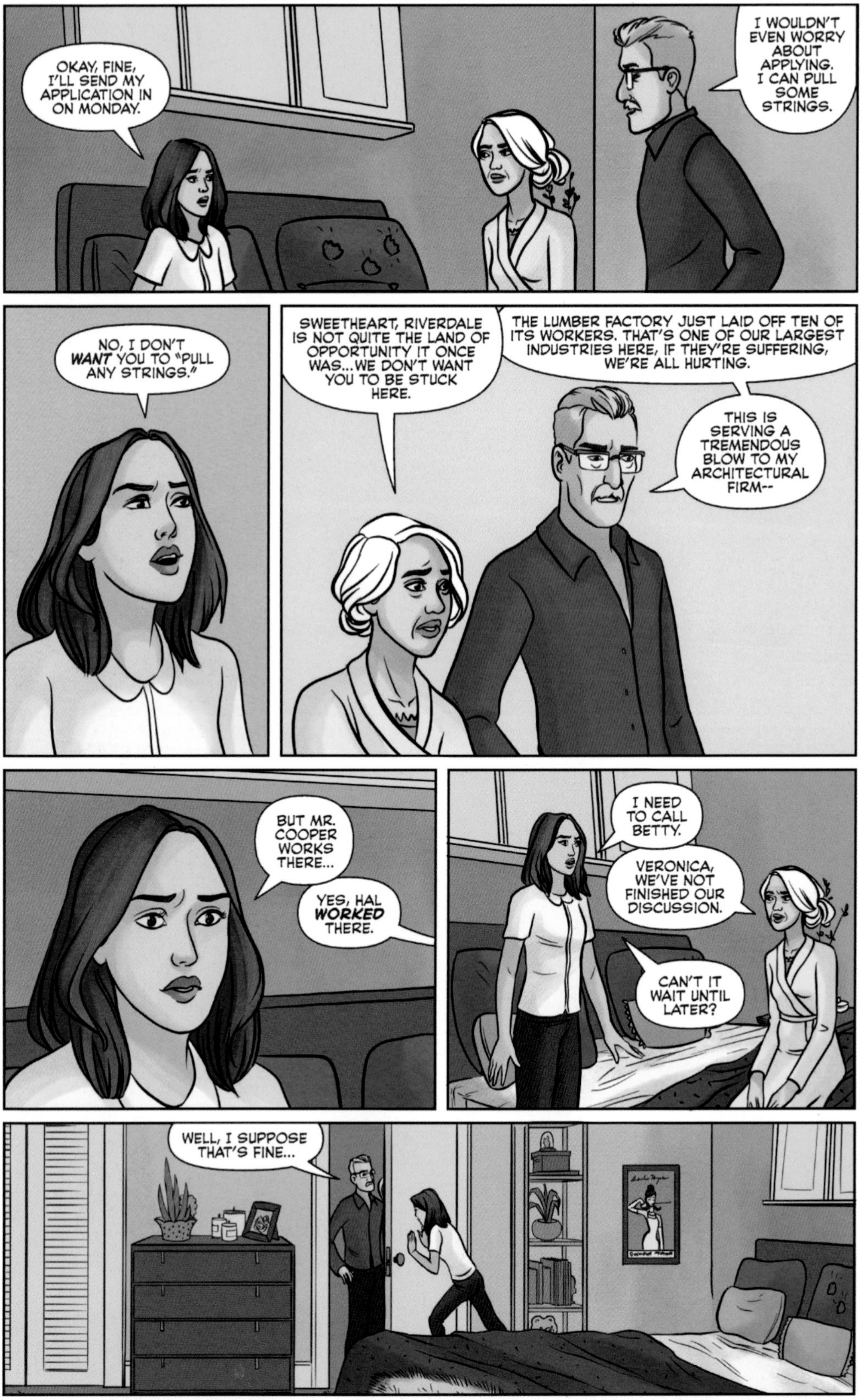
OKAY, FINE, I'LL SEND MY APPLICATION IN ON MONDAY.
I WOULDN'T EVEN WORRY ABOUT APPLYING. I CAN PULL SOME STRINGS.
NO, I DON'T WANT YOU TO "PULL ANY STRINGS."
SWEETHEART, RIVERDALE IS NOT QUITE THE LAND OF OPPORTUNITY IT ONCE WAS...WE DON'T WANT YOU TO BE STUCK HERE.
THE LUMBER FACTORY JUST LAID OFF TEN OF ITS WORKERS. THAT'S ONE OF OUR LARGEST INDUSTRIES HERE, IF THEY'RE SUFFERING, WE'RE ALL HURTING.
THIS IS SERVING A TREMENDOUS BLOW TO MY ARCHITECTURAL FIRM--
BUT MR. COOPER WORKS THERE...
YES, HAL WORKED THERE.
I NEED TO CALL BETTY.
VERONICA, WE'VE NOT FINISHED OUR DISCUSSION.
CAN'T IT WAIT UNTIL LATER?
WELL, I SUPPOSE THAT'S FINE...

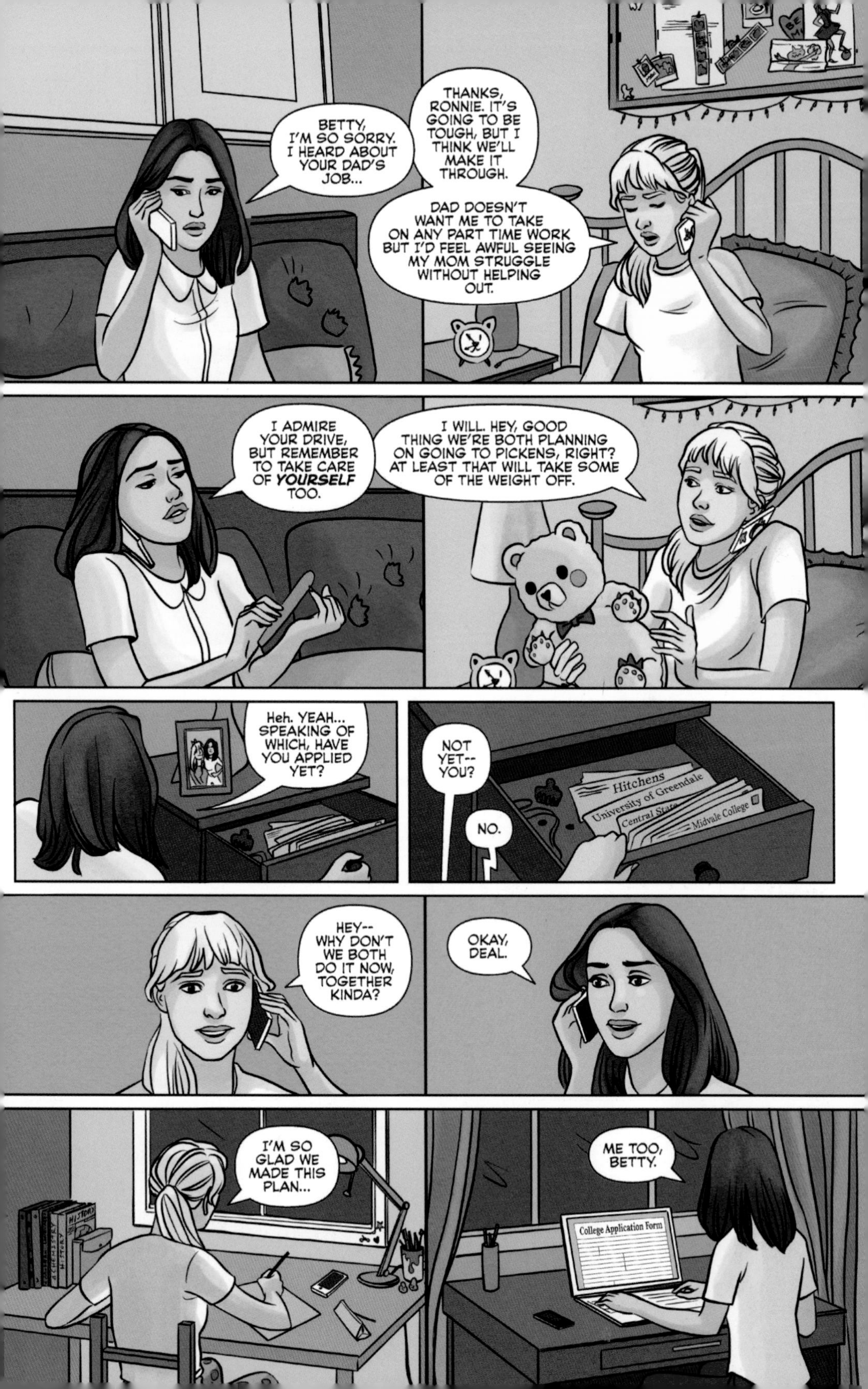
BETTY, I'M SO SORRY. I HEARD ABOUT YOUR DAD'S JOB...
THANKS, RONNIE. IT'S GOING TO BE TOUGH, BUT I THINK WE'LL MAKE IT THROUGH.
DAD DOESN'T WANT ME TO TAKE ON ANY PART TIME WORK BUT I'D FEEL AWFUL SEEING MY MOM STRUGGLE WITHOUT HELPING OUT.
I ADMIRE YOUR DRIVE, BUT REMEMBER TO TAKE CARE OF *YOURSELF* TOO.
I WILL. HEY, GOOD THING WE'RE BOTH PLANNING ON GOING TO PICKENS, RIGHT? AT LEAST THAT WILL TAKE SOME OF THE WEIGHT OFF.
Heh. YEAH... SPEAKING OF WHICH, HAVE YOU APPLIED YET?
NOT YET-- YOU?
NO.
Hitchens
University of Greendale
Midvale College
HEY-- WHY DON'T WE BOTH DO IT NOW, TOGETHER KINDA?
OKAY, DEAL.
I'M SO GLAD WE MADE THIS PLAN...
ME TOO, BETTY.
College Application Form

HOW ARE COLLEGE APPLICATIONS GOING?

FINE, I'VE SENT OUT A BUNCH, FOCUSING ON SCHOLARSHIP ESSAYS NOW. YOU?

EH. I'VE SENT ONE SO FAR. BUT WHEN IT COSTS LIKE SIXTY DOLLARS A POP JUST TO *APPLY*, IT SORTA LIMITS MY OPTIONS, YA KNOW?

GEE, TONI, I NEVER THOUGHT OF IT THAT WAY. MY PARENTS HAVE BEEN HELPING ME OUT WITH THAT...

LUCKY.

YEAH-- I GUESS SO.

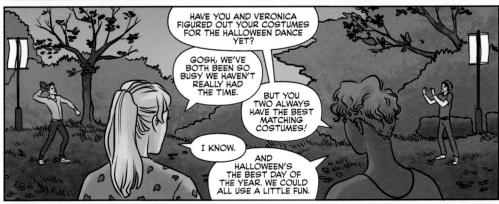

HAVE YOU AND VERONICA FIGURED OUT YOUR COSTUMES FOR THE HALLOWEEN DANCE YET?

GOSH, WE'VE BOTH BEEN SO BUSY WE HAVEN'T REALLY HAD THE TIME.

BUT YOU TWO ALWAYS HAVE THE BEST MATCHING COSTUMES!

I KNOW.

AND HALLOWEEN'S THE BEST DAY OF THE YEAR. WE COULD ALL USE A LITTLE FUN.

Heh, YEAH...

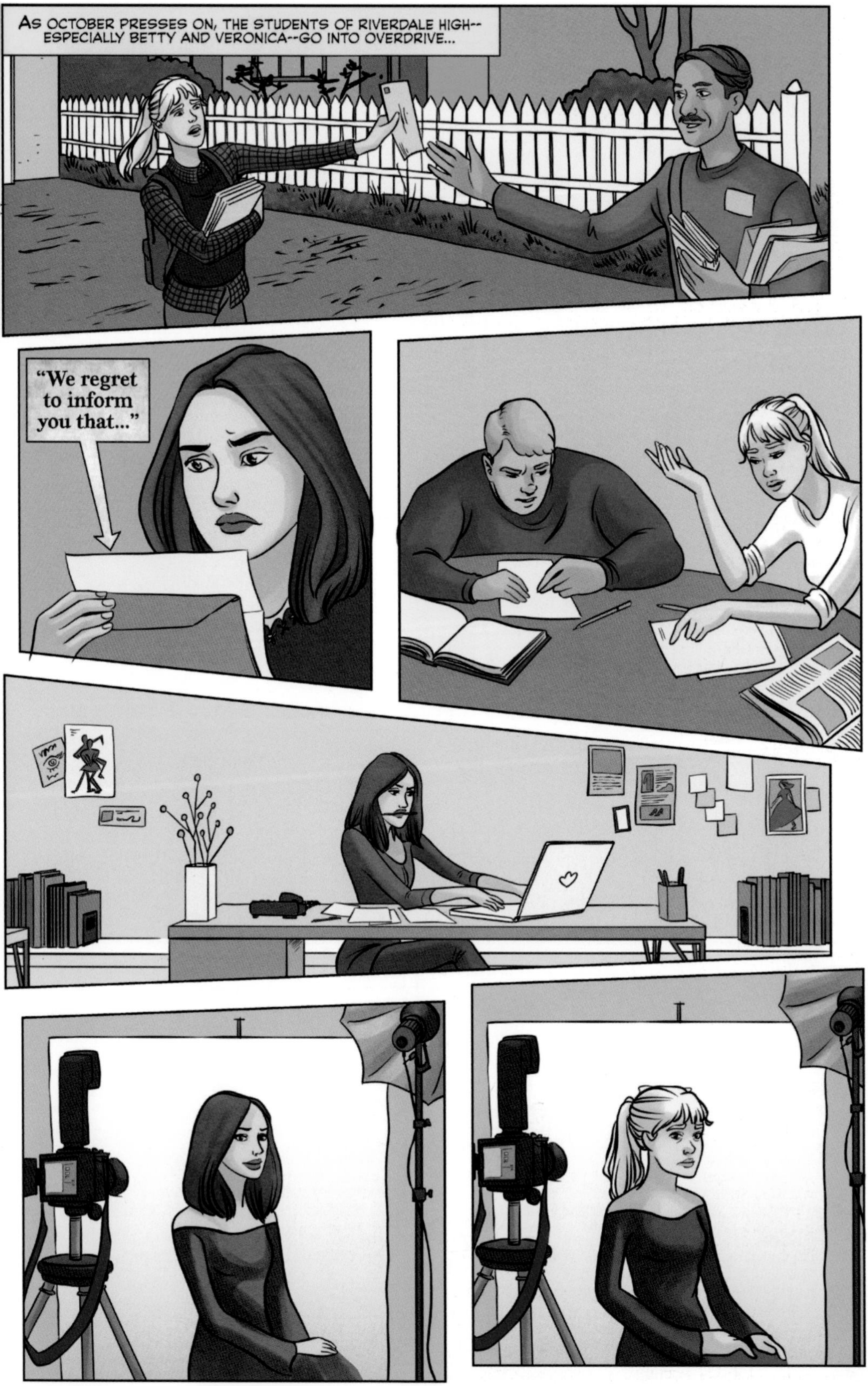
As October presses on, the students of Riverdale High--especially Betty and Veronica--go into overdrive...
"We regret to inform you that..."

RIVERDALE HIGH SCHOOL. MONDAY MORNING.

GOOD MORNING, *NIGHT OF THE LIVING DEAD.*

≩GROAN≨

CRAZY NIGHT?

KLONK

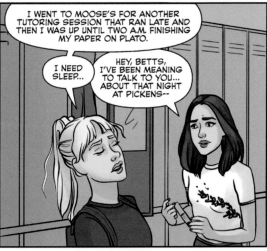

I WENT TO MOOSE'S FOR ANOTHER TUTORING SESSION THAT RAN LATE AND THEN I WAS UP UNTIL TWO A.M. FINISHING MY PAPER ON PLATO.

I NEED SLEEP...

HEY, BETTS, I'VE BEEN MEANING TO TALK TO YOU... ABOUT THAT NIGHT AT PICKENS--

BETTY! THERE YOU ARE!

Huh?!

WHY AREN'T YOU IN THE CAFETERIA? WE'RE HAVING OUR STUDENT ELECTION MEETING AND YOU NEED TO BE THERE!

I *DO?*

Um, YOU'RE MY CAMPAIGN MANAGER AND POTENTIAL *VICE PRESIDENT* OF STUDENT COUNCIL!

NOW C'MON, LET'S *GO!*

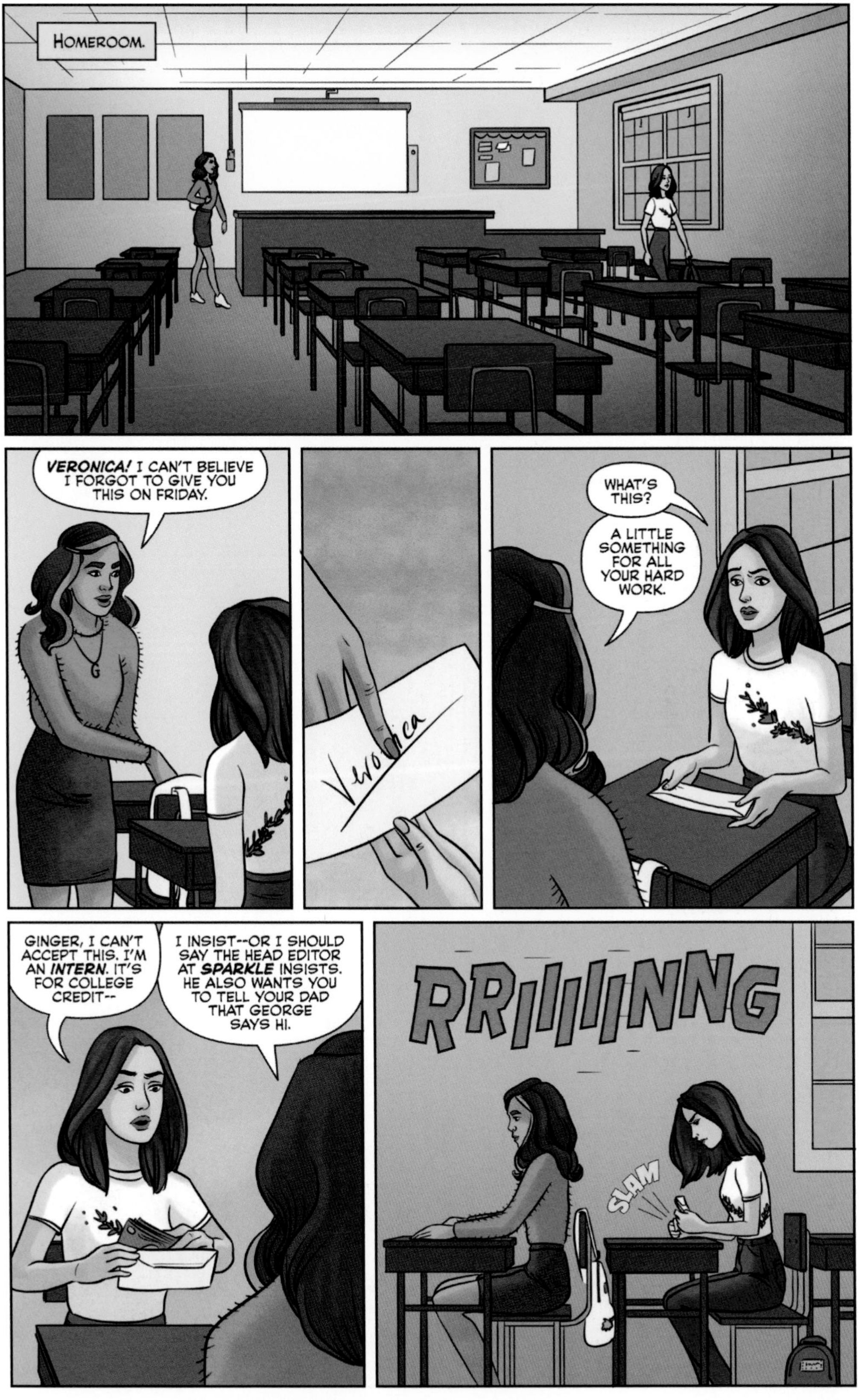
HOMEROOM.
VERONICA! I CAN'T BELIEVE I FORGOT TO GIVE YOU THIS ON FRIDAY.
Veronica
WHAT'S THIS?
A LITTLE SOMETHING FOR ALL YOUR HARD WORK.
GINGER, I CAN'T ACCEPT THIS. I'M AN INTERN. IT'S FOR COLLEGE CREDIT--
I INSIST--OR I SHOULD SAY THE HEAD EDITOR AT SPARKLE INSISTS. HE ALSO WANTS YOU TO TELL YOUR DAD THAT GEORGE SAYS HI.
RRIIIIINNG
SLAM

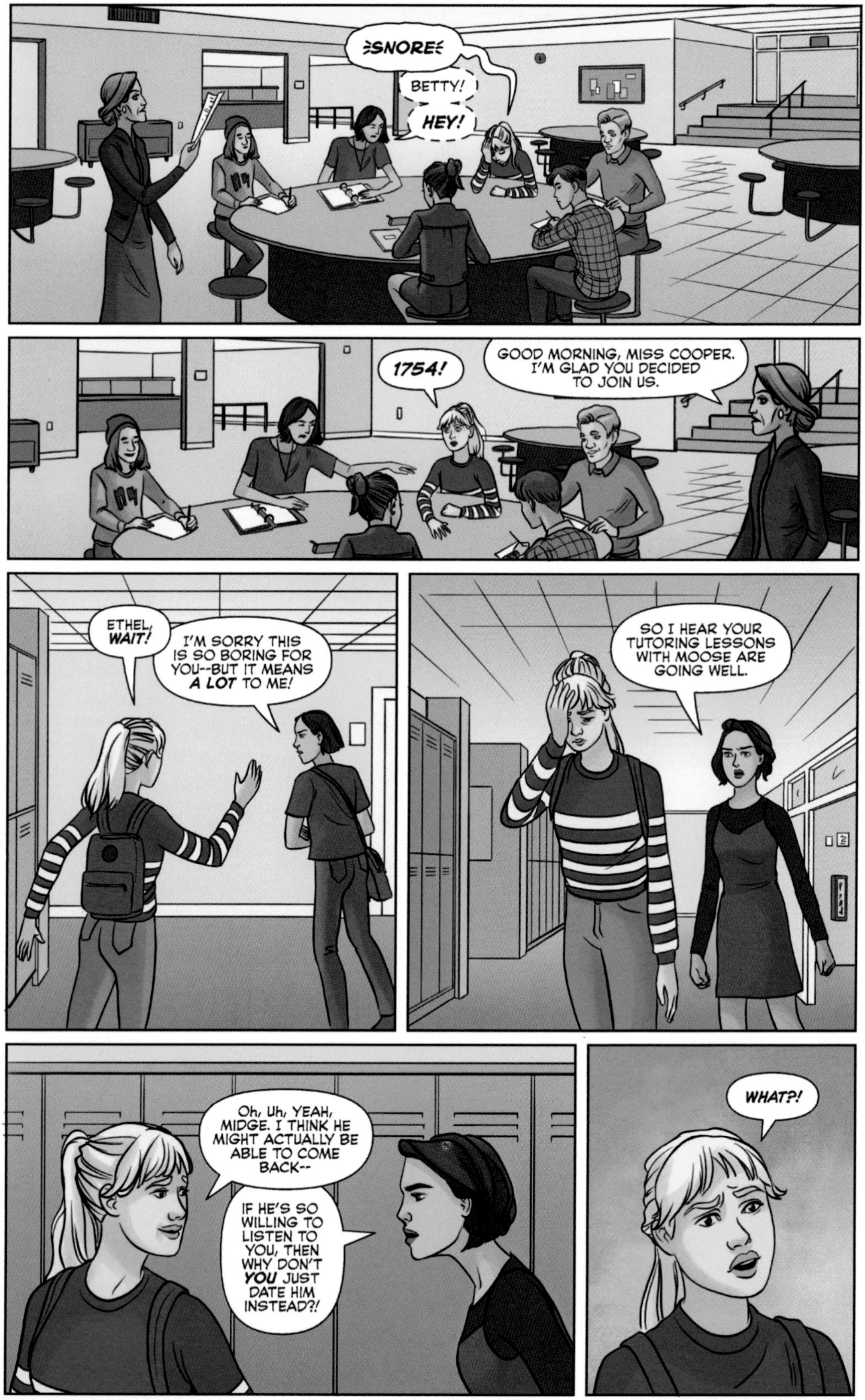

SNORE
BETTY!
HEY!
1754!
GOOD MORNING, MISS COOPER. I'M GLAD YOU DECIDED TO JOIN US.
ETHEL, WAIT!
I'M SORRY THIS IS SO BORING FOR YOU--BUT IT MEANS A LOT TO ME!
SO I HEAR YOUR TUTORING LESSONS WITH MOOSE ARE GOING WELL.
Oh, Uh, YEAH, MIDGE. I THINK HE MIGHT ACTUALLY BE ABLE TO COME BACK--
IF HE'S SO WILLING TO LISTEN TO YOU, THEN WHY DON'T YOU JUST DATE HIM INSTEAD?!
WHAT?!

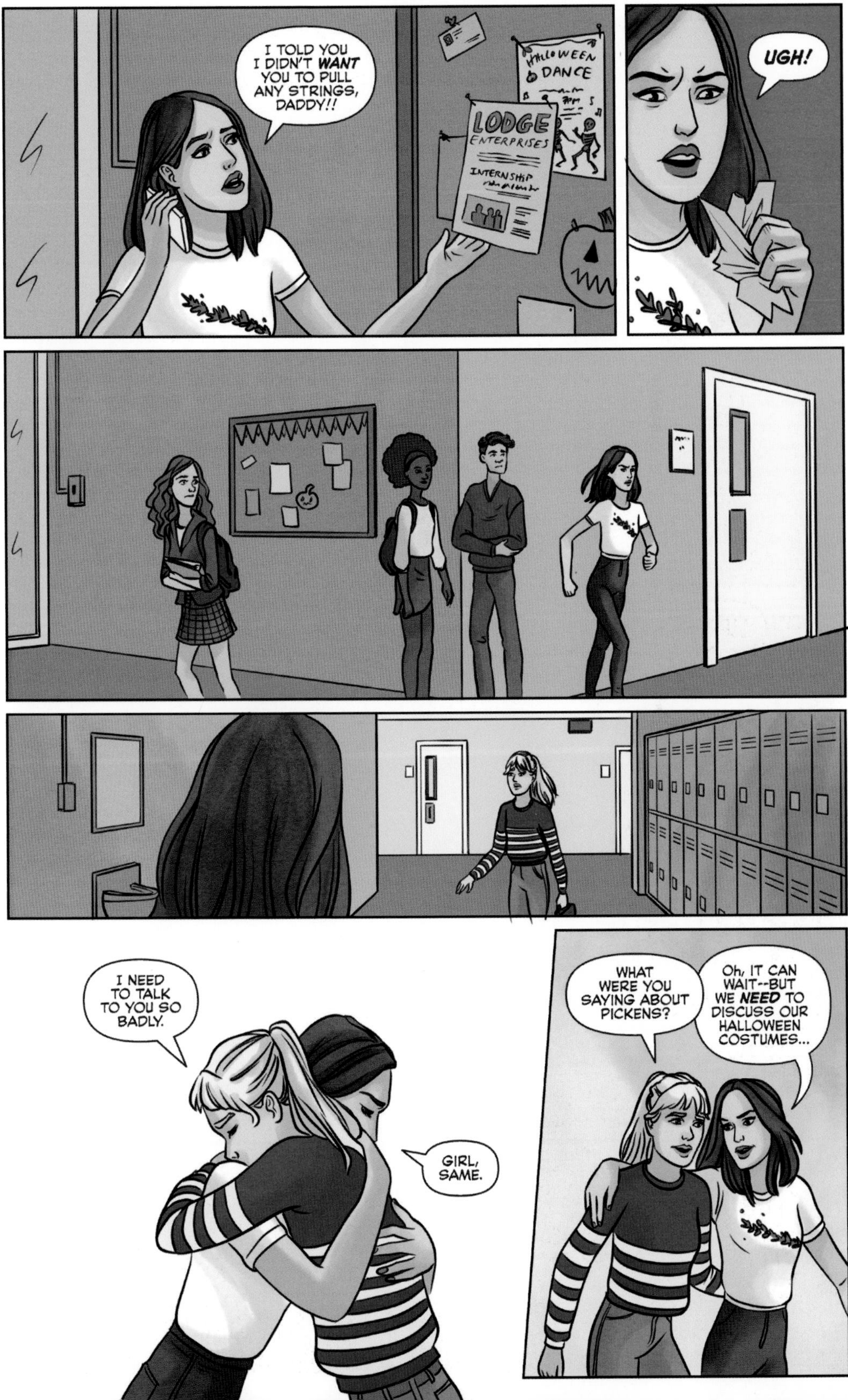

I TOLD YOU I DIDN'T WANT YOU TO PULL ANY STRINGS, DADDY!!
HALLOWEEN DANCE
LODGE ENTERPRISES
INTERNSHIP
UGH!
I NEED TO TALK TO YOU SO BADLY.
GIRL, SAME.
WHAT WERE YOU SAYING ABOUT PICKENS?
Oh, IT CAN WAIT--BUT WE NEED TO DISCUSS OUR HALLOWEEN COSTUMES...

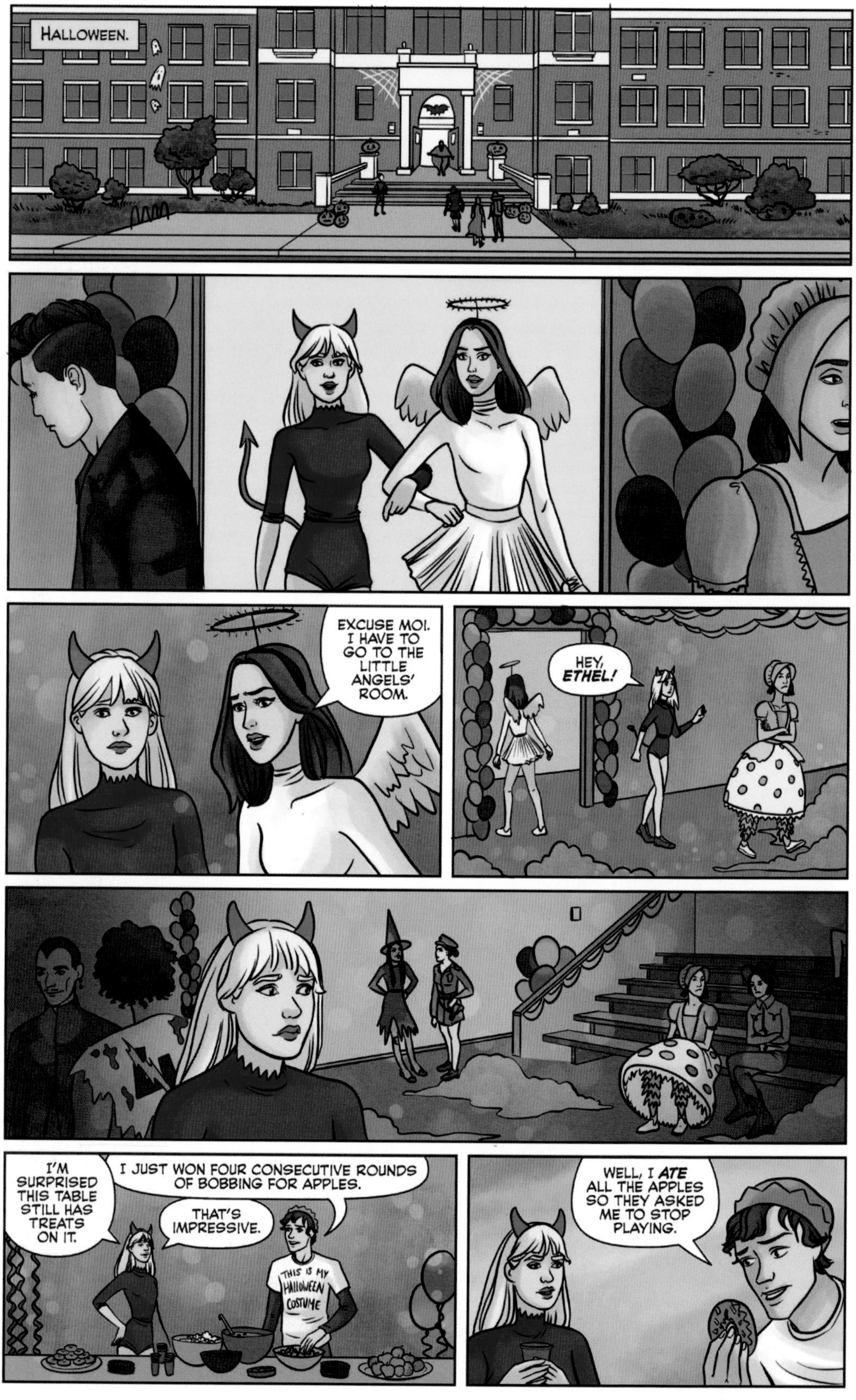
HALLOWEEN.
EXCUSE MOI. I HAVE TO GO TO THE LITTLE ANGELS' ROOM.
HEY, ETHEL!
I'M SURPRISED THIS TABLE STILL HAS TREATS ON IT.
I JUST WON FOUR CONSECUTIVE ROUNDS OF BOBBING FOR APPLES.
THAT'S IMPRESSIVE.
THIS IS MY HALLOWEEN COSTUME
WELL, I ATE ALL THE APPLES SO THEY ASKED ME TO STOP PLAYING.

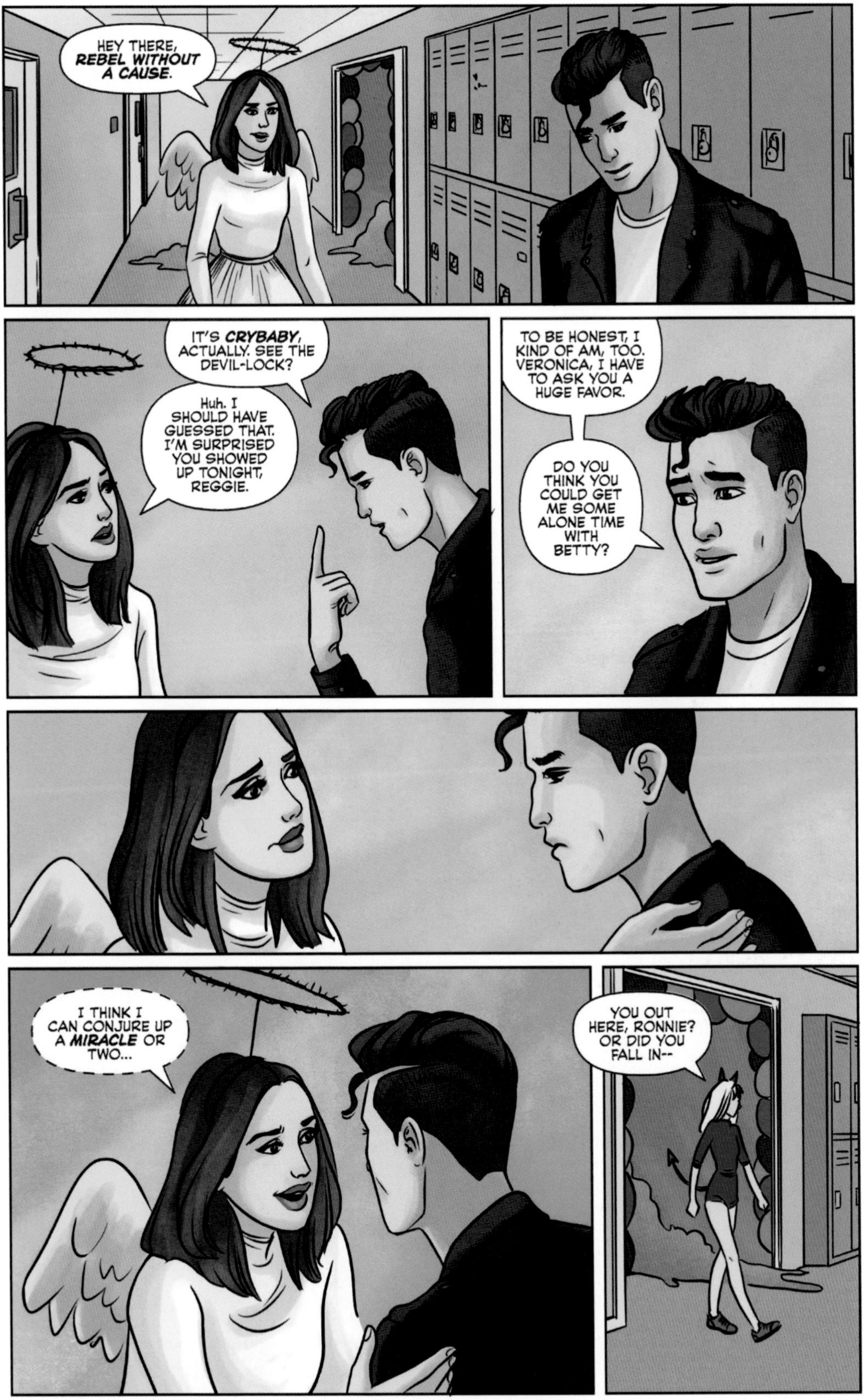
HEY THERE, **REBEL WITHOUT A CAUSE**.
IT'S **CRYBABY**, ACTUALLY. SEE THE DEVIL-LOCK?
Huh. I SHOULD HAVE GUESSED THAT. I'M SURPRISED YOU SHOWED UP TONIGHT, REGGIE.
TO BE HONEST, I KIND OF AM, TOO. VERONICA, I HAVE TO ASK YOU A HUGE FAVOR.
DO YOU THINK YOU COULD GET ME SOME ALONE TIME WITH BETTY?
I THINK I CAN CONJURE UP A **MIRACLE** OR TWO...
YOU OUT HERE, RONNIE? OR DID YOU FALL IN--

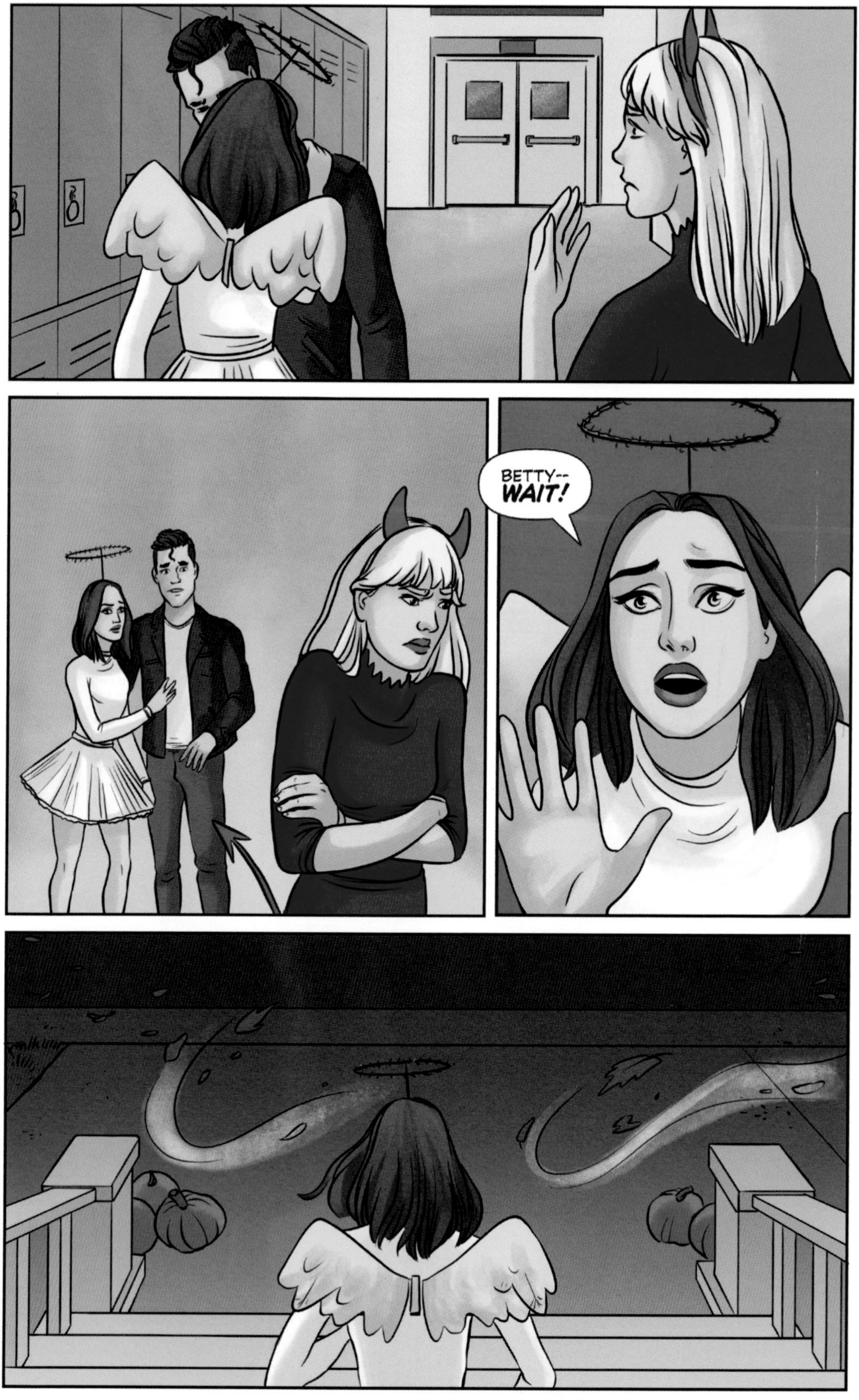
BETTY--
WAIT!

TO BE CONTINUED...

03

STORY BY
JAMIE LEE ROTANTE
LETTERING BY
JACK MORELLI

ART BY
SANDRA LANZ
COLORS BY
KELLY FITZPATRICK

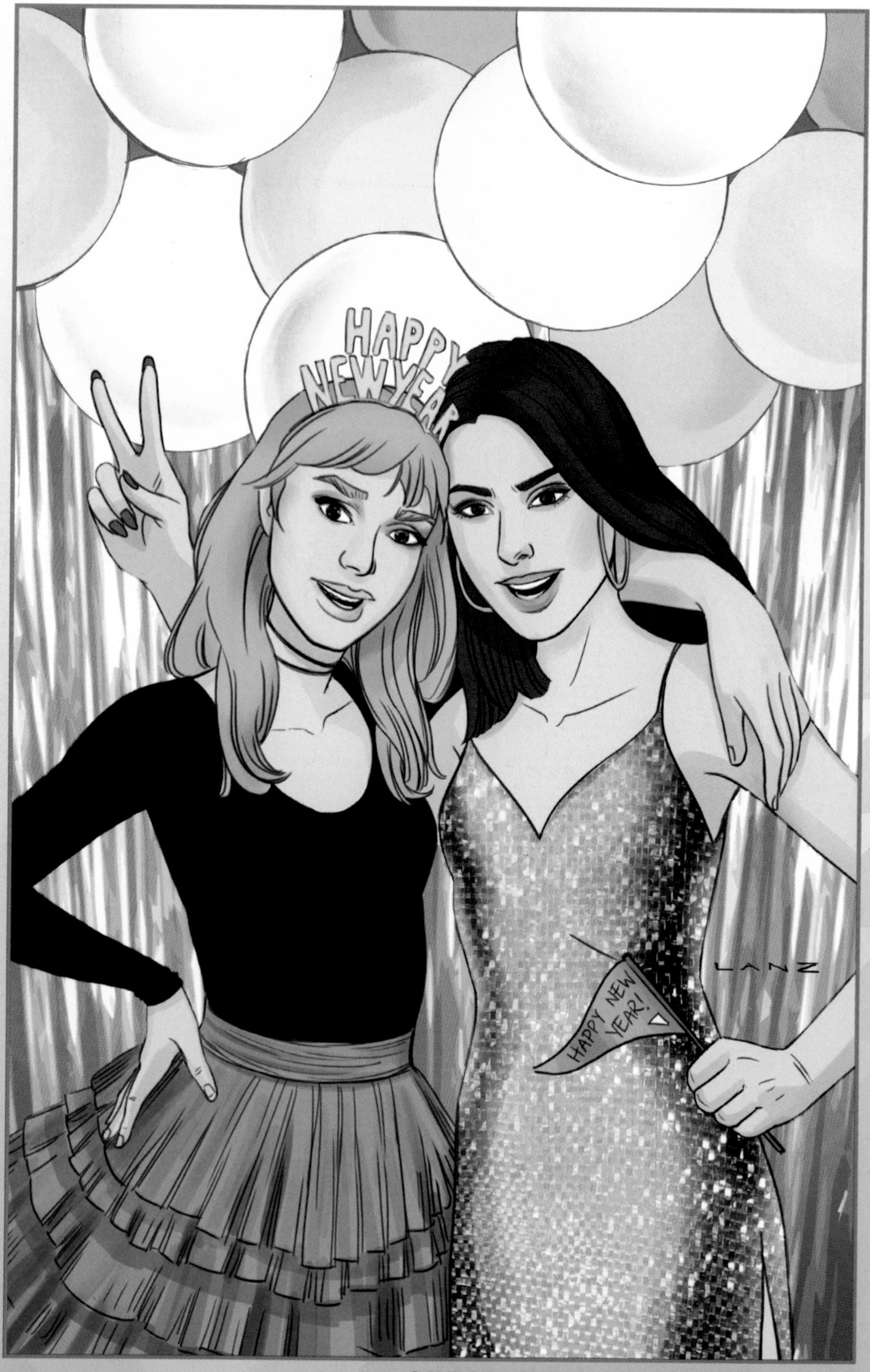

HAPPY NEW YEAR
LANZ
HAPPY NEW YEAR!

COVER ART: **SANDRA LANZ**

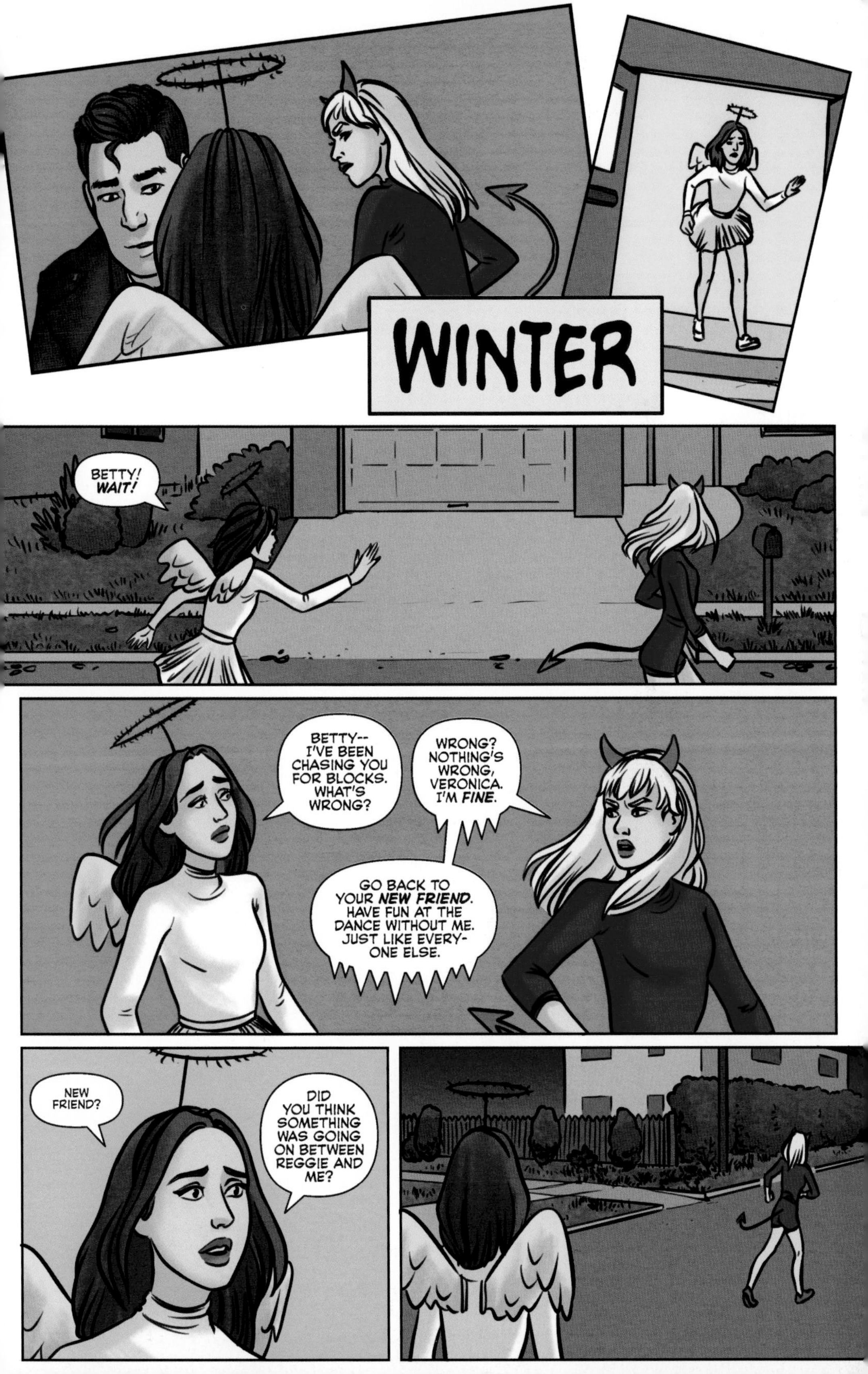
WINTER
BETTY! WAIT!
BETTY-- I'VE BEEN CHASING YOU FOR BLOCKS. WHAT'S WRONG?
WRONG? NOTHING'S WRONG, VERONICA. I'M FINE.
GO BACK TO YOUR NEW FRIEND. HAVE FUN AT THE DANCE WITHOUT ME. JUST LIKE EVERY-ONE ELSE.
NEW FRIEND?
DID YOU THINK SOMETHING WAS GOING ON BETWEEN REGGIE AND ME?

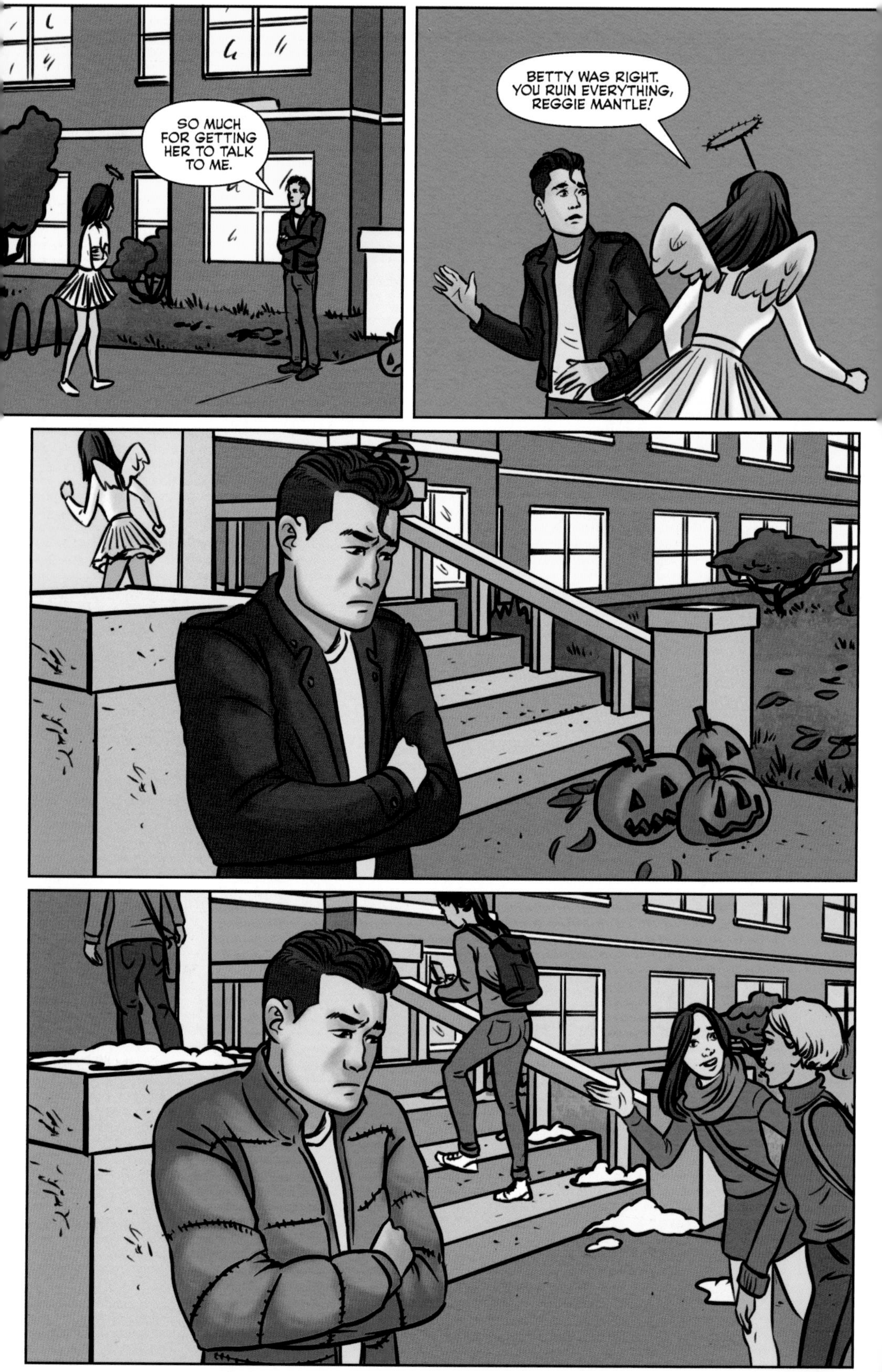
SO MUCH FOR GETTING HER TO TALK TO ME.
BETTY WAS RIGHT. YOU RUIN EVERYTHING, REGGIE MANTLE!

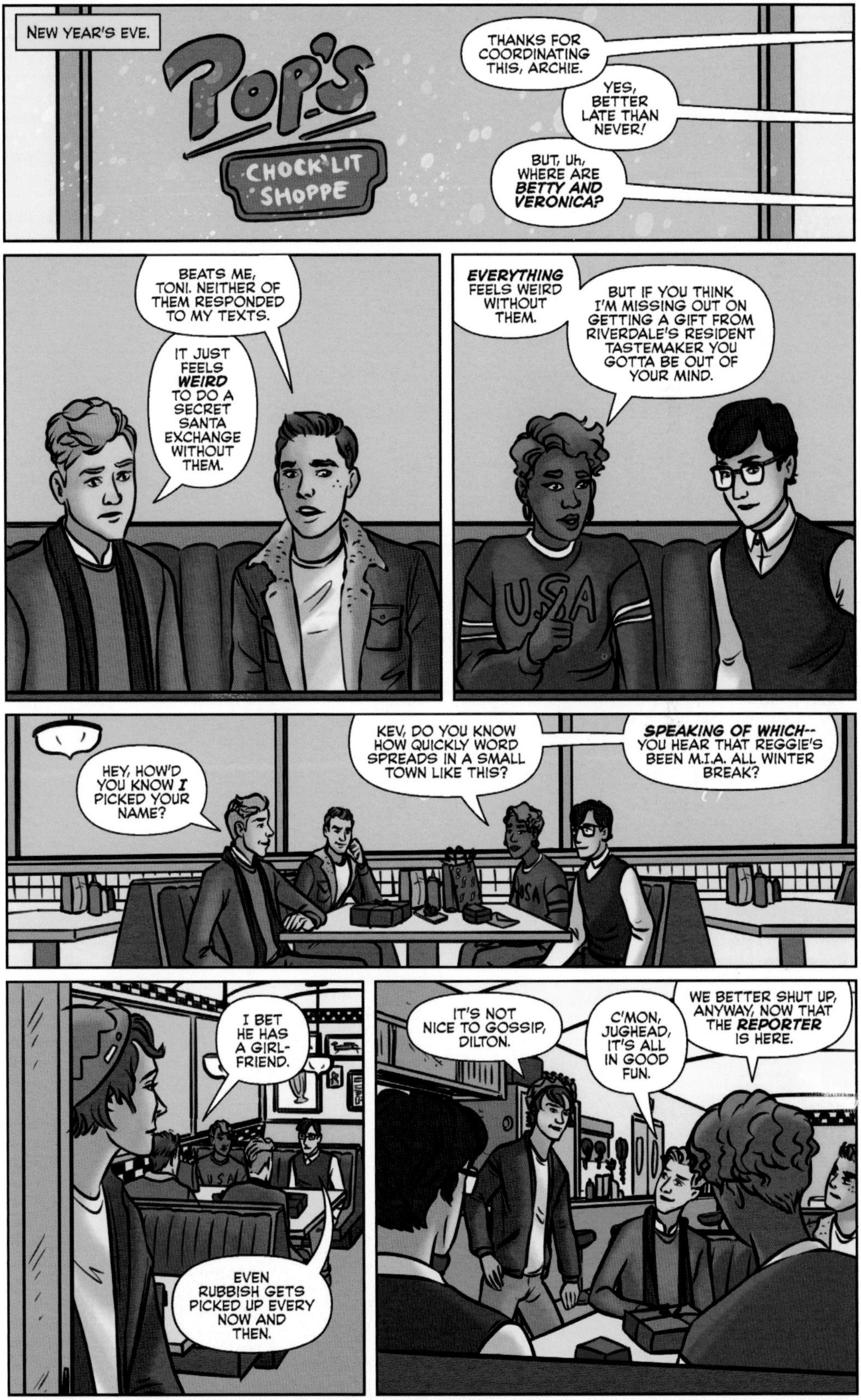

NEW YEAR'S EVE.
POP'S
CHOCK'LIT SHOPPE
THANKS FOR COORDINATING THIS, ARCHIE.
YES, BETTER LATE THAN NEVER!
BUT, Uh, WHERE ARE BETTY AND VERONICA?
BEATS ME, TONI. NEITHER OF THEM RESPONDED TO MY TEXTS.
IT JUST FEELS WEIRD TO DO A SECRET SANTA EXCHANGE WITHOUT THEM.
EVERYTHING FEELS WEIRD WITHOUT THEM.
BUT IF YOU THINK I'M MISSING OUT ON GETTING A GIFT FROM RIVERDALE'S RESIDENT TASTEMAKER YOU GOTTA BE OUT OF YOUR MIND.
USA
HEY, HOW'D YOU KNOW I PICKED YOUR NAME?
KEV, DO YOU KNOW HOW QUICKLY WORD SPREADS IN A SMALL TOWN LIKE THIS?
SPEAKING OF WHICH-- YOU HEAR THAT REGGIE'S BEEN M.I.A. ALL WINTER BREAK?
I BET HE HAS A GIRL-FRIEND.
EVEN RUBBISH GETS PICKED UP EVERY NOW AND THEN.
IT'S NOT NICE TO GOSSIP, DILTON.
C'MON, JUGHEAD, IT'S ALL IN GOOD FUN.
WE BETTER SHUT UP, ANYWAY, NOW THAT THE REPORTER IS HERE.

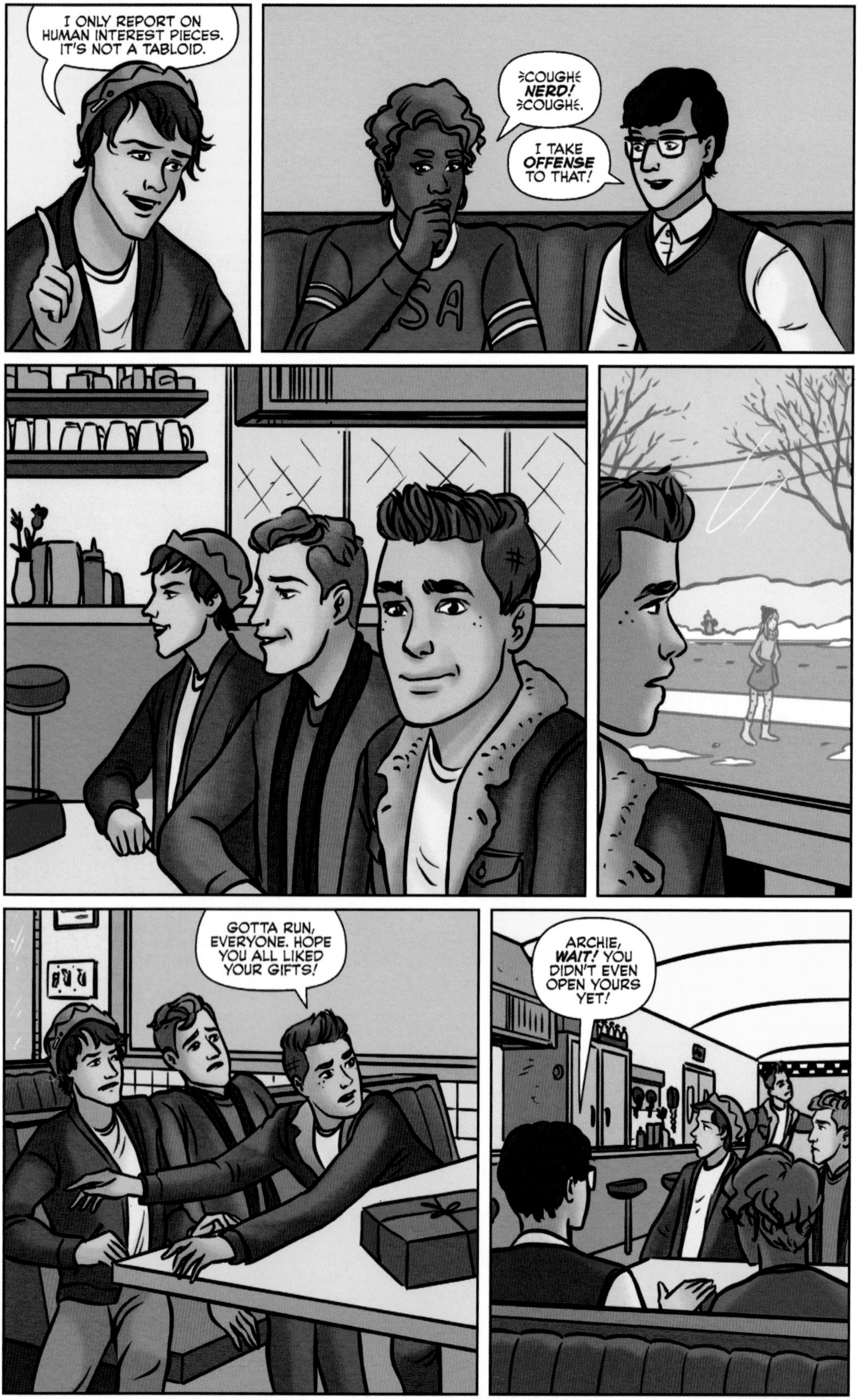
I ONLY REPORT ON HUMAN INTEREST PIECES. IT'S NOT A TABLOID.
COUGH *NERD!* COUGH.
I TAKE *OFFENSE* TO THAT!
GOTTA RUN, EVERYONE. HOPE YOU ALL LIKED YOUR GIFTS!
ARCHIE, *WAIT!* YOU DIDN'T EVEN OPEN YOURS YET!

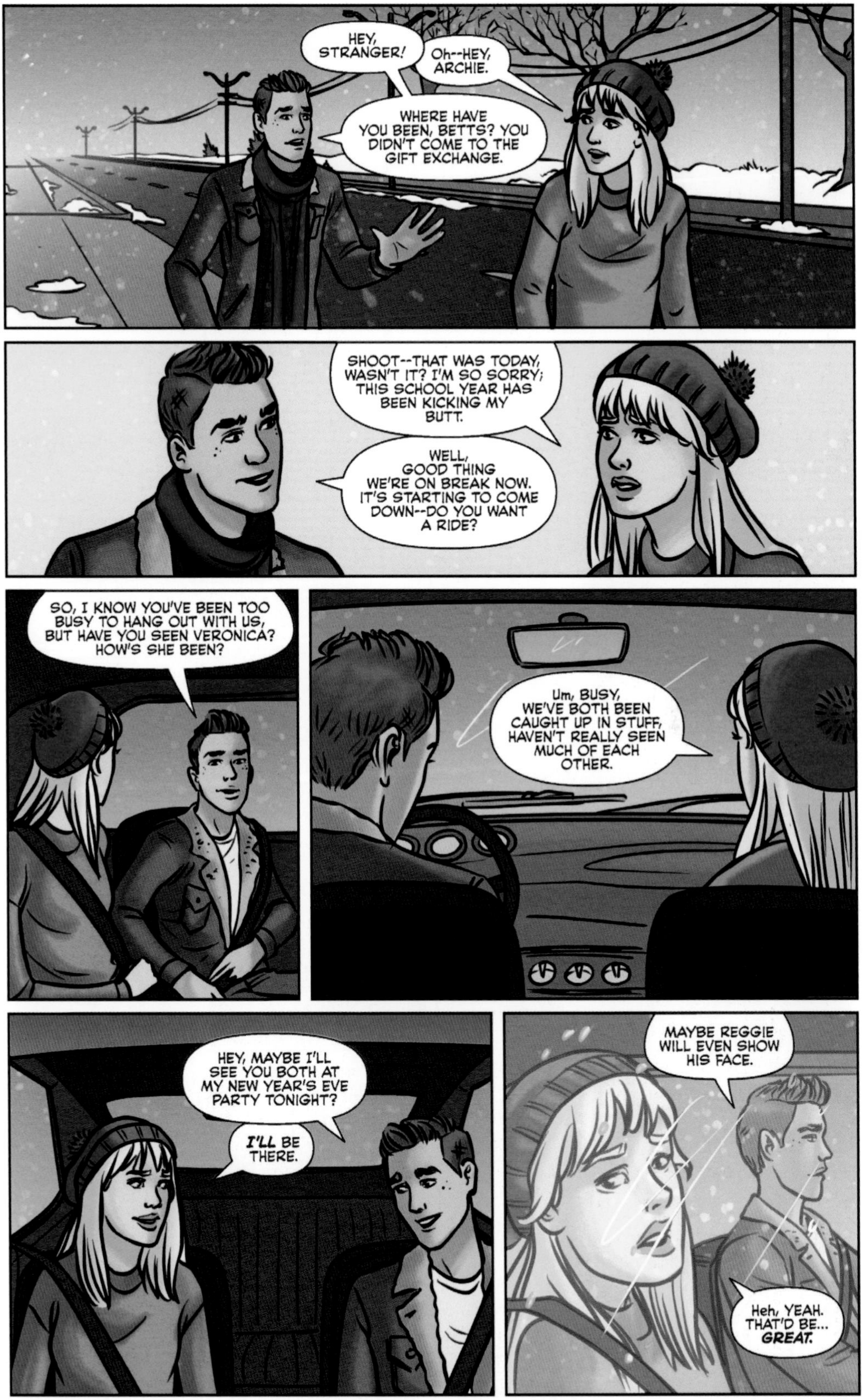
HEY, STRANGER!
Oh--HEY, ARCHIE.
WHERE HAVE YOU BEEN, BETTS? YOU DIDN'T COME TO THE GIFT EXCHANGE.
SHOOT--THAT WAS TODAY, WASN'T IT? I'M SO SORRY; THIS SCHOOL YEAR HAS BEEN KICKING MY BUTT.
WELL, GOOD THING WE'RE ON BREAK NOW. IT'S STARTING TO COME DOWN--DO YOU WANT A RIDE?
SO, I KNOW YOU'VE BEEN TOO BUSY TO HANG OUT WITH US, BUT HAVE YOU SEEN VERONICA? HOW'S SHE BEEN?
Um, BUSY, WE'VE BOTH BEEN CAUGHT UP IN STUFF, HAVEN'T REALLY SEEN MUCH OF EACH OTHER.
HEY, MAYBE I'LL SEE YOU BOTH AT MY NEW YEAR'S EVE PARTY TONIGHT?
I'LL BE THERE.
MAYBE REGGIE WILL EVEN SHOW HIS FACE.
Heh, YEAH. THAT'D BE... ***GREAT.***

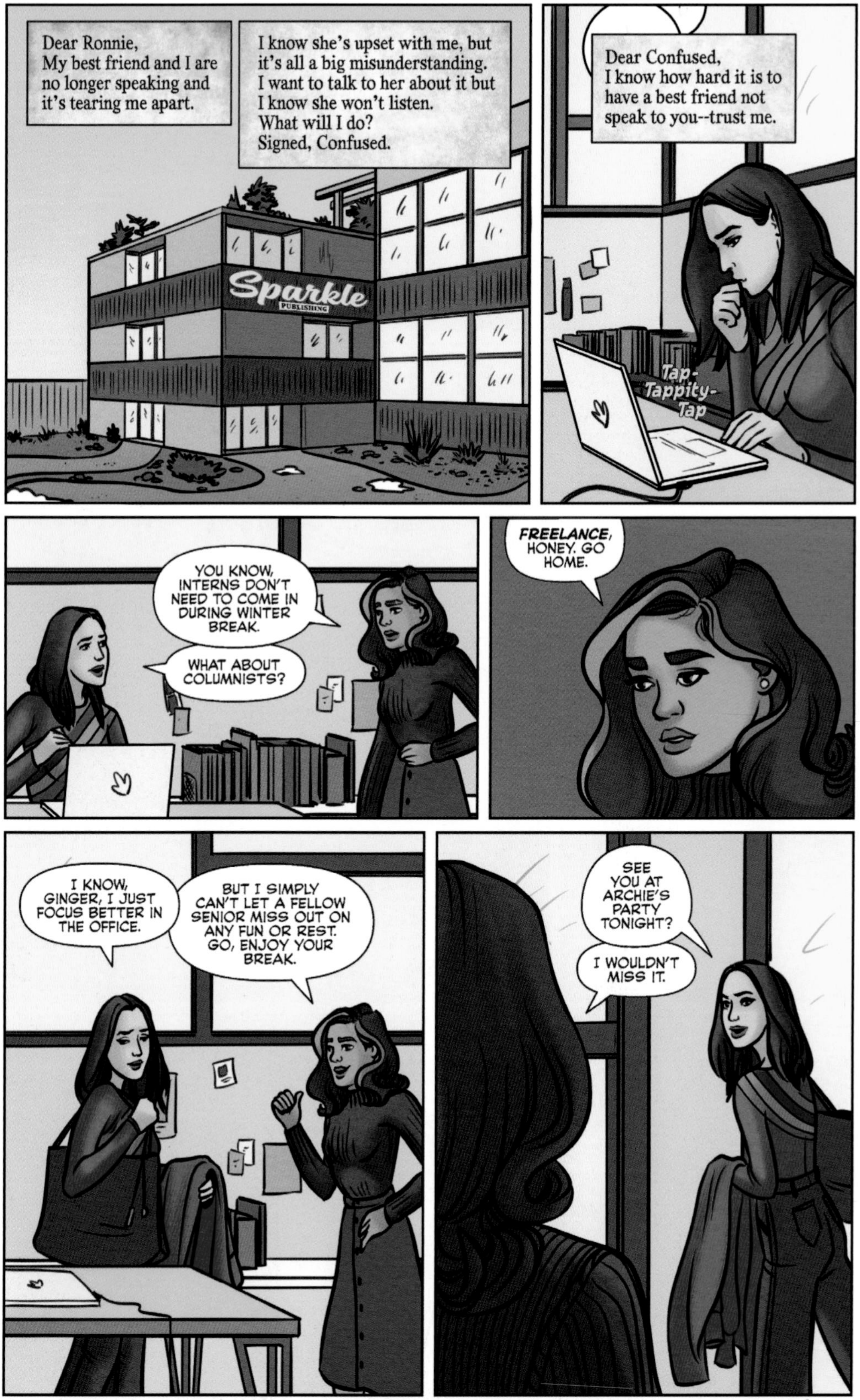
Dear Ronnie,
My best friend and I are no longer speaking and it's tearing me apart.
I know she's upset with me, but it's all a big misunderstanding. I want to talk to her about it but I know she won't listen. What will I do? Signed, Confused.
Sparkle PUBLISHING
Dear Confused, I know how hard it is to have a best friend not speak to you--trust me.
Tap-Tappity-Tap
YOU KNOW, INTERNS DON'T NEED TO COME IN DURING WINTER BREAK.
WHAT ABOUT COLUMNISTS?
FREELANCE, HONEY. GO HOME.
I KNOW, GINGER, I JUST FOCUS BETTER IN THE OFFICE.
BUT I SIMPLY CAN'T LET A FELLOW SENIOR MISS OUT ON ANY FUN OR REST. GO, ENJOY YOUR BREAK.
SEE YOU AT ARCHIE'S PARTY TONIGHT?
I WOULDN'T MISS IT.

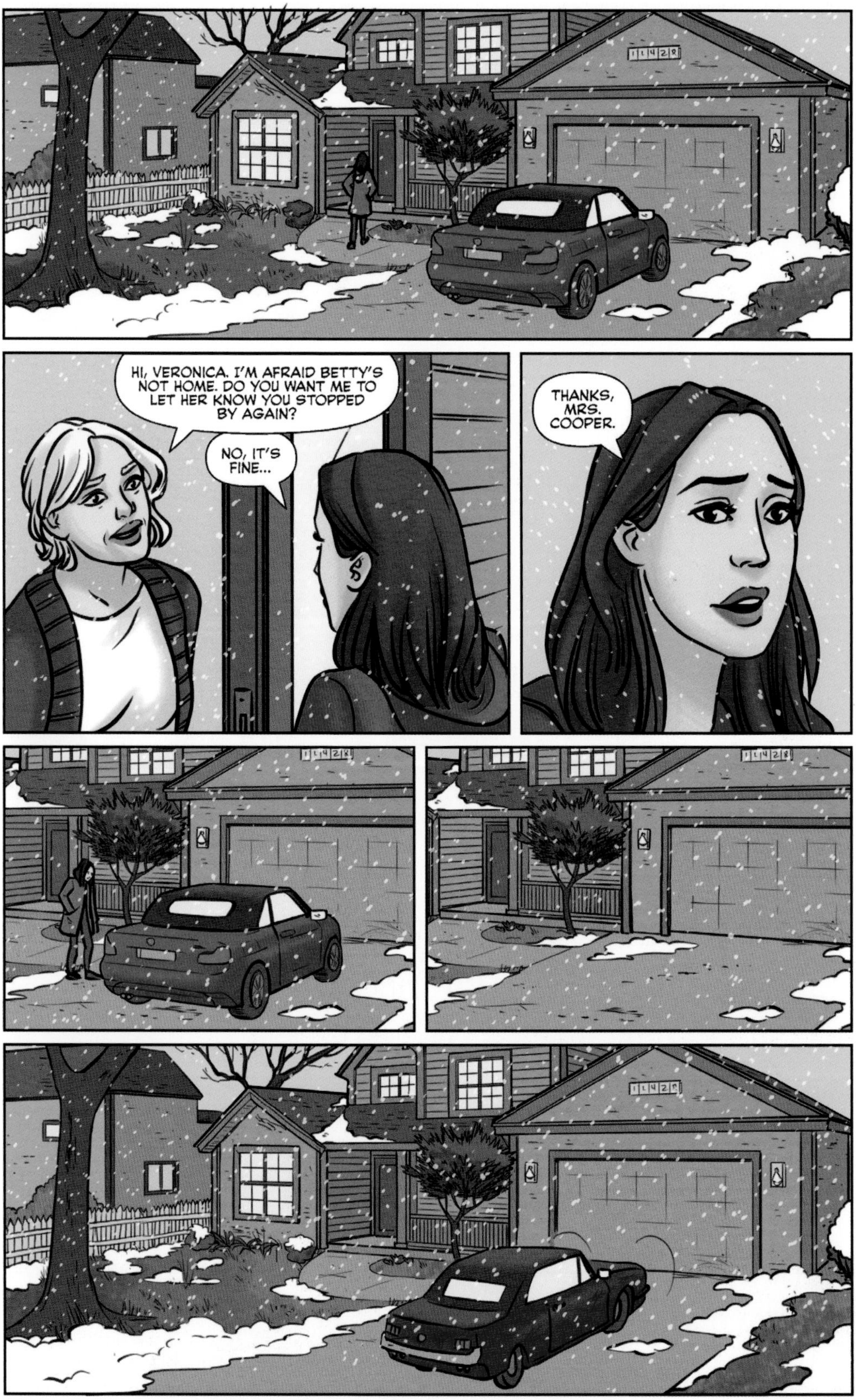
HI, VERONICA. I'M AFRAID BETTY'S NOT HOME. DO YOU WANT ME TO LET HER KNOW YOU STOPPED BY AGAIN?
NO, IT'S FINE...
THANKS, MRS. COOPER.

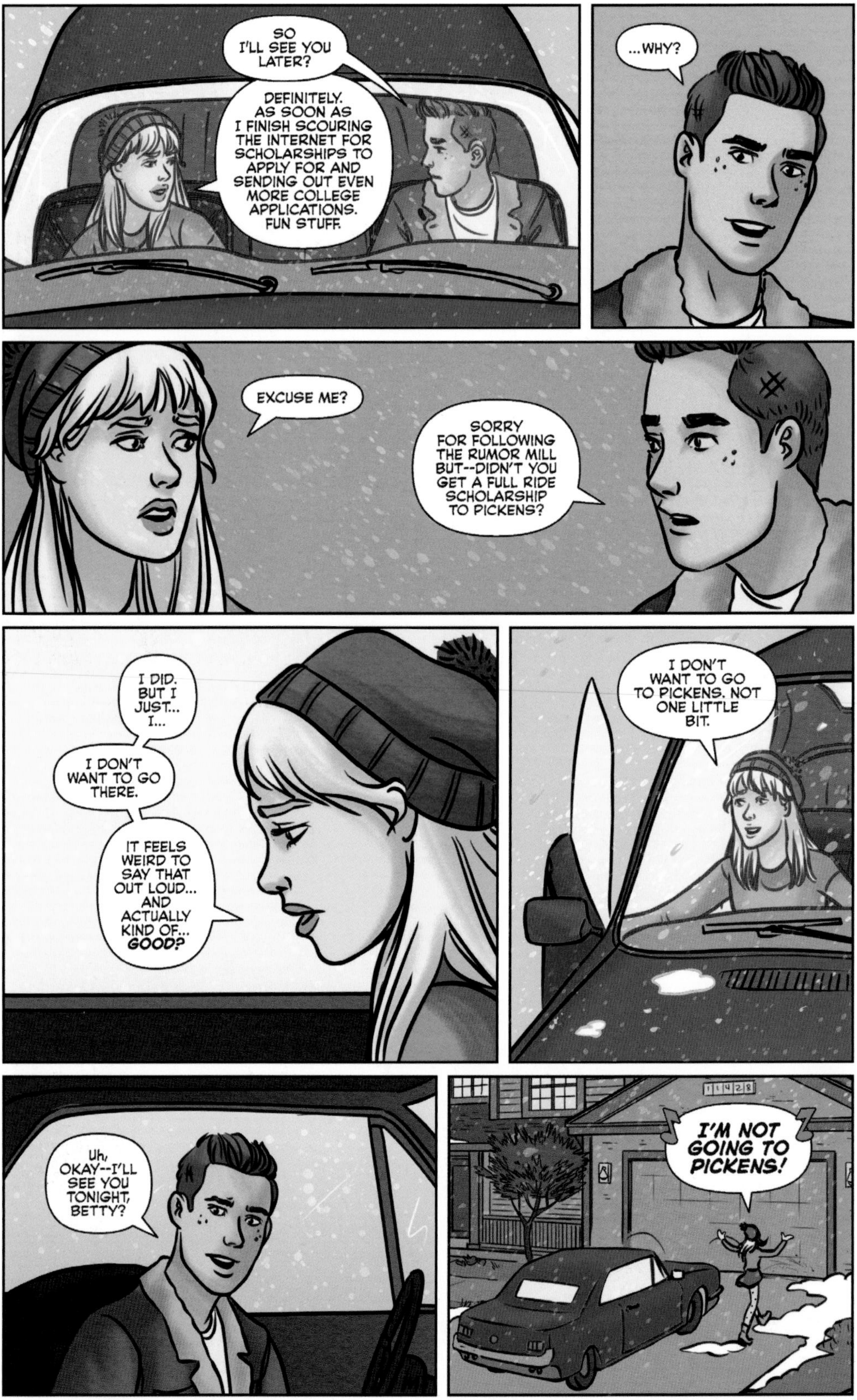
SO I'LL SEE YOU LATER?
DEFINITELY. AS SOON AS I FINISH SCOURING THE INTERNET FOR SCHOLARSHIPS TO APPLY FOR AND SENDING OUT EVEN MORE COLLEGE APPLICATIONS. FUN STUFF.
...WHY?
EXCUSE ME?
SORRY FOR FOLLOWING THE RUMOR MILL BUT--DIDN'T YOU GET A FULL RIDE SCHOLARSHIP TO PICKENS?
I DID. BUT I JUST... I...
I DON'T WANT TO GO THERE.
IT FEELS WEIRD TO SAY THAT OUT LOUD... AND ACTUALLY KIND OF... GOOD?
I DON'T WANT TO GO TO PICKENS. NOT ONE LITTLE BIT.
Uh, OKAY--I'LL SEE YOU TONIGHT, BETTY?
11428
I'M NOT GOING TO PICKENS!

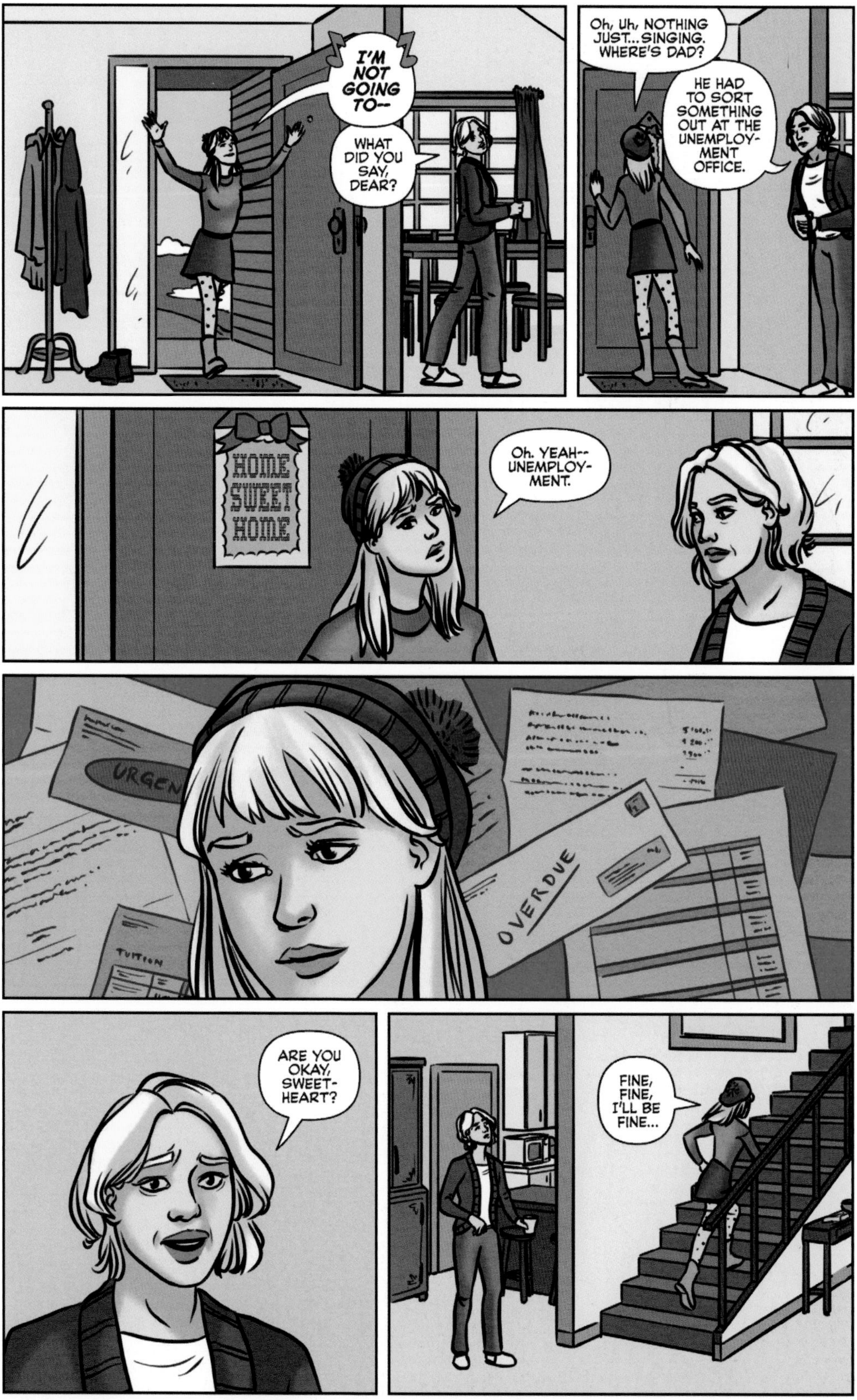
I'M NOT GOING TO--
WHAT DID YOU SAY, DEAR?
Oh, Uh, NOTHING JUST...SINGING. WHERE'S DAD?
HE HAD TO SORT SOMETHING OUT AT THE UNEMPLOYMENT OFFICE.
HOME SWEET HOME
Oh. YEAH--UNEMPLOYMENT.
URGEN
OVERDUE
TUITION
ARE YOU OKAY, SWEETHEART?
FINE, FINE, I'LL BE FINE...

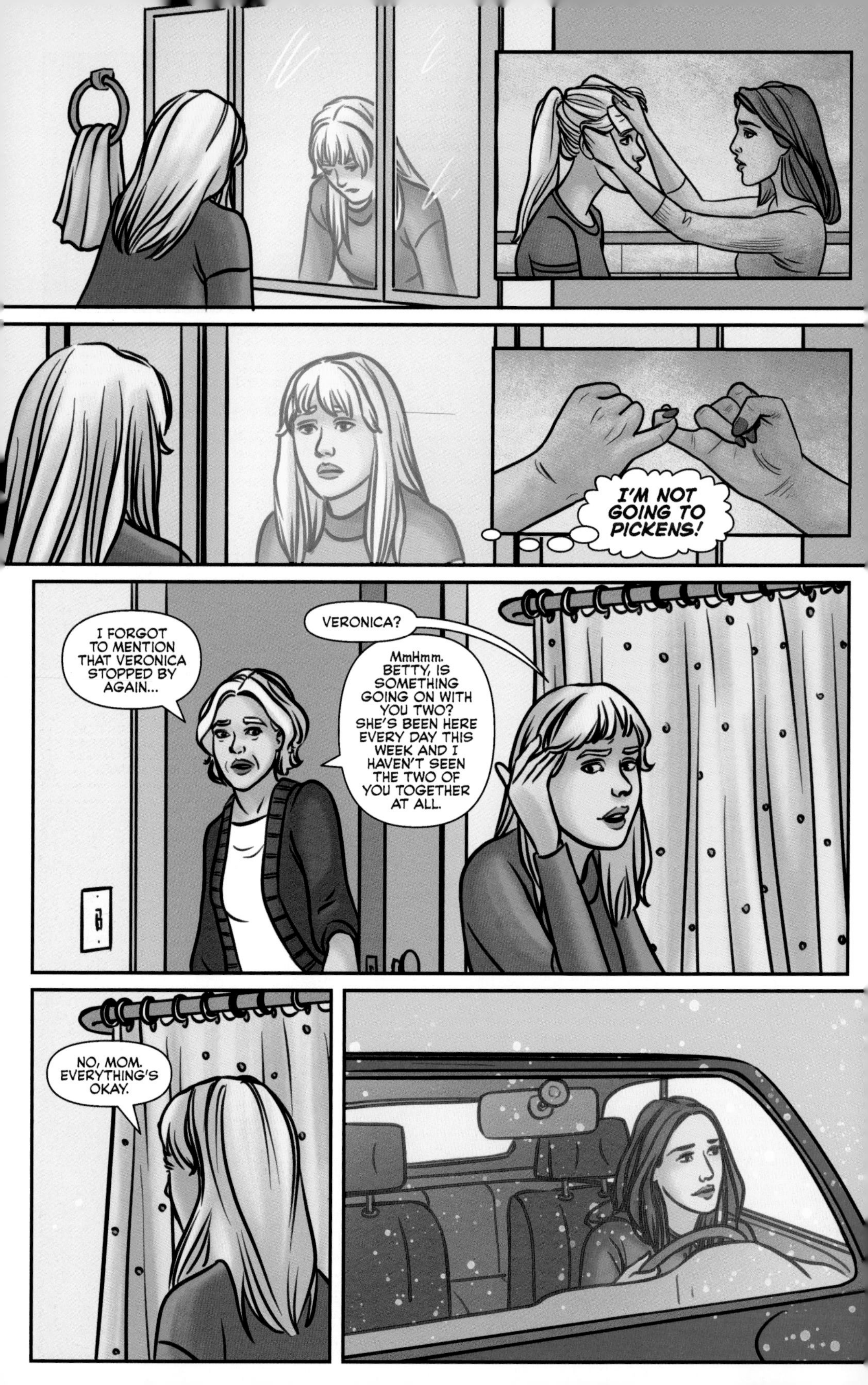
I'M NOT GOING TO PICKENS!
I FORGOT TO MENTION THAT VERONICA STOPPED BY AGAIN...
VERONICA?
MmHmm. BETTY, IS SOMETHING GOING ON WITH YOU TWO? SHE'S BEEN HERE EVERY DAY THIS WEEK AND I HAVEN'T SEEN THE TWO OF YOU TOGETHER AT ALL.
NO, MOM. EVERYTHING'S OKAY.

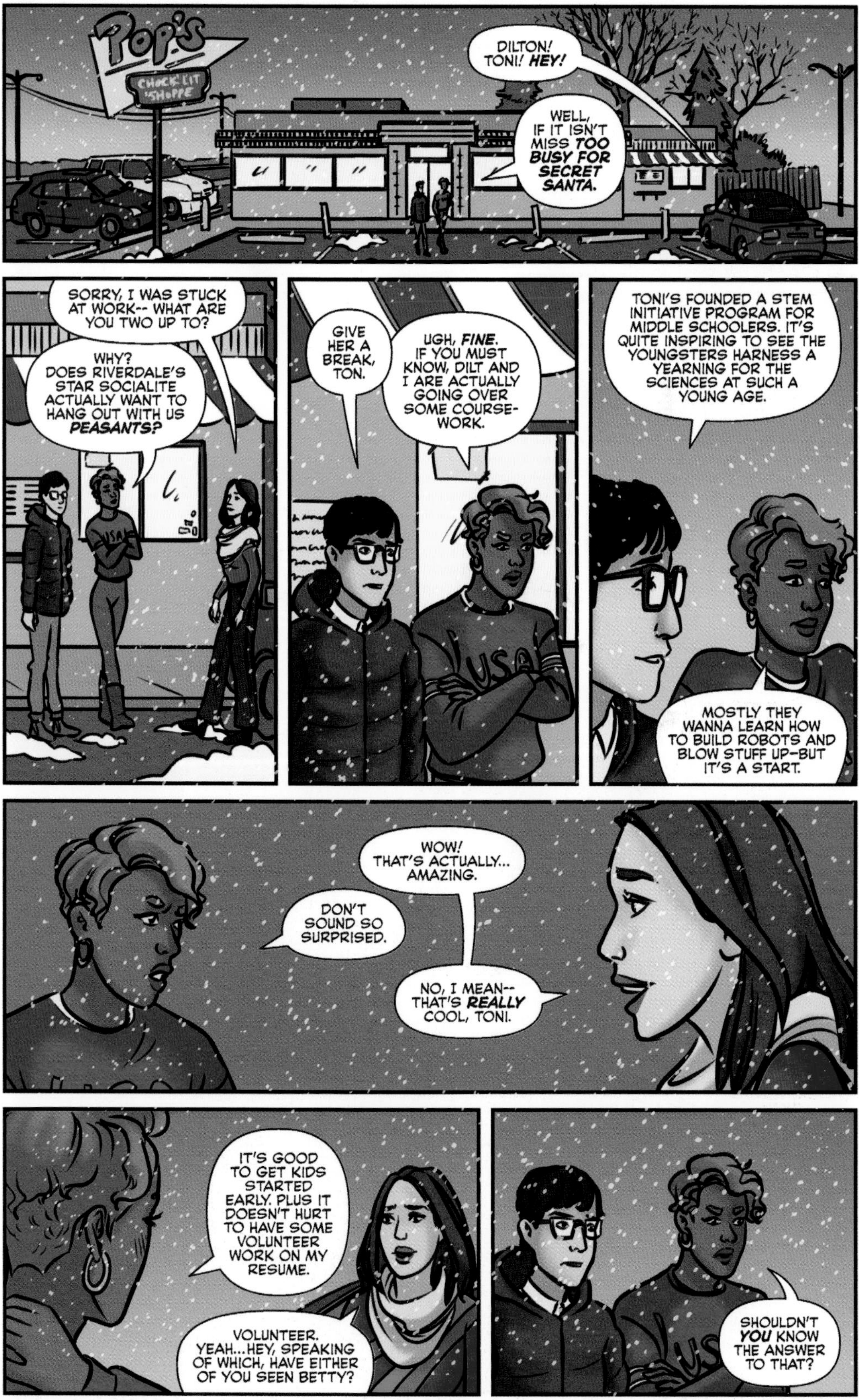
POP'S
CHOCK'LIT SHOPPE
DILTON! TONI! HEY!
WELL, IF IT ISN'T MISS TOO BUSY FOR SECRET SANTA.
SORRY, I WAS STUCK AT WORK-- WHAT ARE YOU TWO UP TO?
WHY? DOES RIVERDALE'S STAR SOCIALITE ACTUALLY WANT TO HANG OUT WITH US PEASANTS?
GIVE HER A BREAK, TON.
UGH, FINE. IF YOU MUST KNOW, DILT AND I ARE ACTUALLY GOING OVER SOME COURSE-WORK.
TONI'S FOUNDED A STEM INITIATIVE PROGRAM FOR MIDDLE SCHOOLERS. IT'S QUITE INSPIRING TO SEE THE YOUNGSTERS HARNESS A YEARNING FOR THE SCIENCES AT SUCH A YOUNG AGE.
MOSTLY THEY WANNA LEARN HOW TO BUILD ROBOTS AND BLOW STUFF UP—BUT IT'S A START.
WOW! THAT'S ACTUALLY... AMAZING.
DON'T SOUND SO SURPRISED.
NO, I MEAN-- THAT'S REALLY COOL, TONI.
IT'S GOOD TO GET KIDS STARTED EARLY. PLUS IT DOESN'T HURT TO HAVE SOME VOLUNTEER WORK ON MY RESUME.
VOLUNTEER. YEAH...HEY, SPEAKING OF WHICH, HAVE EITHER OF YOU SEEN BETTY?
SHOULDN'T YOU KNOW THE ANSWER TO THAT?

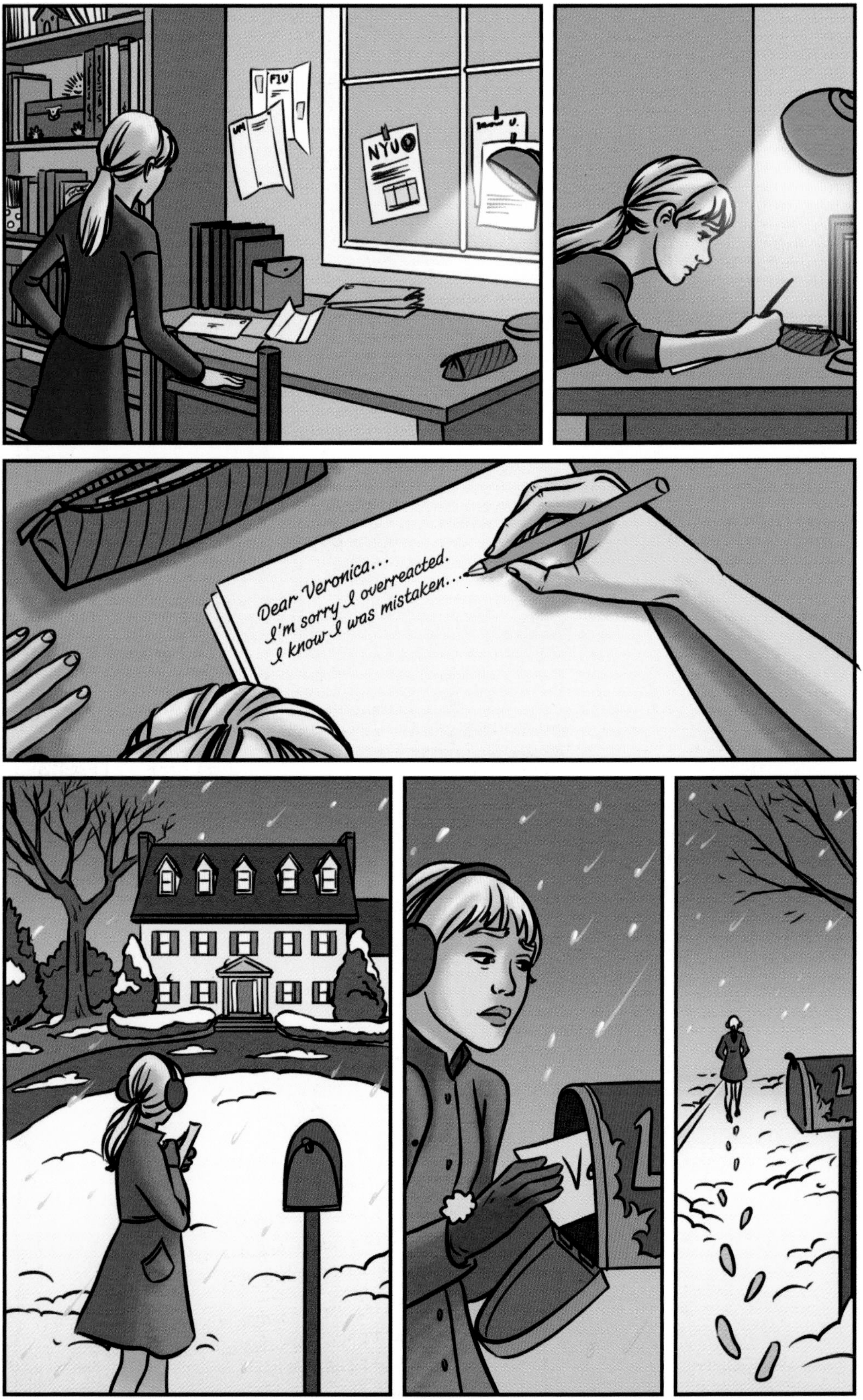
FIU
NYU
Dear Veronica...
I'm sorry I overreacted.
I know I was mistaken...

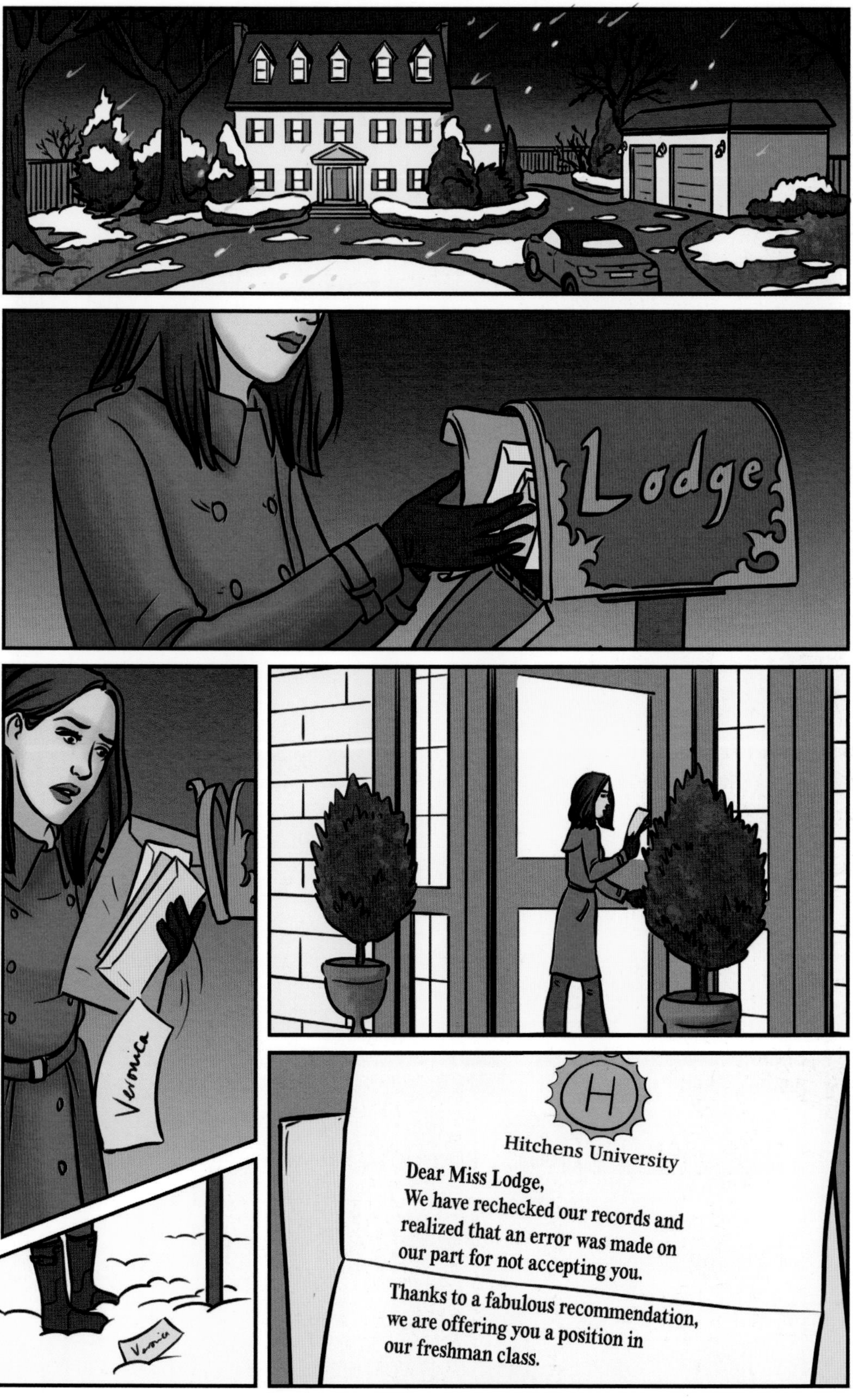
Lodge
Veronica
Veronica
Hitchens University
Dear Miss Lodge,
We have rechecked our records and realized that an error was made on our part for not accepting you.
Thanks to a fabulous recommendation, we are offering you a position in our freshman class.

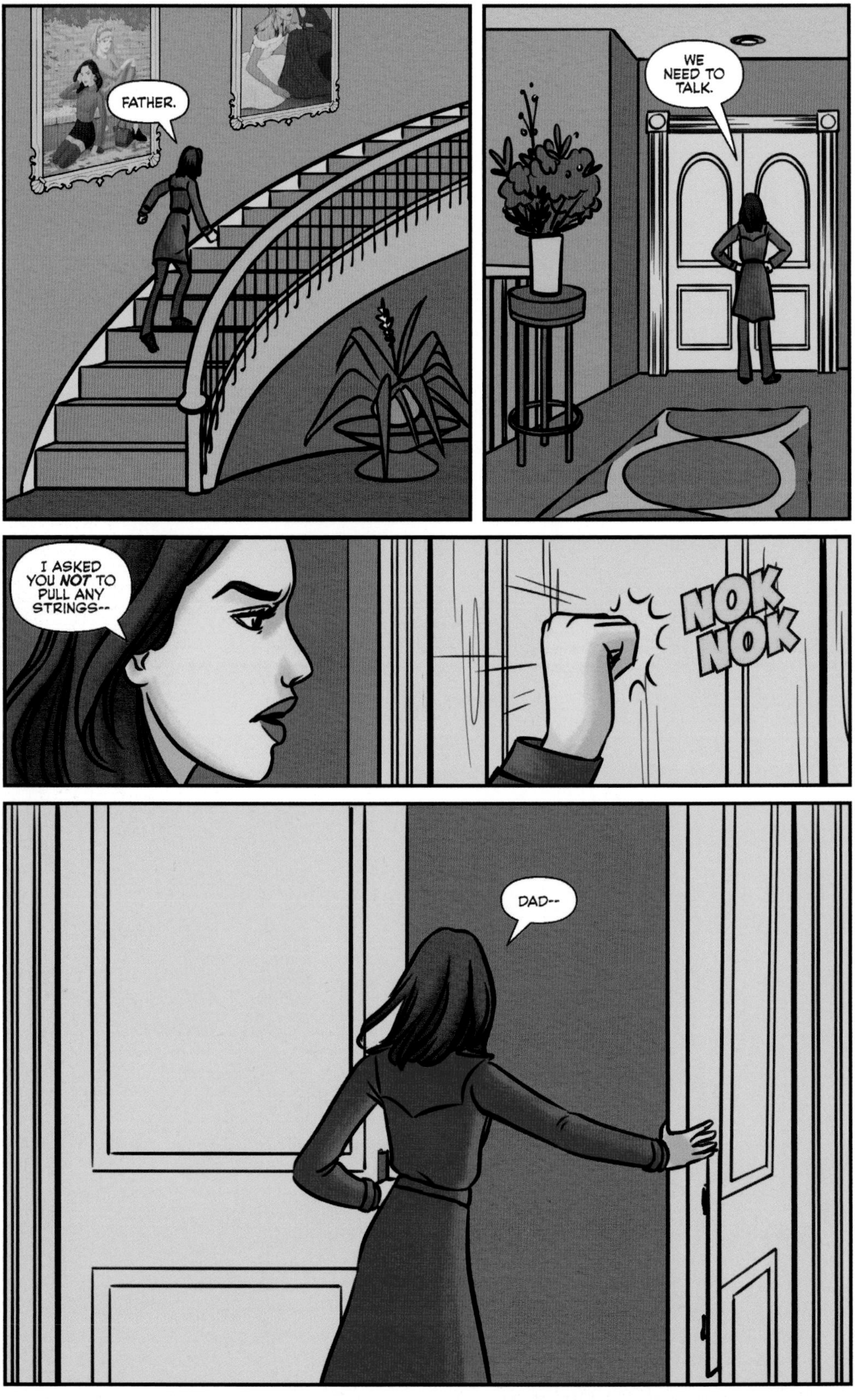
FATHER.
WE NEED TO TALK.
I ASKED YOU *NOT* TO PULL ANY STRINGS--
NOK NOK
DAD--

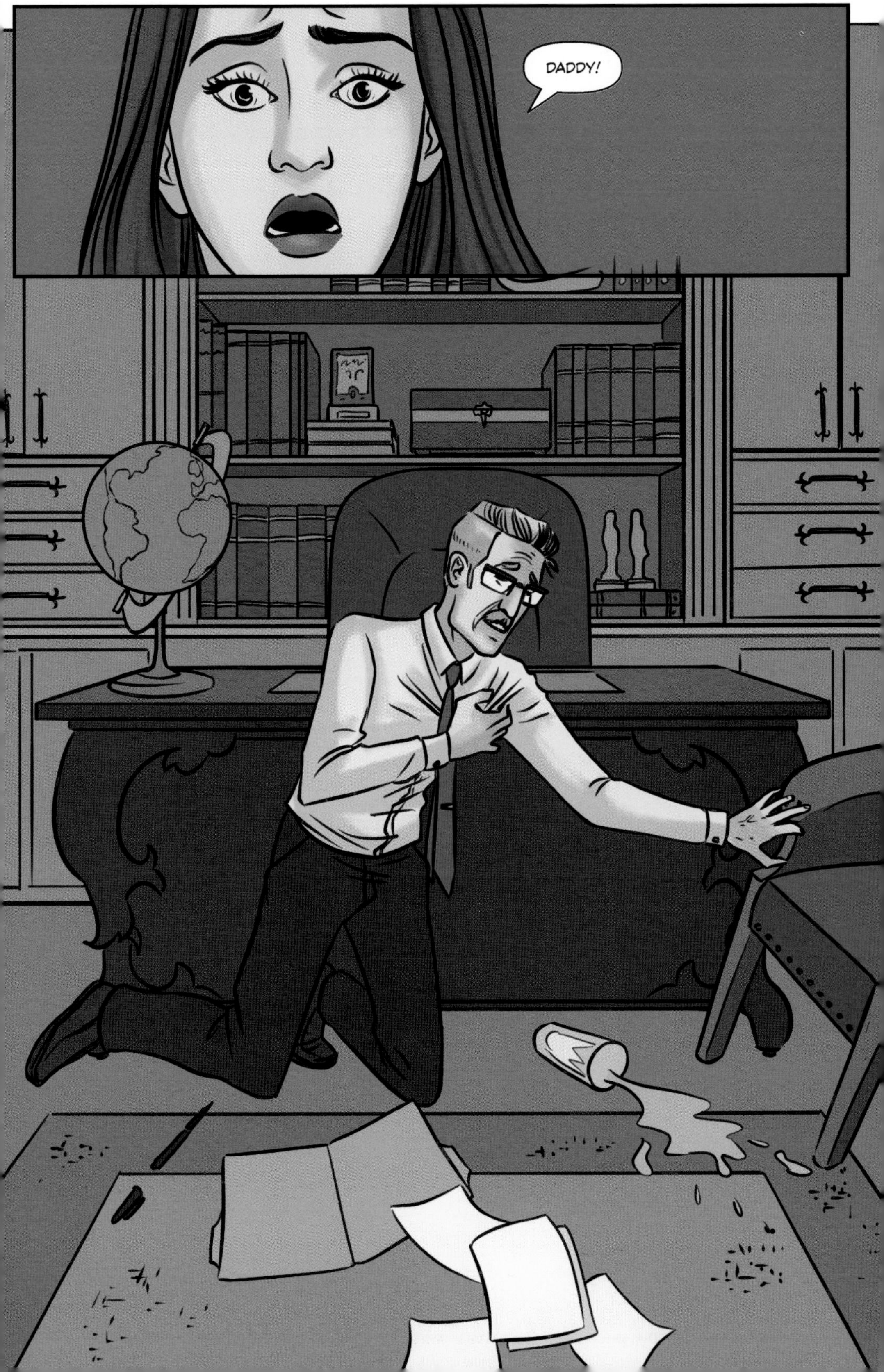
DADDY!

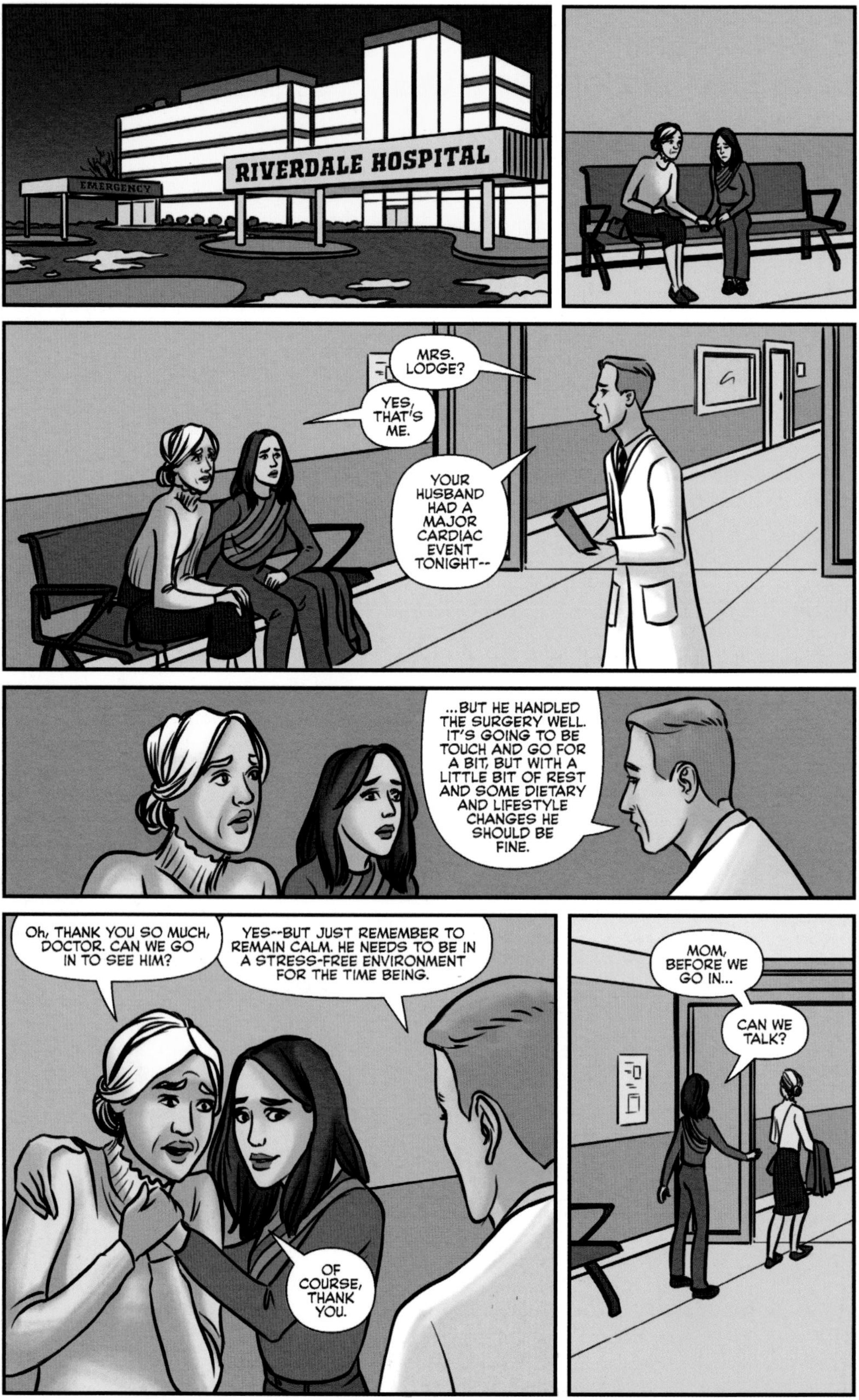
RIVERDALE HOSPITAL
EMERGENCY
MRS. LODGE?
YES, THAT'S ME.
YOUR HUSBAND HAD A MAJOR CARDIAC EVENT TONIGHT--
...BUT HE HANDLED THE SURGERY WELL. IT'S GOING TO BE TOUCH AND GO FOR A BIT, BUT WITH A LITTLE BIT OF REST AND SOME DIETARY AND LIFESTYLE CHANGES HE SHOULD BE FINE.
Oh, THANK YOU SO MUCH, DOCTOR. CAN WE GO IN TO SEE HIM?
YES--BUT JUST REMEMBER TO REMAIN CALM. HE NEEDS TO BE IN A STRESS-FREE ENVIRONMENT FOR THE TIME BEING.
OF COURSE, THANK YOU.
MOM, BEFORE WE GO IN...
CAN WE TALK?

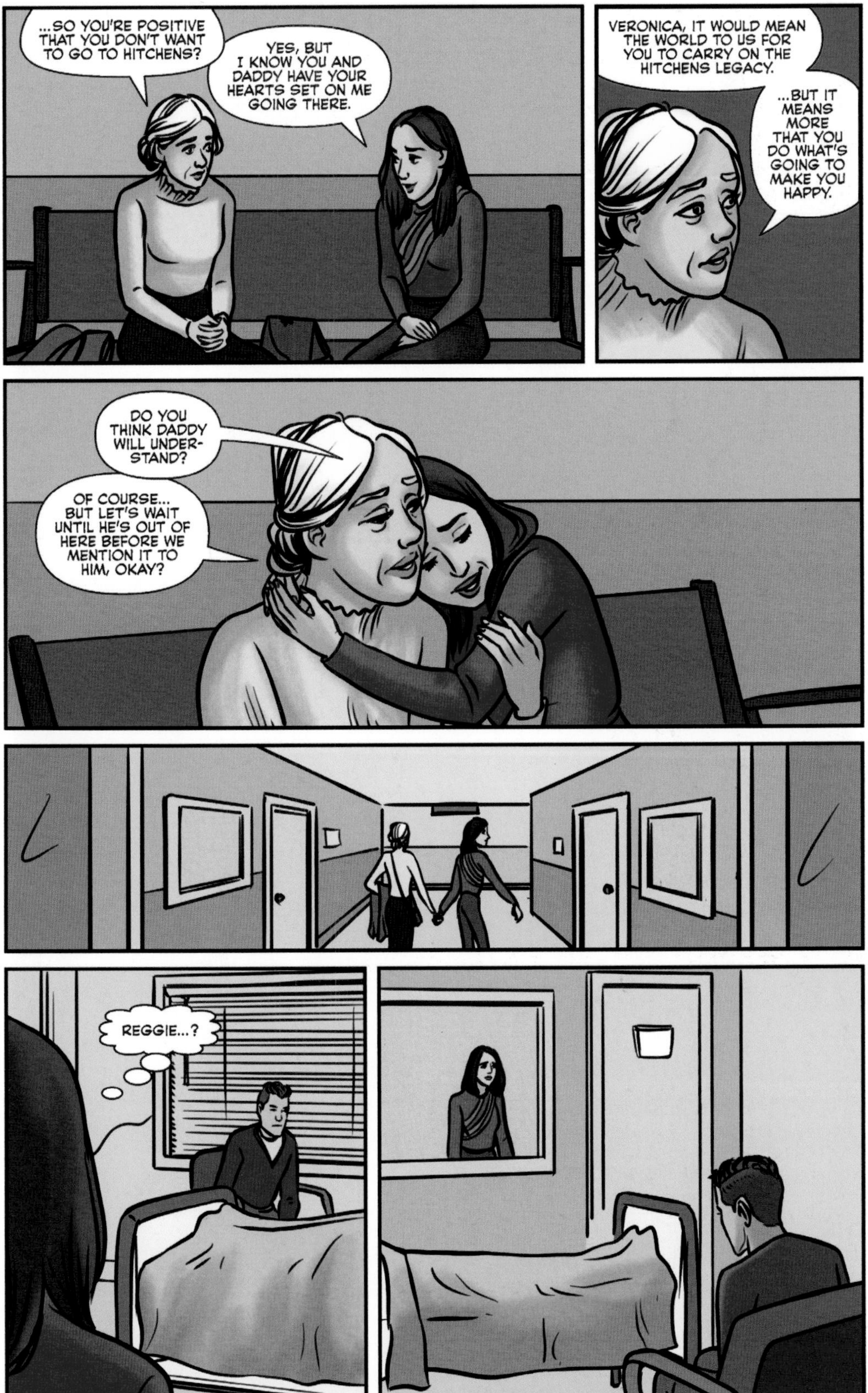
...SO YOU'RE POSITIVE THAT YOU DON'T WANT TO GO TO HITCHENS?
YES, BUT I KNOW YOU AND DADDY HAVE YOUR HEARTS SET ON ME GOING THERE.
VERONICA, IT WOULD MEAN THE WORLD TO US FOR YOU TO CARRY ON THE HITCHENS LEGACY.
...BUT IT MEANS MORE THAT YOU DO WHAT'S GOING TO MAKE YOU HAPPY.
DO YOU THINK DADDY WILL UNDER-STAND?
OF COURSE... BUT LET'S WAIT UNTIL HE'S OUT OF HERE BEFORE WE MENTION IT TO HIM, OKAY?
REGGIE...?

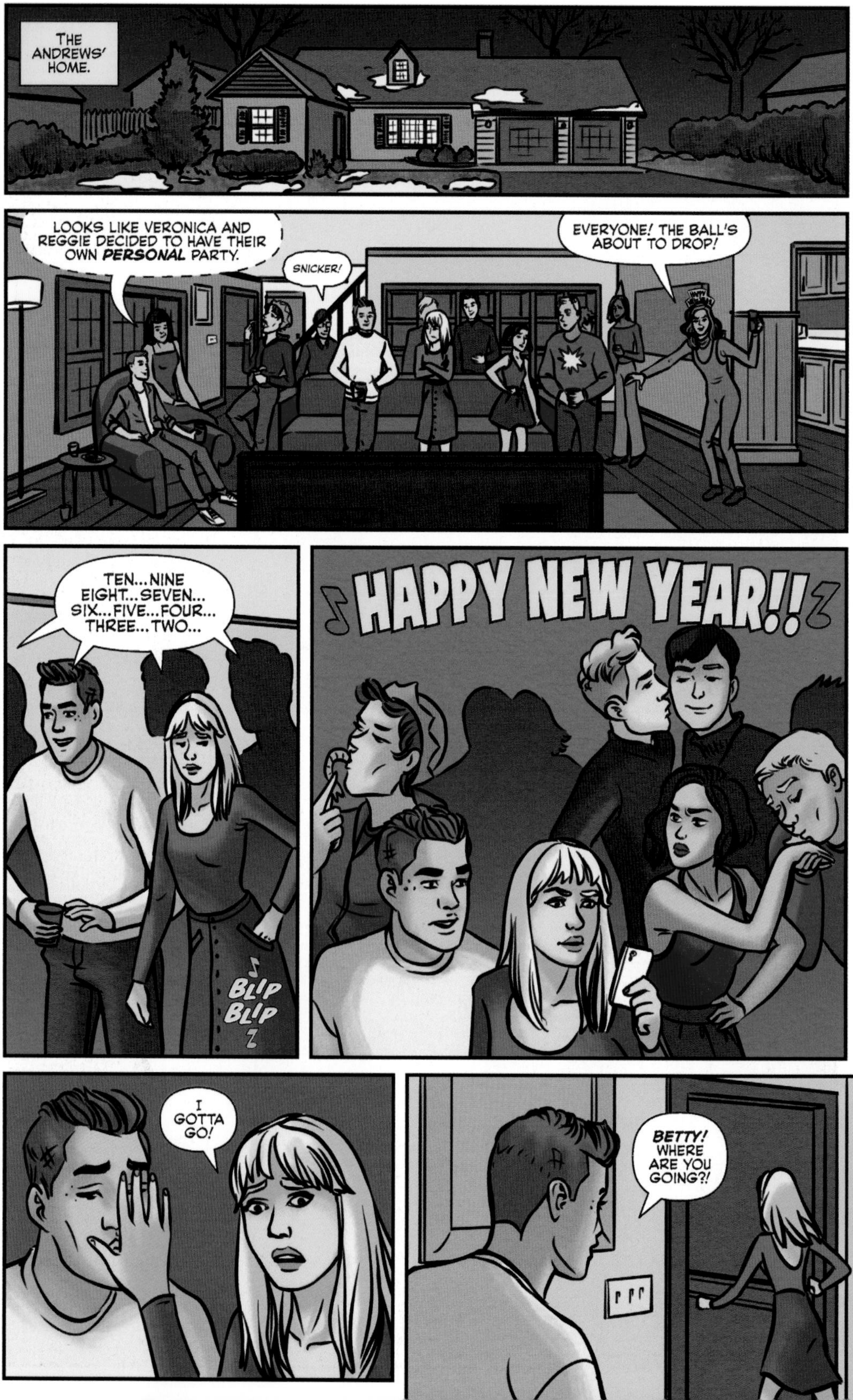
THE ANDREWS' HOME.
LOOKS LIKE VERONICA AND REGGIE DECIDED TO HAVE THEIR OWN **PERSONAL** PARTY.
SNICKER!
EVERYONE! THE BALL'S ABOUT TO DROP!
TEN...NINE EIGHT...SEVEN... SIX...FIVE...FOUR... THREE...TWO...
BLIP BLIP
HAPPY NEW YEAR!!
I GOTTA GO!
BETTY! WHERE ARE YOU GOING?!

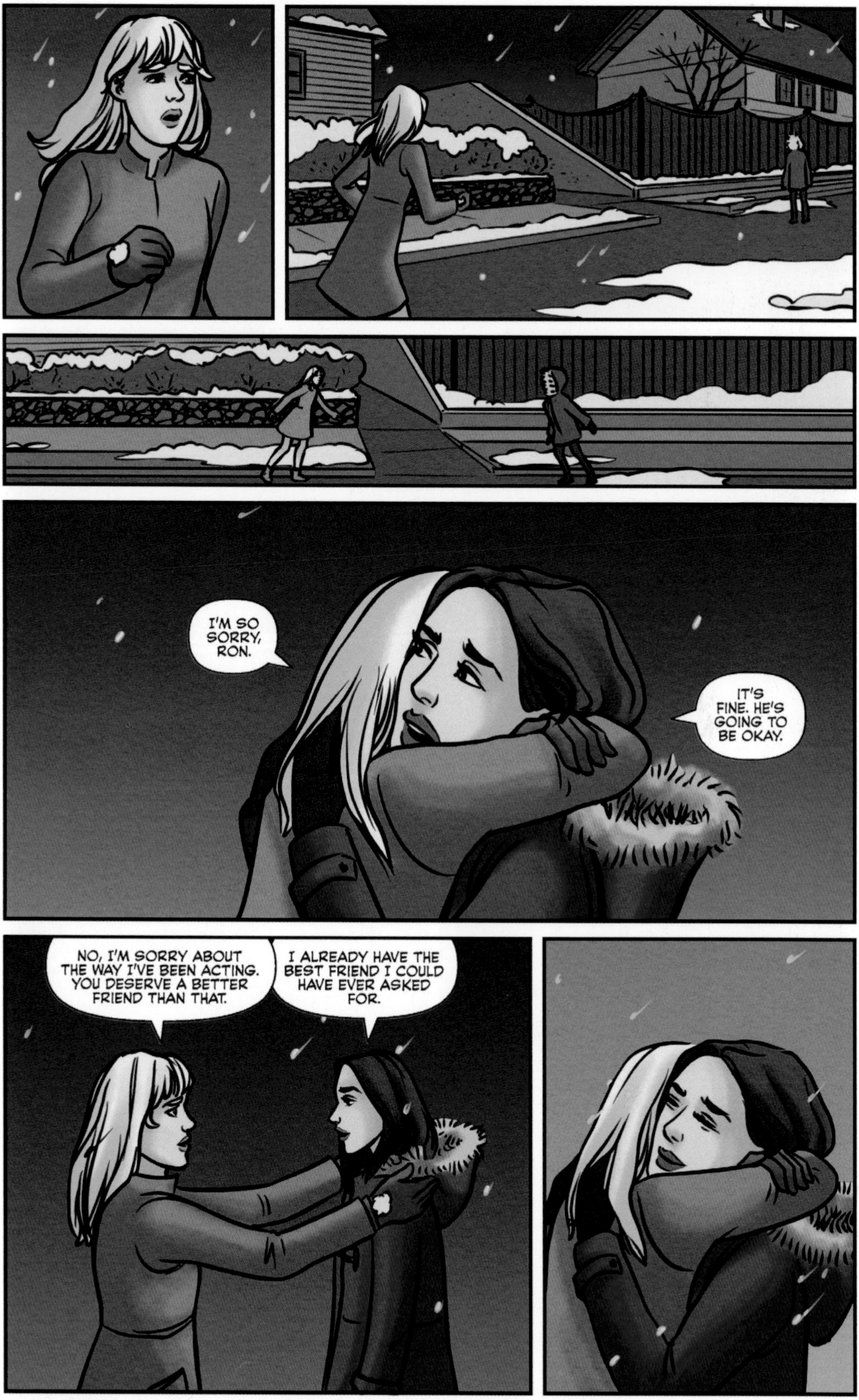
I'M SO SORRY, RON.
IT'S FINE. HE'S GOING TO BE OKAY.
NO, I'M SORRY ABOUT THE WAY I'VE BEEN ACTING. YOU DESERVE A BETTER FRIEND THAN THAT.
I ALREADY HAVE THE BEST FRIEND I COULD HAVE EVER ASKED FOR.

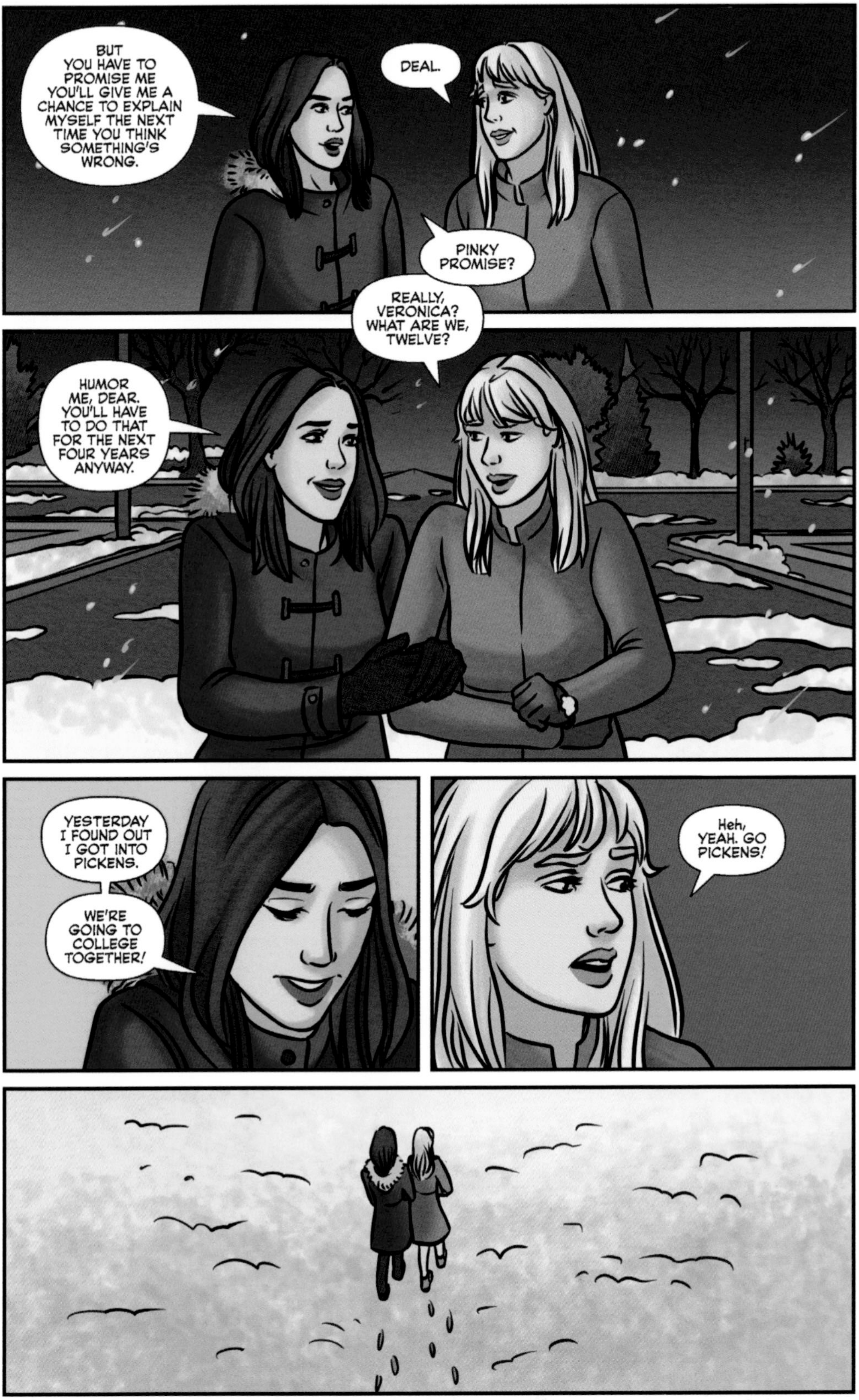
BUT YOU HAVE TO PROMISE ME YOU'LL GIVE ME A CHANCE TO EXPLAIN MYSELF THE NEXT TIME YOU THINK SOMETHING'S WRONG.
DEAL.
PINKY PROMISE?
REALLY, VERONICA? WHAT ARE WE, TWELVE?
HUMOR ME, DEAR. YOU'LL HAVE TO DO THAT FOR THE NEXT FOUR YEARS ANYWAY.
YESTERDAY I FOUND OUT I GOT INTO PICKENS.
WE'RE GOING TO COLLEGE TOGETHER!
Heh, YEAH. GO PICKENS!

TO BE CONTINUED...

04

STORY BY
JAMIE LEE ROTANTE

LETTERING BY
JACK MORELLI

ART BY
SANDRA LANZ

COLORS BY
KELLY FITZPATRICK

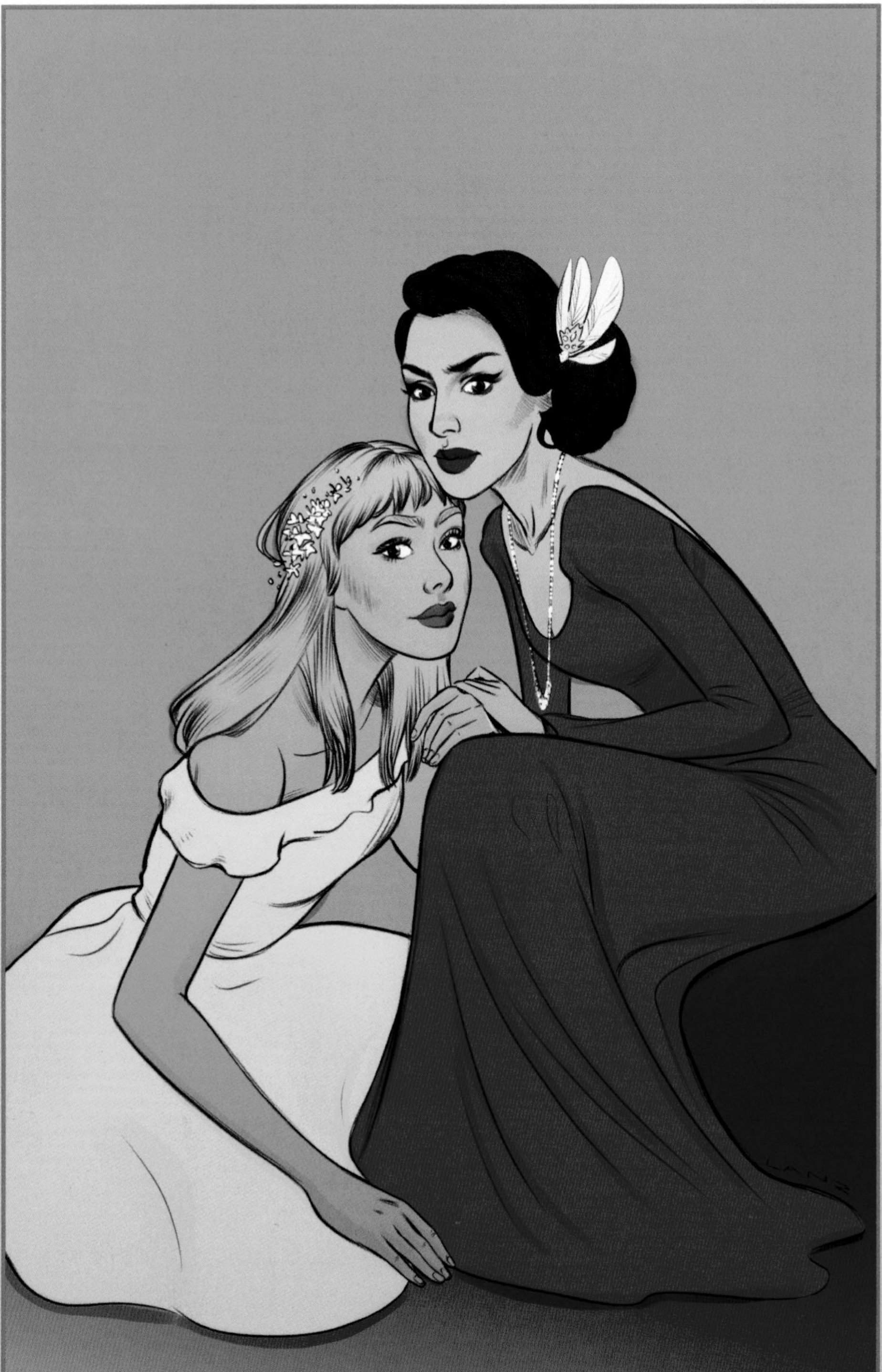
LANZ

COVER ART: **SANDRA LANZ**

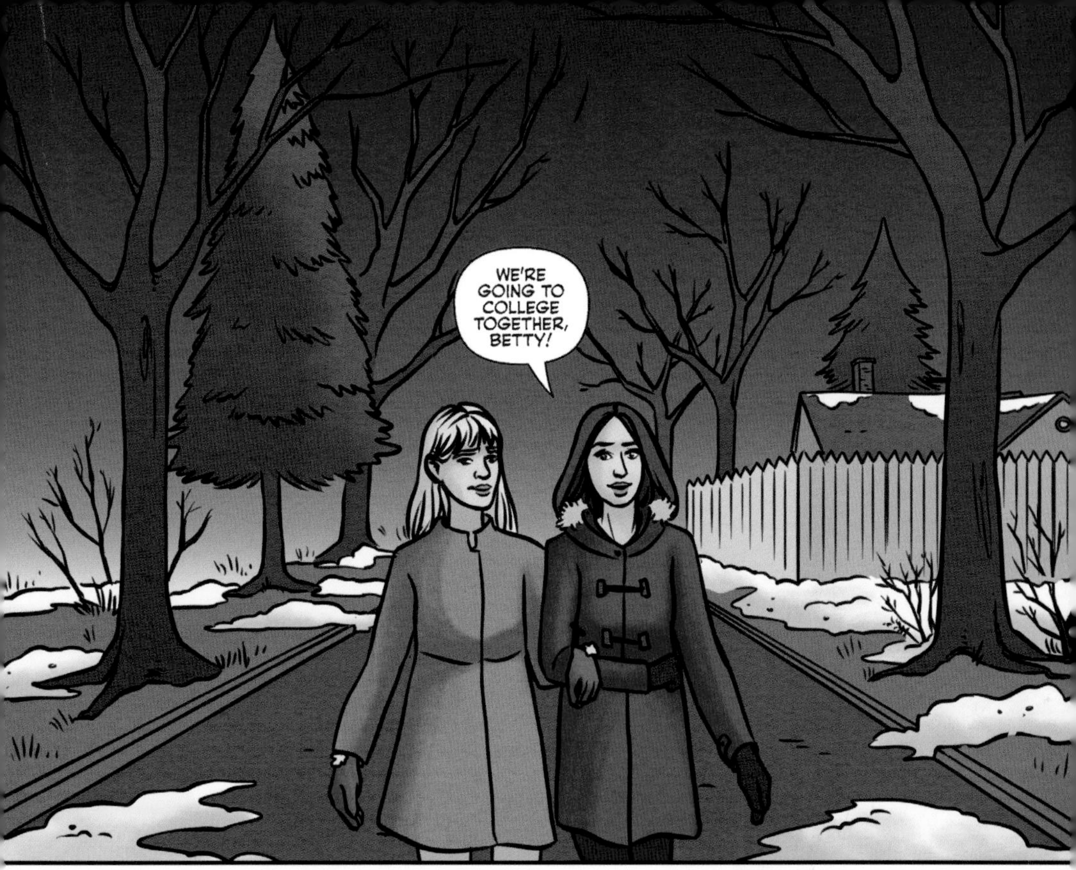
WE'RE GOING TO COLLEGE TOGETHER, BETTY!

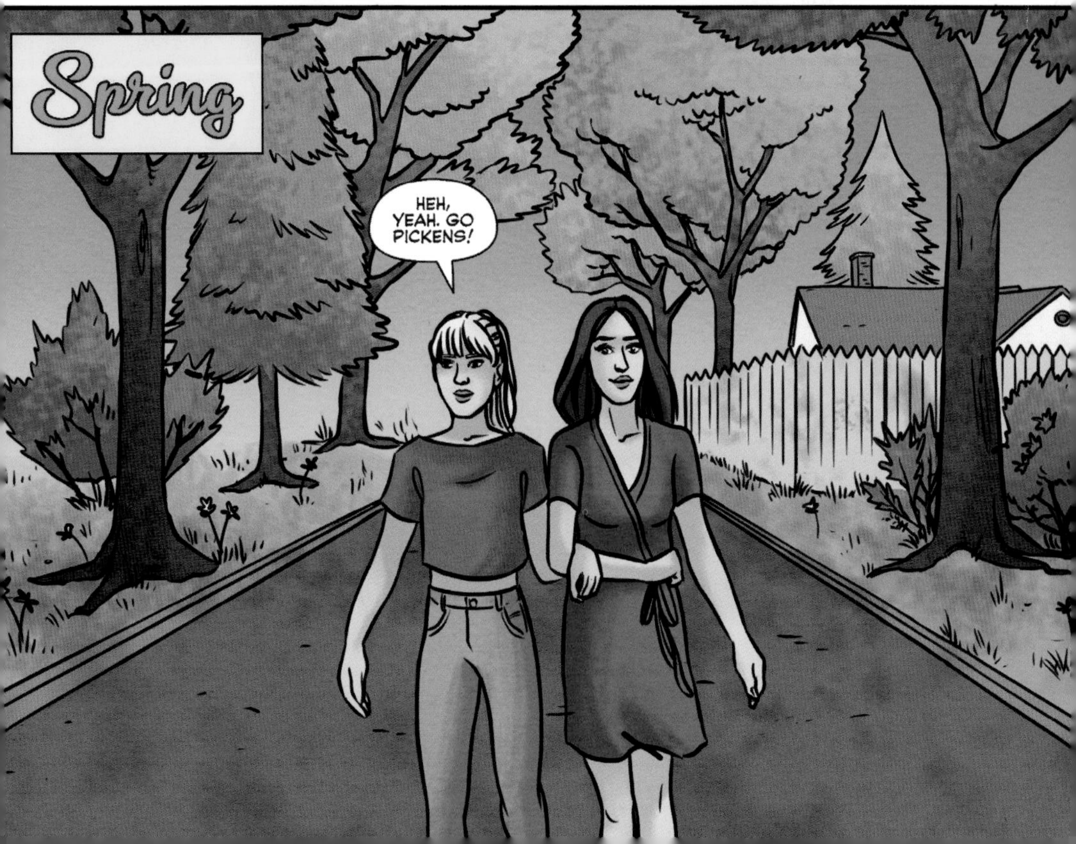
Spring
HEH, YEAH. GO PICKENS!

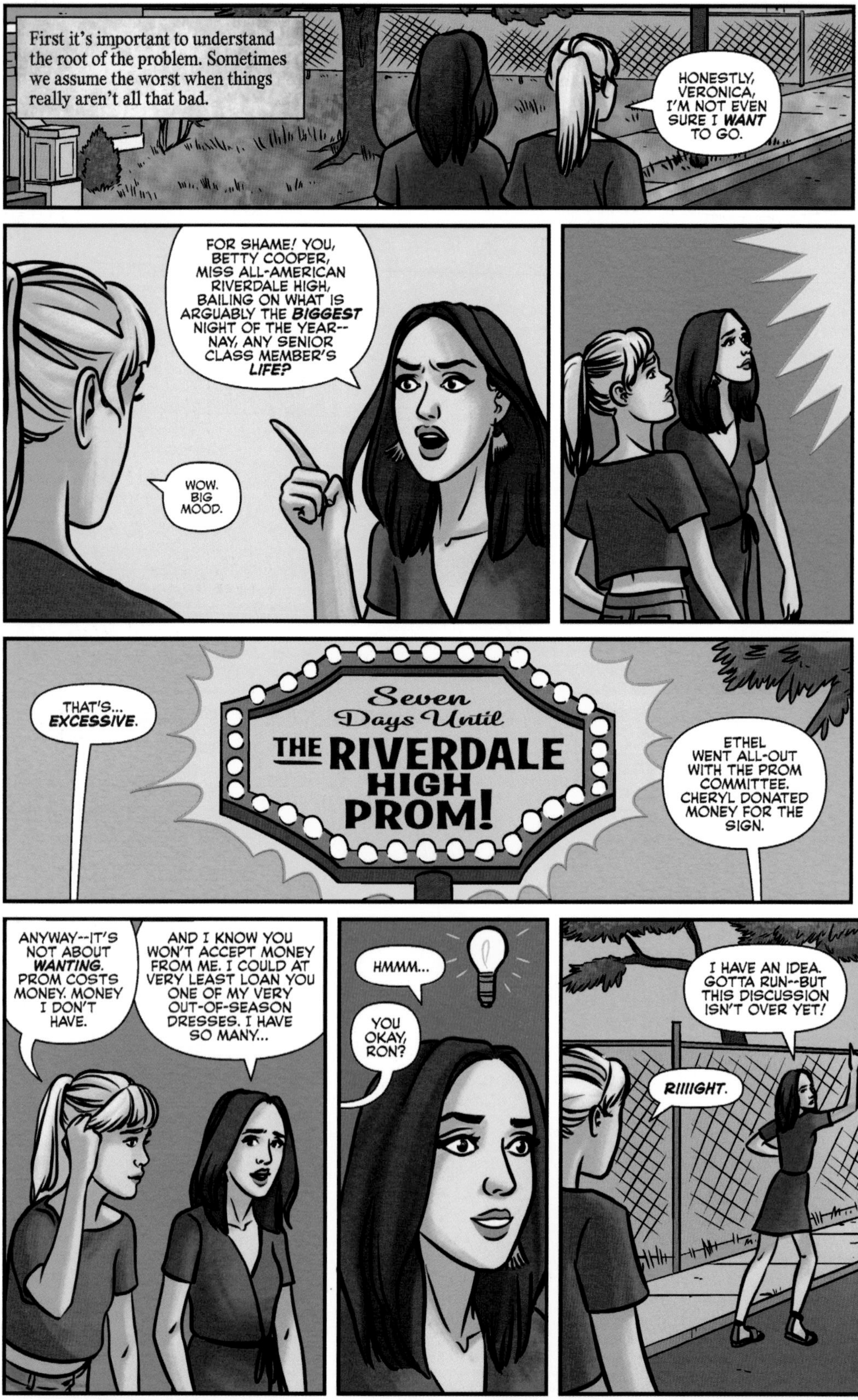
First it's important to understand the root of the problem. Sometimes we assume the worst when things really aren't all that bad.
HONESTLY, VERONICA, I'M NOT EVEN SURE I WANT TO GO.
FOR SHAME! YOU, BETTY COOPER, MISS ALL-AMERICAN RIVERDALE HIGH, BAILING ON WHAT IS ARGUABLY THE BIGGEST NIGHT OF THE YEAR-- NAY, ANY SENIOR CLASS MEMBER'S LIFE?
WOW. BIG MOOD.
THAT'S... EXCESSIVE.
Seven Days Until THE RIVERDALE HIGH PROM!
ETHEL WENT ALL-OUT WITH THE PROM COMMITTEE. CHERYL DONATED MONEY FOR THE SIGN.
ANYWAY--IT'S NOT ABOUT WANTING. PROM COSTS MONEY. MONEY I DON'T HAVE.
AND I KNOW YOU WON'T ACCEPT MONEY FROM ME. I COULD AT VERY LEAST LOAN YOU ONE OF MY VERY OUT-OF-SEASON DRESSES. I HAVE SO MANY...
HMMM...
YOU OKAY, RON?
I HAVE AN IDEA. GOTTA RUN--BUT THIS DISCUSSION ISN'T OVER YET!
RIIIIGHT.

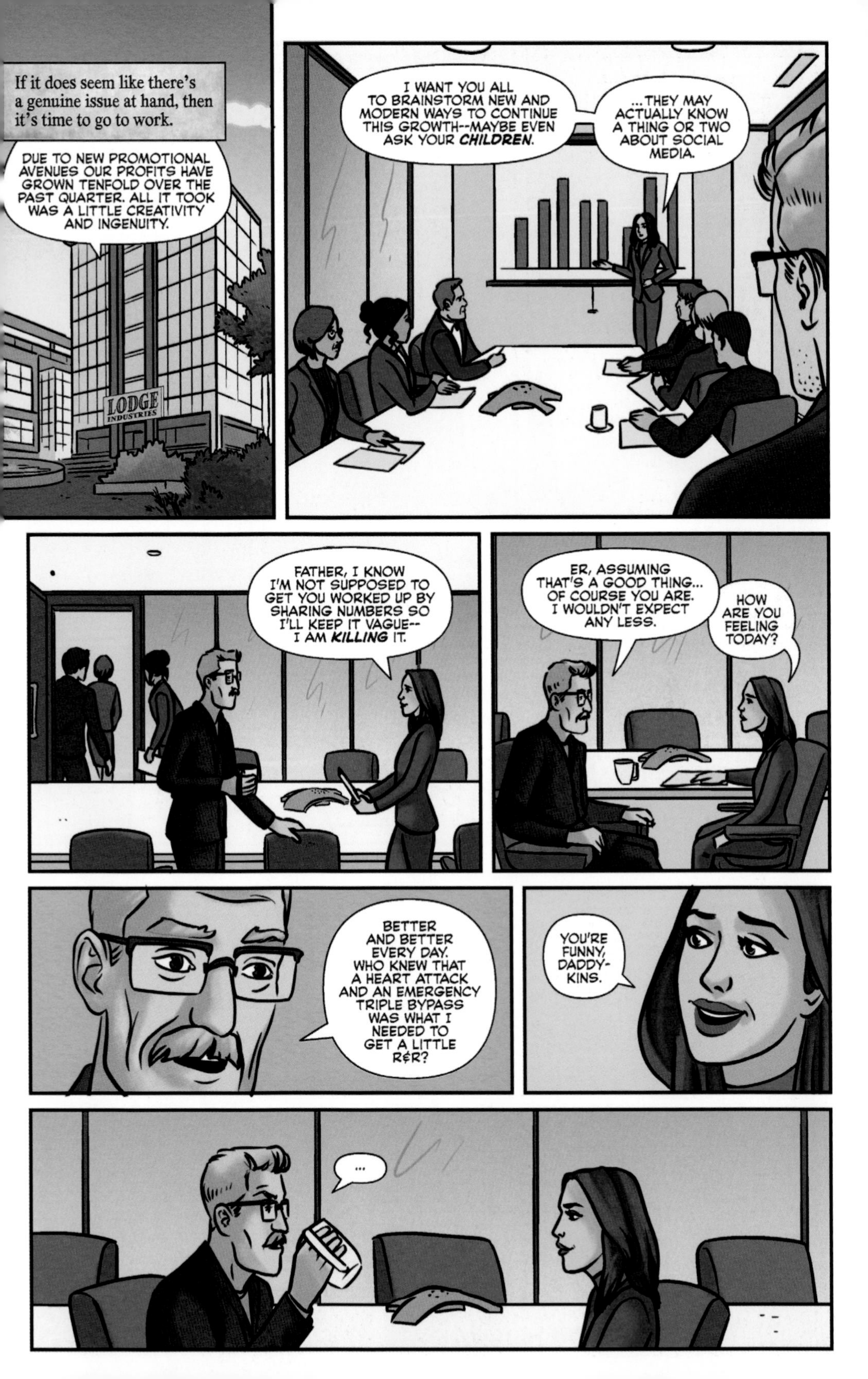
If it does seem like there's a genuine issue at hand, then it's time to go to work.
DUE TO NEW PROMOTIONAL AVENUES OUR PROFITS HAVE GROWN TENFOLD OVER THE PAST QUARTER. ALL IT TOOK WAS A LITTLE CREATIVITY AND INGENUITY.
LODGE INDUSTRIES
I WANT YOU ALL TO BRAINSTORM NEW AND MODERN WAYS TO CONTINUE THIS GROWTH--MAYBE EVEN ASK YOUR CHILDREN.
...THEY MAY ACTUALLY KNOW A THING OR TWO ABOUT SOCIAL MEDIA.
FATHER, I KNOW I'M NOT SUPPOSED TO GET YOU WORKED UP BY SHARING NUMBERS SO I'LL KEEP IT VAGUE-- I AM KILLING IT.
ER, ASSUMING THAT'S A GOOD THING... OF COURSE YOU ARE. I WOULDN'T EXPECT ANY LESS.
HOW ARE YOU FEELING TODAY?
BETTER AND BETTER EVERY DAY. WHO KNEW THAT A HEART ATTACK AND AN EMERGENCY TRIPLE BYPASS WAS WHAT I NEEDED TO GET A LITTLE R&R?
YOU'RE FUNNY, DADDY-KINS.
...

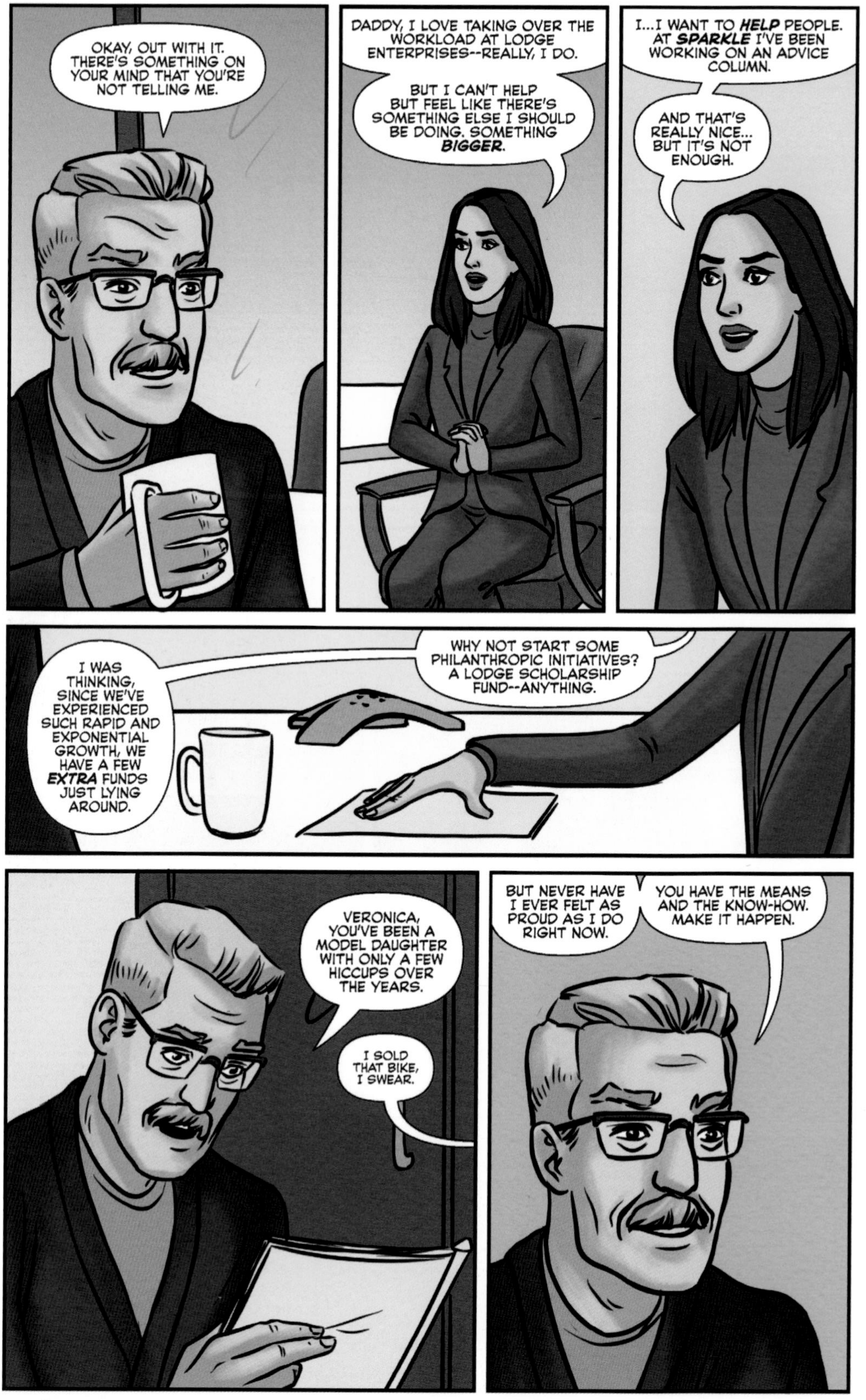
OKAY, OUT WITH IT. THERE'S SOMETHING ON YOUR MIND THAT YOU'RE NOT TELLING ME.
DADDY, I LOVE TAKING OVER THE WORKLOAD AT LODGE ENTERPRISES--REALLY, I DO.
BUT I CAN'T HELP BUT FEEL LIKE THERE'S SOMETHING ELSE I SHOULD BE DOING. SOMETHING ***BIGGER***.
I...I WANT TO ***HELP*** PEOPLE. AT ***SPARKLE*** I'VE BEEN WORKING ON AN ADVICE COLUMN.
AND THAT'S REALLY NICE... BUT IT'S NOT ENOUGH.
I WAS THINKING, SINCE WE'VE EXPERIENCED SUCH RAPID AND EXPONENTIAL GROWTH, WE HAVE A FEW ***EXTRA*** FUNDS JUST LYING AROUND.
WHY NOT START SOME PHILANTHROPIC INITIATIVES? A LODGE SCHOLARSHIP FUND--ANYTHING.
VERONICA, YOU'VE BEEN A MODEL DAUGHTER WITH ONLY A FEW HICCUPS OVER THE YEARS.
I SOLD THAT BIKE, I SWEAR.
BUT NEVER HAVE I EVER FELT AS PROUD AS I DO RIGHT NOW.
YOU HAVE THE MEANS AND THE KNOW-HOW. MAKE IT HAPPEN.

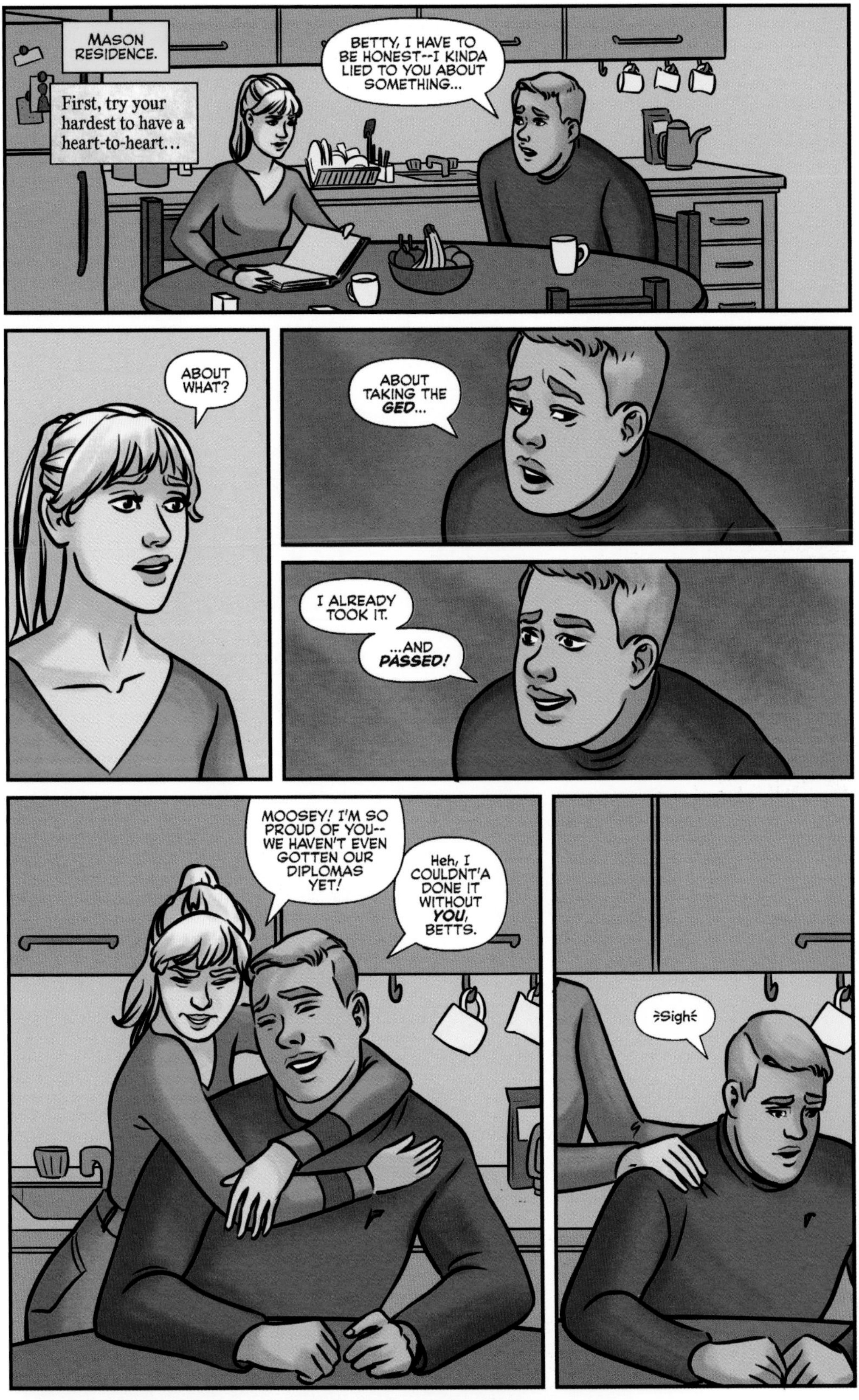
MASON RESIDENCE.
First, try your hardest to have a heart-to-heart…
BETTY, I HAVE TO BE HONEST--I KINDA LIED TO YOU ABOUT SOMETHING...
ABOUT WHAT?
ABOUT TAKING THE GED...
I ALREADY TOOK IT.
...AND PASSED!
MOOSEY! I'M SO PROUD OF YOU--WE HAVEN'T EVEN GOTTEN OUR DIPLOMAS YET!
Heh, I COULDNT'A DONE IT WITHOUT YOU, BETTS.
Sigh

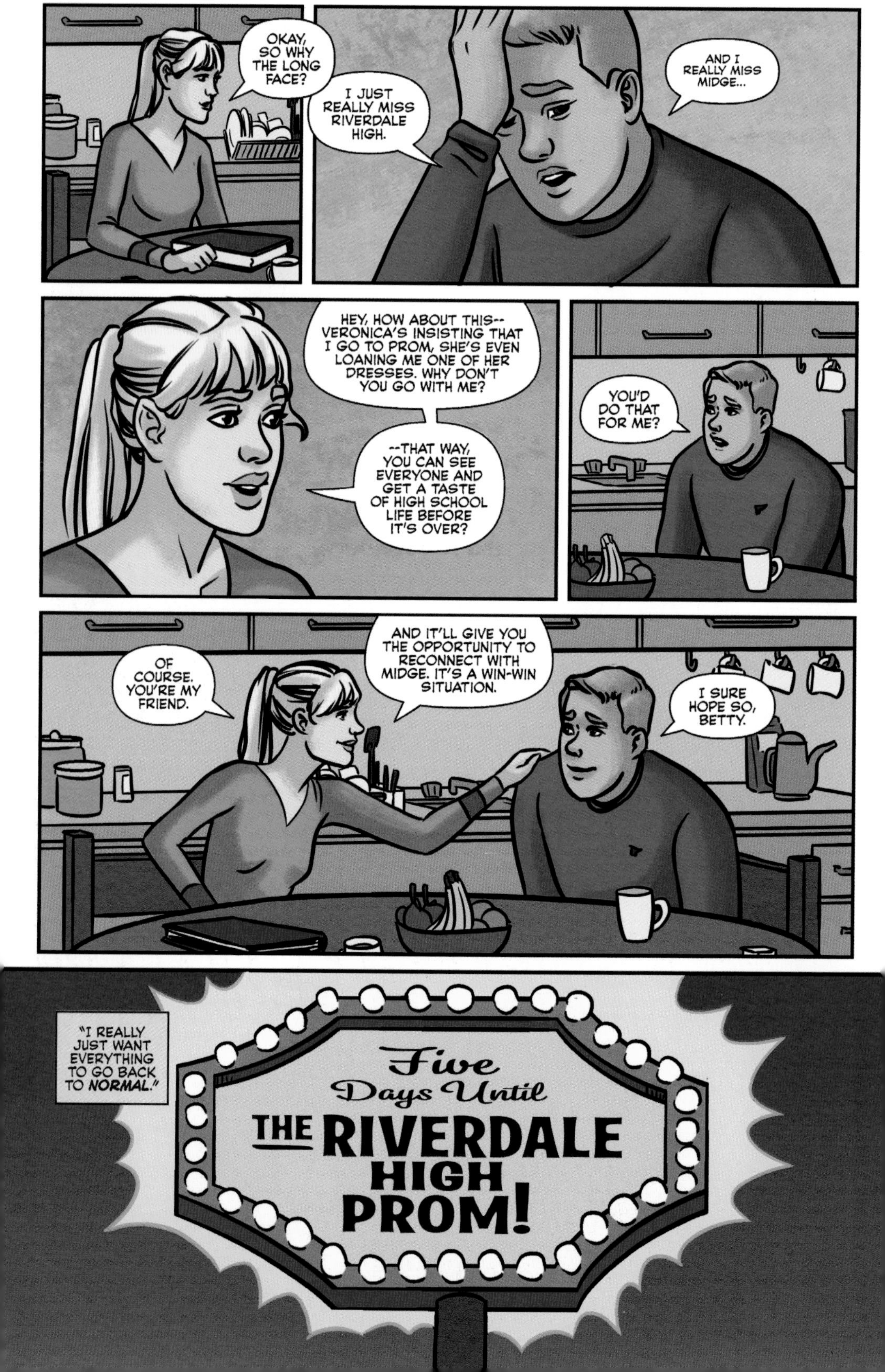
OKAY, SO WHY THE LONG FACE?
I JUST REALLY MISS RIVERDALE HIGH.
AND I REALLY MISS MIDGE...
HEY, HOW ABOUT THIS-- VERONICA'S INSISTING THAT I GO TO PROM, SHE'S EVEN LOANING ME ONE OF HER DRESSES. WHY DON'T YOU GO WITH ME?
--THAT WAY, YOU CAN SEE EVERYONE AND GET A TASTE OF HIGH SCHOOL LIFE BEFORE IT'S OVER?
YOU'D DO THAT FOR ME?
OF COURSE. YOU'RE MY FRIEND.
AND IT'LL GIVE YOU THE OPPORTUNITY TO RECONNECT WITH MIDGE. IT'S A WIN-WIN SITUATION.
I SURE HOPE SO, BETTY.
"I REALLY JUST WANT EVERYTHING TO GO BACK TO *NORMAL*."
Five Days Until THE RIVERDALE HIGH PROM!

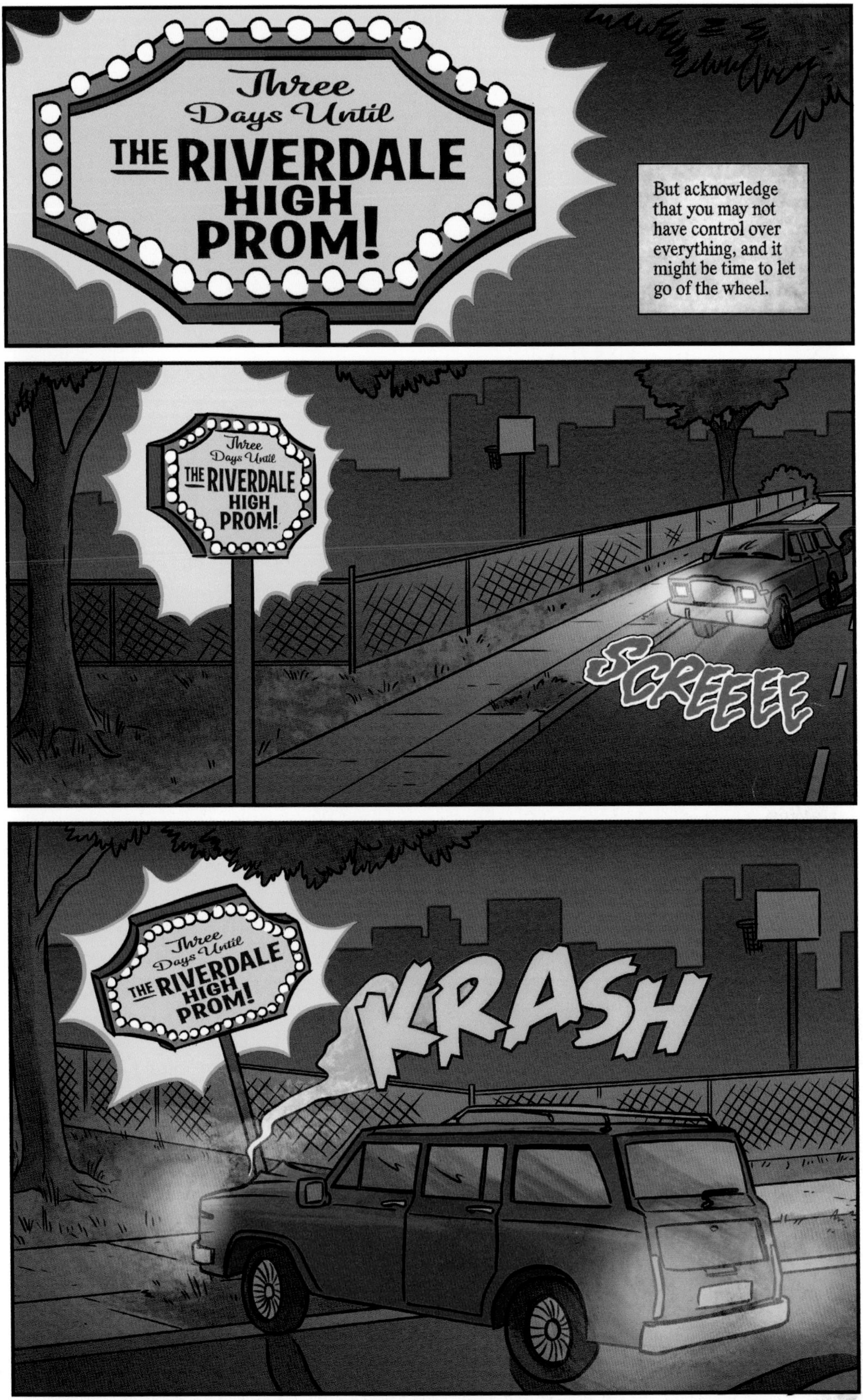
Three Days Until THE RIVERDALE HIGH PROM!
But acknowledge that you may not have control over everything, and it might be time to let go of the wheel.
Three Days Until THE RIVERDALE HIGH PROM!
SCREEEEE
Three Days Until THE RIVERDALE HIGH PROM!
KRASH

THE NEXT MORNING.

Think about what it is that you're going to say. Don't leave it up to the moment, your emotions may take control.

POLLY, IS THIS REALLY NECESSARY?

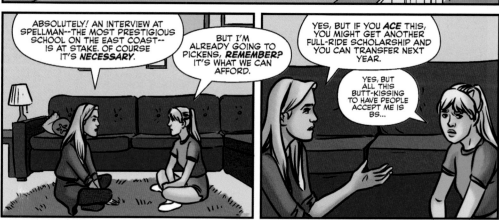

ABSOLUTELY! AN INTERVIEW AT SPELLMAN--THE MOST PRESTIGIOUS SCHOOL ON THE EAST COAST-- IS AT STAKE. OF COURSE IT'S *NECESSARY*.

BUT I'M ALREADY GOING TO PICKENS, *REMEMBER?* IT'S WHAT WE CAN AFFORD.

YES, BUT IF YOU *ACE* THIS, YOU MIGHT GET ANOTHER FULL-RIDE SCHOLARSHIP AND YOU CAN TRANSFER NEXT YEAR.

YES, BUT ALL THIS BUTT-KISSING TO HAVE PEOPLE ACCEPT ME IS BS...

HI, LADIES. DON'T MEAN TO INTERRUPT. BETTY, DID YOU HEAR ABOUT WHAT HAPPENED LAST NIGHT?

NO, MOM, WHAT?

THERE WAS A BIG ACCIDENT IN TOWN SQUARE. SOMEONE CRASHED INTO THAT PROM SIGN.

I HEAR IT MIGHT HAVE BEEN THE MANTLE BOY.

R-REGGIE?

PROBABLY DID IT ON PURPOSE, KNOWING THAT KID. HE'S NOTHING BUT TROUBLE...

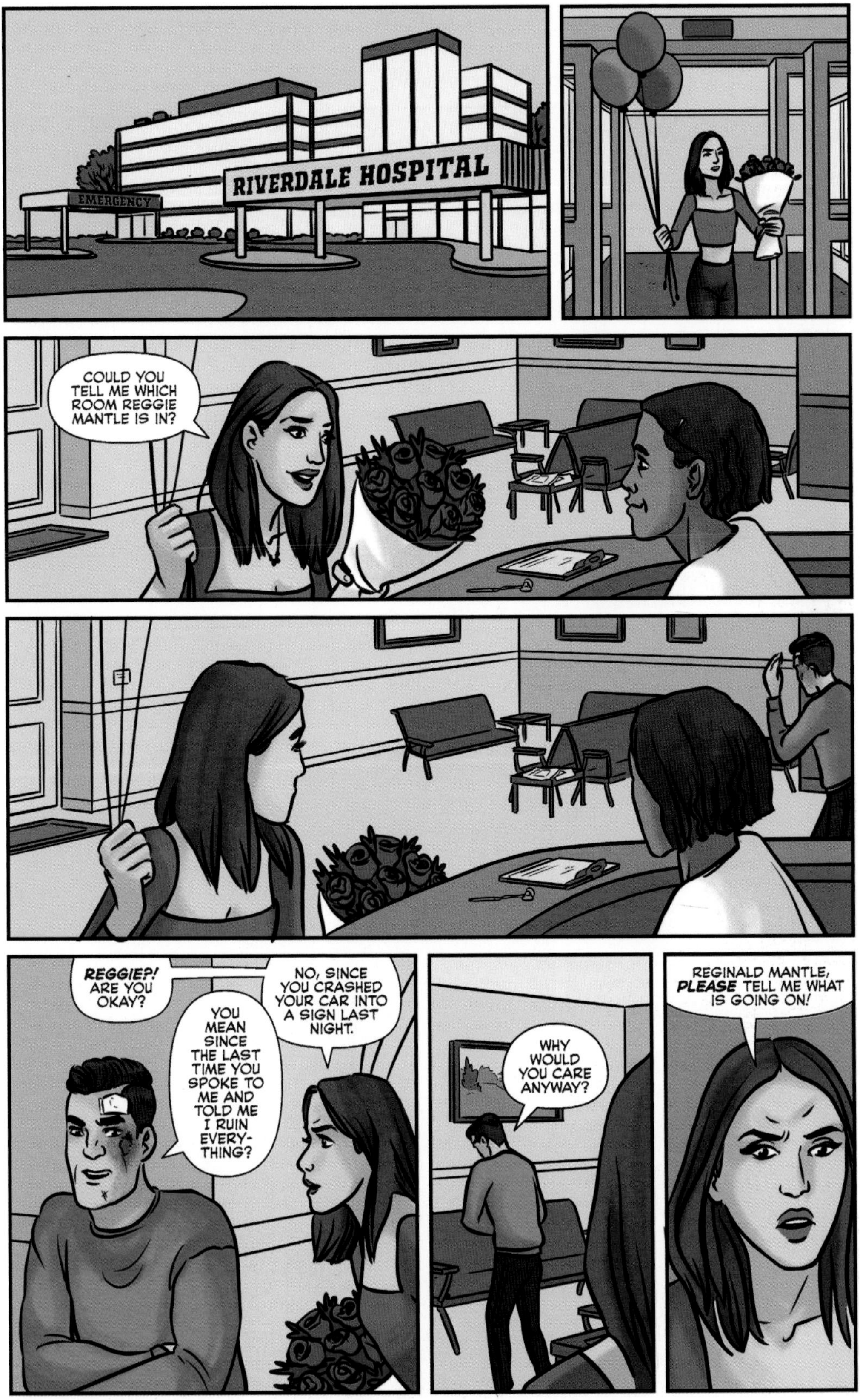
RIVERDALE HOSPITAL
EMERGENCY
COULD YOU TELL ME WHICH ROOM REGGIE MANTLE IS IN?
REGGIE?! ARE YOU OKAY?
YOU MEAN SINCE THE LAST TIME YOU SPOKE TO ME AND TOLD ME I RUIN EVERY-THING?
NO, SINCE YOU CRASHED YOUR CAR INTO A SIGN LAST NIGHT.
WHY WOULD YOU CARE ANYWAY?
REGINALD MANTLE, PLEASE TELL ME WHAT IS GOING ON!

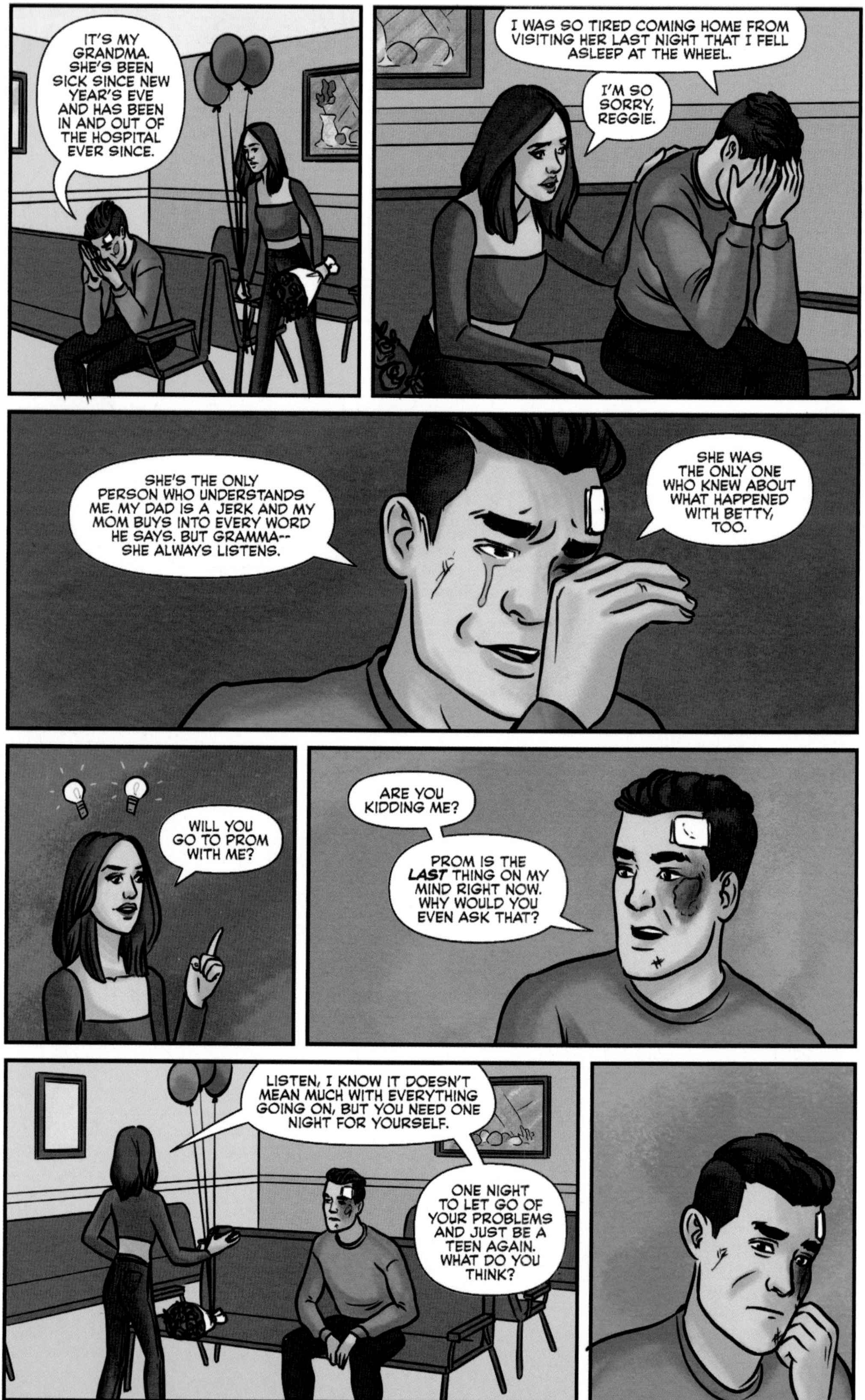
IT'S MY GRANDMA. SHE'S BEEN SICK SINCE NEW YEAR'S EVE AND HAS BEEN IN AND OUT OF THE HOSPITAL EVER SINCE.
I WAS SO TIRED COMING HOME FROM VISITING HER LAST NIGHT THAT I FELL ASLEEP AT THE WHEEL.
I'M SO SORRY, REGGIE.
SHE'S THE ONLY PERSON WHO UNDERSTANDS ME. MY DAD IS A JERK AND MY MOM BUYS INTO EVERY WORD HE SAYS. BUT GRAMMA-- SHE ALWAYS LISTENS.
SHE WAS THE ONLY ONE WHO KNEW ABOUT WHAT HAPPENED WITH BETTY, TOO.
WILL YOU GO TO PROM WITH ME?
ARE YOU KIDDING ME?
PROM IS THE *LAST* THING ON MY MIND RIGHT NOW. WHY WOULD YOU EVEN ASK THAT?
LISTEN, I KNOW IT DOESN'T MEAN MUCH WITH EVERYTHING GOING ON, BUT YOU NEED ONE NIGHT FOR YOURSELF.
ONE NIGHT TO LET GO OF YOUR PROBLEMS AND JUST BE A TEEN AGAIN. WHAT DO YOU THINK?

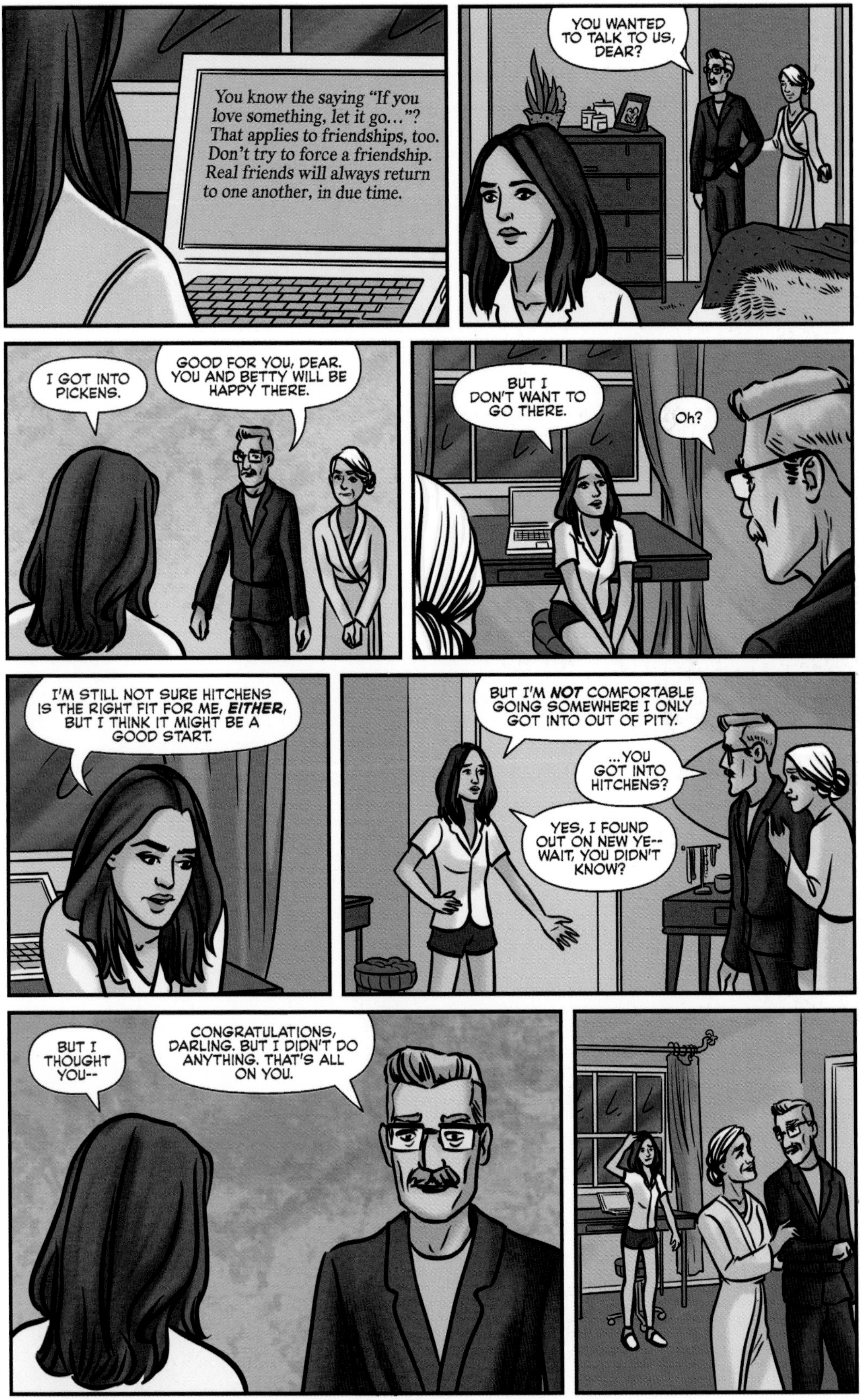
You know the saying "If you love something, let it go…"? That applies to friendships, too. Don't try to force a friendship. Real friends will always return to one another, in due time.
YOU WANTED TO TALK TO US, DEAR?
I GOT INTO PICKENS.
GOOD FOR YOU, DEAR. YOU AND BETTY WILL BE HAPPY THERE.
BUT I DON'T WANT TO GO THERE.
Oh?
I'M STILL NOT SURE HITCHENS IS THE RIGHT FIT FOR ME, *EITHER*, BUT I THINK IT MIGHT BE A GOOD START.
BUT I'M *NOT* COMFORTABLE GOING SOMEWHERE I ONLY GOT INTO OUT OF PITY.
...YOU GOT INTO HITCHENS?
YES, I FOUND OUT ON NEW YE-- WAIT, YOU DIDN'T KNOW?
BUT I THOUGHT YOU--
CONGRATULATIONS, DARLING. BUT I DIDN'T DO ANYTHING. THAT'S ALL ON YOU.

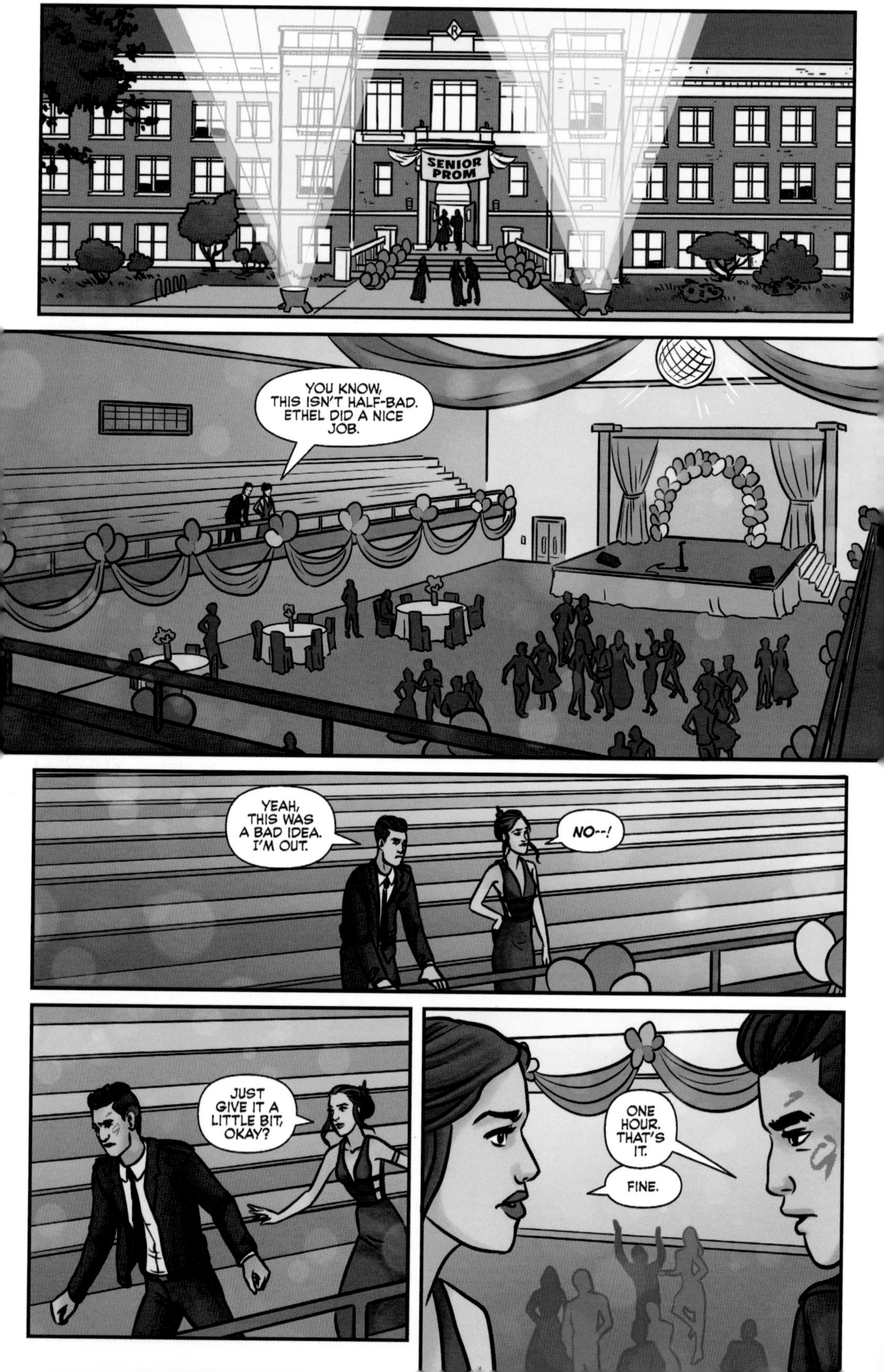
SENIOR PROM
YOU KNOW, THIS ISN'T HALF-BAD. ETHEL DID A NICE JOB.
YEAH, THIS WAS A BAD IDEA. I'M OUT.
NO--!
JUST GIVE IT A LITTLE BIT, OKAY?
ONE HOUR. THAT'S IT.
FINE.

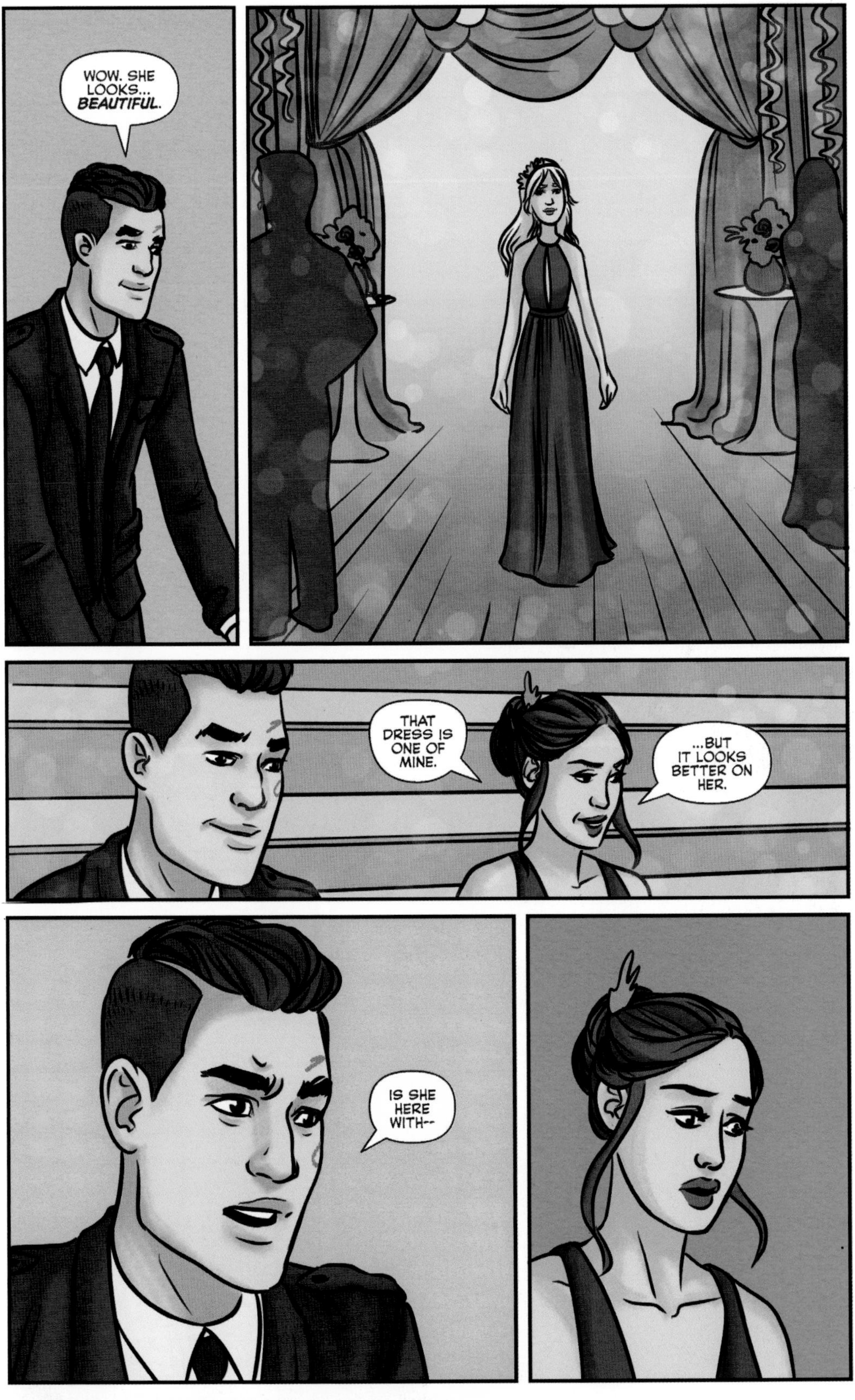
WOW. SHE LOOKS... *BEAUTIFUL*.
THAT DRESS IS ONE OF MINE.
...BUT IT LOOKS BETTER ON HER.
IS SHE HERE WITH--

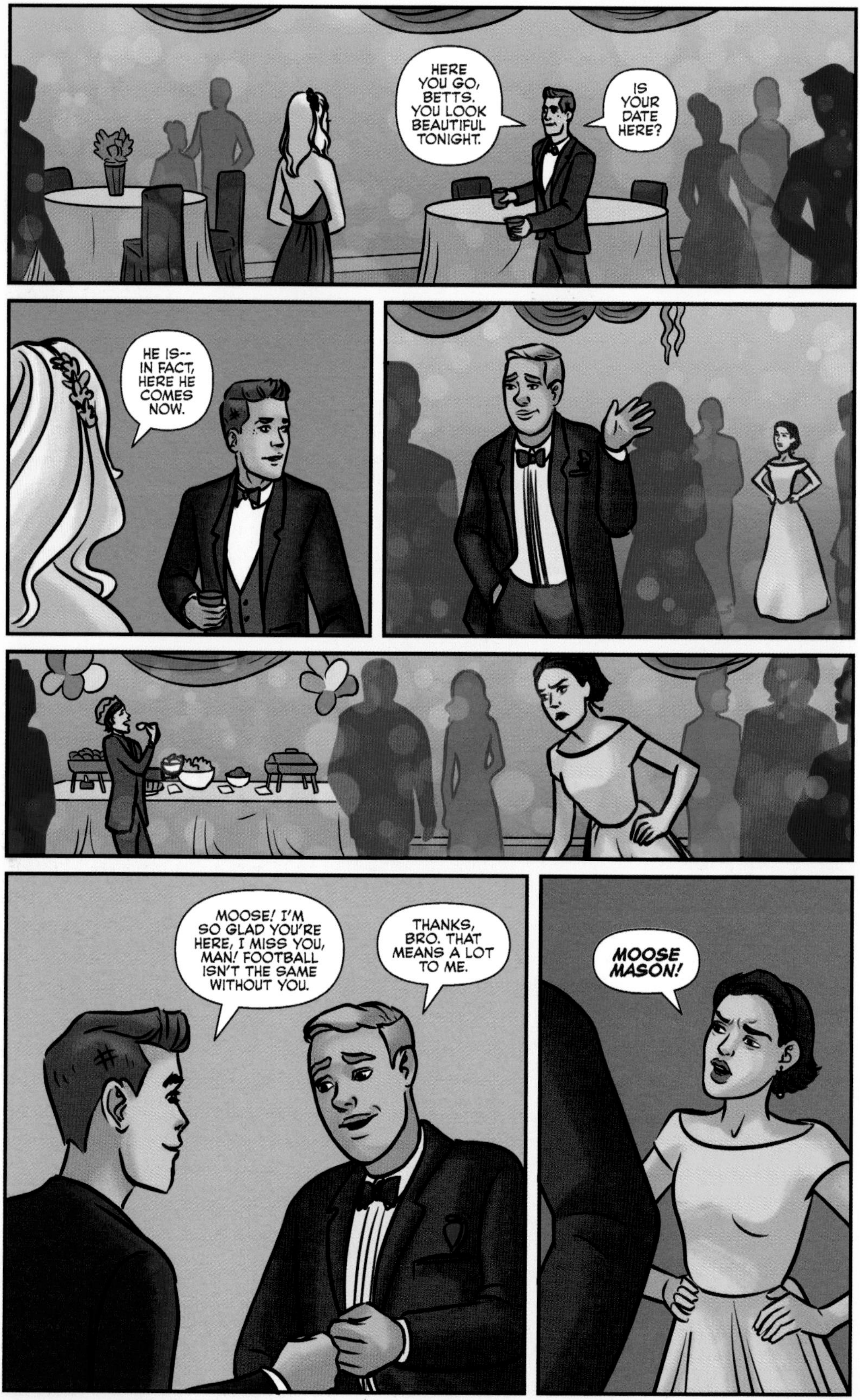
HERE YOU GO, BETTS. YOU LOOK BEAUTIFUL TONIGHT.
IS YOUR DATE HERE?
HE IS-- IN FACT, HERE HE COMES NOW.
MOOSE! I'M SO GLAD YOU'RE HERE, I MISS YOU, MAN! FOOTBALL ISN'T THE SAME WITHOUT YOU.
THANKS, BRO. THAT MEANS A LOT TO ME.
MOOSE MASON!

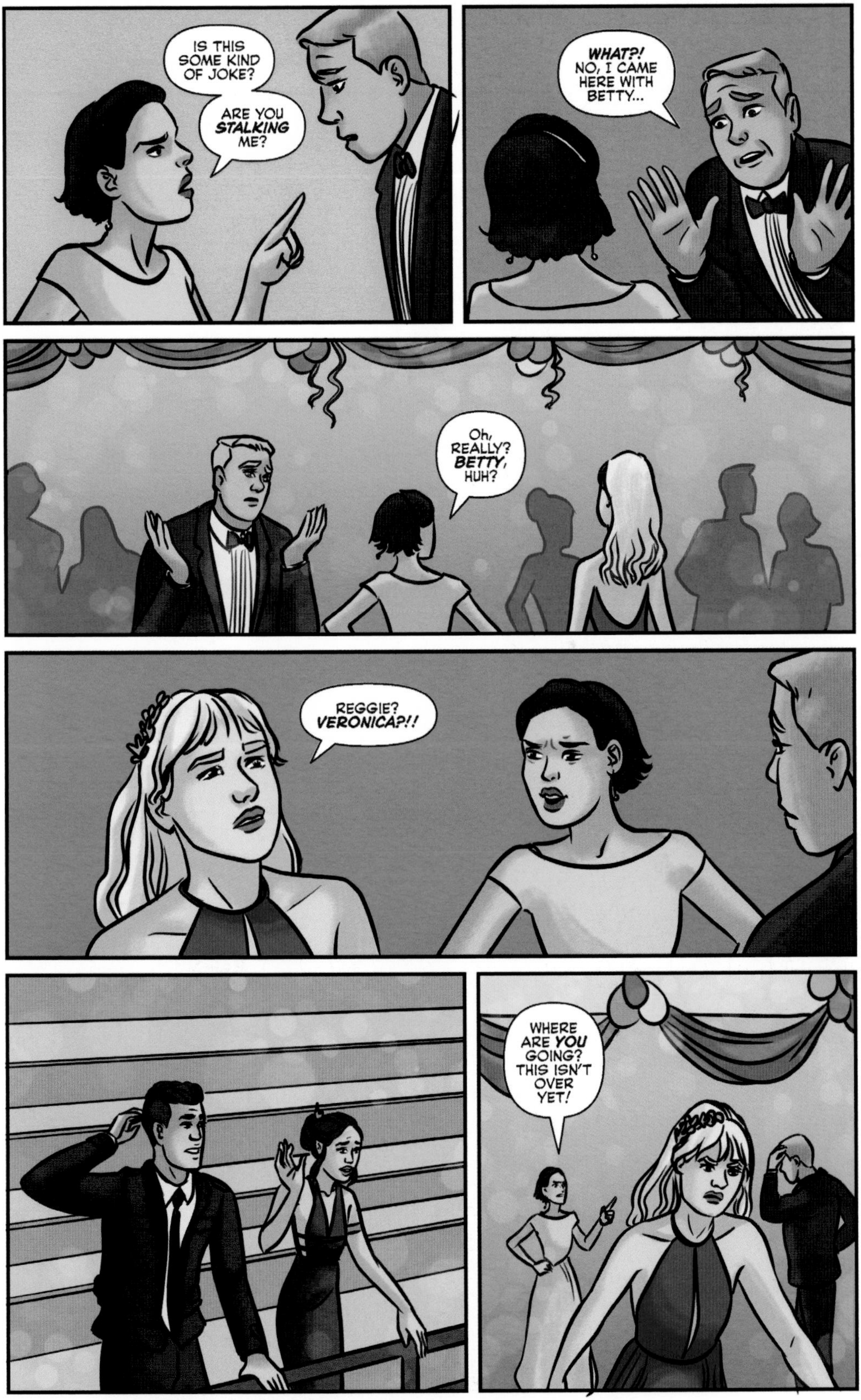
IS THIS SOME KIND OF JOKE?
ARE YOU STALKING ME?
WHAT?! NO, I CAME HERE WITH BETTY...
Oh, REALLY? BETTY, HUH?
REGGIE? VERONICA?!!
WHERE ARE YOU GOING? THIS ISN'T OVER YET!

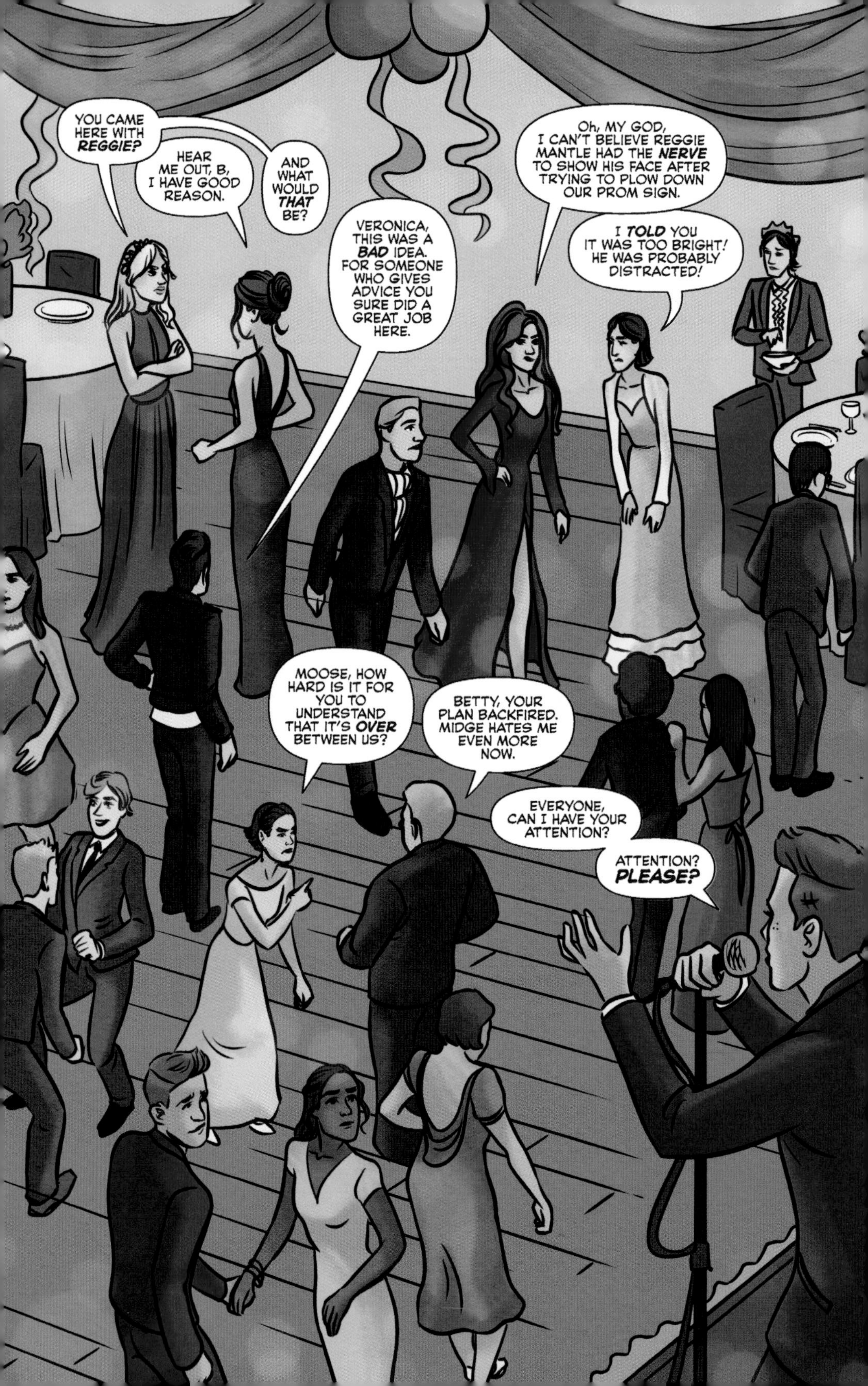
YOU CAME HERE WITH REGGIE?
HEAR ME OUT, B, I HAVE GOOD REASON.
AND WHAT WOULD THAT BE?
VERONICA, THIS WAS A BAD IDEA. FOR SOMEONE WHO GIVES ADVICE YOU SURE DID A GREAT JOB HERE.
Oh, MY GOD, I CAN'T BELIEVE REGGIE MANTLE HAD THE NERVE TO SHOW HIS FACE AFTER TRYING TO PLOW DOWN OUR PROM SIGN.
I TOLD YOU IT WAS TOO BRIGHT! HE WAS PROBABLY DISTRACTED!
MOOSE, HOW HARD IS IT FOR YOU TO UNDERSTAND THAT IT'S OVER BETWEEN US?
BETTY, YOUR PLAN BACKFIRED. MIDGE HATES ME EVEN MORE NOW.
EVERYONE, CAN I HAVE YOUR ATTENTION?
ATTENTION? PLEASE?

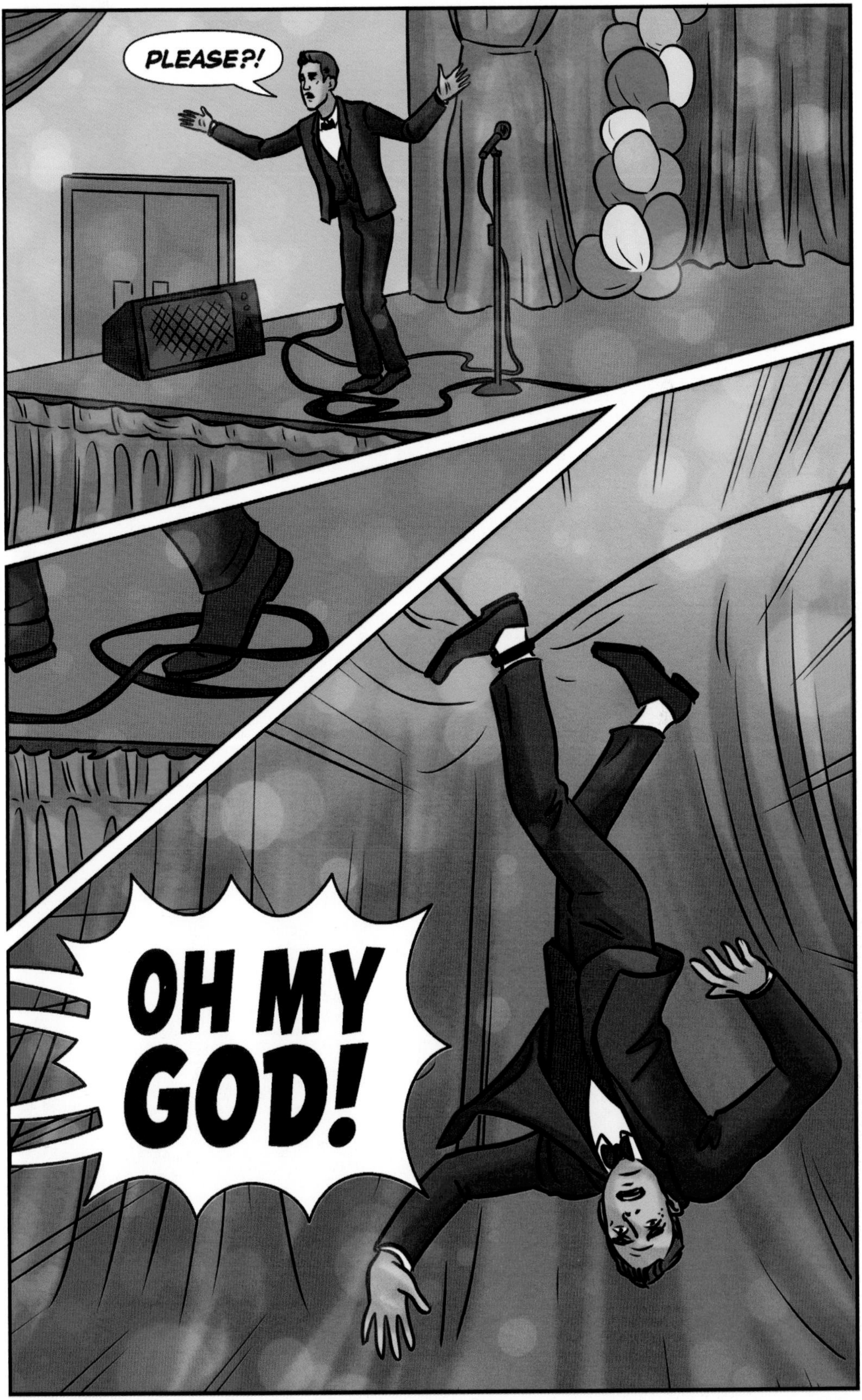
PLEASE?!
OH MY GOD!

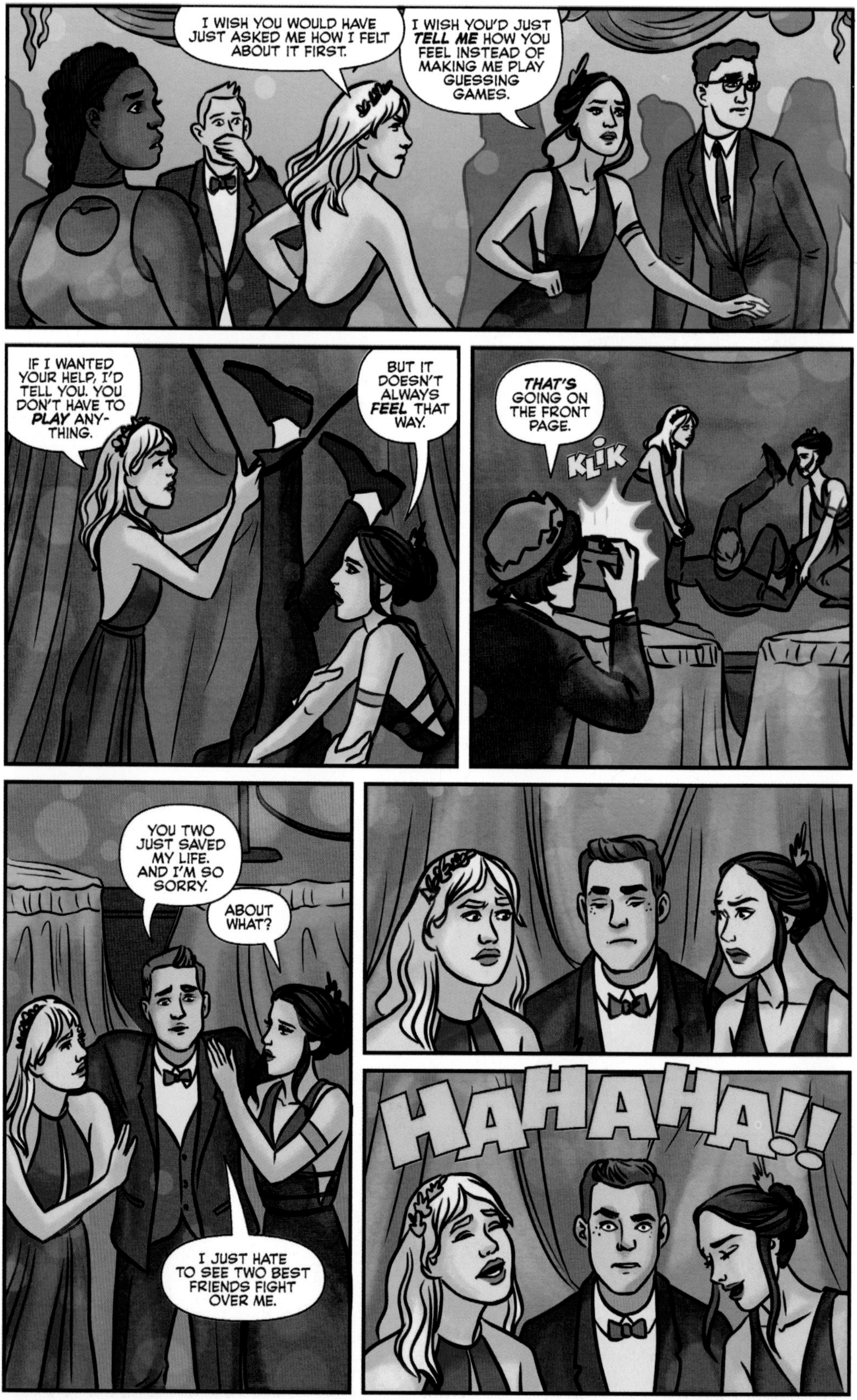
I WISH YOU WOULD HAVE JUST ASKED ME HOW I FELT ABOUT IT FIRST.
I WISH YOU'D JUST **TELL ME** HOW YOU FEEL INSTEAD OF MAKING ME PLAY GUESSING GAMES.
IF I WANTED YOUR HELP, I'D TELL YOU. YOU DON'T HAVE TO **PLAY** ANY-THING.
BUT IT DOESN'T ALWAYS **FEEL** THAT WAY.
THAT'S GOING ON THE FRONT PAGE.
KLIK
YOU TWO JUST SAVED MY LIFE. AND I'M SO SORRY.
ABOUT WHAT?
I JUST HATE TO SEE TWO BEST FRIENDS FIGHT OVER ME.
HAHAHA!!

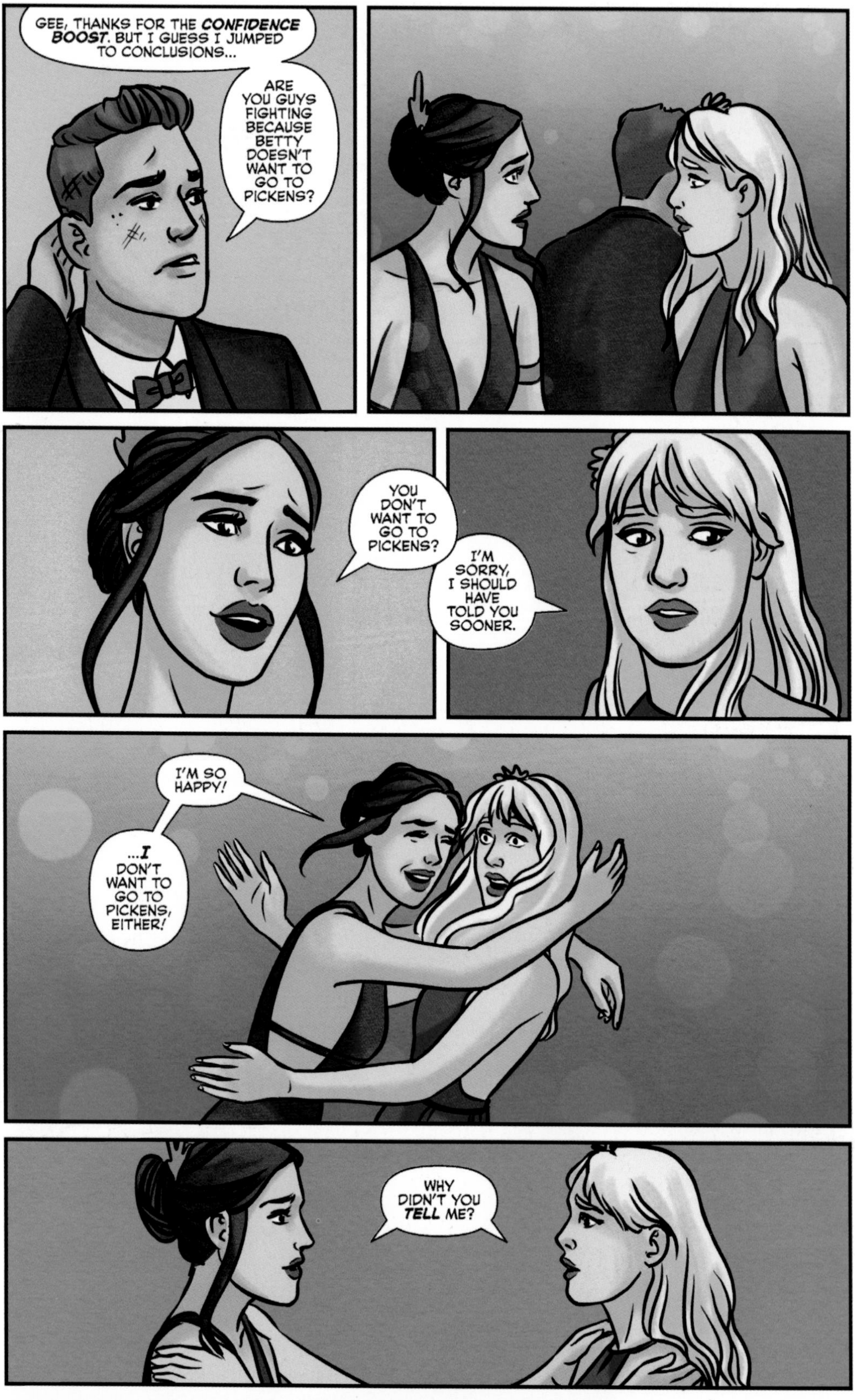
GEE, THANKS FOR THE **CONFIDENCE BOOST**. BUT I GUESS I JUMPED TO CONCLUSIONS...
ARE YOU GUYS FIGHTING BECAUSE BETTY DOESN'T WANT TO GO TO PICKENS?
YOU DON'T WANT TO GO TO PICKENS?
I'M SORRY, I SHOULD HAVE TOLD YOU SOONER.
I'M SO HAPPY!
...*I* DON'T WANT TO GO TO PICKENS, EITHER!
WHY DIDN'T YOU ***TELL*** ME?

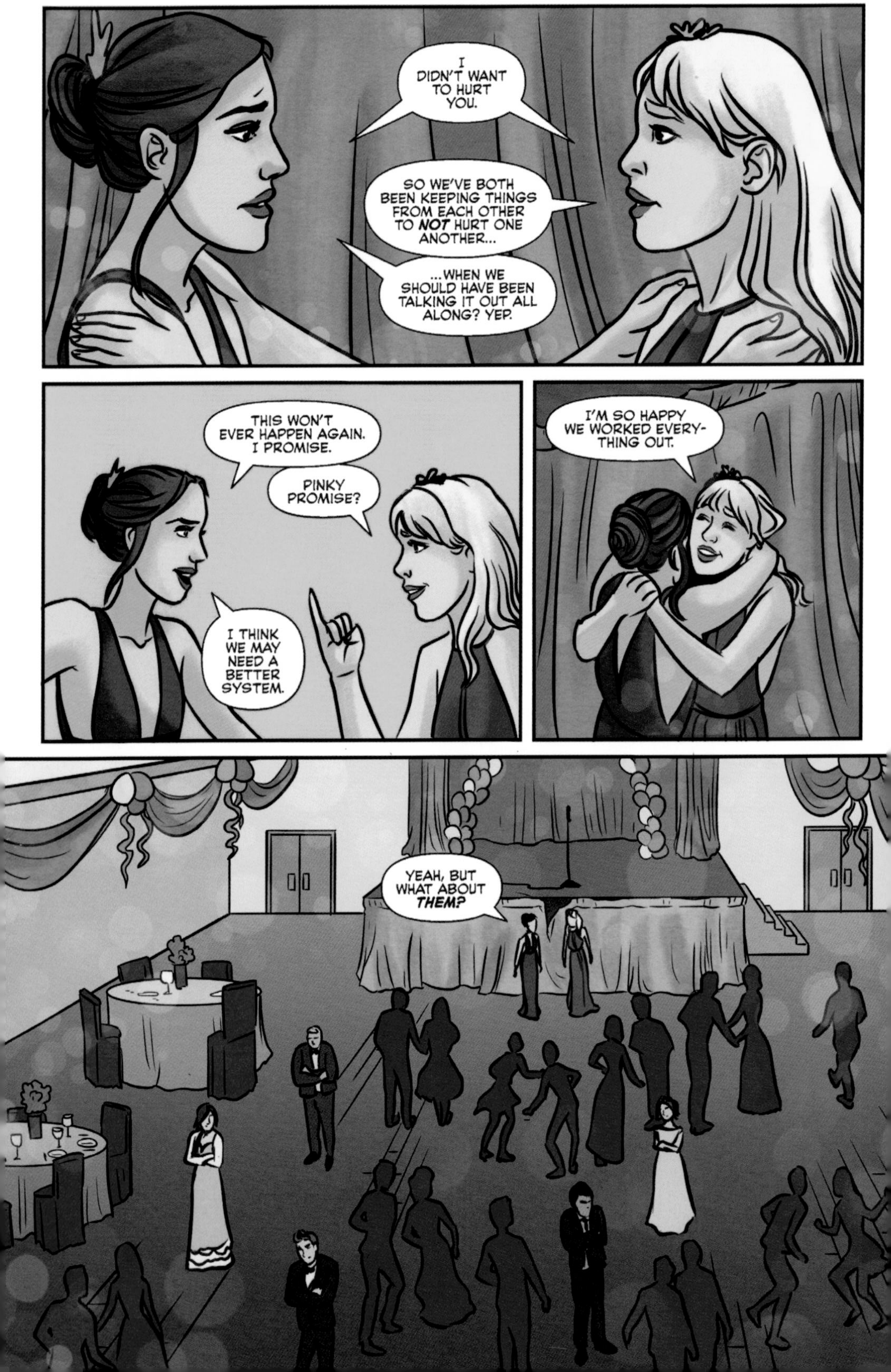
I DIDN'T WANT TO HURT YOU.
SO WE'VE BOTH BEEN KEEPING THINGS FROM EACH OTHER TO *NOT* HURT ONE ANOTHER...
...WHEN WE SHOULD HAVE BEEN TALKING IT OUT ALL ALONG? YEP.
THIS WON'T EVER HAPPEN AGAIN. I PROMISE.
PINKY PROMISE?
I THINK WE MAY NEED A BETTER SYSTEM.
I'M SO HAPPY WE WORKED EVERYTHING OUT.
YEAH, BUT WHAT ABOUT *THEM?*

TO BE CONTINUED...

05

STORY BY
JAMIE LEE ROTANTE

ART BY
SANDRA LANZ

LETTERING BY
JACK MORELLI

COLORS BY
KELLY FITZPATRICK

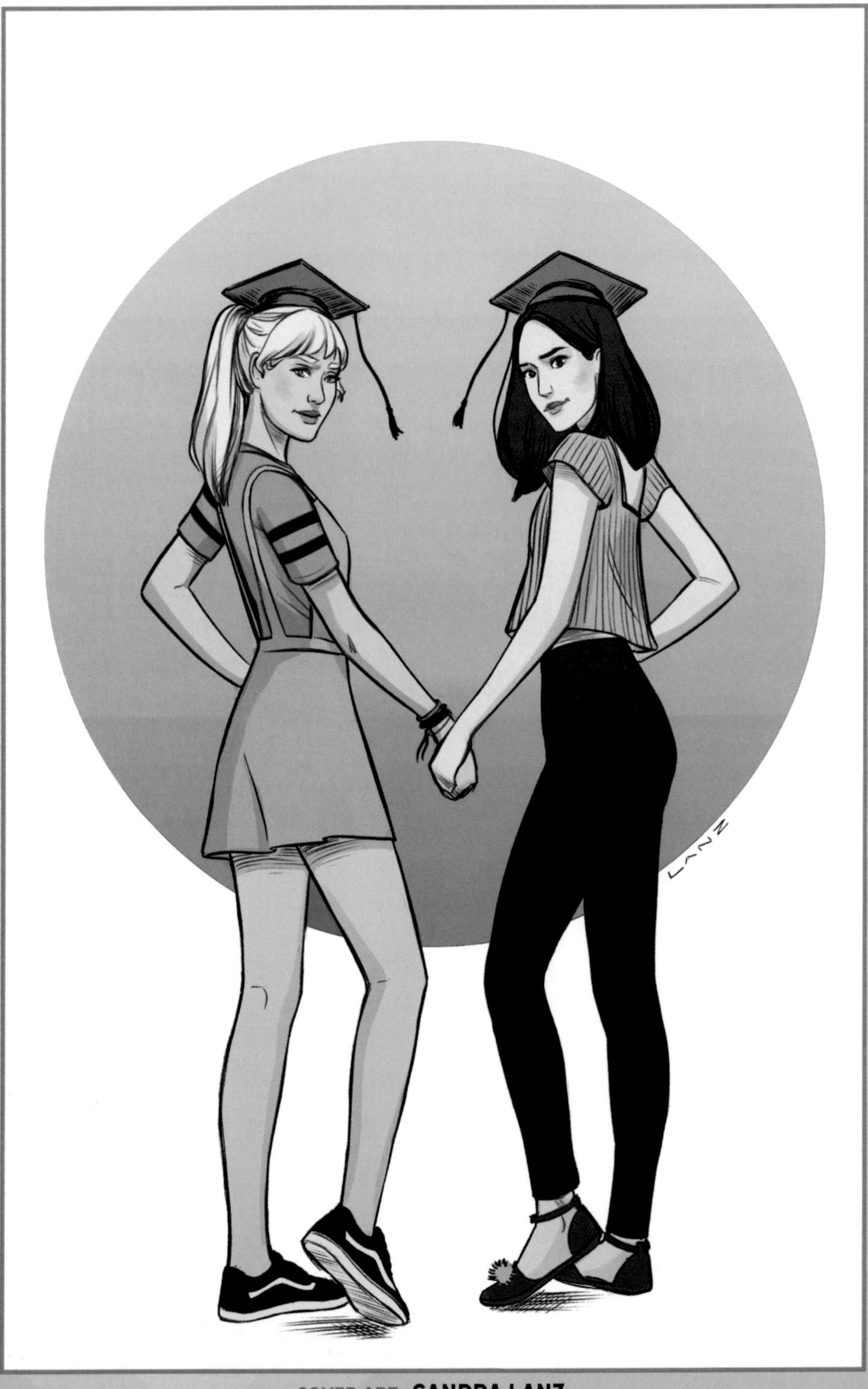
LANZ

COVER ART: **SANDRA LANZ**

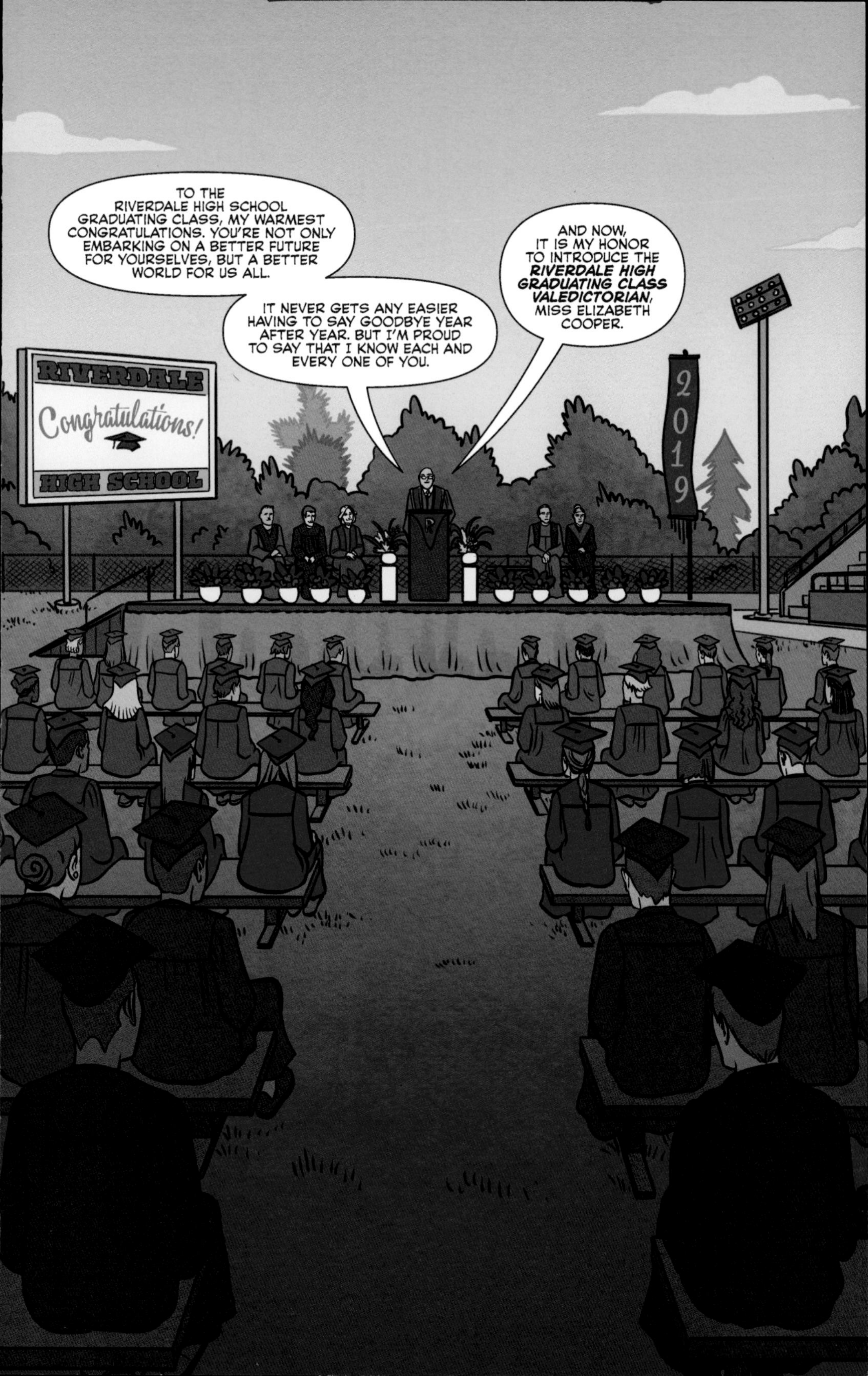
TO THE RIVERDALE HIGH SCHOOL GRADUATING CLASS, MY WARMEST CONGRATULATIONS. YOU'RE NOT ONLY EMBARKING ON A BETTER FUTURE FOR YOURSELVES, BUT A BETTER WORLD FOR US ALL.
IT NEVER GETS ANY EASIER HAVING TO SAY GOODBYE YEAR AFTER YEAR. BUT I'M PROUD TO SAY THAT I KNOW EACH AND EVERY ONE OF YOU.
AND NOW, IT IS MY HONOR TO INTRODUCE THE ***RIVERDALE HIGH GRADUATING CLASS VALEDICTORIAN***, MISS ELIZABETH COOPER.
RIVERDALE
Congratulations!
HIGH SCHOOL
2019

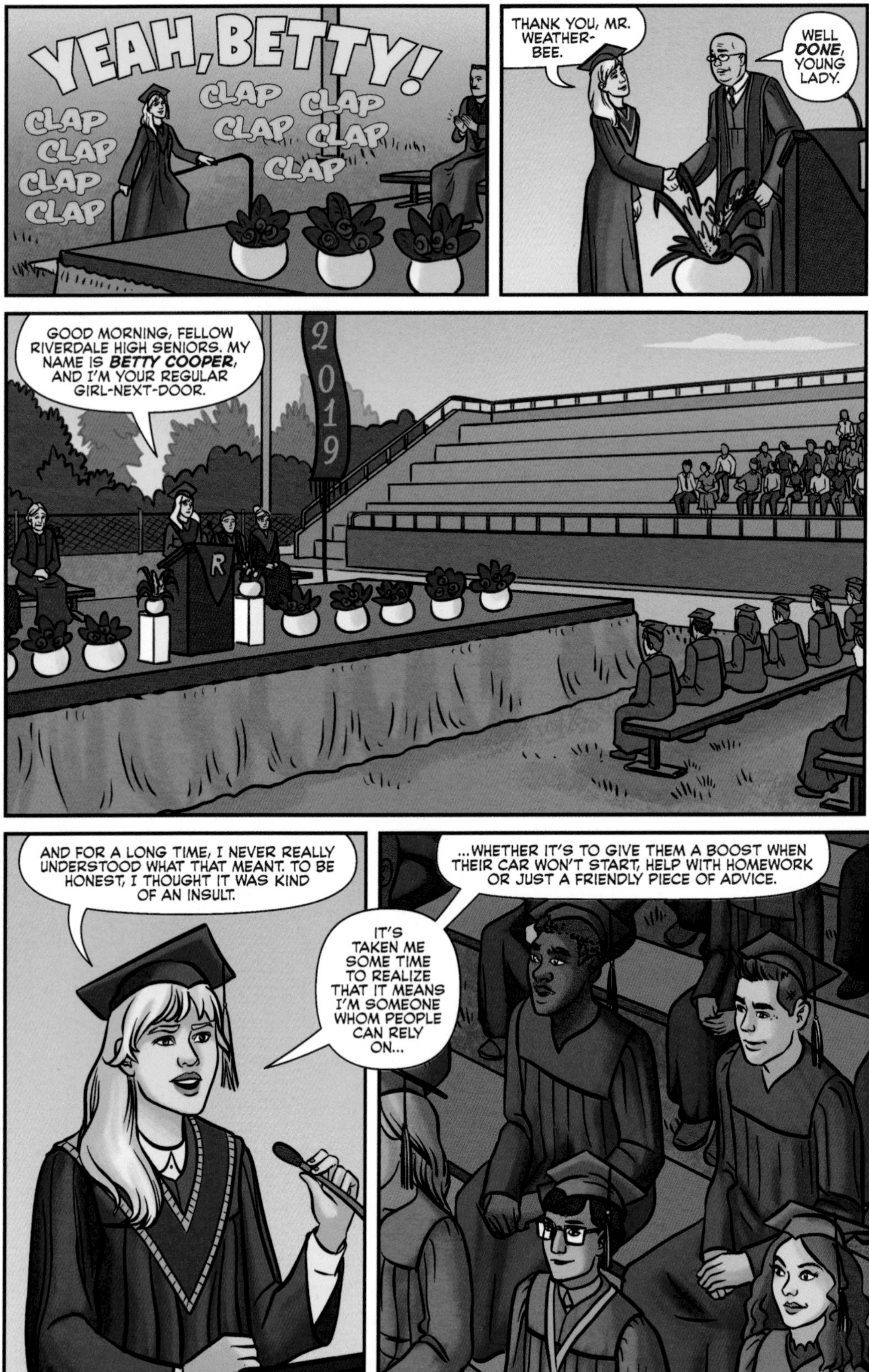
YEAH, BETTY!
CLAP CLAP CLAP CLAP
CLAP CLAP
CLAP CLAP
CLAP
THANK YOU, MR. WEATHERBEE.
WELL **DONE**, YOUNG LADY.
2019
GOOD MORNING, FELLOW RIVERDALE HIGH SENIORS. MY NAME IS **BETTY COOPER**, AND I'M YOUR REGULAR GIRL-NEXT-DOOR.
R
AND FOR A LONG TIME, I NEVER REALLY UNDERSTOOD WHAT THAT MEANT. TO BE HONEST, I THOUGHT IT WAS KIND OF AN INSULT.
IT'S TAKEN ME SOME TIME TO REALIZE THAT IT MEANS I'M SOMEONE WHOM PEOPLE CAN RELY ON...
...WHETHER IT'S TO GIVE THEM A BOOST WHEN THEIR CAR WON'T START, HELP WITH HOMEWORK OR JUST A FRIENDLY PIECE OF ADVICE.

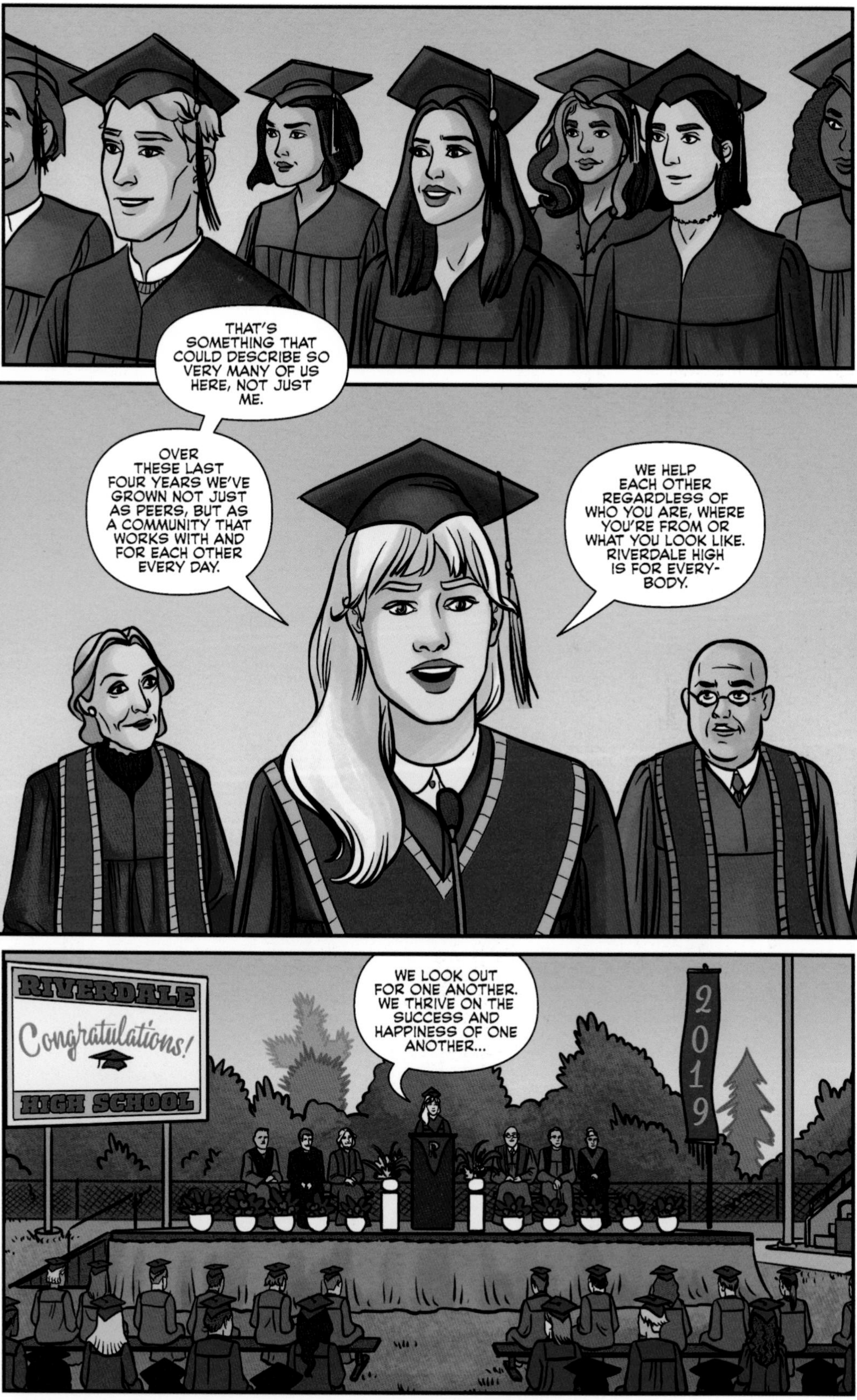

THAT'S SOMETHING THAT COULD DESCRIBE SO VERY MANY OF US HERE, NOT JUST ME.
OVER THESE LAST FOUR YEARS WE'VE GROWN NOT JUST AS PEERS, BUT AS A COMMUNITY THAT WORKS WITH AND FOR EACH OTHER EVERY DAY.
WE HELP EACH OTHER REGARDLESS OF WHO YOU ARE, WHERE YOU'RE FROM OR WHAT YOU LOOK LIKE. RIVERDALE HIGH IS FOR EVERY-BODY.
RIVERDALE
Congratulations!
HIGH SCHOOL
WE LOOK OUT FOR ONE ANOTHER. WE THRIVE ON THE SUCCESS AND HAPPINESS OF ONE ANOTHER...
2019

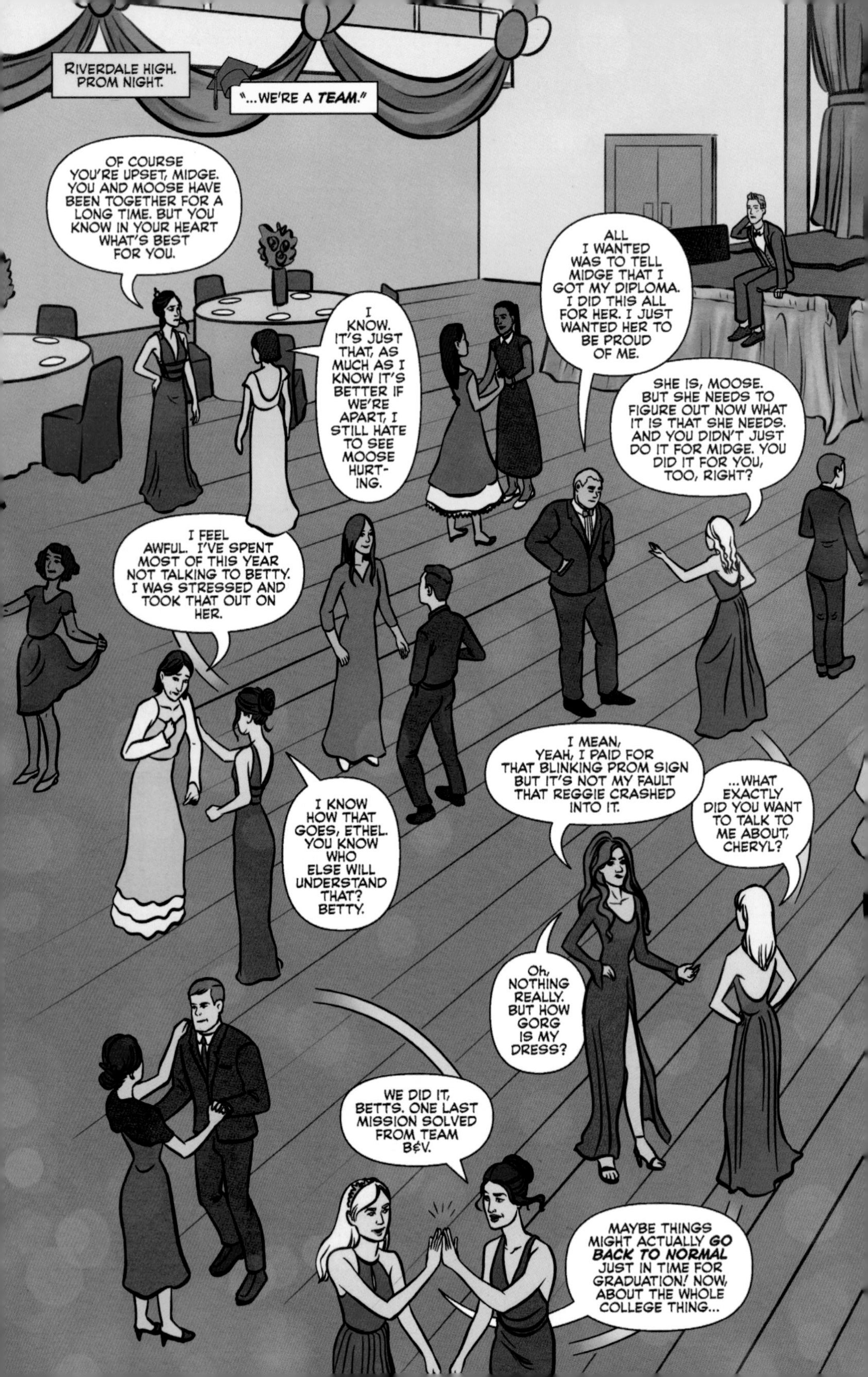
RIVERDALE HIGH. PROM NIGHT.
"...WE'RE A TEAM."
OF COURSE YOU'RE UPSET, MIDGE. YOU AND MOOSE HAVE BEEN TOGETHER FOR A LONG TIME. BUT YOU KNOW IN YOUR HEART WHAT'S BEST FOR YOU.
I KNOW. IT'S JUST THAT, AS MUCH AS I KNOW IT'S BETTER IF WE'RE APART, I STILL HATE TO SEE MOOSE HURT-ING.
ALL I WANTED WAS TO TELL MIDGE THAT I GOT MY DIPLOMA. I DID THIS ALL FOR HER. I JUST WANTED HER TO BE PROUD OF ME.
SHE IS, MOOSE. BUT SHE NEEDS TO FIGURE OUT NOW WHAT IT IS THAT SHE NEEDS. AND YOU DIDN'T JUST DO IT FOR MIDGE. YOU DID IT FOR YOU, TOO, RIGHT?
I FEEL AWFUL. I'VE SPENT MOST OF THIS YEAR NOT TALKING TO BETTY. I WAS STRESSED AND TOOK THAT OUT ON HER.
I KNOW HOW THAT GOES, ETHEL. YOU KNOW WHO ELSE WILL UNDERSTAND THAT? BETTY.
I MEAN, YEAH, I PAID FOR THAT BLINKING PROM SIGN BUT IT'S NOT MY FAULT THAT REGGIE CRASHED INTO IT.
...WHAT EXACTLY DID YOU WANT TO TALK TO ME ABOUT, CHERYL?
Oh, NOTHING REALLY. BUT HOW GORG IS MY DRESS?
WE DID IT, BETTS. ONE LAST MISSION SOLVED FROM TEAM B&V.
MAYBE THINGS MIGHT ACTUALLY GO BACK TO NORMAL JUST IN TIME FOR GRADUATION! NOW, ABOUT THE WHOLE COLLEGE THING...

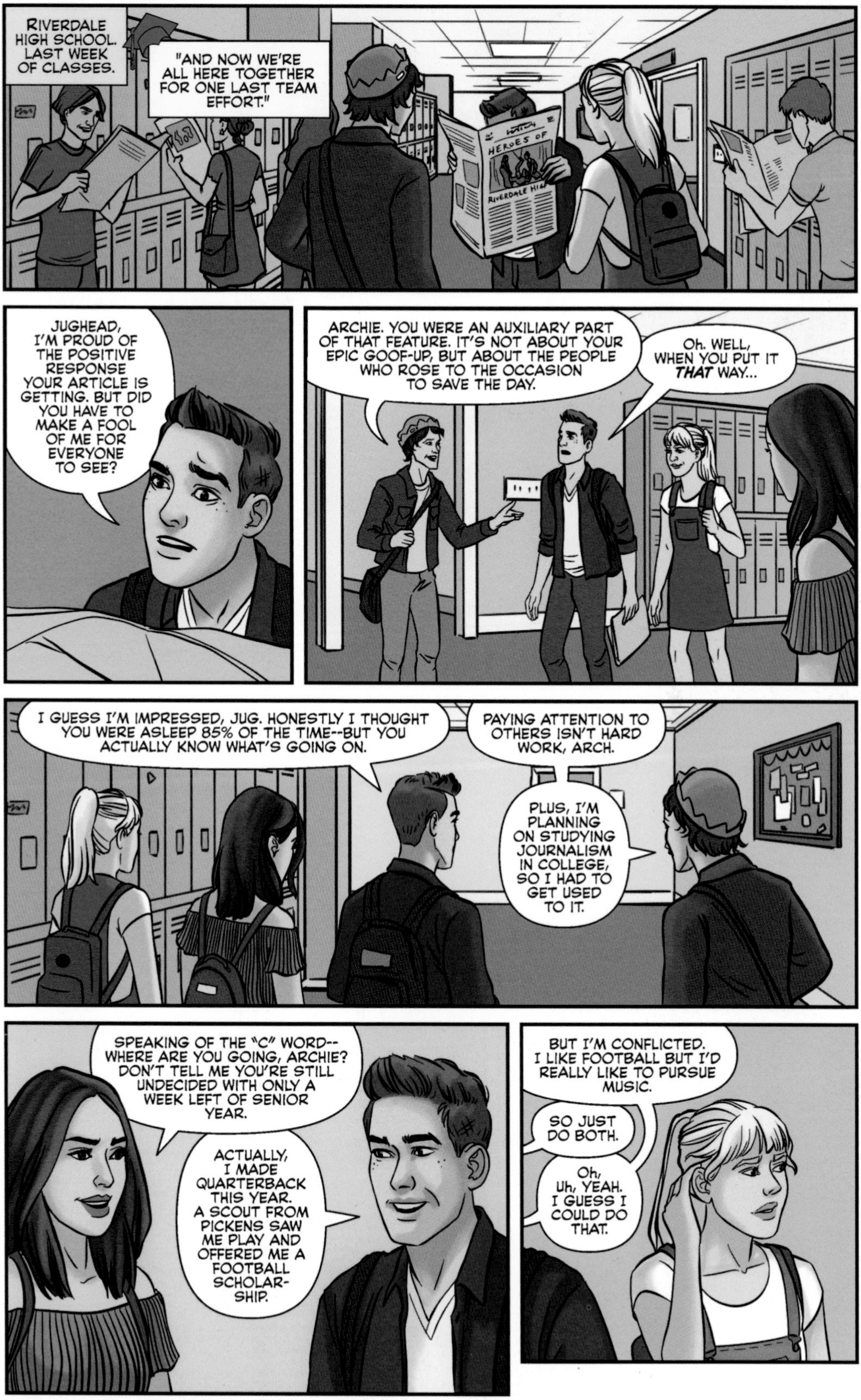
RIVERDALE HIGH SCHOOL. LAST WEEK OF CLASSES.
"AND NOW WE'RE ALL HERE TOGETHER FOR ONE LAST TEAM EFFORT."
HEROES OF
RIVERDALE HIGH
JUGHEAD, I'M PROUD OF THE POSITIVE RESPONSE YOUR ARTICLE IS GETTING. BUT DID YOU HAVE TO MAKE A FOOL OF ME FOR EVERYONE TO SEE?
ARCHIE. YOU WERE AN AUXILIARY PART OF THAT FEATURE. IT'S NOT ABOUT YOUR EPIC GOOF-UP, BUT ABOUT THE PEOPLE WHO ROSE TO THE OCCASION TO SAVE THE DAY.
Oh. WELL, WHEN YOU PUT IT *THAT* WAY...
I GUESS I'M IMPRESSED, JUG. HONESTLY I THOUGHT YOU WERE ASLEEP 85% OF THE TIME--BUT YOU ACTUALLY KNOW WHAT'S GOING ON.
PAYING ATTENTION TO OTHERS ISN'T HARD WORK, ARCH.
PLUS, I'M PLANNING ON STUDYING JOURNALISM IN COLLEGE, SO I HAD TO GET USED TO IT.
SPEAKING OF THE "C" WORD--WHERE ARE YOU GOING, ARCHIE? DON'T TELL ME YOU'RE STILL UNDECIDED WITH ONLY A WEEK LEFT OF SENIOR YEAR.
ACTUALLY, I MADE QUARTERBACK THIS YEAR. A SCOUT FROM PICKENS SAW ME PLAY AND OFFERED ME A FOOTBALL SCHOLAR-SHIP.
BUT I'M CONFLICTED. I LIKE FOOTBALL BUT I'D REALLY LIKE TO PURSUE MUSIC.
SO JUST DO BOTH.
Oh, Uh, YEAH. I GUESS I COULD DO THAT.

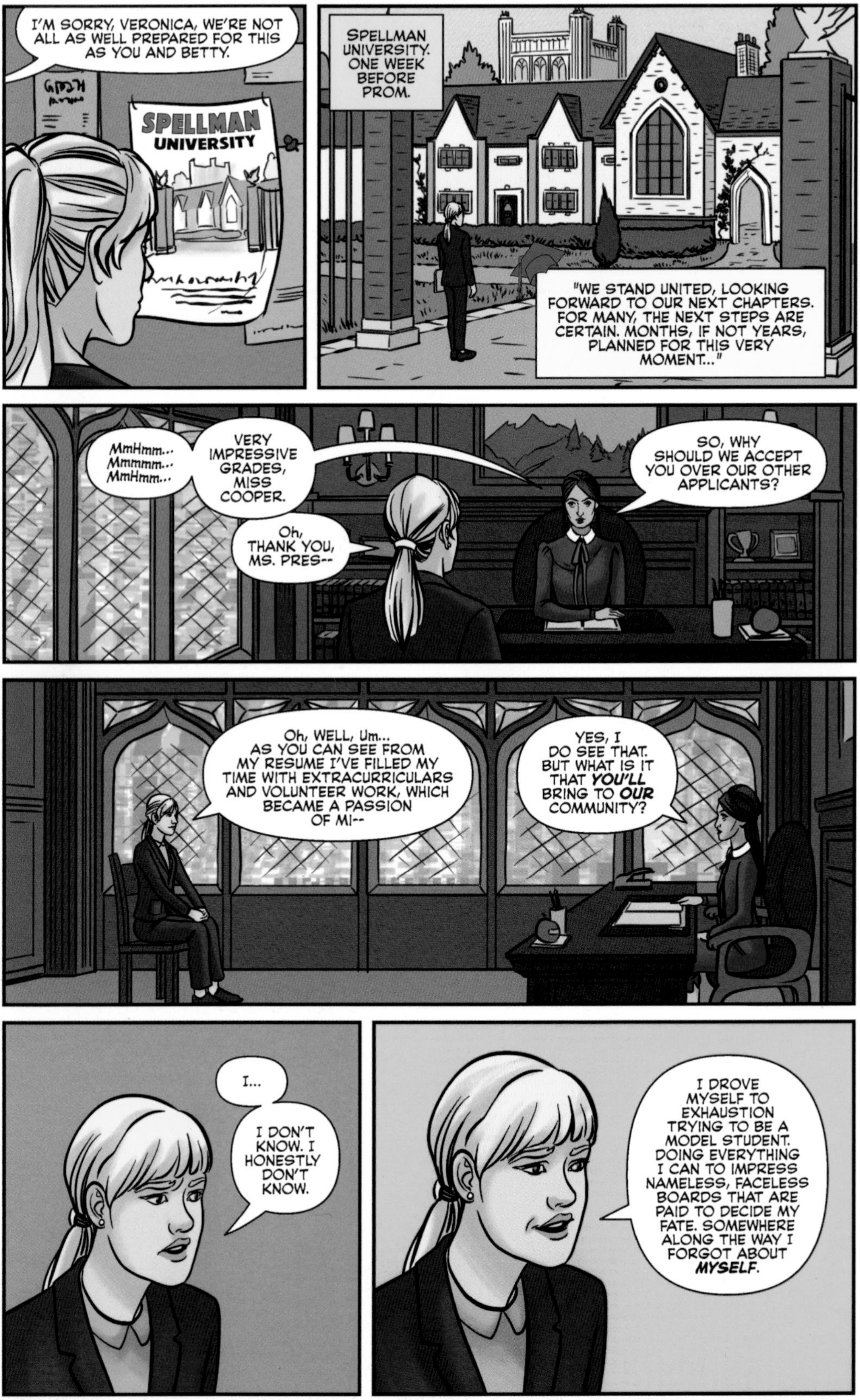
I'M SORRY, VERONICA, WE'RE NOT ALL AS WELL PREPARED FOR THIS AS YOU AND BETTY.
SPELLMAN UNIVERSITY
SPELLMAN UNIVERSITY. ONE WEEK BEFORE PROM.
"WE STAND UNITED, LOOKING FORWARD TO OUR NEXT CHAPTERS. FOR MANY, THE NEXT STEPS ARE CERTAIN. MONTHS, IF NOT YEARS, PLANNED FOR THIS VERY MOMENT..."
MmHmm... Mmmmm... MmHmm...
VERY IMPRESSIVE GRADES, MISS COOPER.
Oh, THANK YOU, MS. PRES--
SO, WHY SHOULD WE ACCEPT YOU OVER OUR OTHER APPLICANTS?
Oh, WELL, Um... AS YOU CAN SEE FROM MY RESUME I'VE FILLED MY TIME WITH EXTRACURRICULARS AND VOLUNTEER WORK, WHICH BECAME A PASSION OF MI--
YES, I DO SEE THAT. BUT WHAT IS IT THAT ***YOU'LL*** BRING TO ***OUR*** COMMUNITY?
I...
I DON'T KNOW. I HONESTLY DON'T KNOW.
I DROVE MYSELF TO EXHAUSTION TRYING TO BE A MODEL STUDENT. DOING EVERYTHING I CAN TO IMPRESS NAMELESS, FACELESS BOARDS THAT ARE PAID TO DECIDE MY FATE. SOMEWHERE ALONG THE WAY I FORGOT ABOUT ***MYSELF***.

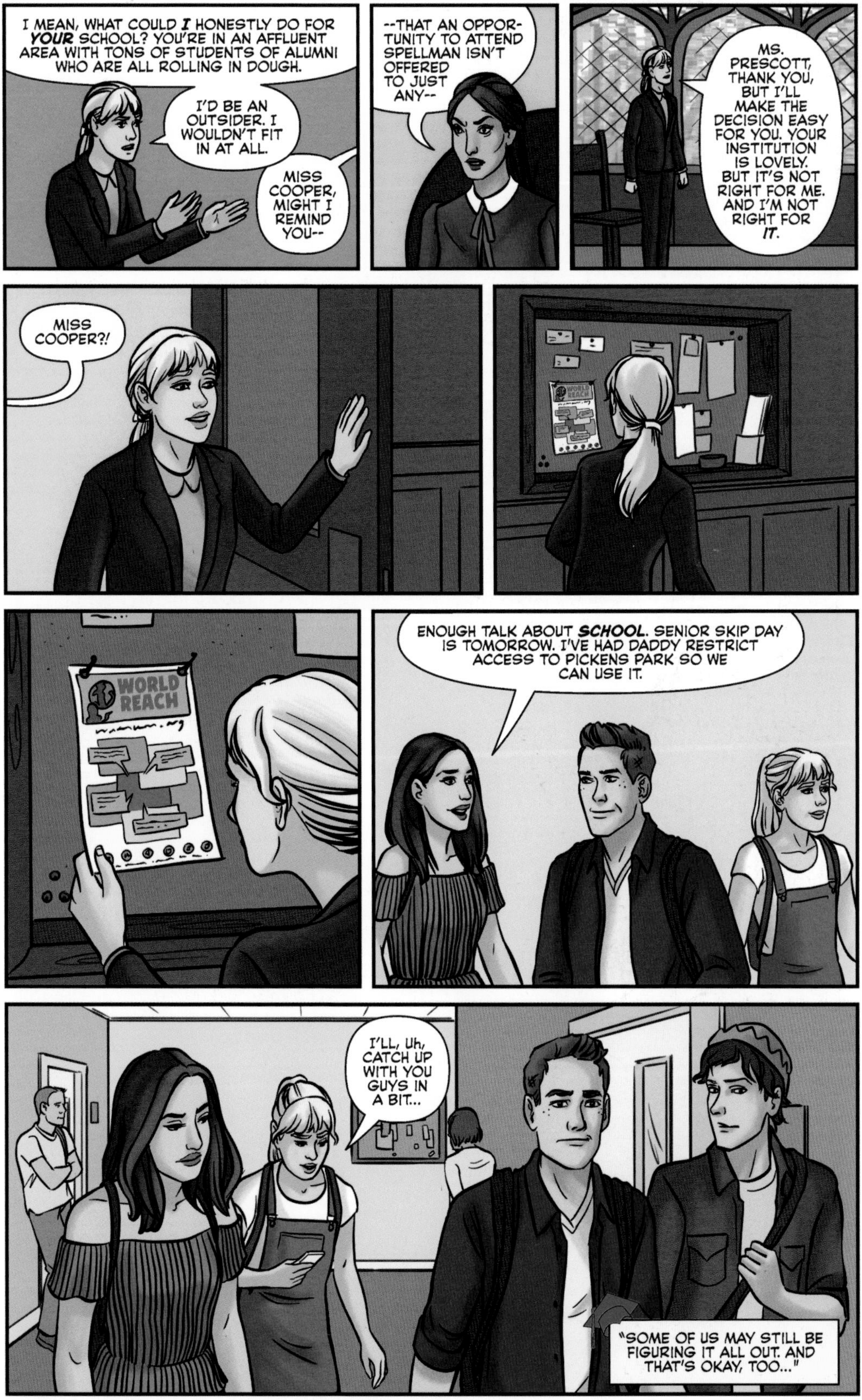
I MEAN, WHAT COULD I HONESTLY DO FOR YOUR SCHOOL? YOU'RE IN AN AFFLUENT AREA WITH TONS OF STUDENTS OF ALUMNI WHO ARE ALL ROLLING IN DOUGH.
I'D BE AN OUTSIDER. I WOULDN'T FIT IN AT ALL.
MISS COOPER, MIGHT I REMIND YOU--
--THAT AN OPPORTUNITY TO ATTEND SPELLMAN ISN'T OFFERED TO JUST ANY--
MS. PRESCOTT, THANK YOU, BUT I'LL MAKE THE DECISION EASY FOR YOU. YOUR INSTITUTION IS LOVELY. BUT IT'S NOT RIGHT FOR ME. AND I'M NOT RIGHT FOR IT.
MISS COOPER?!
WORLD REACH
ENOUGH TALK ABOUT SCHOOL. SENIOR SKIP DAY IS TOMORROW. I'VE HAD DADDY RESTRICT ACCESS TO PICKENS PARK SO WE CAN USE IT.
I'LL, UH, CATCH UP WITH YOU GUYS IN A BIT...
"SOME OF US MAY STILL BE FIGURING IT ALL OUT. AND THAT'S OKAY, TOO..."

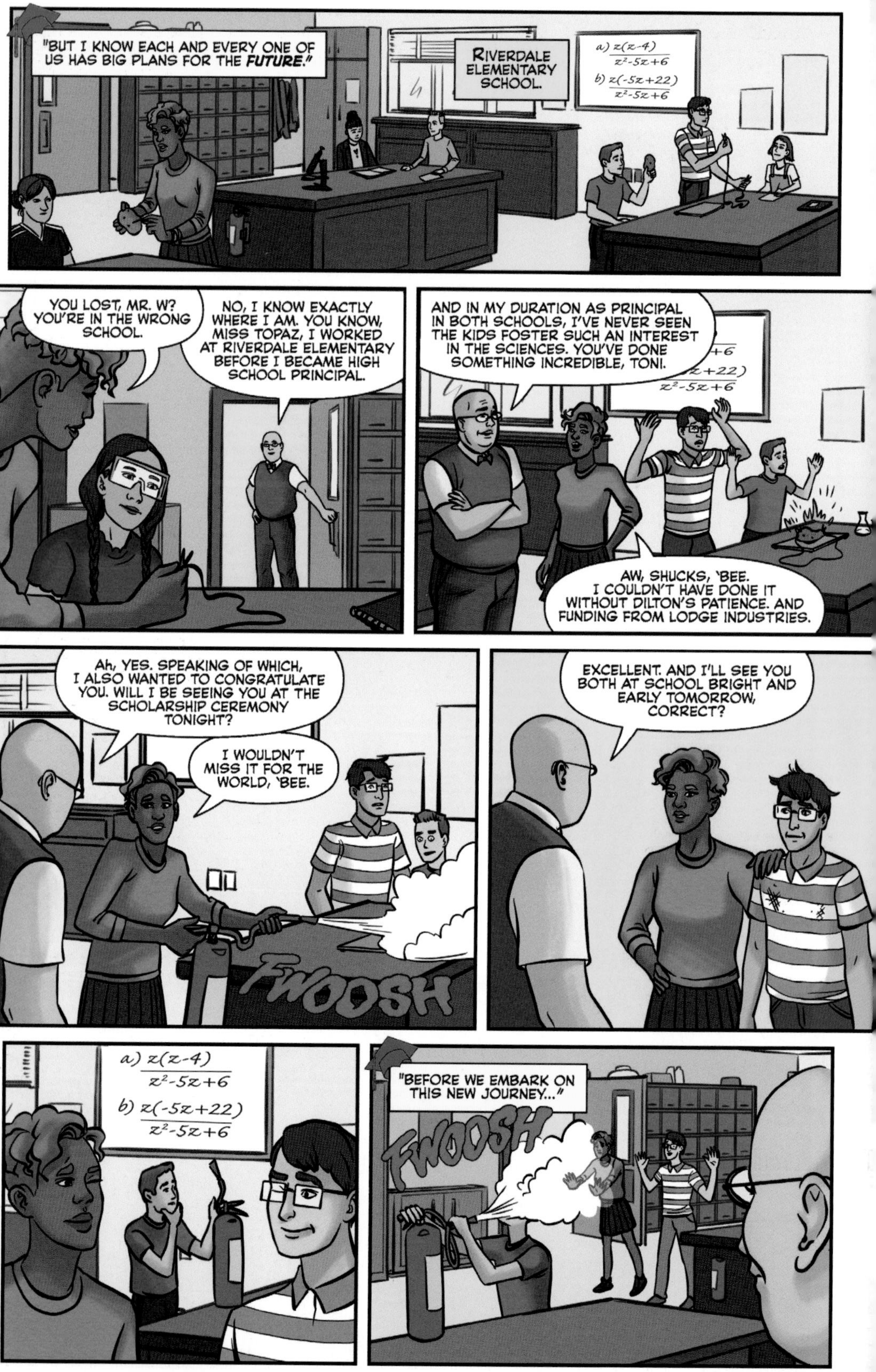

"BUT I KNOW EACH AND EVERY ONE OF US HAS BIG PLANS FOR THE FUTURE."
RIVERDALE ELEMENTARY SCHOOL.
a) z(z-4) / z²-5z+6
b) z(-5z+22) / z²-5z+6
YOU LOST, MR. W? YOU'RE IN THE WRONG SCHOOL.
NO, I KNOW EXACTLY WHERE I AM. YOU KNOW, MISS TOPAZ, I WORKED AT RIVERDALE ELEMENTARY BEFORE I BECAME HIGH SCHOOL PRINCIPAL.
AND IN MY DURATION AS PRINCIPAL IN BOTH SCHOOLS, I'VE NEVER SEEN THE KIDS FOSTER SUCH AN INTEREST IN THE SCIENCES. YOU'VE DONE SOMETHING INCREDIBLE, TONI.
AW, SHUCKS, 'BEE. I COULDN'T HAVE DONE IT WITHOUT DILTON'S PATIENCE. AND FUNDING FROM LODGE INDUSTRIES.
Ah, YES. SPEAKING OF WHICH, I ALSO WANTED TO CONGRATULATE YOU. WILL I BE SEEING YOU AT THE SCHOLARSHIP CEREMONY TONIGHT?
I WOULDN'T MISS IT FOR THE WORLD, 'BEE.
FWOOSH
EXCELLENT. AND I'LL SEE YOU BOTH AT SCHOOL BRIGHT AND EARLY TOMORROW, CORRECT?
a) z(z-4) / z²-5z+6
b) z(-5z+22) / z²-5z+6
"BEFORE WE EMBARK ON THIS NEW JOURNEY..."
FWOOSH

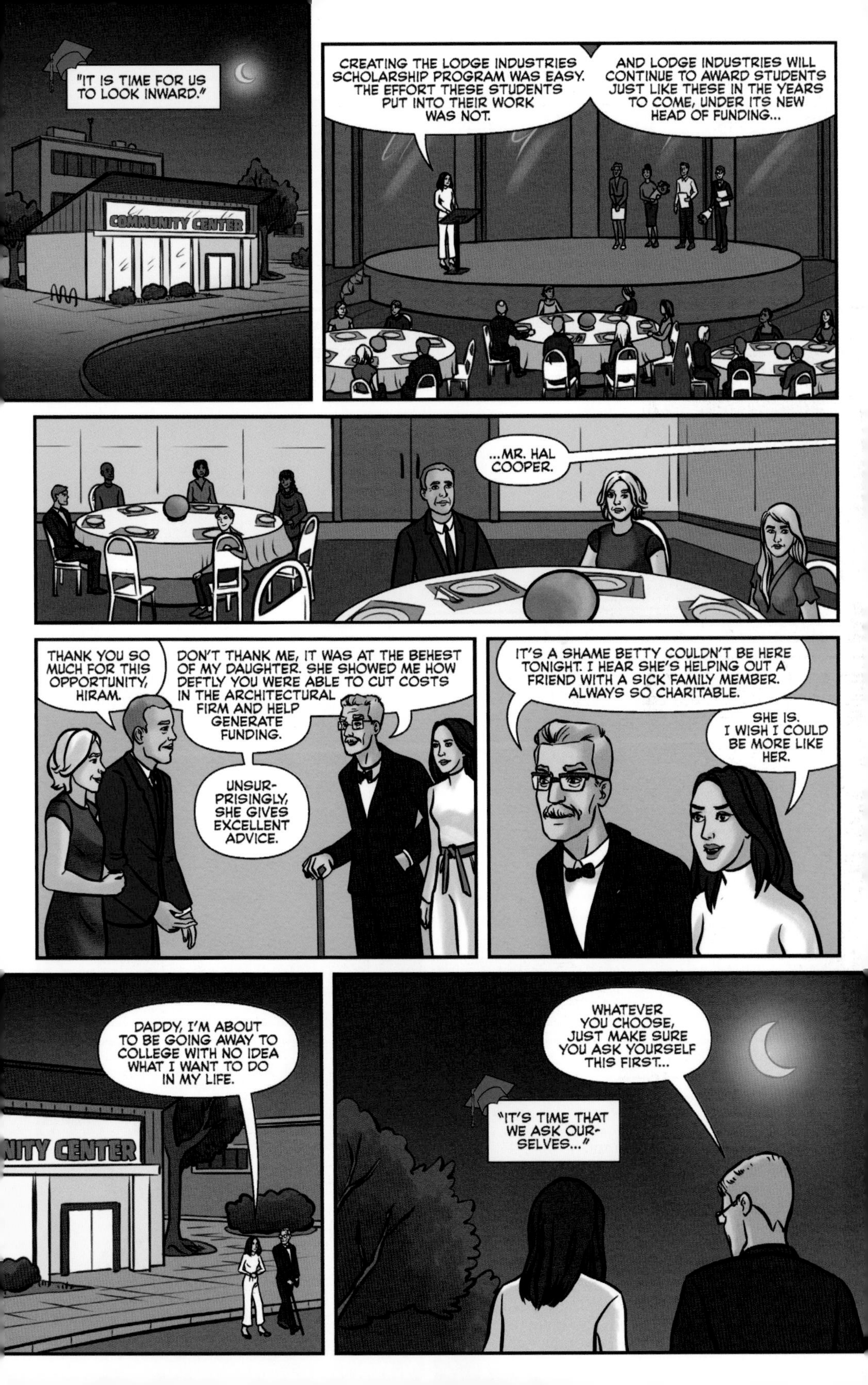
"IT IS TIME FOR US TO LOOK INWARD."
COMMUNITY CENTER
CREATING THE LODGE INDUSTRIES SCHOLARSHIP PROGRAM WAS EASY. THE EFFORT THESE STUDENTS PUT INTO THEIR WORK WAS NOT.
AND LODGE INDUSTRIES WILL CONTINUE TO AWARD STUDENTS JUST LIKE THESE IN THE YEARS TO COME, UNDER ITS NEW HEAD OF FUNDING...
...MR. HAL COOPER.
THANK YOU SO MUCH FOR THIS OPPORTUNITY, HIRAM.
DON'T THANK ME, IT WAS AT THE BEHEST OF MY DAUGHTER. SHE SHOWED ME HOW DEFTLY YOU WERE ABLE TO CUT COSTS IN THE ARCHITECTURAL FIRM AND HELP GENERATE FUNDING.
UNSURPRISINGLY, SHE GIVES EXCELLENT ADVICE.
IT'S A SHAME BETTY COULDN'T BE HERE TONIGHT. I HEAR SHE'S HELPING OUT A FRIEND WITH A SICK FAMILY MEMBER. ALWAYS SO CHARITABLE.
SHE IS. I WISH I COULD BE MORE LIKE HER.
DADDY, I'M ABOUT TO BE GOING AWAY TO COLLEGE WITH NO IDEA WHAT I WANT TO DO IN MY LIFE.
NITY CENTER
WHATEVER YOU CHOOSE, JUST MAKE SURE YOU ASK YOURSELF THIS FIRST...
"IT'S TIME THAT WE ASK OURSELVES..."

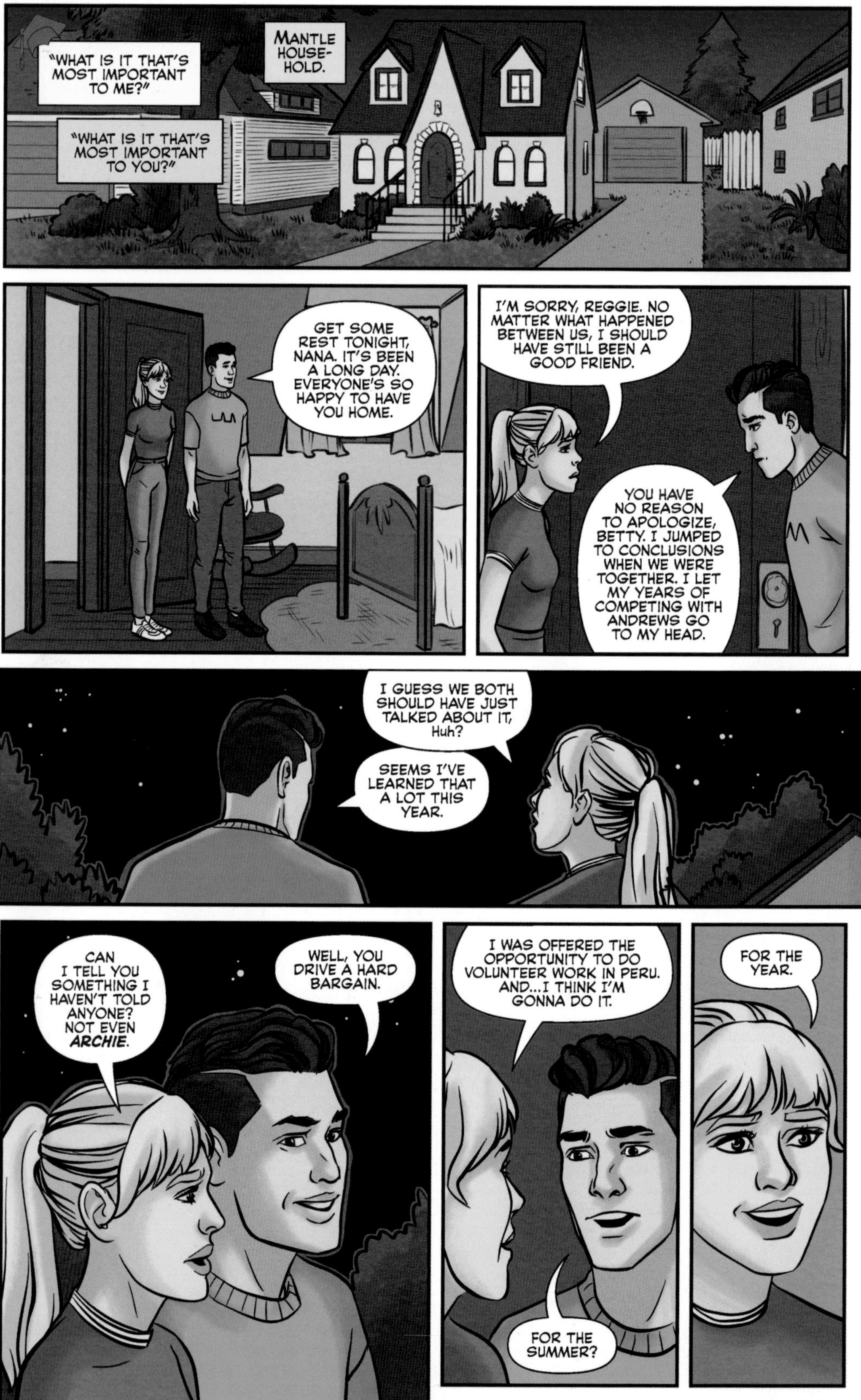
"WHAT IS IT THAT'S MOST IMPORTANT TO ME?"
"WHAT IS IT THAT'S MOST IMPORTANT TO YOU?"
MANTLE HOUSE-HOLD.
GET SOME REST TONIGHT, NANA. IT'S BEEN A LONG DAY. EVERYONE'S SO HAPPY TO HAVE YOU HOME.
I'M SORRY, REGGIE. NO MATTER WHAT HAPPENED BETWEEN US, I SHOULD HAVE STILL BEEN A GOOD FRIEND.
YOU HAVE NO REASON TO APOLOGIZE, BETTY. I JUMPED TO CONCLUSIONS WHEN WE WERE TOGETHER. I LET MY YEARS OF COMPETING WITH ANDREWS GO TO MY HEAD.
I GUESS WE BOTH SHOULD HAVE JUST TALKED ABOUT IT, Huh?
SEEMS I'VE LEARNED THAT A LOT THIS YEAR.
CAN I TELL YOU SOMETHING I HAVEN'T TOLD ANYONE? NOT EVEN ARCHIE.
WELL, YOU DRIVE A HARD BARGAIN.
I WAS OFFERED THE OPPORTUNITY TO DO VOLUNTEER WORK IN PERU. AND...I THINK I'M GONNA DO IT.
FOR THE SUMMER?
FOR THE YEAR.

BUT WHAT ABOUT COLLEGE?

COLLEGE WILL STILL BE THERE WHEN I GET BACK. BUT THIS, THIS IS SOMETHING I NEED TO DO RIGHT NOW.

YOU'RE AMAZING, BETTY COOPER.

AND WHAT ABOUT YOU?

I FELT SO POWERLESS WATCHING MY GRANDMA SUFFER.

SO I'M THINKING OF ENROLLING IN SOME NURSING CLASSES AT RIVERDALE COMMUNITY COLLEGE IN THE FALL.

WELL THEN, YOU'RE NOT SO BAD YOURSELF, ARE YOU, MR. MANTLE?

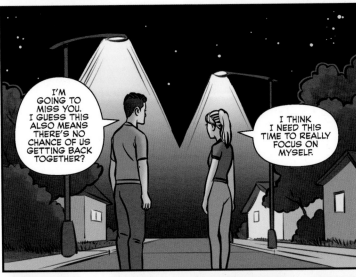

I'M GOING TO MISS YOU. I GUESS THIS ALSO MEANS THERE'S NO CHANCE OF US GETTING BACK TOGETHER?

I THINK I NEED THIS TIME TO REALLY FOCUS ON MYSELF.

...BUT WE DO STILL HAVE THE SUMMER. AND MAYBE THIS TIME IT WON'T BE IN SECRET.

DON'T WORRY, THE CAMERA'S AT HOME.

HAHA HA!

"WHAT TRULY MAKES ME HAPPY?"

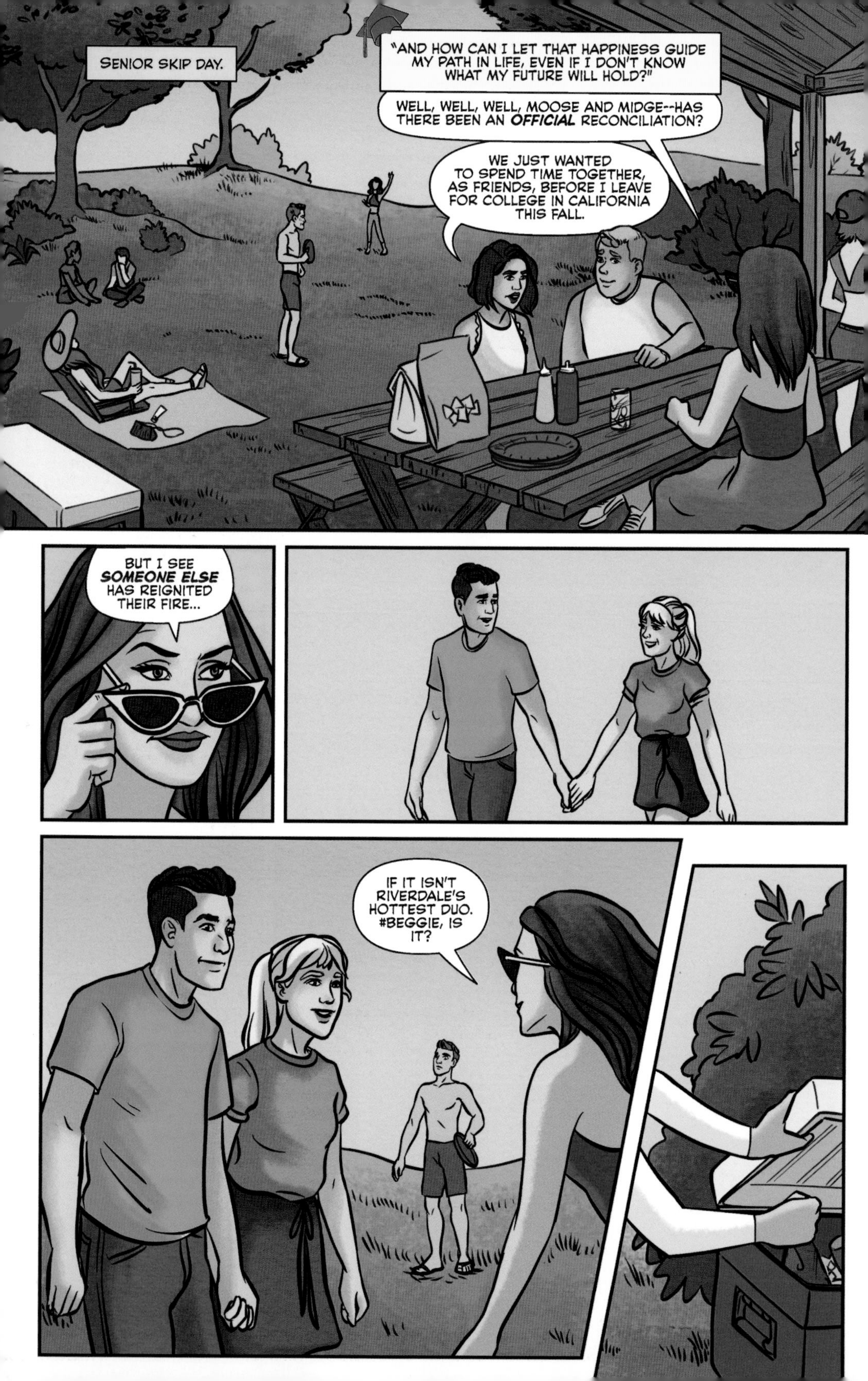
SENIOR SKIP DAY.
"AND HOW CAN I LET THAT HAPPINESS GUIDE MY PATH IN LIFE, EVEN IF I DON'T KNOW WHAT MY FUTURE WILL HOLD?"
WELL, WELL, WELL, MOOSE AND MIDGE--HAS THERE BEEN AN OFFICIAL RECONCILIATION?
WE JUST WANTED TO SPEND TIME TOGETHER, AS FRIENDS, BEFORE I LEAVE FOR COLLEGE IN CALIFORNIA THIS FALL.
BUT I SEE SOMEONE ELSE HAS REIGNITED THEIR FIRE...
IF IT ISN'T RIVERDALE'S HOTTEST DUO. #BEGGIE, IS IT?

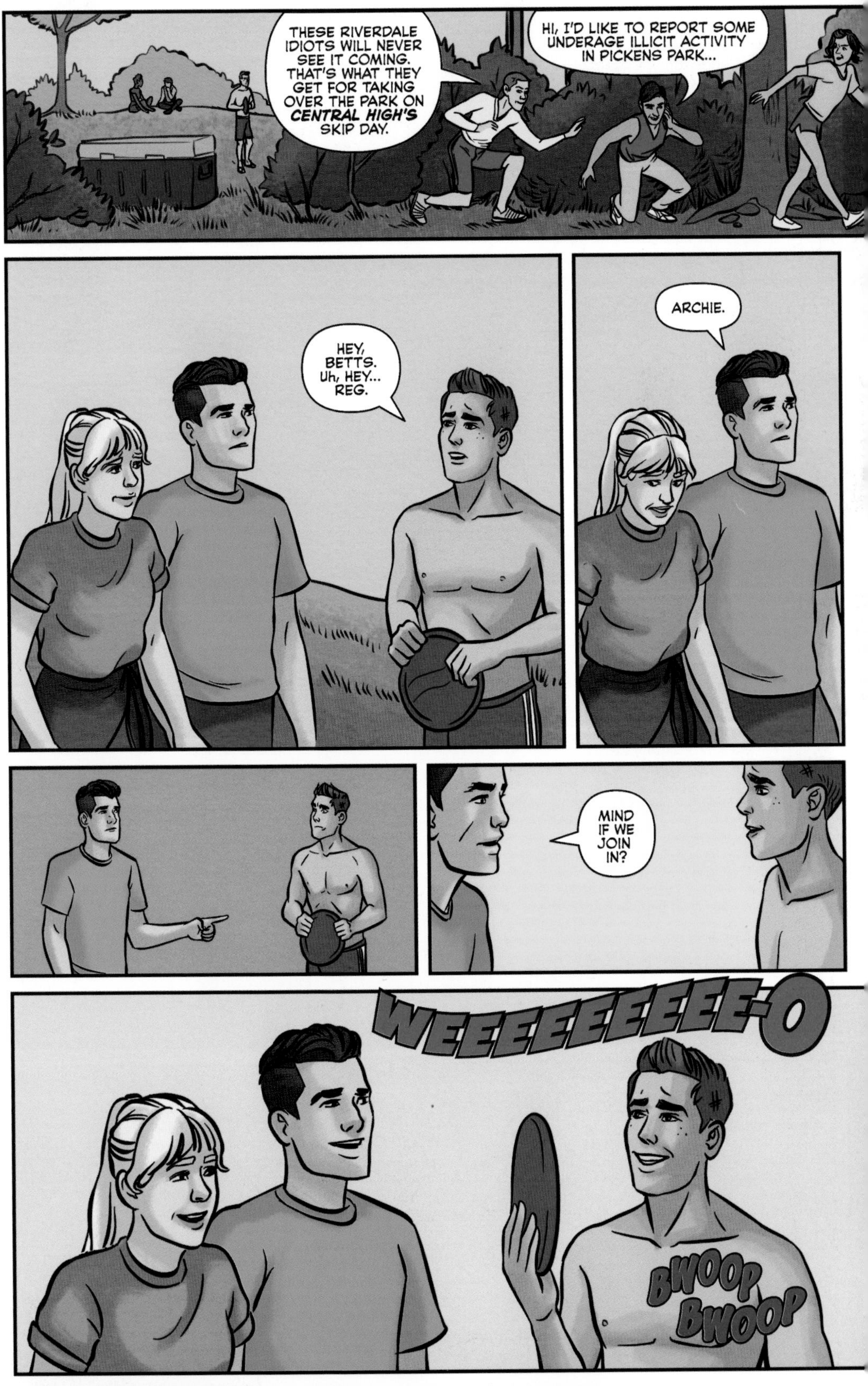
THESE RIVERDALE IDIOTS WILL NEVER SEE IT COMING. THAT'S WHAT THEY GET FOR TAKING OVER THE PARK ON **CENTRAL HIGH'S** SKIP DAY.
HI, I'D LIKE TO REPORT SOME UNDERAGE ILLICIT ACTIVITY IN PICKENS PARK...
HEY, BETTS. Uh, HEY... REG.
ARCHIE.
MIND IF WE JOIN IN?
WEEEEEEEEE-O
BWOOP BWOOP

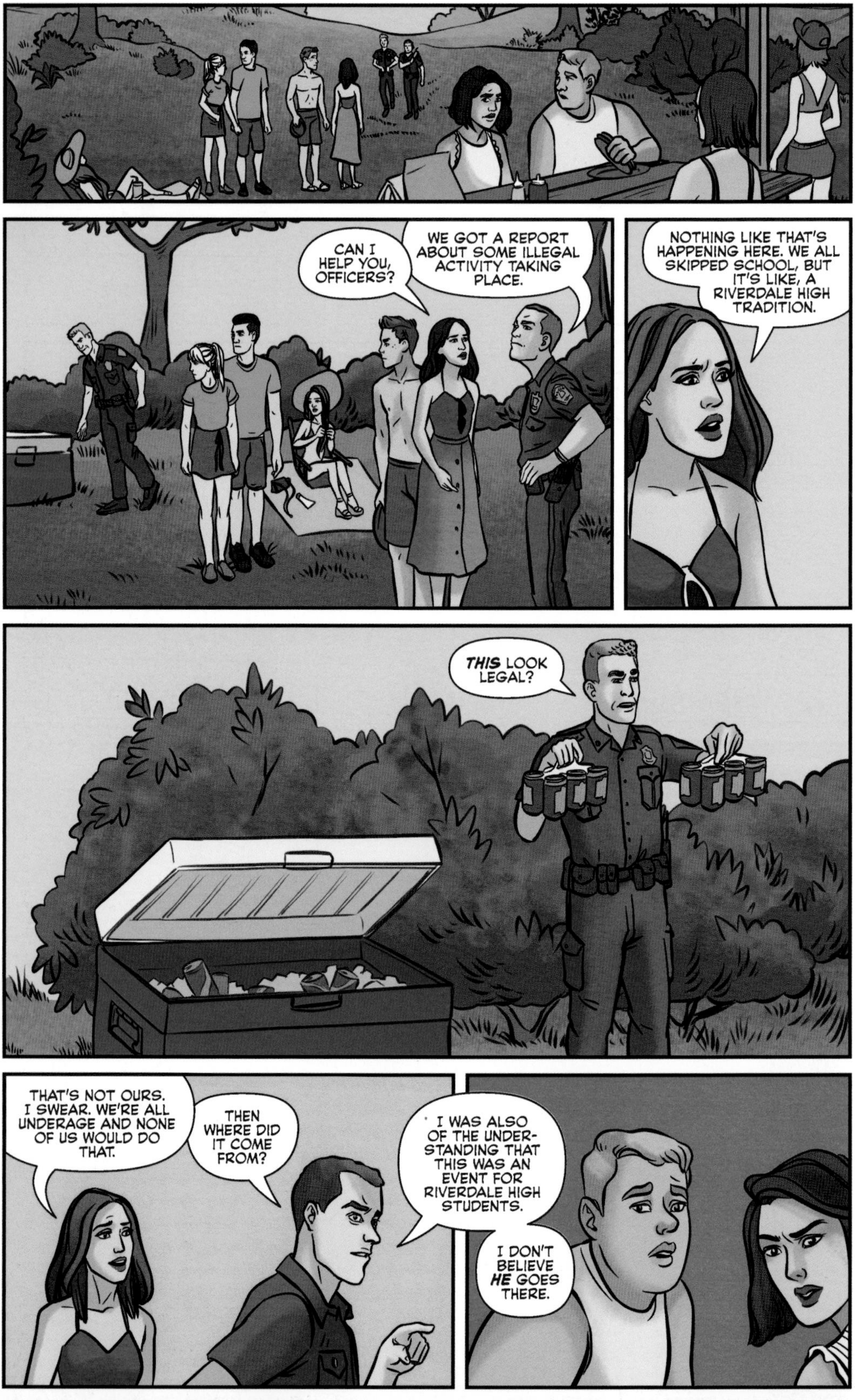
CAN I HELP YOU, OFFICERS?
WE GOT A REPORT ABOUT SOME ILLEGAL ACTIVITY TAKING PLACE.
NOTHING LIKE THAT'S HAPPENING HERE. WE ALL SKIPPED SCHOOL, BUT IT'S LIKE, A RIVERDALE HIGH TRADITION.
THIS LOOK LEGAL?
THAT'S NOT OURS. I SWEAR. WE'RE ALL UNDERAGE AND NONE OF US WOULD DO THAT.
THEN WHERE DID IT COME FROM?
I WAS ALSO OF THE UNDER-STANDING THAT THIS WAS AN EVENT FOR RIVERDALE HIGH STUDENTS.
I DON'T BELIEVE *HE* GOES THERE.

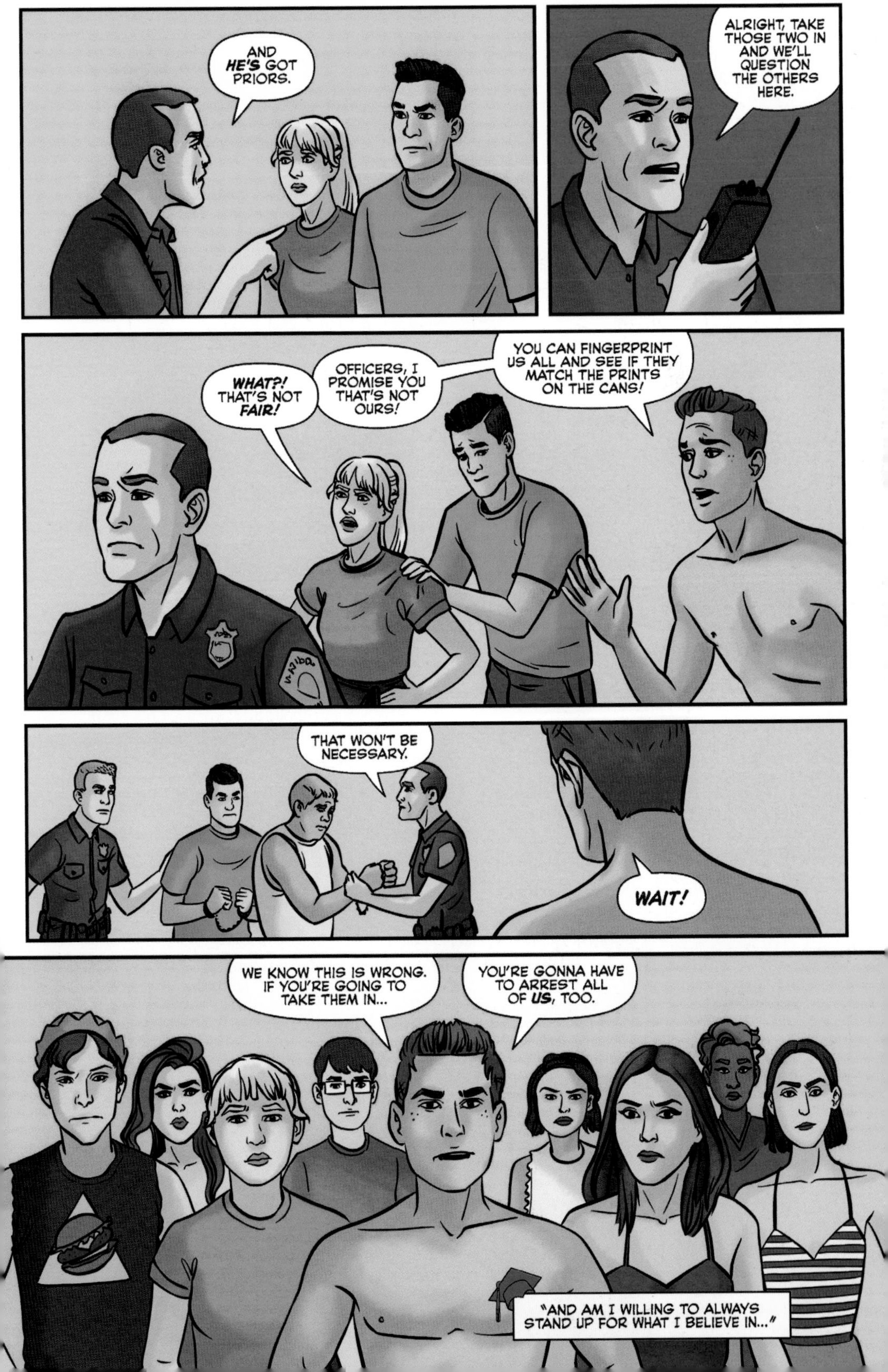
AND HE'S GOT PRIORS.
ALRIGHT, TAKE THOSE TWO IN AND WE'LL QUESTION THE OTHERS HERE.
WHAT?! THAT'S NOT FAIR!
OFFICERS, I PROMISE YOU THAT'S NOT OURS!
YOU CAN FINGERPRINT US ALL AND SEE IF THEY MATCH THE PRINTS ON THE CANS!
THAT WON'T BE NECESSARY.
WAIT!
WE KNOW THIS IS WRONG. IF YOU'RE GOING TO TAKE THEM IN...
YOU'RE GONNA HAVE TO ARREST ALL OF US, TOO.
"AND AM I WILLING TO ALWAYS STAND UP FOR WHAT I BELIEVE IN..."

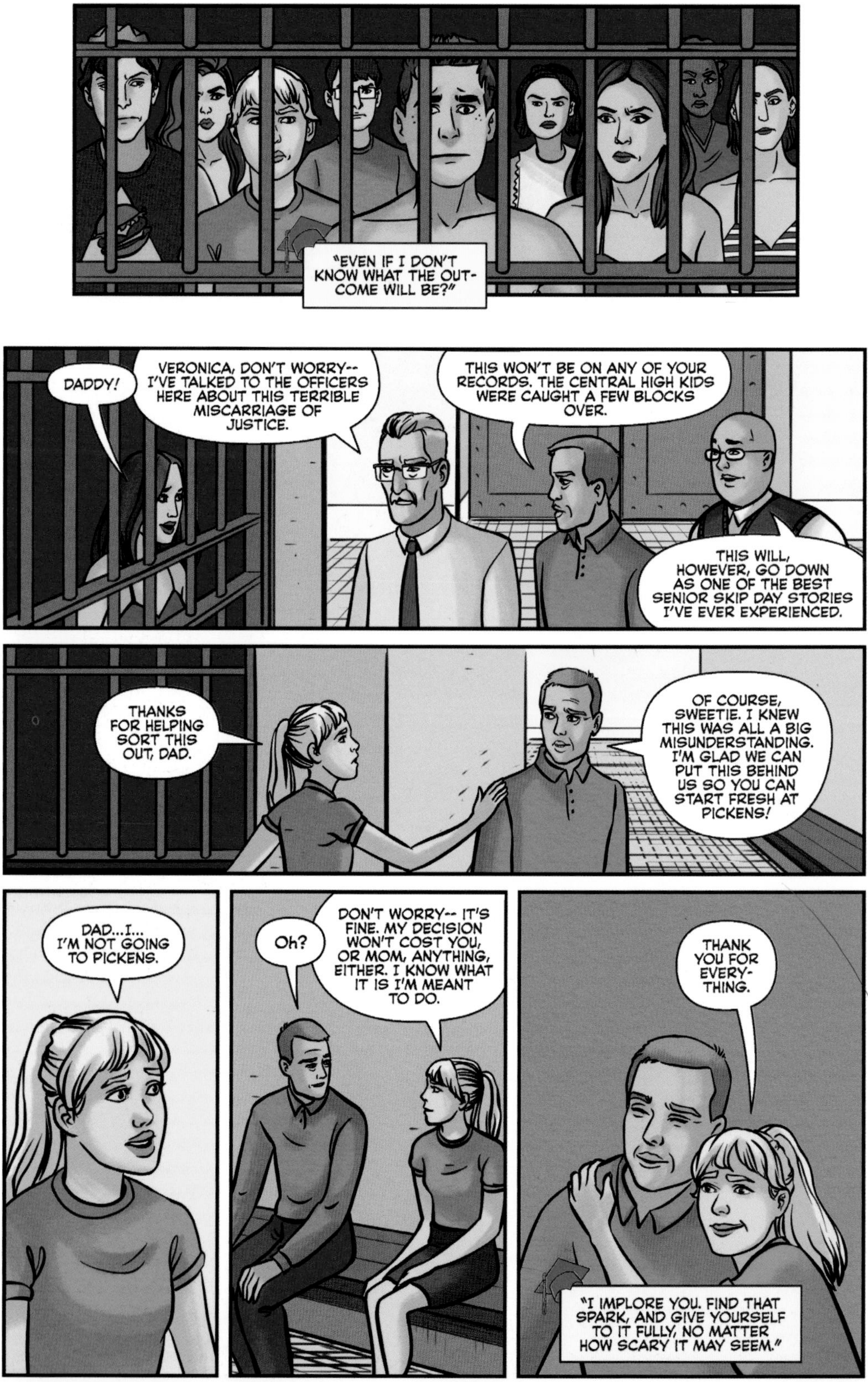
"EVEN IF I DON'T KNOW WHAT THE OUT-COME WILL BE?"
DADDY!
VERONICA, DON'T WORRY-- I'VE TALKED TO THE OFFICERS HERE ABOUT THIS TERRIBLE MISCARRIAGE OF JUSTICE.
THIS WON'T BE ON ANY OF YOUR RECORDS. THE CENTRAL HIGH KIDS WERE CAUGHT A FEW BLOCKS OVER.
THIS WILL, HOWEVER, GO DOWN AS ONE OF THE BEST SENIOR SKIP DAY STORIES I'VE EVER EXPERIENCED.
THANKS FOR HELPING SORT THIS OUT, DAD.
OF COURSE, SWEETIE. I KNEW THIS WAS ALL A BIG MISUNDERSTANDING. I'M GLAD WE CAN PUT THIS BEHIND US SO YOU CAN START FRESH AT PICKENS!
DAD...I... I'M NOT GOING TO PICKENS.
Oh?
DON'T WORRY-- IT'S FINE. MY DECISION WON'T COST YOU, OR MOM, ANYTHING, EITHER. I KNOW WHAT IT IS I'M MEANT TO DO.
THANK YOU FOR EVERY-THING.
"I IMPLORE YOU. FIND THAT SPARK, AND GIVE YOURSELF TO IT FULLY, NO MATTER HOW SCARY IT MAY SEEM."

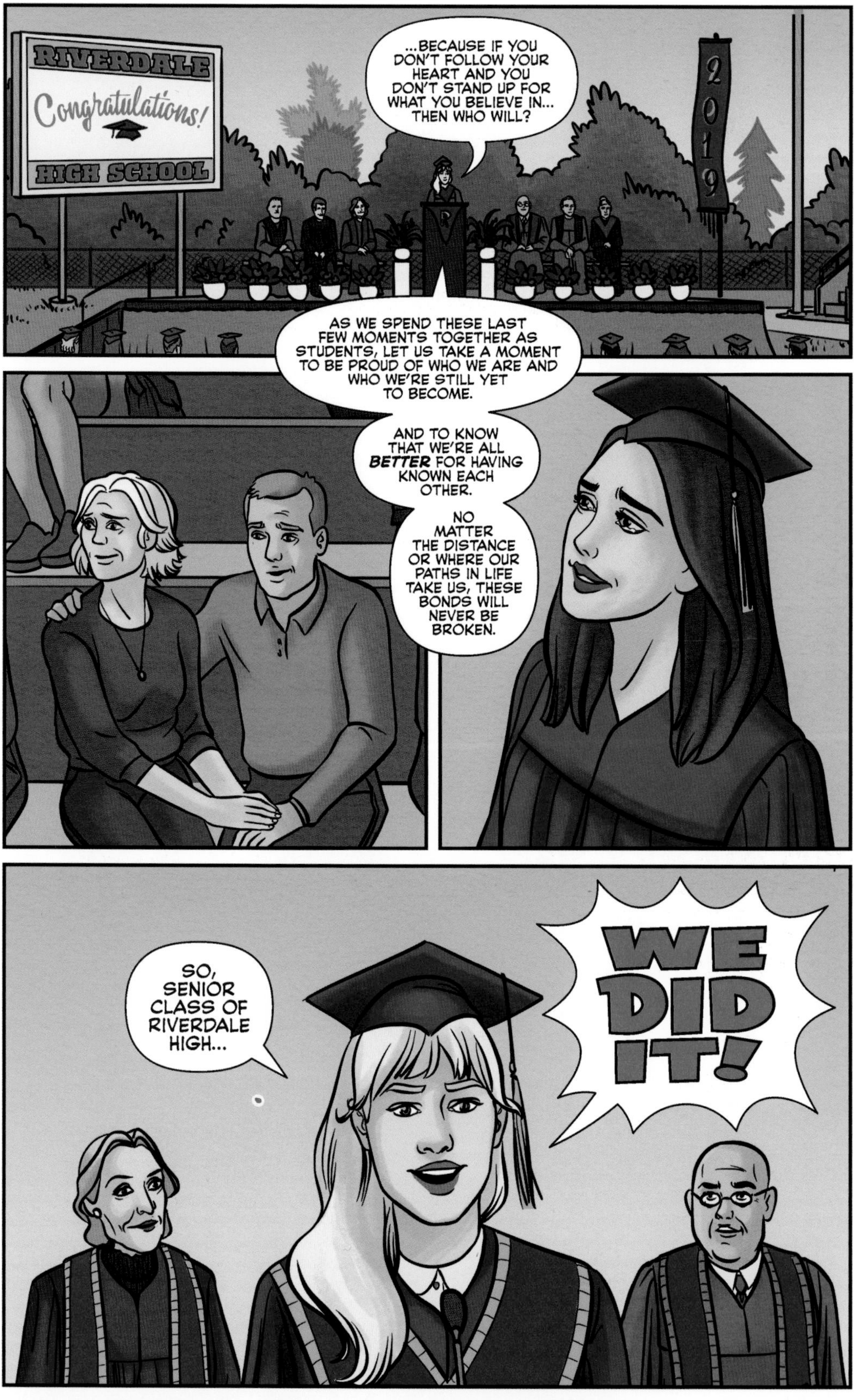
RIVERDALE
Congratulations!
HIGH SCHOOL
2019
...BECAUSE IF YOU DON'T FOLLOW YOUR HEART AND YOU DON'T STAND UP FOR WHAT YOU BELIEVE IN... THEN WHO WILL?
AS WE SPEND THESE LAST FEW MOMENTS TOGETHER AS STUDENTS, LET US TAKE A MOMENT TO BE PROUD OF WHO WE ARE AND WHO WE'RE STILL YET TO BECOME.
AND TO KNOW THAT WE'RE ALL **BETTER** FOR HAVING KNOWN EACH OTHER.
NO MATTER THE DISTANCE OR WHERE OUR PATHS IN LIFE TAKE US, THESE BONDS WILL NEVER BE BROKEN.
SO, SENIOR CLASS OF RIVERDALE HIGH...
WE DID IT!

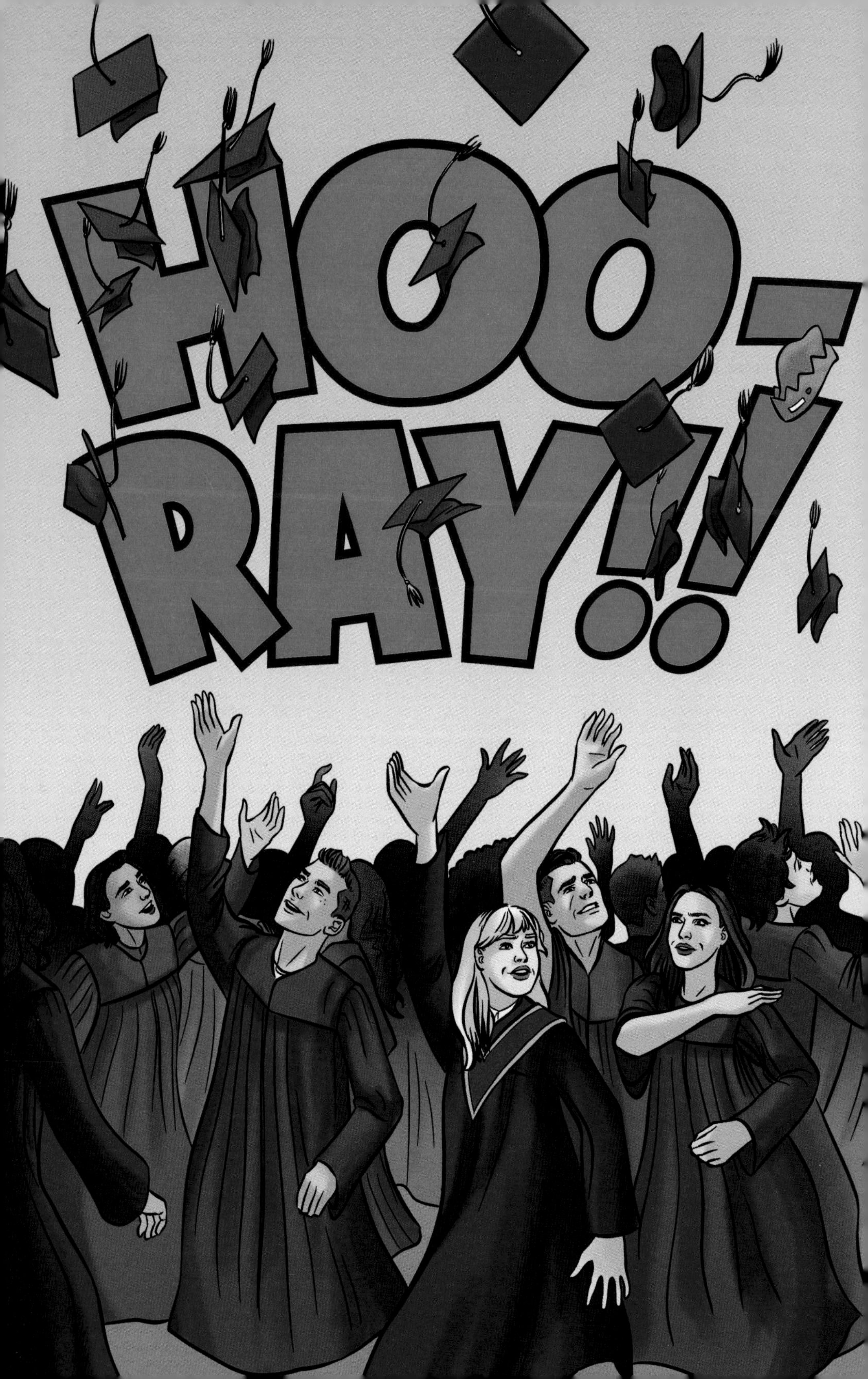
HOO-
RAY!!

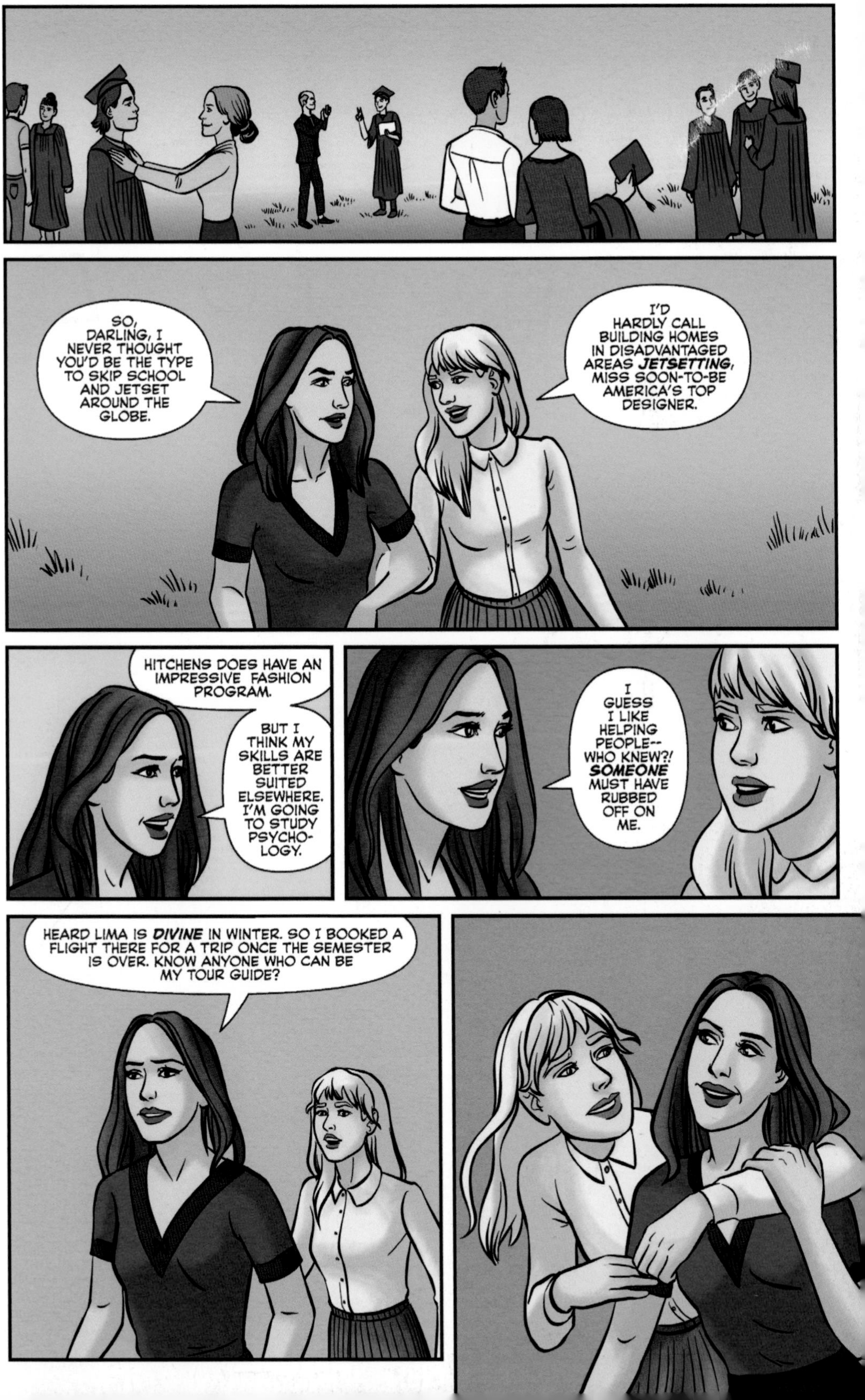
SO, DARLING, I NEVER THOUGHT YOU'D BE THE TYPE TO SKIP SCHOOL AND JETSET AROUND THE GLOBE.
I'D HARDLY CALL BUILDING HOMES IN DISADVANTAGED AREAS *JETSETTING*, MISS SOON-TO-BE AMERICA'S TOP DESIGNER.
HITCHENS DOES HAVE AN IMPRESSIVE FASHION PROGRAM.
BUT I THINK MY SKILLS ARE BETTER SUITED ELSEWHERE. I'M GOING TO STUDY PSYCHO-LOGY.
I GUESS I LIKE HELPING PEOPLE-- WHO KNEW?! *SOMEONE* MUST HAVE RUBBED OFF ON ME.
HEARD LIMA IS *DIVINE* IN WINTER. SO I BOOKED A FLIGHT THERE FOR A TRIP ONCE THE SEMESTER IS OVER. KNOW ANYONE WHO CAN BE MY TOUR GUIDE?

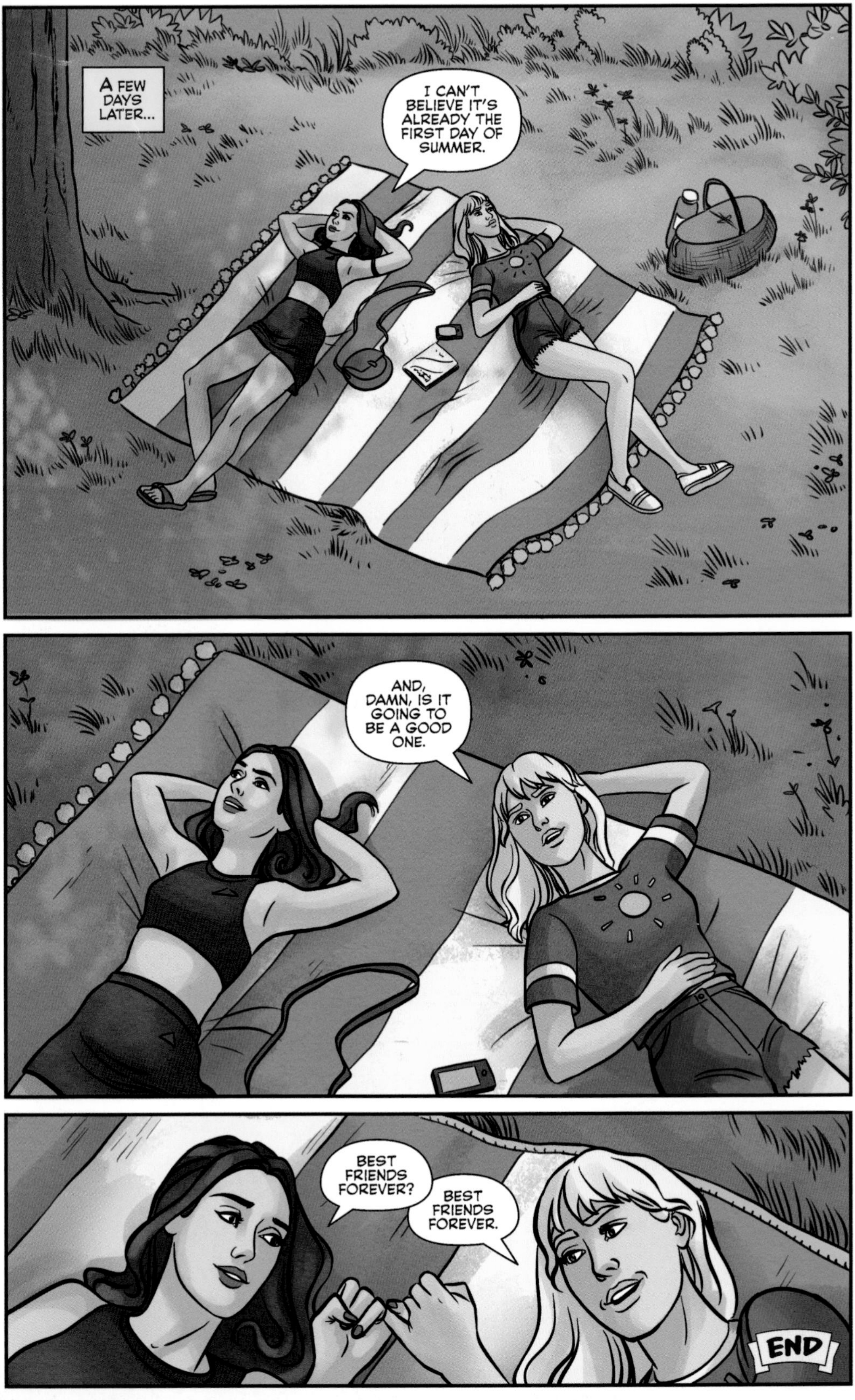
A FEW DAYS LATER...
I CAN'T BELIEVE IT'S ALREADY THE FIRST DAY OF SUMMER.
AND, DAMN, IS IT GOING TO BE A GOOD ONE.
BEST FRIENDS FOREVER?
BEST FRIENDS FOREVER.
END

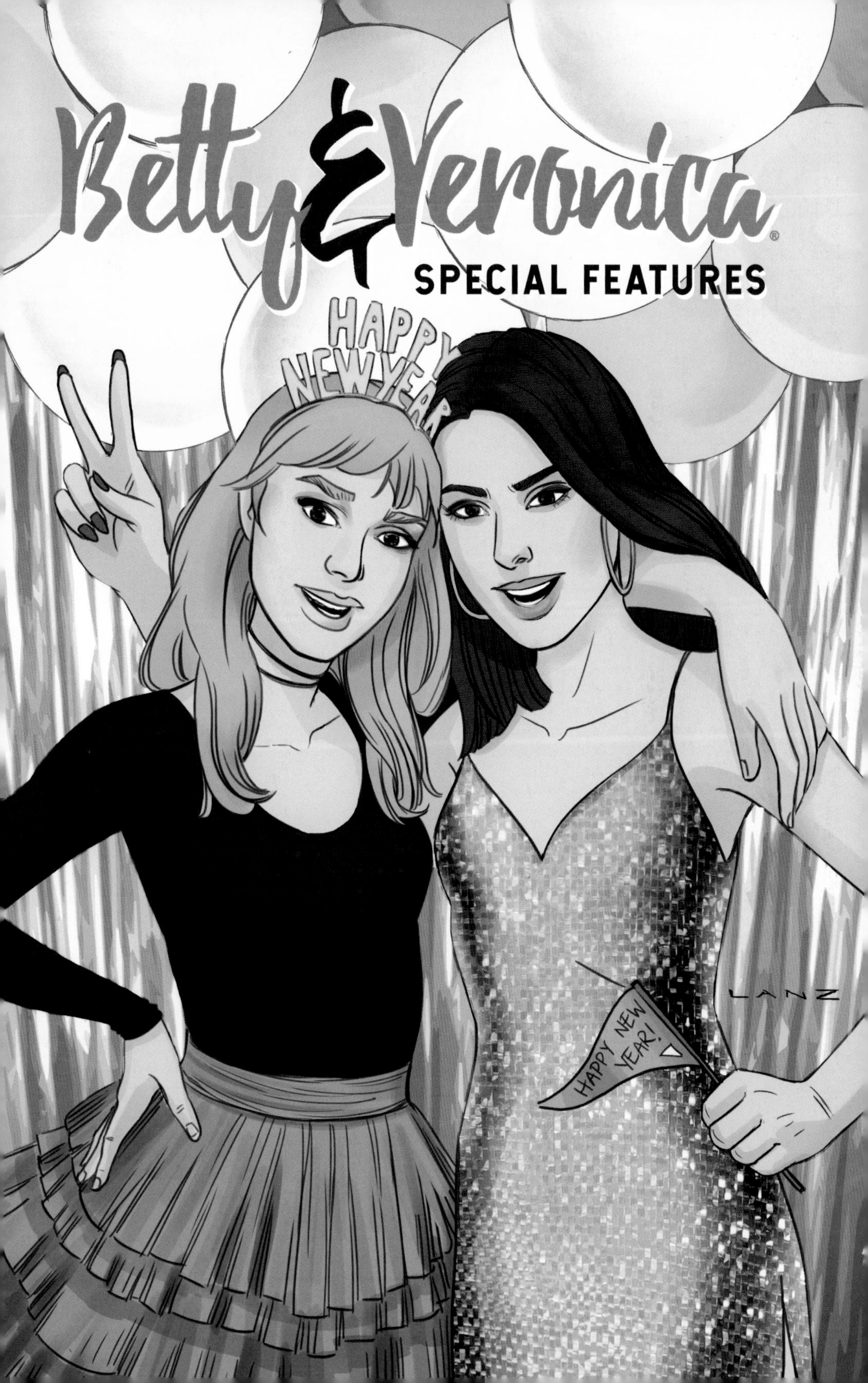
Betty & Veronica®
SPECIAL FEATURES
HAPPY NEW YEAR
HAPPY NEW YEAR!
LANZ

Betty & Veronica®

VARIANT COVER GALLERY

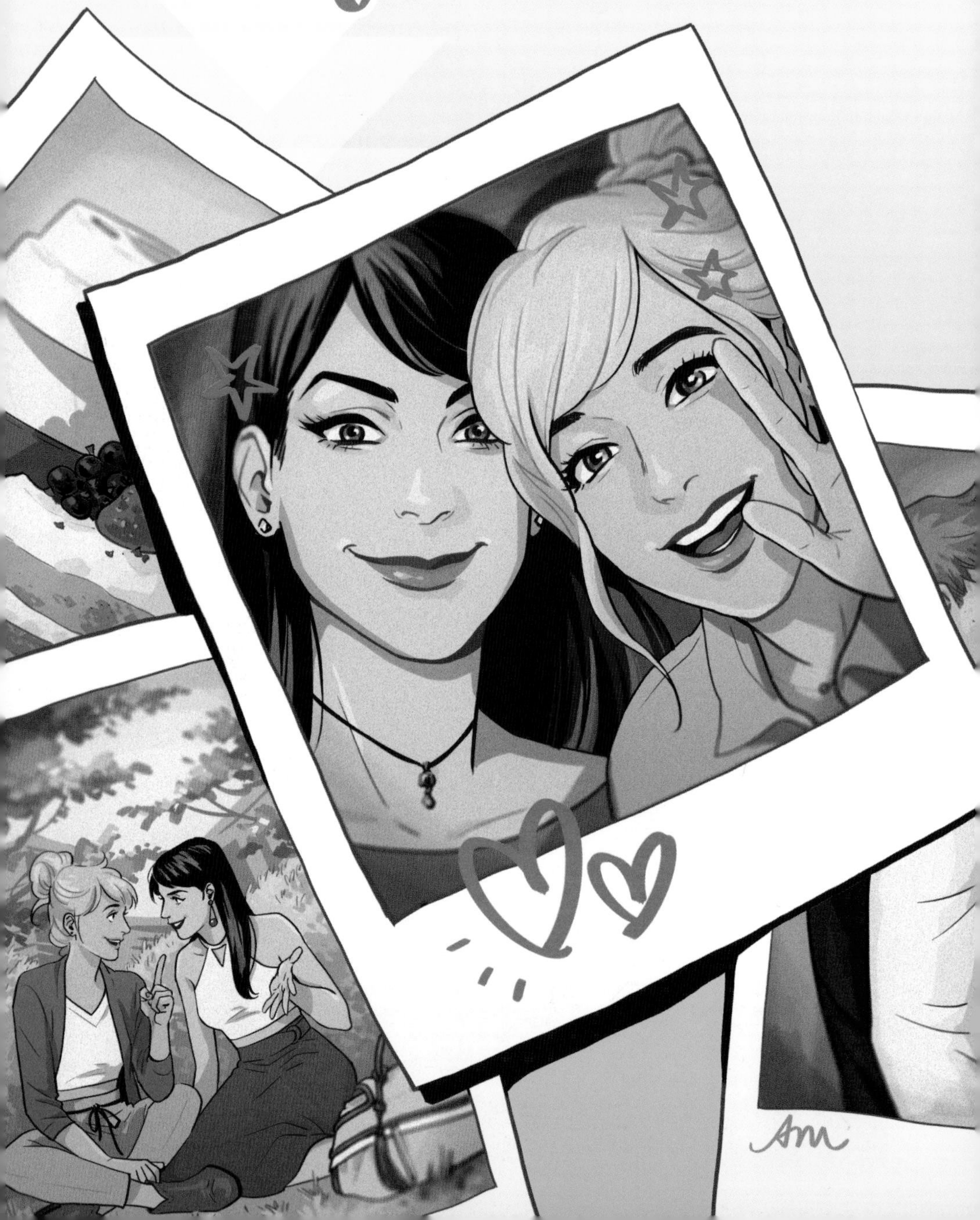

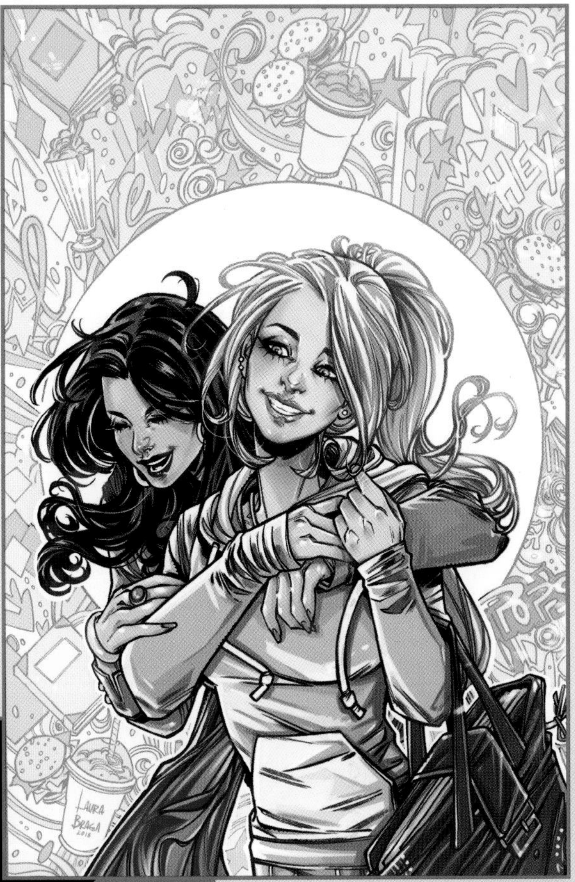

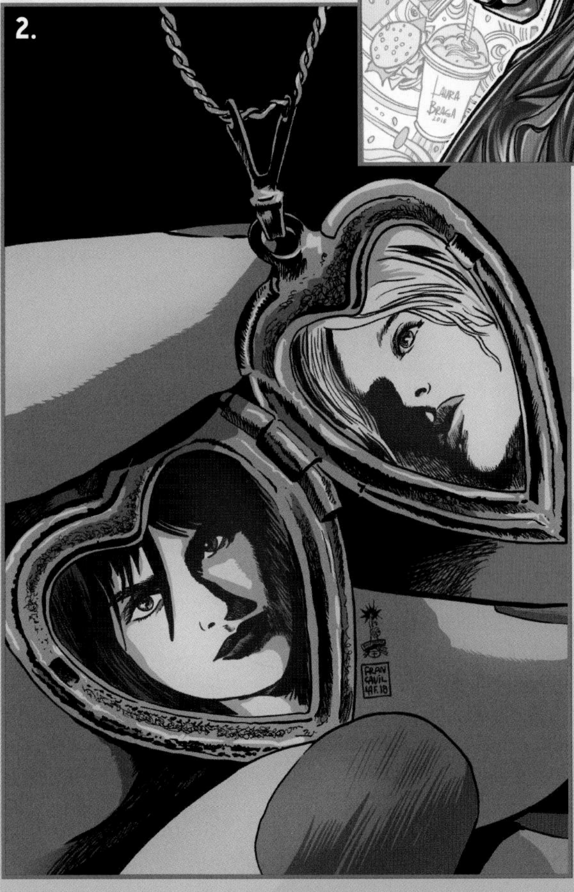

2.

ISSUE 01

1. LAURA BRAGA

2. FRANCESCO FRANCAVILLA

ISSUE 01

3. AUDREY MOK

4. MARGUERITE SAUVAGE

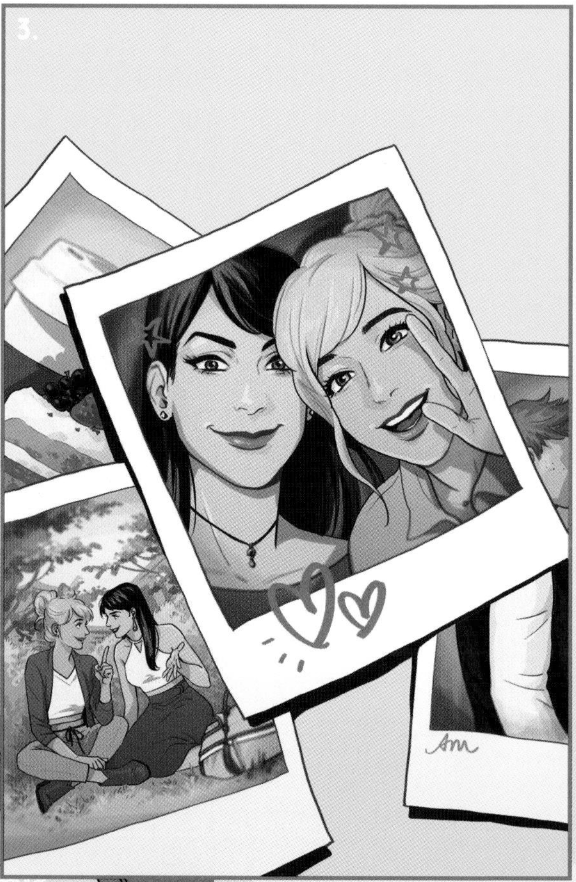
3.
Am

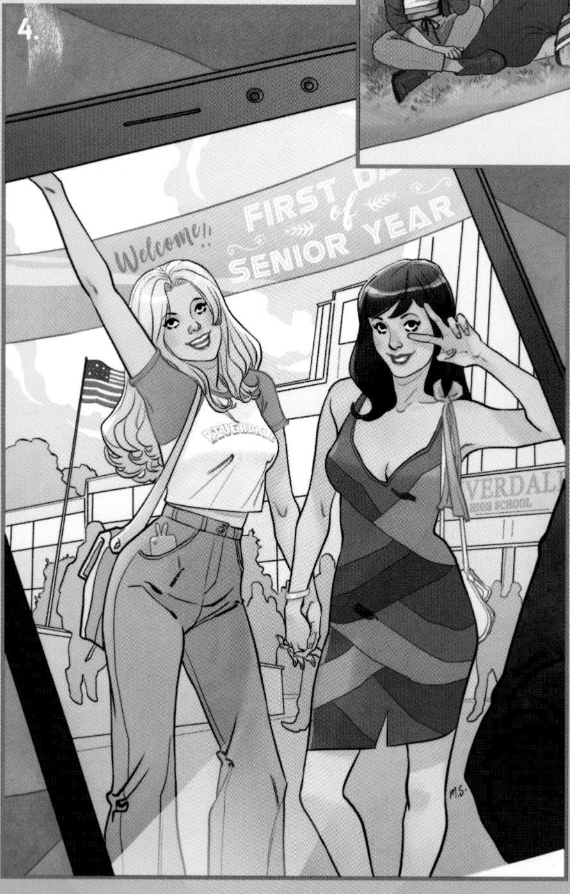
4.
FIRST DAY of SENIOR YEAR
Welcome!!
HIGH SCHOOL
M.S.

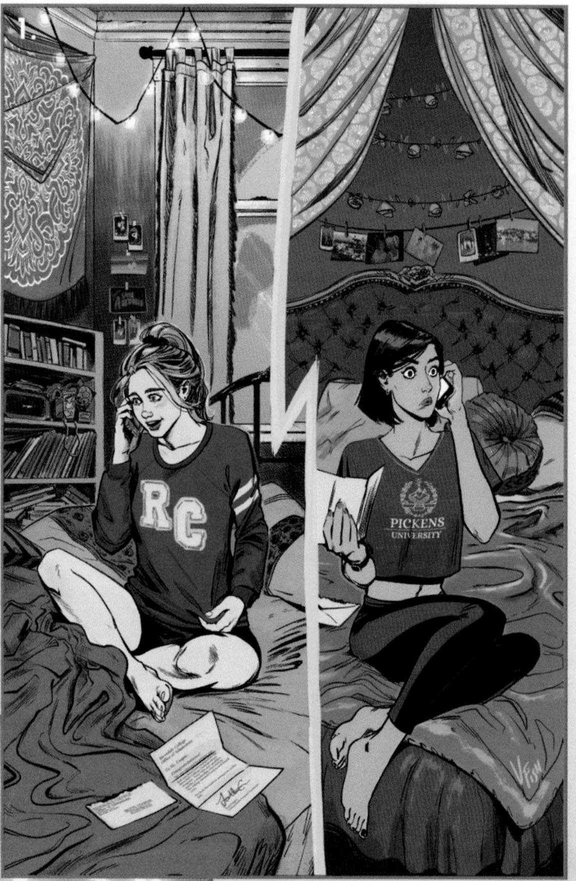
1.
RC
PICKENS
UNIVERSITY

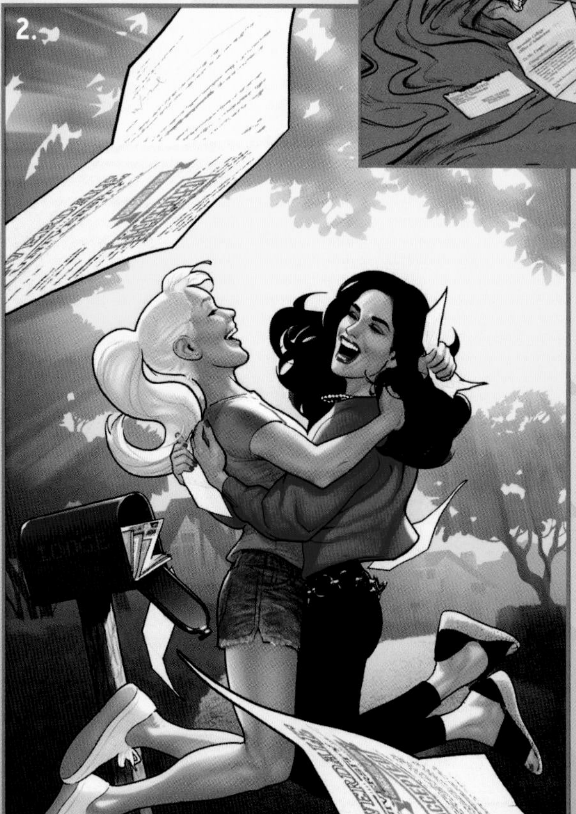
2.

ISSUE 02

1. VERONICA FISH

2. RYAN SOOK

ISSUE 03

1. **JEN BARTEL**

2. **REBEKAH ISAACS** WITH **KELLY FITZPATRICK**

1\.

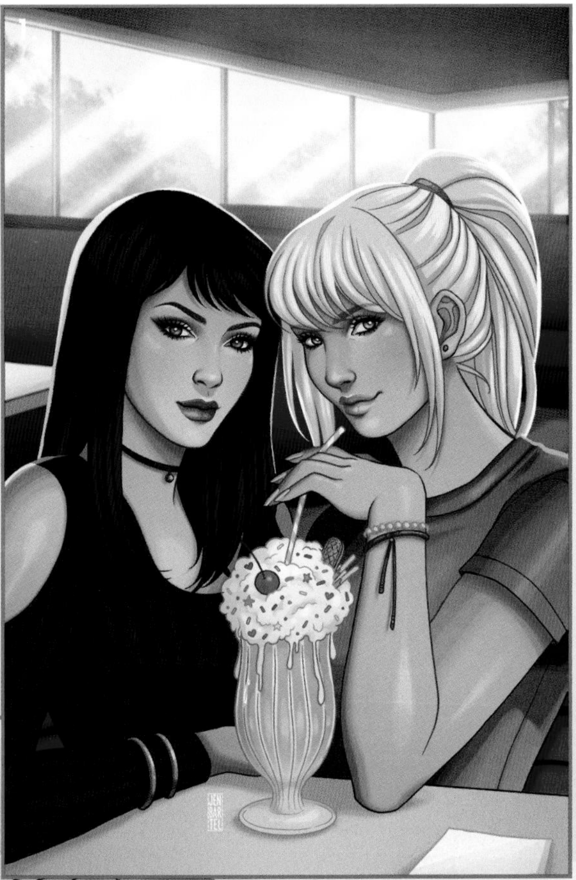
JEN
BAR
TEL

2\.

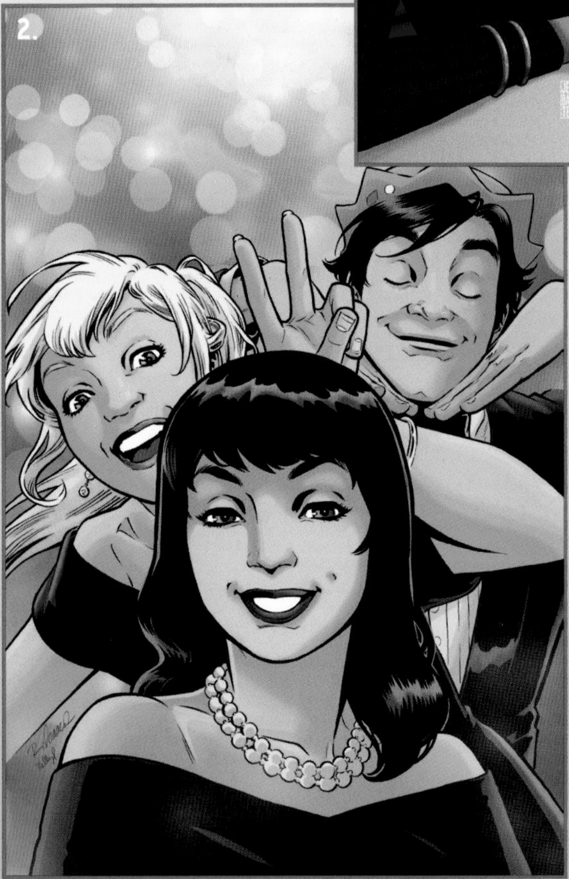

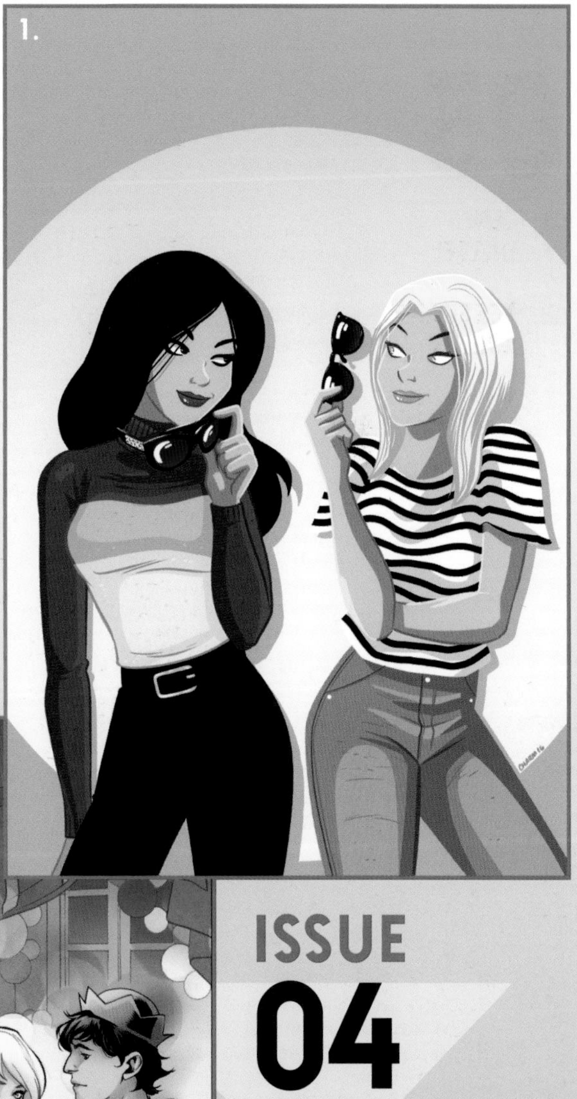
1.

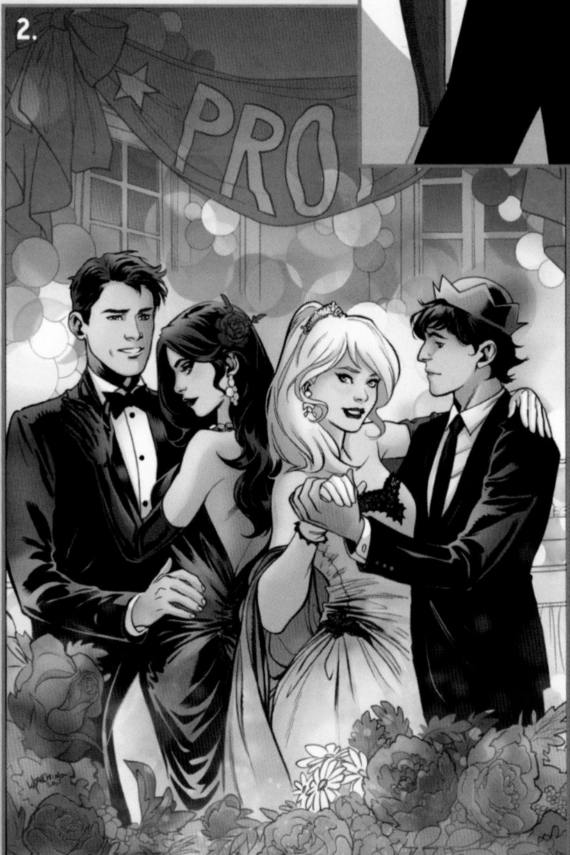
2.
PRO

ISSUE 04

1. DEREK CHARM

2. EMANUELA LUPACCHINO WITH KELLY FITZPATRICK.

ISSUE
05

1. SANYA ANWAR
2. LISSY MARLIN

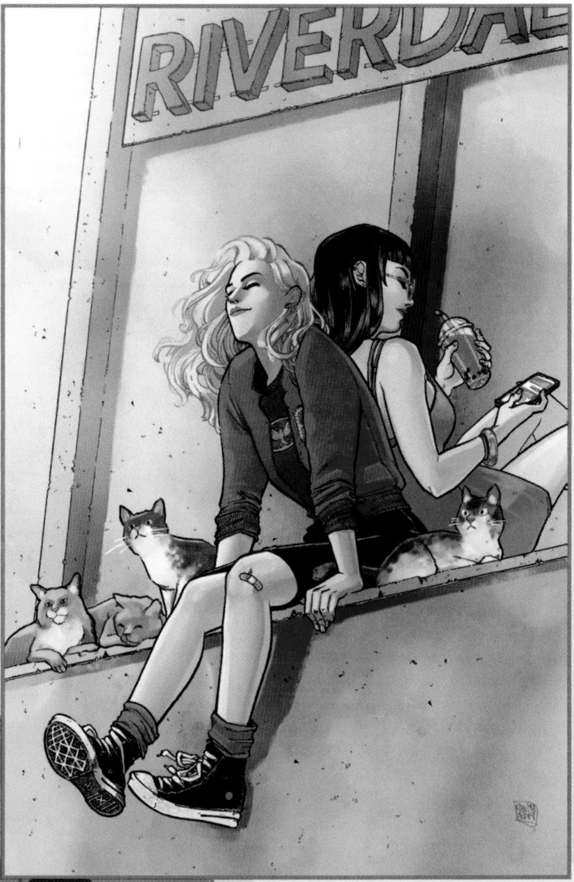
RIVERDAL

2.

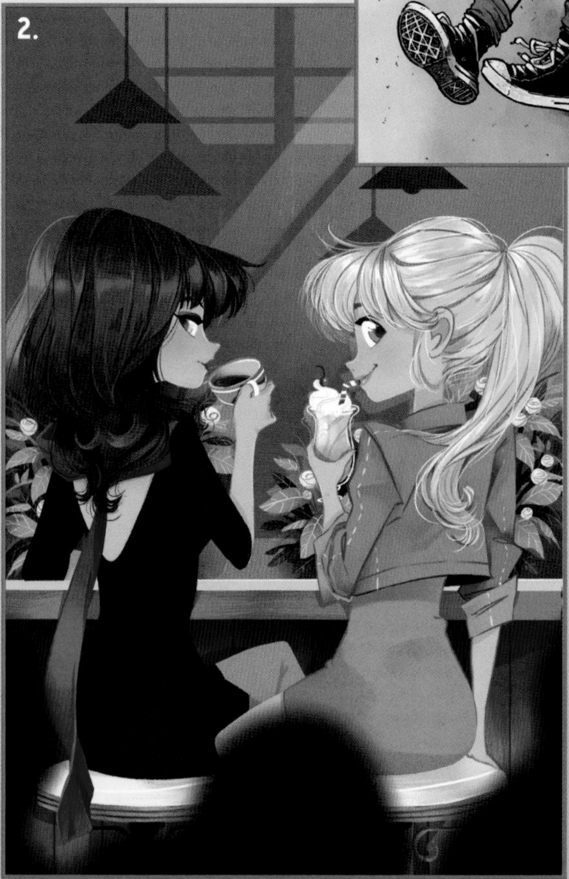

CHARACTER SKETCHES

ORIGINAL CHARACTER SKETCHES BY **SANDRA LANZ**

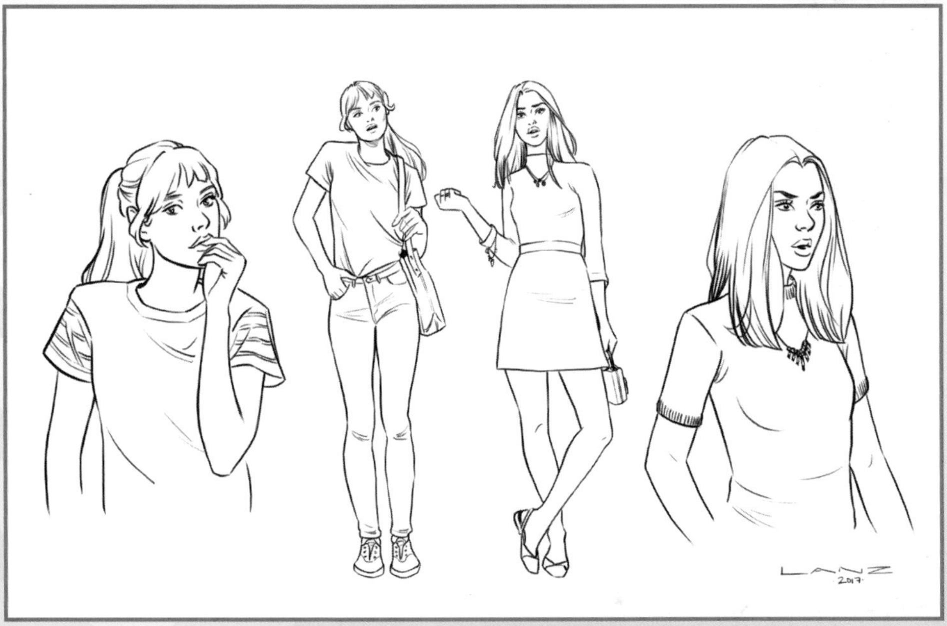
LANZ
2017

BETTY & VERONICA **CHARACTER SKETCHES**

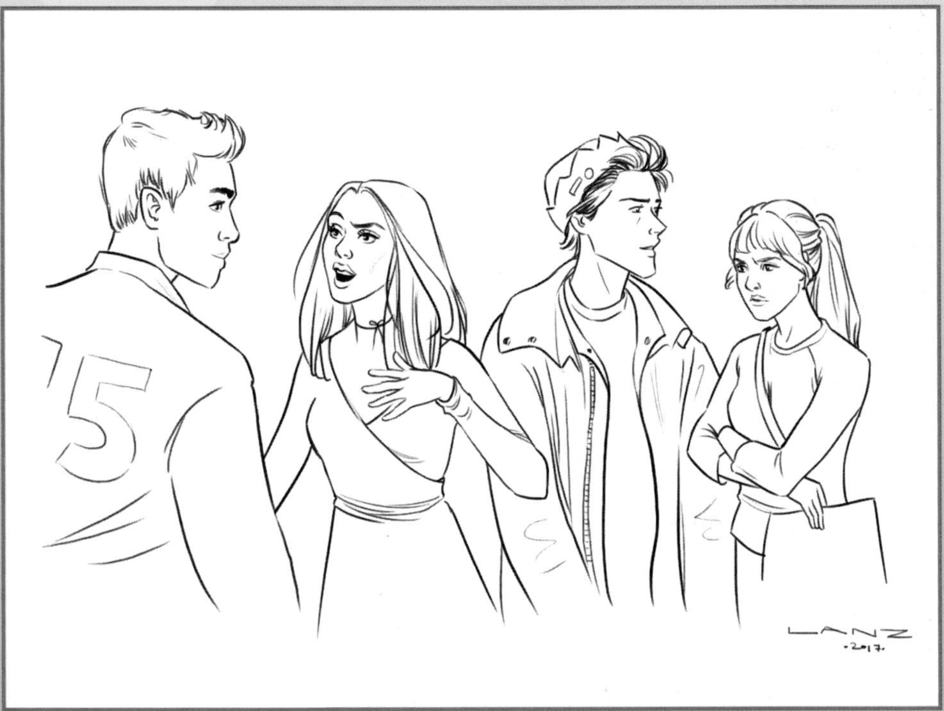
LANZ
2017

BETTY, VERONICA, ARCHIE & JUGHEAD **CHARACTER SKETCHES**

COVER SKETCHES

COVER SKETCHES AND FINAL ART BY **SANDRA LANZ**

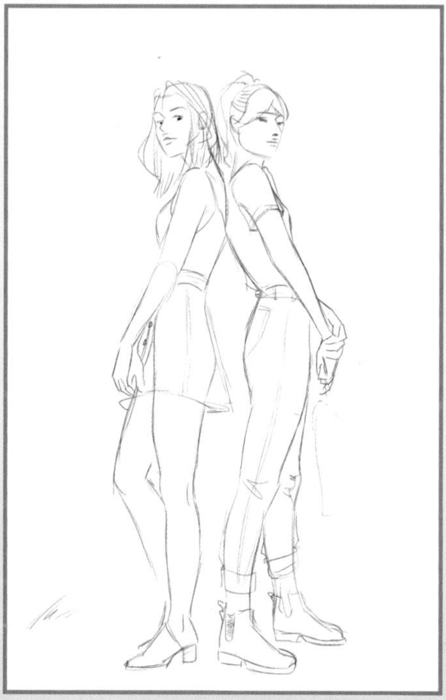

BETTY & VERONICA 01 COVER: **SKETCH**

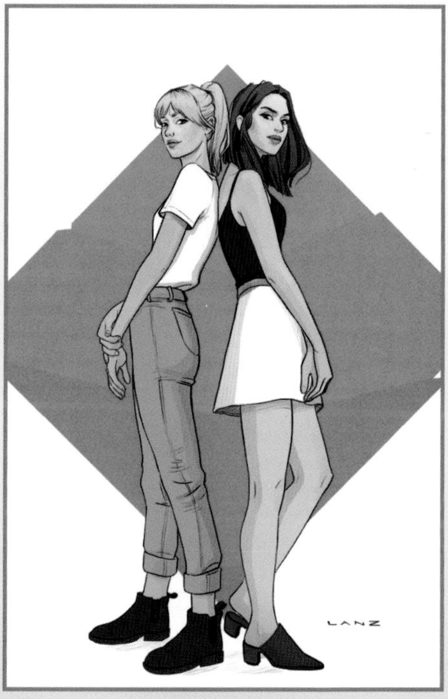
LANZ

BETTY & VERONICA 01 COVER: **FINAL ART**

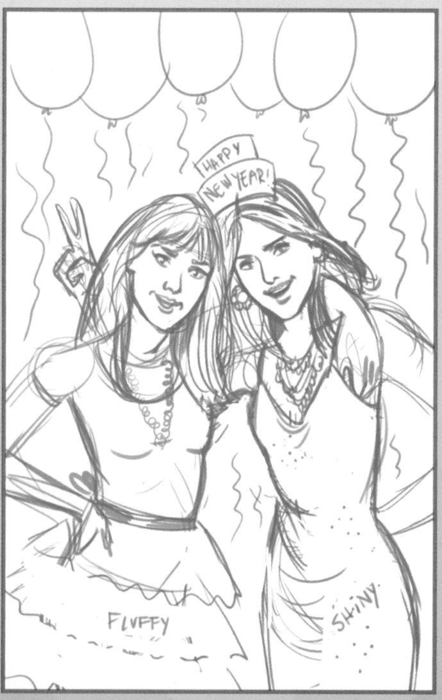
HAPPY NEW YEAR!
FLUFFY
SHINY

BETTY & VERONICA 03 COVER: **SKETCH**

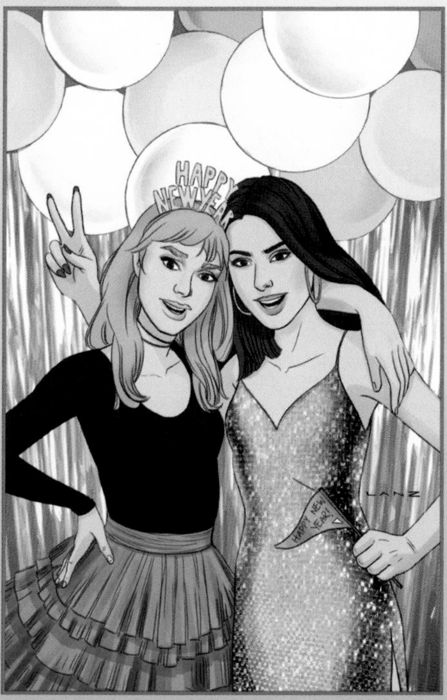
HAPPY NEW YEAR
LANZ
HAPPY NEW YEAR!

BETTY & VERONICA 03 COVER: **FINAL ART**

BONUS COMIC

Sabrina Spellman, a teen witch who's struggling with balancing the double life of high school and her burgeoning powers is trying to make the best of being the new girl in town which so far includes two intriguing love interests, an instant rivalry, a couple of misfits that could turn into BFFs, and trying to save the high school (and maybe the world) from crazy supernatural events. NBD!

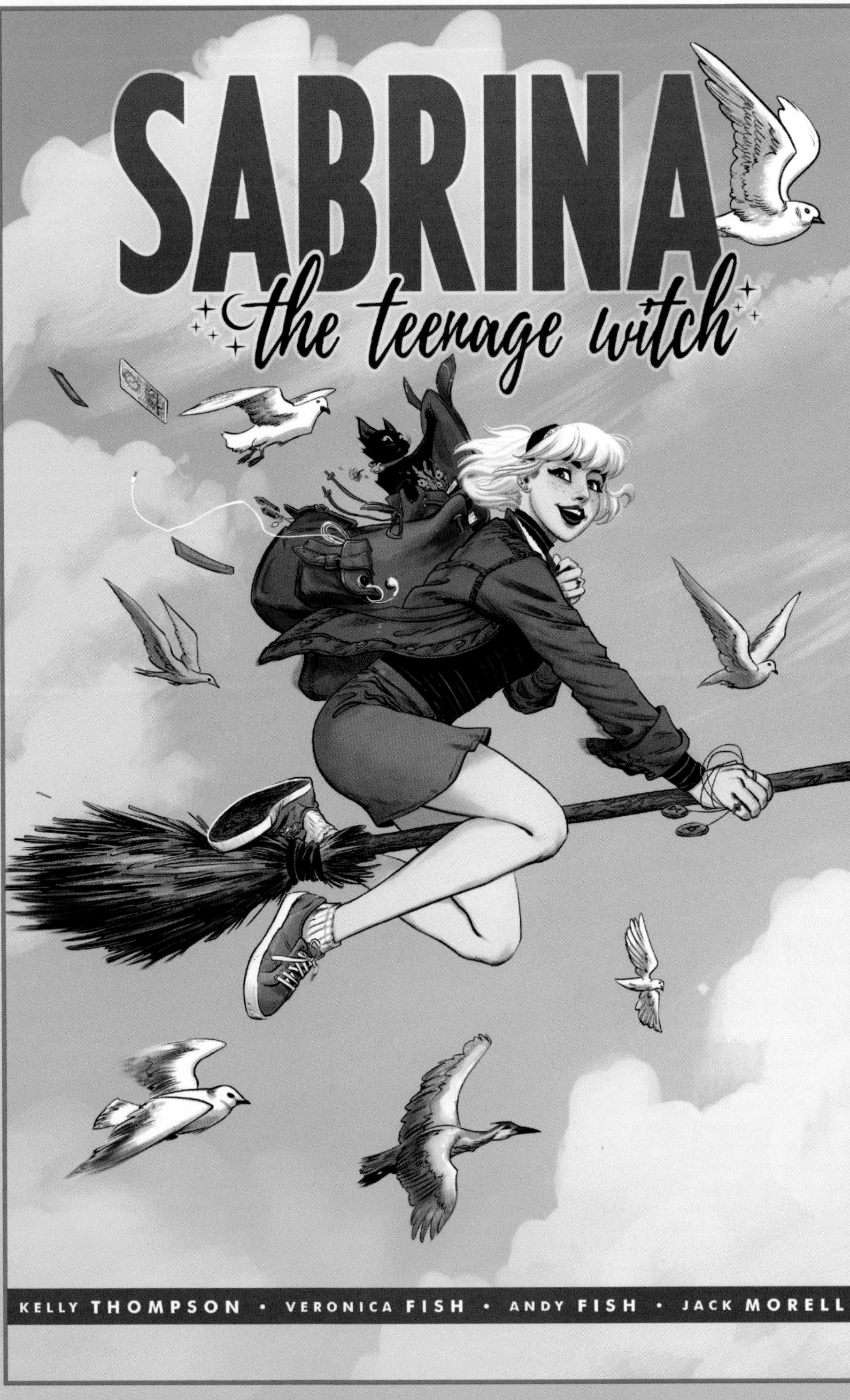
SABRINA
the teenage witch
KELLY THOMPSON • VERONICA FISH • ANDY FISH • JACK MORELLI

01

STORY BY
KELLY THOMPSON
LETTERING BY
JACK MORELLI

ART BY
VERONICA FISH AND **ANDY FISH**

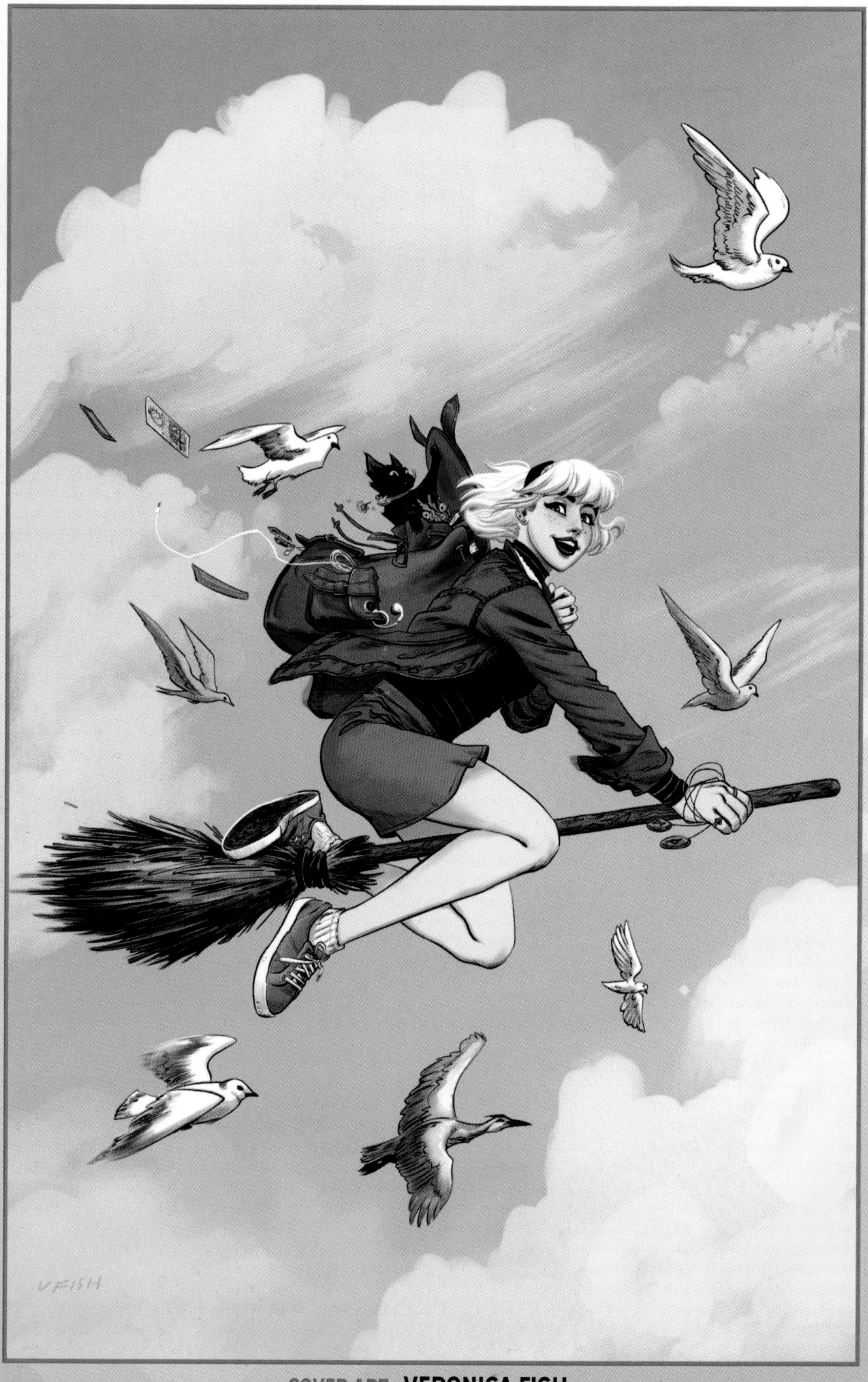
VFISH

COVER ART: **VERONICA FISH**

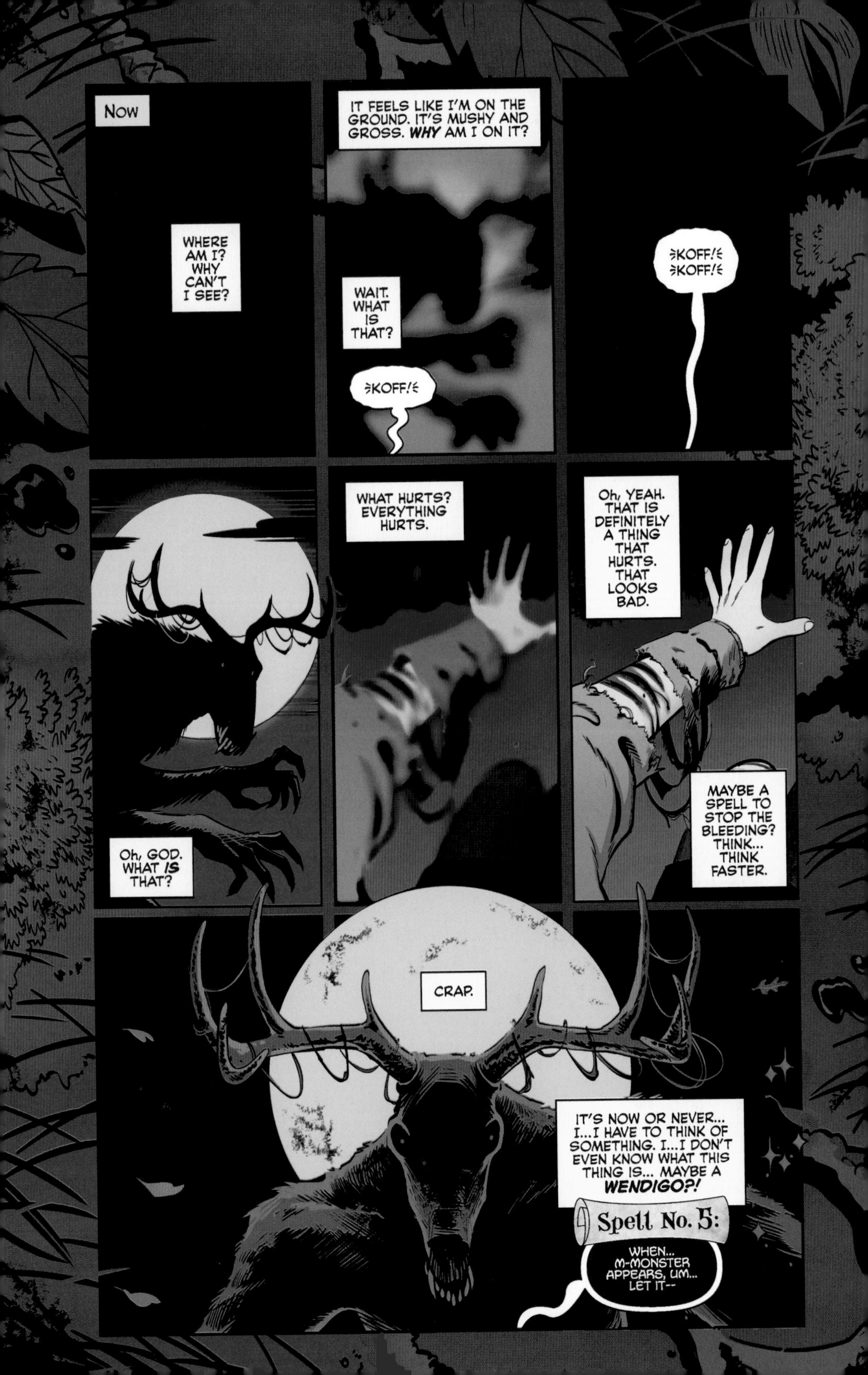
NOW
WHERE AM I? WHY CAN'T I SEE?
IT FEELS LIKE I'M ON THE GROUND. IT'S MUSHY AND GROSS. **WHY** AM I ON IT?
WAIT. WHAT IS THAT?
KOFF!
KOFF! KOFF!
Oh, GOD. WHAT **IS** THAT?
WHAT HURTS? EVERYTHING HURTS.
Oh, YEAH. THAT IS DEFINITELY A THING THAT HURTS. THAT LOOKS BAD.
MAYBE A SPELL TO STOP THE BLEEDING? THINK... THINK FASTER.
CRAP.
IT'S NOW OR NEVER... I...I HAVE TO THINK OF SOMETHING. I...I DON'T EVEN KNOW WHAT THIS THING IS... MAYBE A **WENDIGO?!**
Spell No. 5:
WHEN... M-MONSTER APPEARS, UM... LET IT--

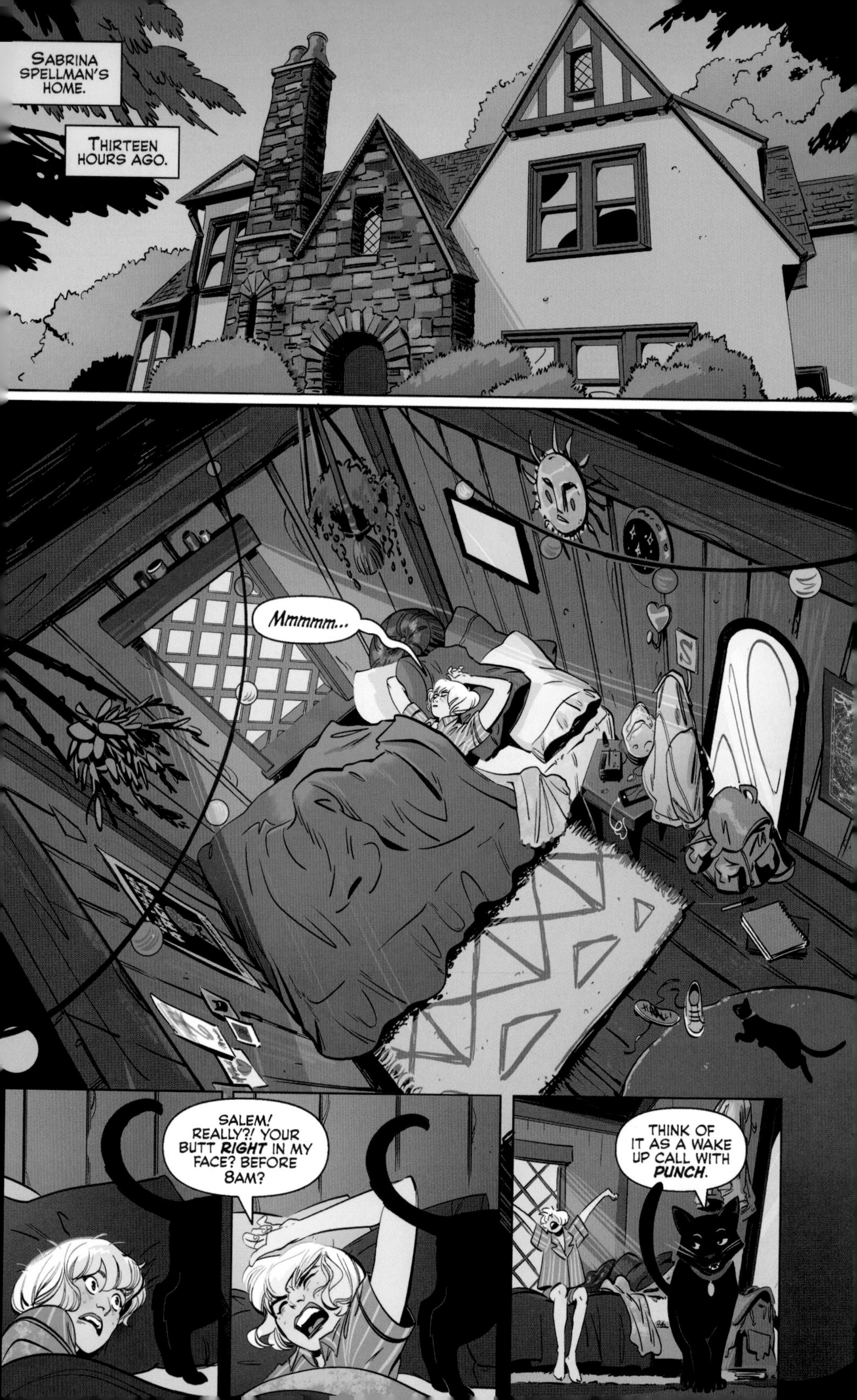
Sabrina Spellman's home.
Thirteen hours ago.
Mmmmm...
Salem! Really?! Your butt right in my face? Before 8AM?
Think of it as a wake up call with punch.

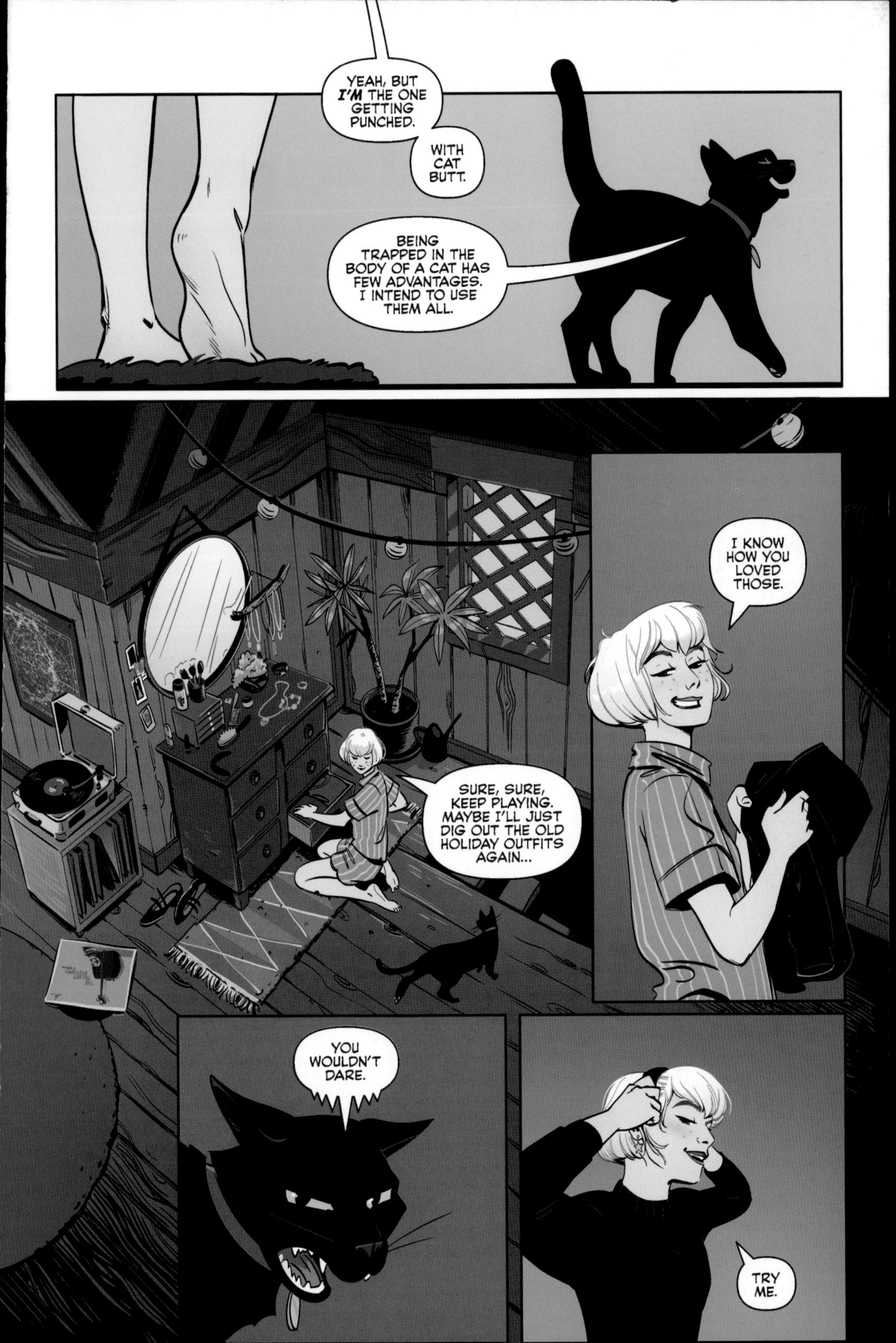
YEAH, BUT I'M THE ONE GETTING PUNCHED.
WITH CAT BUTT.
BEING TRAPPED IN THE BODY OF A CAT HAS FEW ADVANTAGES. I INTEND TO USE THEM ALL.
SURE, SURE, KEEP PLAYING. MAYBE I'LL JUST DIG OUT THE OLD HOLIDAY OUTFITS AGAIN...
I KNOW HOW YOU LOVED THOSE.
YOU WOULDN'T DARE.
TRY ME.

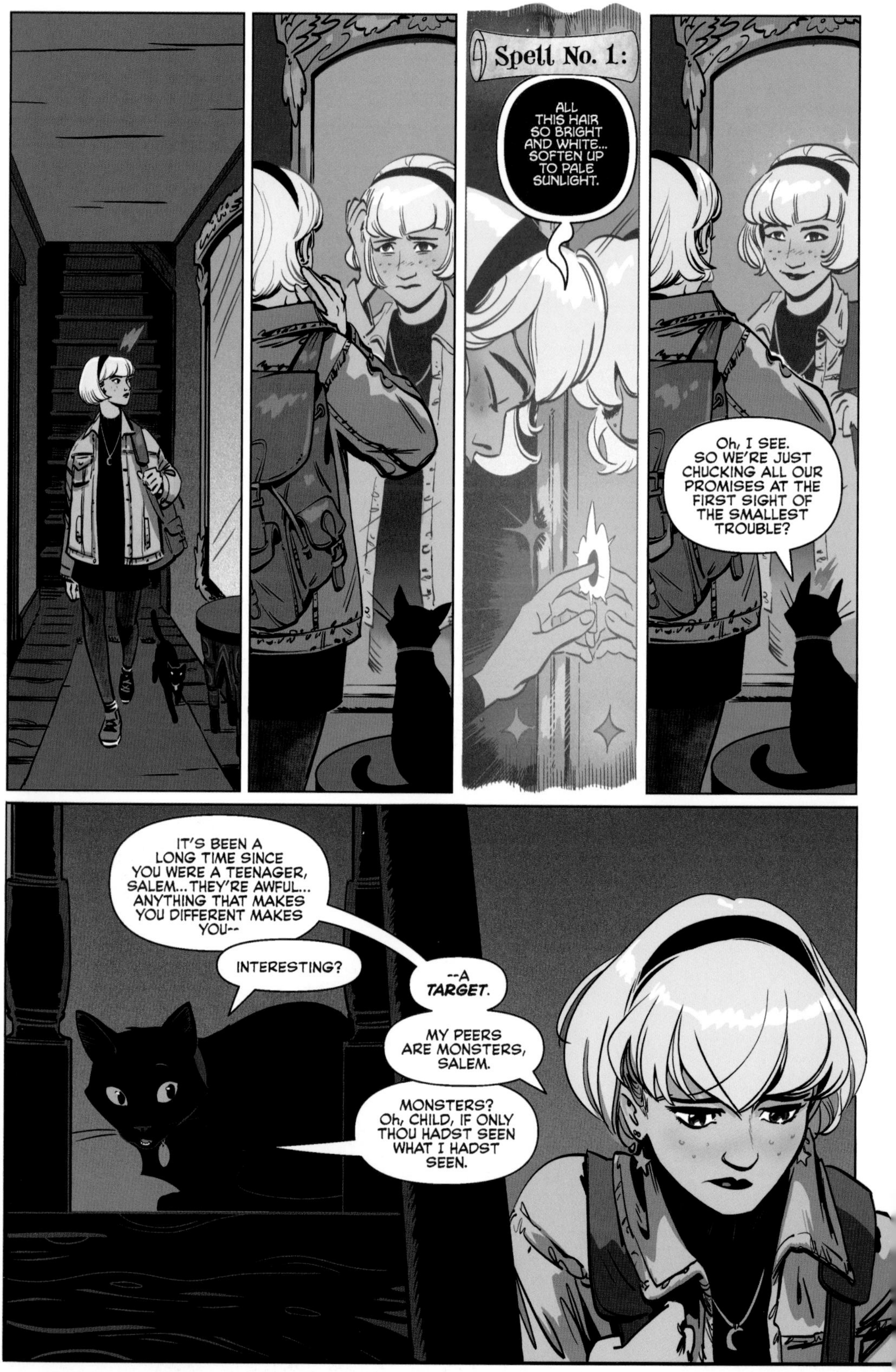
Spell No. 1:
ALL THIS HAIR SO BRIGHT AND WHITE... SOFTEN UP TO PALE SUNLIGHT.
Oh, I SEE. SO WE'RE JUST CHUCKING ALL OUR PROMISES AT THE FIRST SIGHT OF THE SMALLEST TROUBLE?
IT'S BEEN A LONG TIME SINCE YOU WERE A TEENAGER, SALEM...THEY'RE AWFUL... ANYTHING THAT MAKES YOU DIFFERENT MAKES YOU--
INTERESTING?
--A *TARGET*.
MY PEERS ARE MONSTERS, SALEM.
MONSTERS? Oh, CHILD, IF ONLY THOU HADST SEEN WHAT I HADST SEEN.

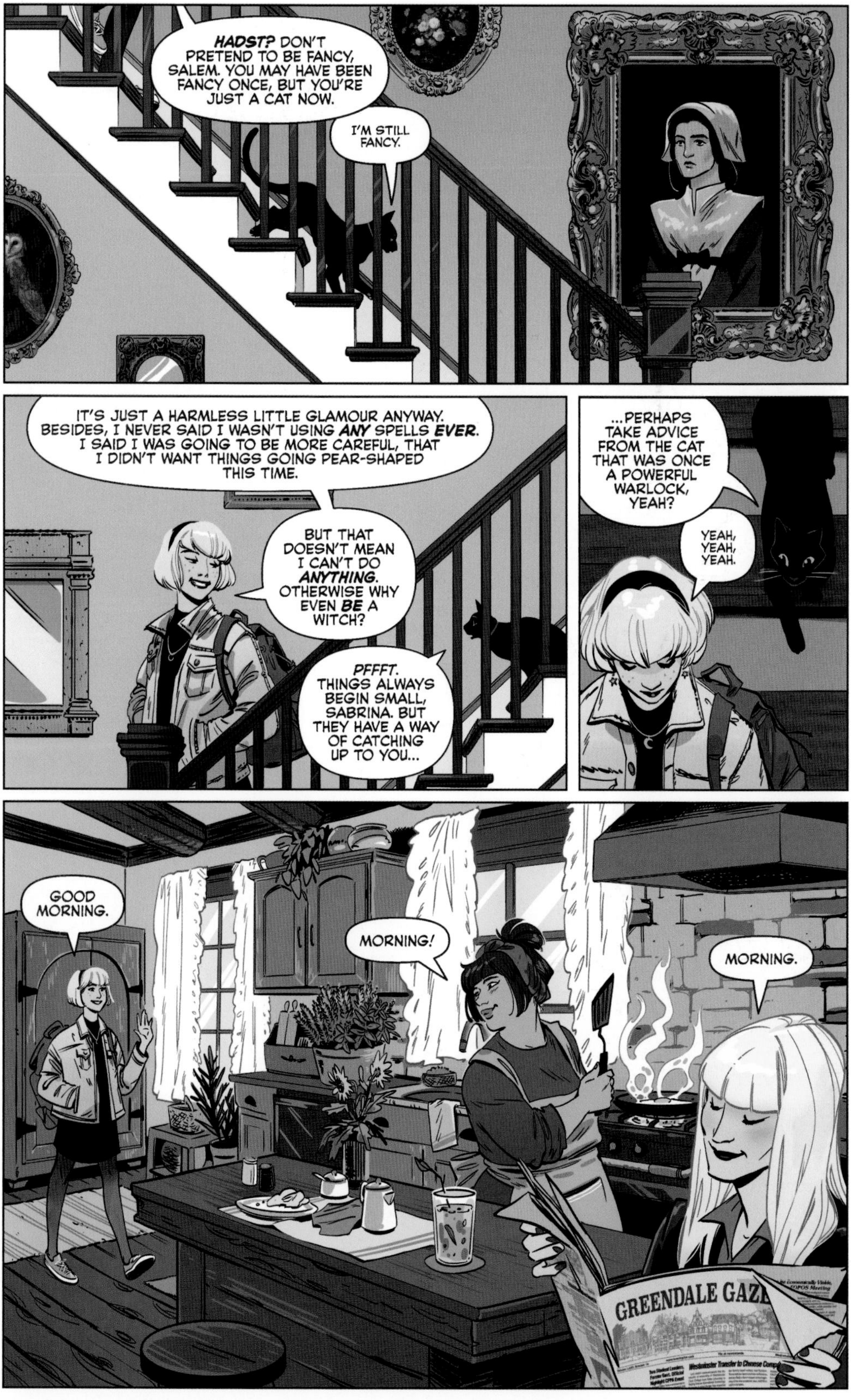
HADST? DON'T PRETEND TO BE FANCY, SALEM. YOU MAY HAVE BEEN FANCY ONCE, BUT YOU'RE JUST A CAT NOW.
I'M STILL FANCY.
IT'S JUST A HARMLESS LITTLE GLAMOUR ANYWAY. BESIDES, I NEVER SAID I WASN'T USING ANY SPELLS EVER. I SAID I WAS GOING TO BE MORE CAREFUL, THAT I DIDN'T WANT THINGS GOING PEAR-SHAPED THIS TIME.
BUT THAT DOESN'T MEAN I CAN'T DO ANYTHING. OTHERWISE WHY EVEN BE A WITCH?
PFFFT. THINGS ALWAYS BEGIN SMALL, SABRINA. BUT THEY HAVE A WAY OF CATCHING UP TO YOU...
...PERHAPS TAKE ADVICE FROM THE CAT THAT WAS ONCE A POWERFUL WARLOCK, YEAH?
YEAH, YEAH, YEAH.
GOOD MORNING.
MORNING!
MORNING.
GREENDALE GAZE

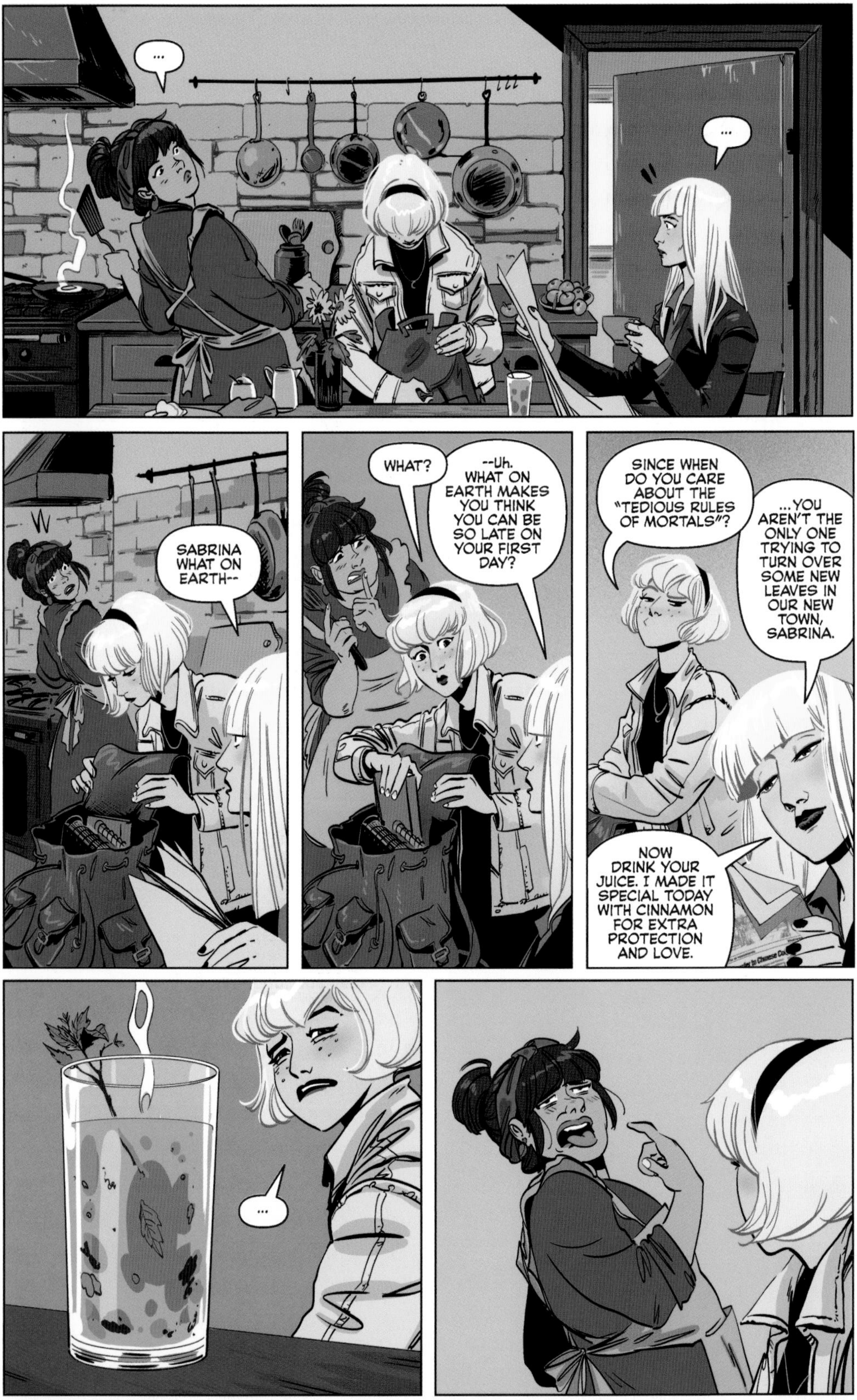
...
...
SABRINA WHAT ON EARTH--
WHAT?
--Uh. WHAT ON EARTH MAKES YOU THINK YOU CAN BE SO LATE ON YOUR FIRST DAY?
SINCE WHEN DO YOU CARE ABOUT THE "TEDIOUS RULES OF MORTALS"?
...YOU AREN'T THE ONLY ONE TRYING TO TURN OVER SOME NEW LEAVES IN OUR NEW TOWN, SABRINA.
NOW DRINK YOUR JUICE. I MADE IT SPECIAL TODAY WITH CINNAMON FOR EXTRA PROTECTION AND LOVE.
...

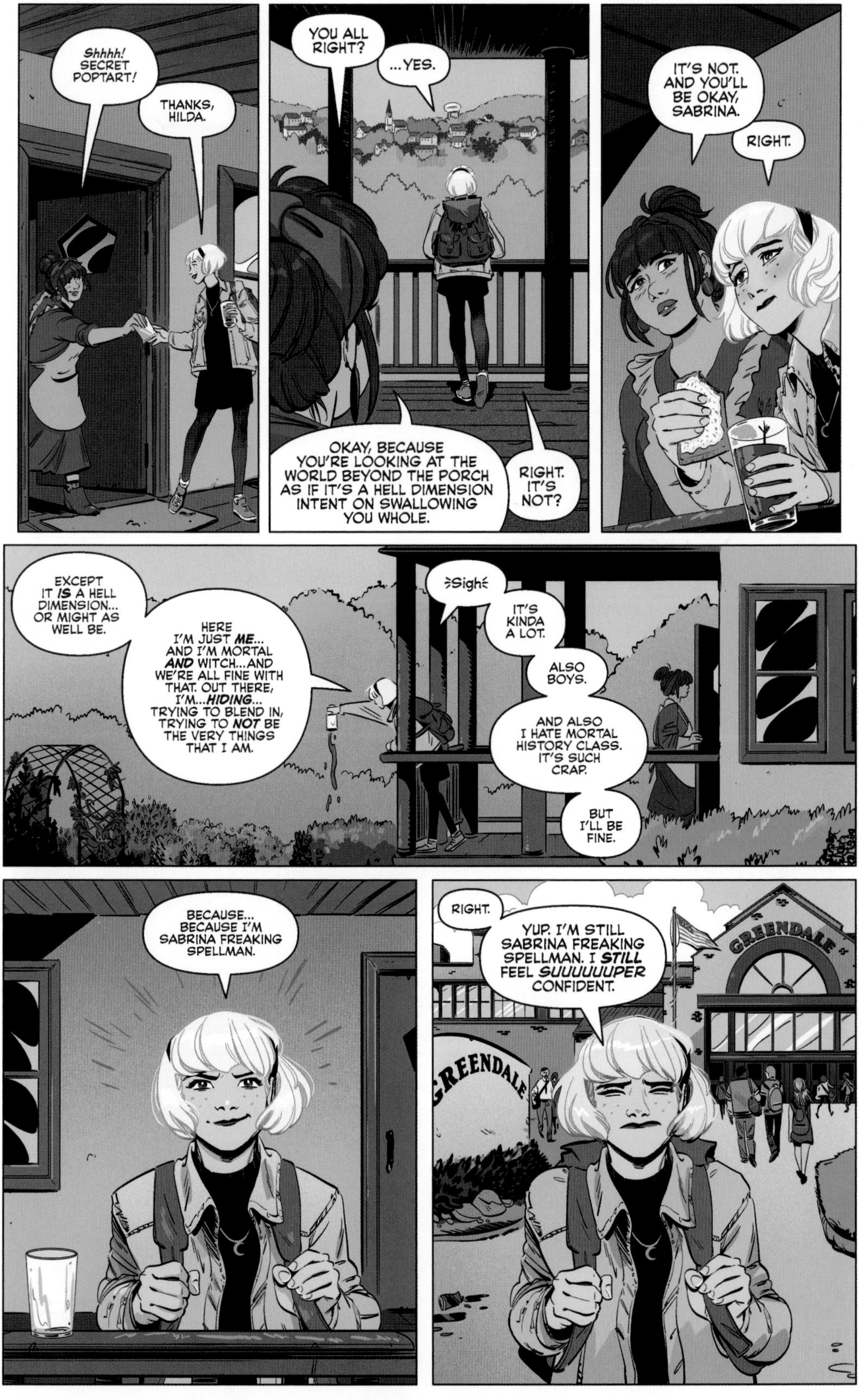
Shhhh! SECRET POPTART!
THANKS, HILDA.
YOU ALL RIGHT?
...YES.
OKAY, BECAUSE YOU'RE LOOKING AT THE WORLD BEYOND THE PORCH AS IF IT'S A HELL DIMENSION INTENT ON SWALLOWING YOU WHOLE.
RIGHT. IT'S NOT?
IT'S NOT. AND YOU'LL BE OKAY, SABRINA.
RIGHT.
EXCEPT IT ***IS*** A HELL DIMENSION... OR MIGHT AS WELL BE.
HERE I'M JUST ***ME***... AND I'M MORTAL ***AND*** WITCH...AND WE'RE ALL FINE WITH THAT. OUT THERE, I'M...***HIDING***... TRYING TO BLEND IN, TRYING TO ***NOT*** BE THE VERY THINGS THAT I AM.
Sigh
IT'S KINDA A LOT.
ALSO BOYS.
AND ALSO I HATE MORTAL HISTORY CLASS. IT'S SUCH CRAP.
BUT I'LL BE FINE.
BECAUSE... BECAUSE I'M SABRINA FREAKING SPELLMAN.
RIGHT.
YUP. I'M STILL SABRINA FREAKING SPELLMAN. I ***STILL*** FEEL ***SUUUUUUPER*** CONFIDENT.
GREENDALE
GREENDALE

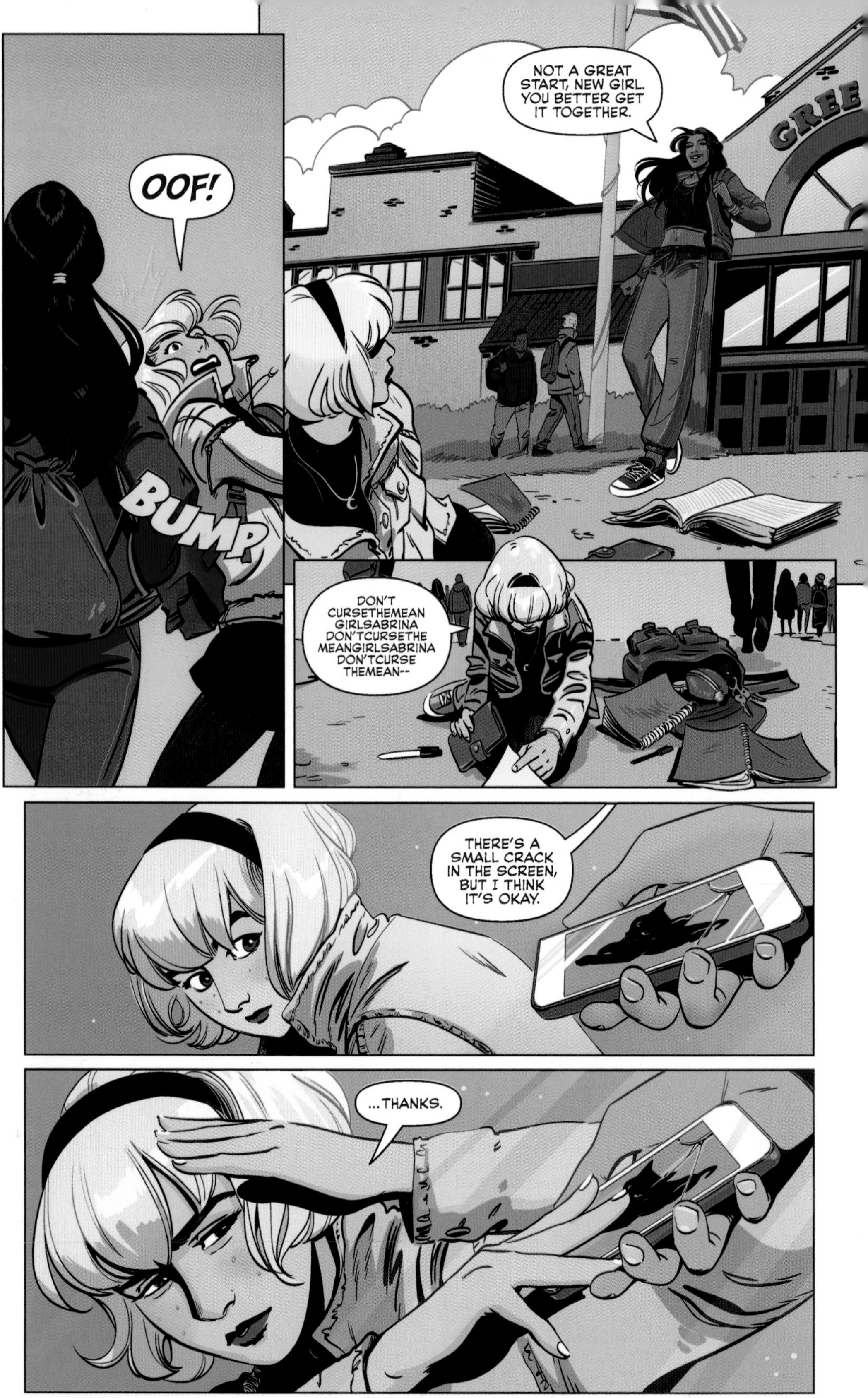
OOF!
BUMP
NOT A GREAT START, NEW GIRL. YOU BETTER GET IT TOGETHER.
GREE
DON'T CURSETHEMEAN GIRLSABRINA DON'TCURSETHE MEANGIRLSABRINA DON'TCURSE THEMEAN--
THERE'S A SMALL CRACK IN THE SCREEN, BUT I THINK IT'S OKAY.
...THANKS.

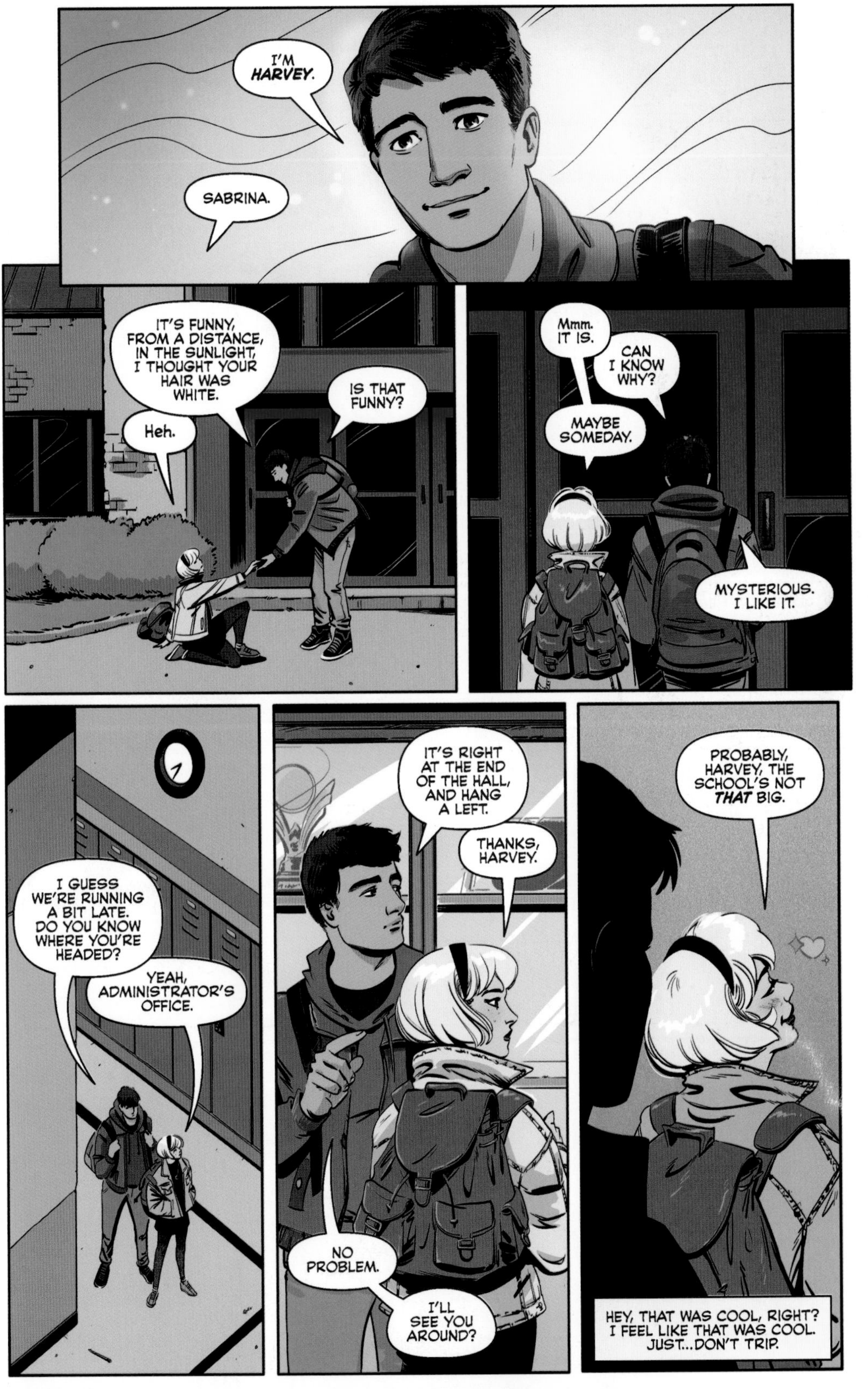
I'M *HARVEY*.
SABRINA.
IT'S FUNNY, FROM A DISTANCE, IN THE SUNLIGHT, I THOUGHT YOUR HAIR WAS WHITE.
Heh.
IS THAT FUNNY?
Mmm. IT IS.
CAN I KNOW WHY?
MAYBE SOMEDAY.
MYSTERIOUS. I LIKE IT.
I GUESS WE'RE RUNNING A BIT LATE. DO YOU KNOW WHERE YOU'RE HEADED?
YEAH, ADMINISTRATOR'S OFFICE.
IT'S RIGHT AT THE END OF THE HALL, AND HANG A LEFT.
THANKS, HARVEY.
NO PROBLEM.
I'LL SEE YOU AROUND?
PROBABLY, HARVEY, THE SCHOOL'S NOT *THAT* BIG.
HEY, THAT WAS COOL, RIGHT? I FEEL LIKE THAT WAS COOL. JUST...DON'T TRIP.

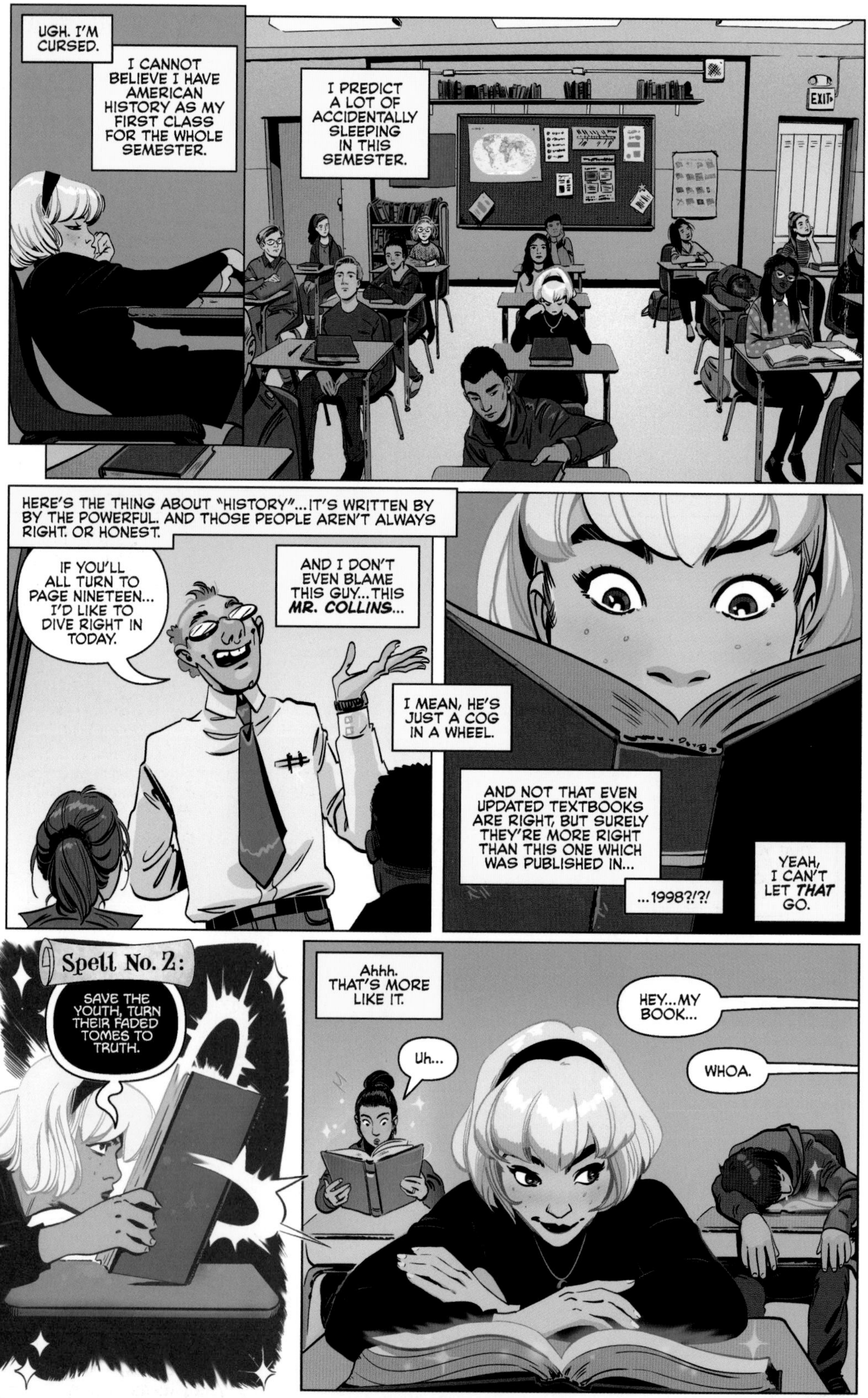
UGH. I'M CURSED.
I CANNOT BELIEVE I HAVE AMERICAN HISTORY AS MY FIRST CLASS FOR THE WHOLE SEMESTER.
I PREDICT A LOT OF ACCIDENTALLY SLEEPING IN THIS SEMESTER.
EXIT
HERE'S THE THING ABOUT "HISTORY"...IT'S WRITTEN BY BY THE POWERFUL. AND THOSE PEOPLE AREN'T ALWAYS RIGHT. OR HONEST.
IF YOU'LL ALL TURN TO PAGE NINETEEN... I'D LIKE TO DIVE RIGHT IN TODAY.
AND I DON'T EVEN BLAME THIS GUY...THIS MR. COLLINS...
I MEAN, HE'S JUST A COG IN A WHEEL.
AND NOT THAT EVEN UPDATED TEXTBOOKS ARE RIGHT, BUT SURELY THEY'RE MORE RIGHT THAN THIS ONE WHICH WAS PUBLISHED IN...
...1998?!?!
YEAH, I CAN'T LET THAT GO.
Spell No. 2:
SAVE THE YOUTH, TURN THEIR FADED TOMES TO TRUTH.
Ahhh. THAT'S MORE LIKE IT.
HEY...MY BOOK...
Uh...
WHOA.

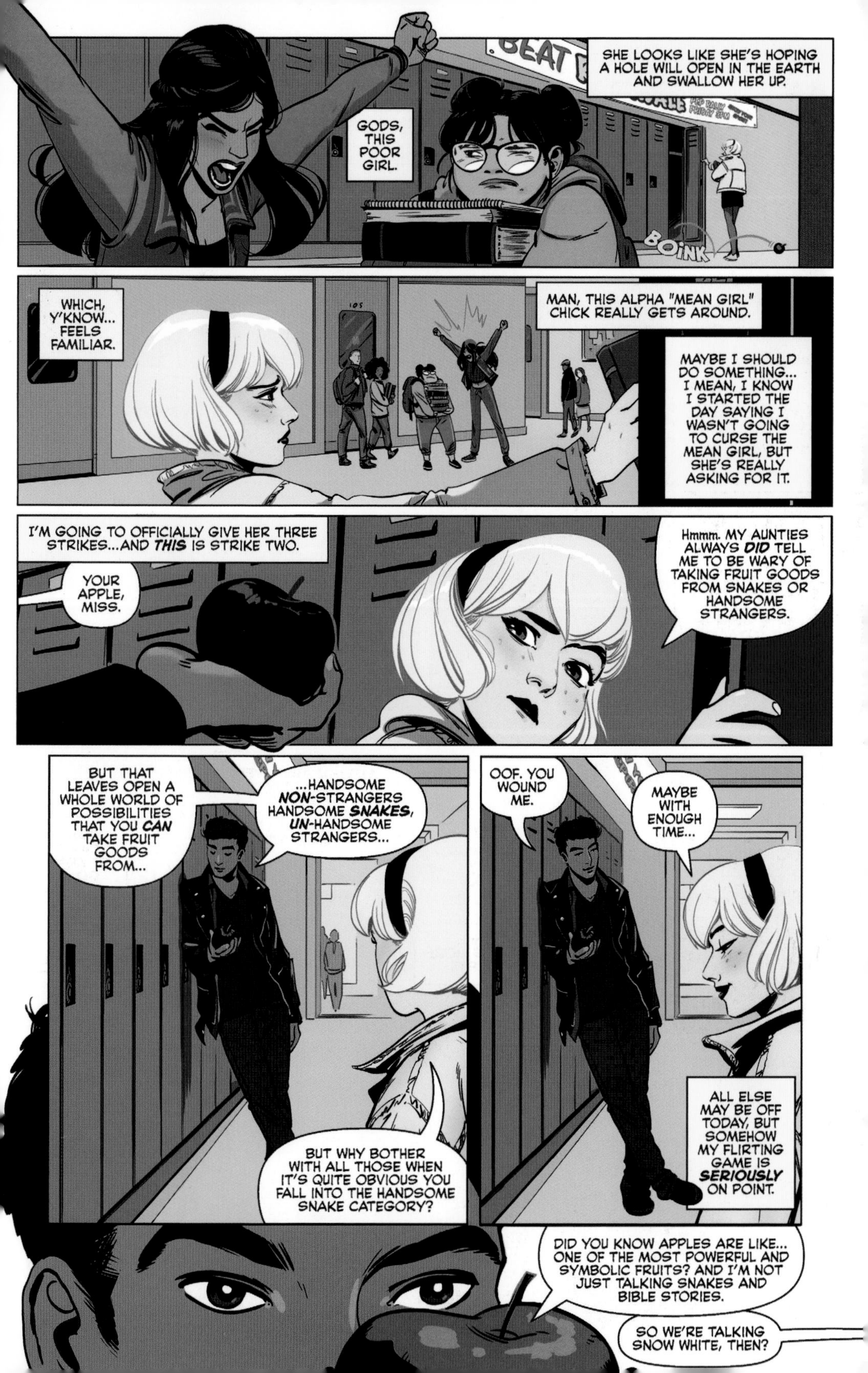
SHE LOOKS LIKE SHE'S HOPING A HOLE WILL OPEN IN THE EARTH AND SWALLOW HER UP.
GODS, THIS POOR GIRL.
BEAT
BOiNK
WHICH, Y'KNOW... FEELS FAMILIAR.
MAN, THIS ALPHA "MEAN GIRL" CHICK REALLY GETS AROUND.
MAYBE I SHOULD DO SOMETHING... I MEAN, I KNOW I STARTED THE DAY SAYING I WASN'T GOING TO CURSE THE MEAN GIRL, BUT SHE'S REALLY ASKING FOR IT.
I'M GOING TO OFFICIALLY GIVE HER THREE STRIKES...AND ***THIS*** IS STRIKE TWO.
YOUR APPLE, MISS.
Hmmm. MY AUNTIES ALWAYS ***DID*** TELL ME TO BE WARY OF TAKING FRUIT GOODS FROM SNAKES OR HANDSOME STRANGERS.
BUT THAT LEAVES OPEN A WHOLE WORLD OF POSSIBILITIES THAT YOU ***CAN*** TAKE FRUIT GOODS FROM...
...HANDSOME ***NON***-STRANGERS HANDSOME ***SNAKES***, ***UN***-HANDSOME STRANGERS...
BUT WHY BOTHER WITH ALL THOSE WHEN IT'S QUITE OBVIOUS YOU FALL INTO THE HANDSOME SNAKE CATEGORY?
OOF. YOU WOUND ME.
MAYBE WITH ENOUGH TIME...
ALL ELSE MAY BE OFF TODAY, BUT SOMEHOW MY FLIRTING GAME IS ***SERIOUSLY*** ON POINT.
DID YOU KNOW APPLES ARE LIKE... ONE OF THE MOST POWERFUL AND SYMBOLIC FRUITS? AND I'M NOT JUST TALKING SNAKES AND BIBLE STORIES.
SO WE'RE TALKING SNOW WHITE, THEN?

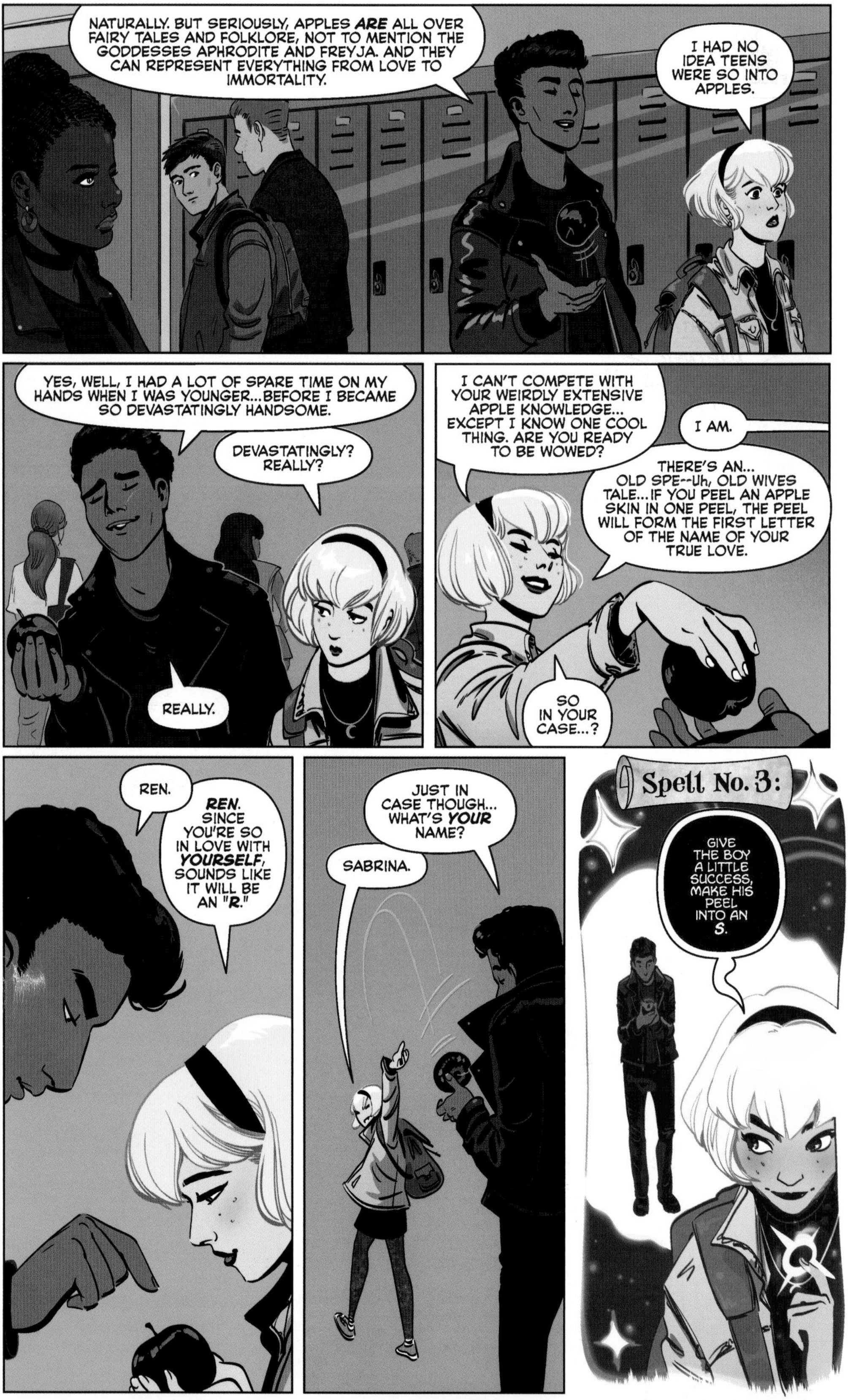
NATURALLY. BUT SERIOUSLY, APPLES ARE ALL OVER FAIRY TALES AND FOLKLORE, NOT TO MENTION THE GODDESSES APHRODITE AND FREYJA. AND THEY CAN REPRESENT EVERYTHING FROM LOVE TO IMMORTALITY.
I HAD NO IDEA TEENS WERE SO INTO APPLES.
YES, WELL, I HAD A LOT OF SPARE TIME ON MY HANDS WHEN I WAS YOUNGER...BEFORE I BECAME SO DEVASTATINGLY HANDSOME.
DEVASTATINGLY? REALLY?
REALLY.
I CAN'T COMPETE WITH YOUR WEIRDLY EXTENSIVE APPLE KNOWLEDGE... EXCEPT I KNOW ONE COOL THING. ARE YOU READY TO BE WOWED?
I AM.
THERE'S AN... OLD SPE--UH, OLD WIVES TALE...IF YOU PEEL AN APPLE SKIN IN ONE PEEL, THE PEEL WILL FORM THE FIRST LETTER OF THE NAME OF YOUR TRUE LOVE.
SO IN YOUR CASE...?
REN.
REN. SINCE YOU'RE SO IN LOVE WITH YOURSELF, SOUNDS LIKE IT WILL BE AN "R."
JUST IN CASE THOUGH... WHAT'S YOUR NAME?
SABRINA.
Spell No. 3:
GIVE THE BOY A LITTLE SUCCESS, MAKE HIS PEEL INTO AN S.

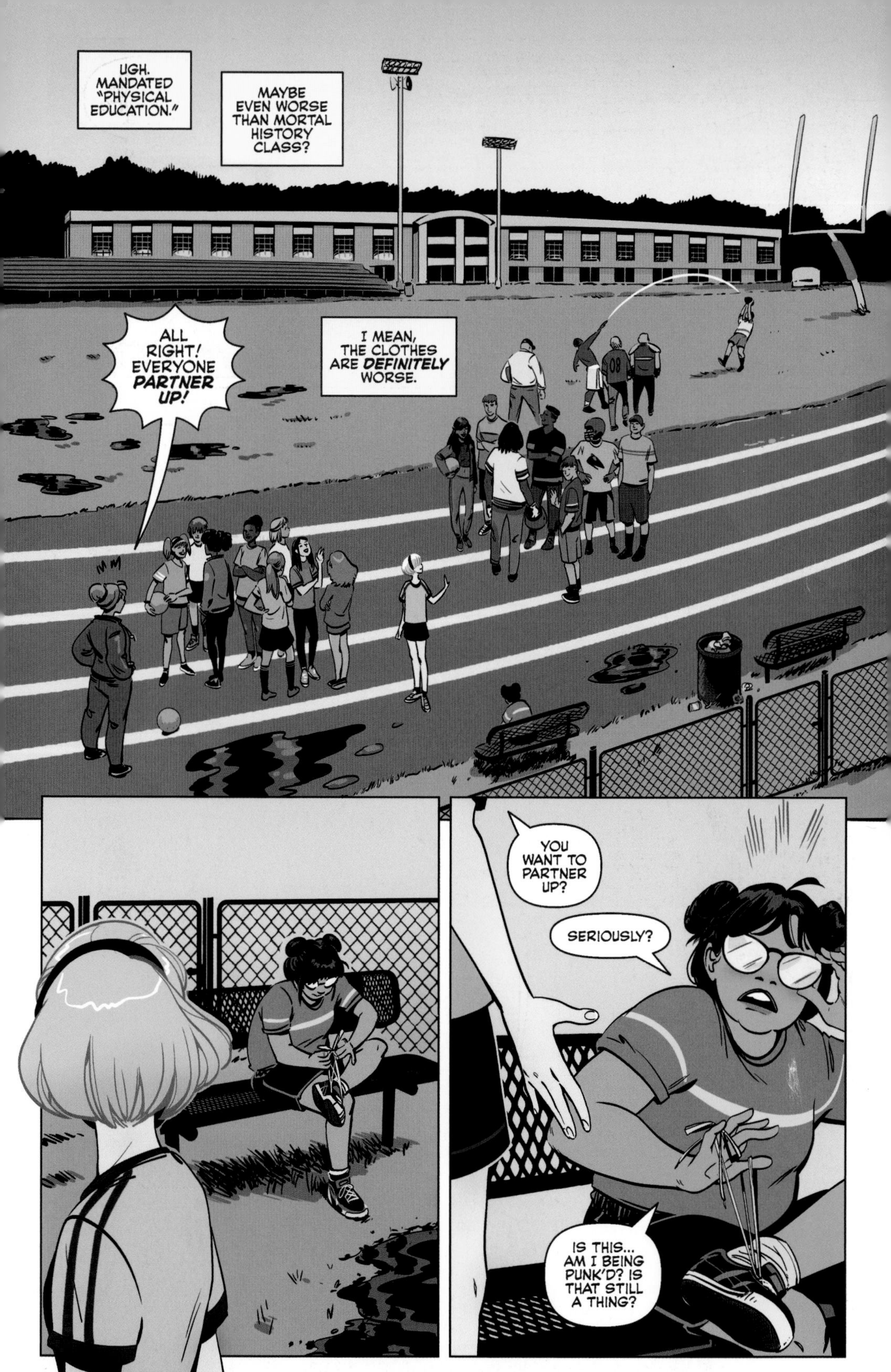
UGH. MANDATED "PHYSICAL EDUCATION."
MAYBE EVEN WORSE THAN MORTAL HISTORY CLASS?
ALL RIGHT! EVERYONE *PARTNER UP!*
I MEAN, THE CLOTHES ARE *DEFINITELY* WORSE.
YOU WANT TO PARTNER UP?
SERIOUSLY?
IS THIS... AM I BEING PUNK'D? IS THAT STILL A THING?

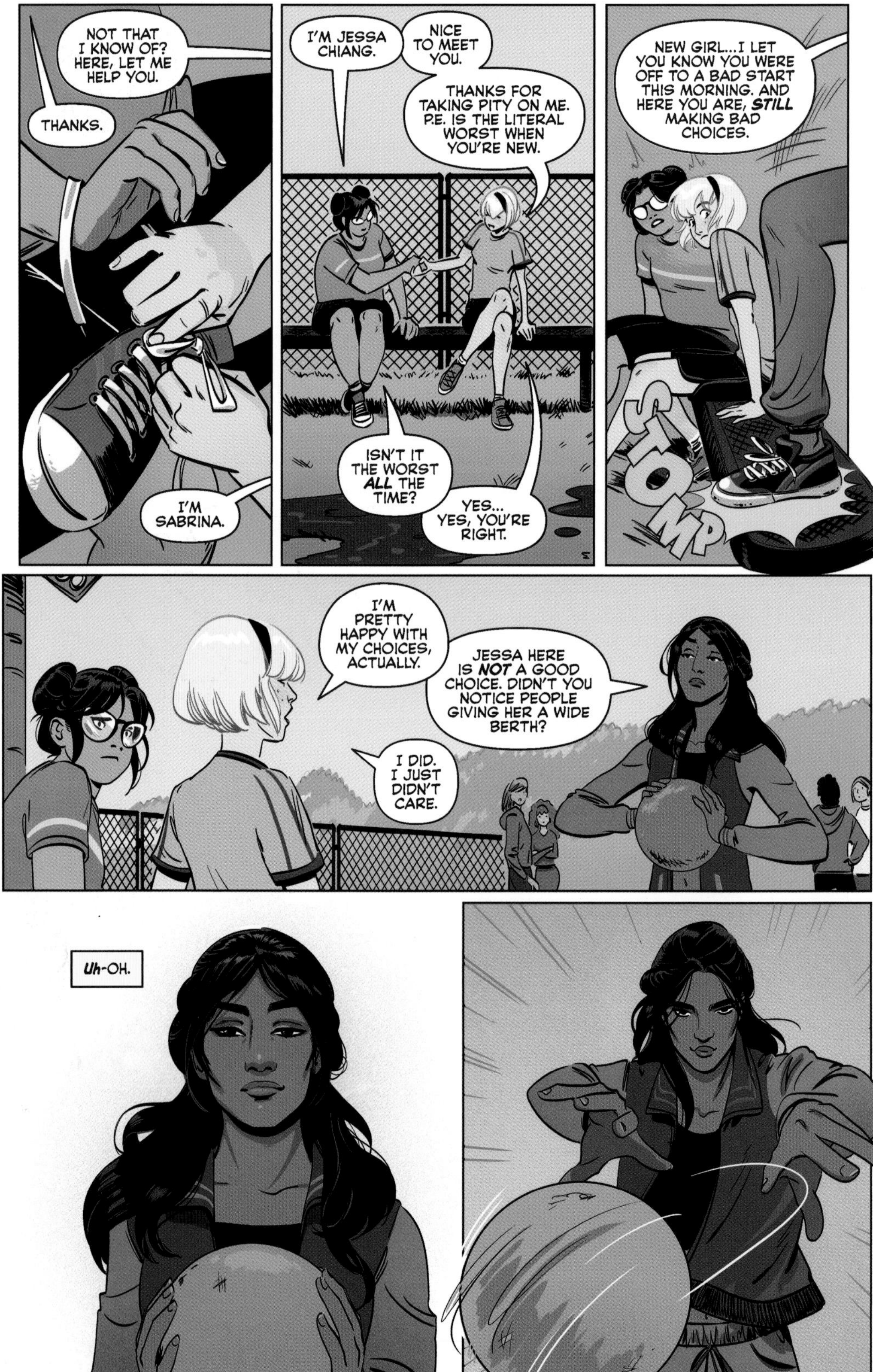
NOT THAT I KNOW OF? HERE, LET ME HELP YOU.
THANKS.
I'M SABRINA.
I'M JESSA CHIANG.
NICE TO MEET YOU.
THANKS FOR TAKING PITY ON ME. P.E. IS THE LITERAL WORST WHEN YOU'RE NEW.
ISN'T IT THE WORST ALL THE TIME?
YES... YES, YOU'RE RIGHT.
NEW GIRL...I LET YOU KNOW YOU WERE OFF TO A BAD START THIS MORNING. AND HERE YOU ARE, STILL MAKING BAD CHOICES.
STOMP
I'M PRETTY HAPPY WITH MY CHOICES, ACTUALLY.
JESSA HERE IS NOT A GOOD CHOICE. DIDN'T YOU NOTICE PEOPLE GIVING HER A WIDE BERTH?
I DID. I JUST DIDN'T CARE.
Uh-OH.

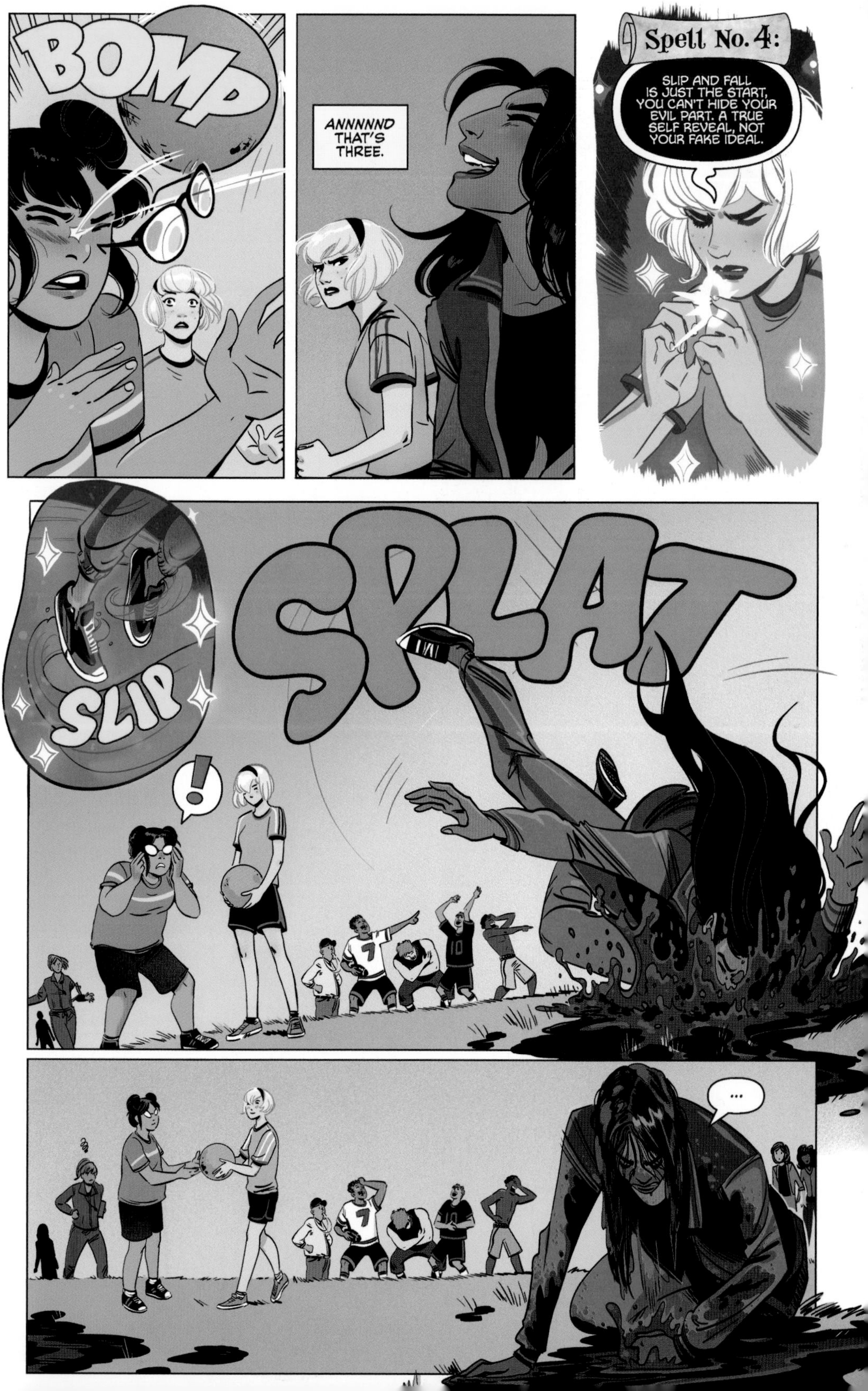

BOMP
ANNNNND THAT'S THREE.
Spell No. 4:
SLIP AND FALL IS JUST THE START, YOU CAN'T HIDE YOUR EVIL PART. A TRUE SELF REVEAL, NOT YOUR FAKE IDEAL.
SLIP
SPLAT
!
...

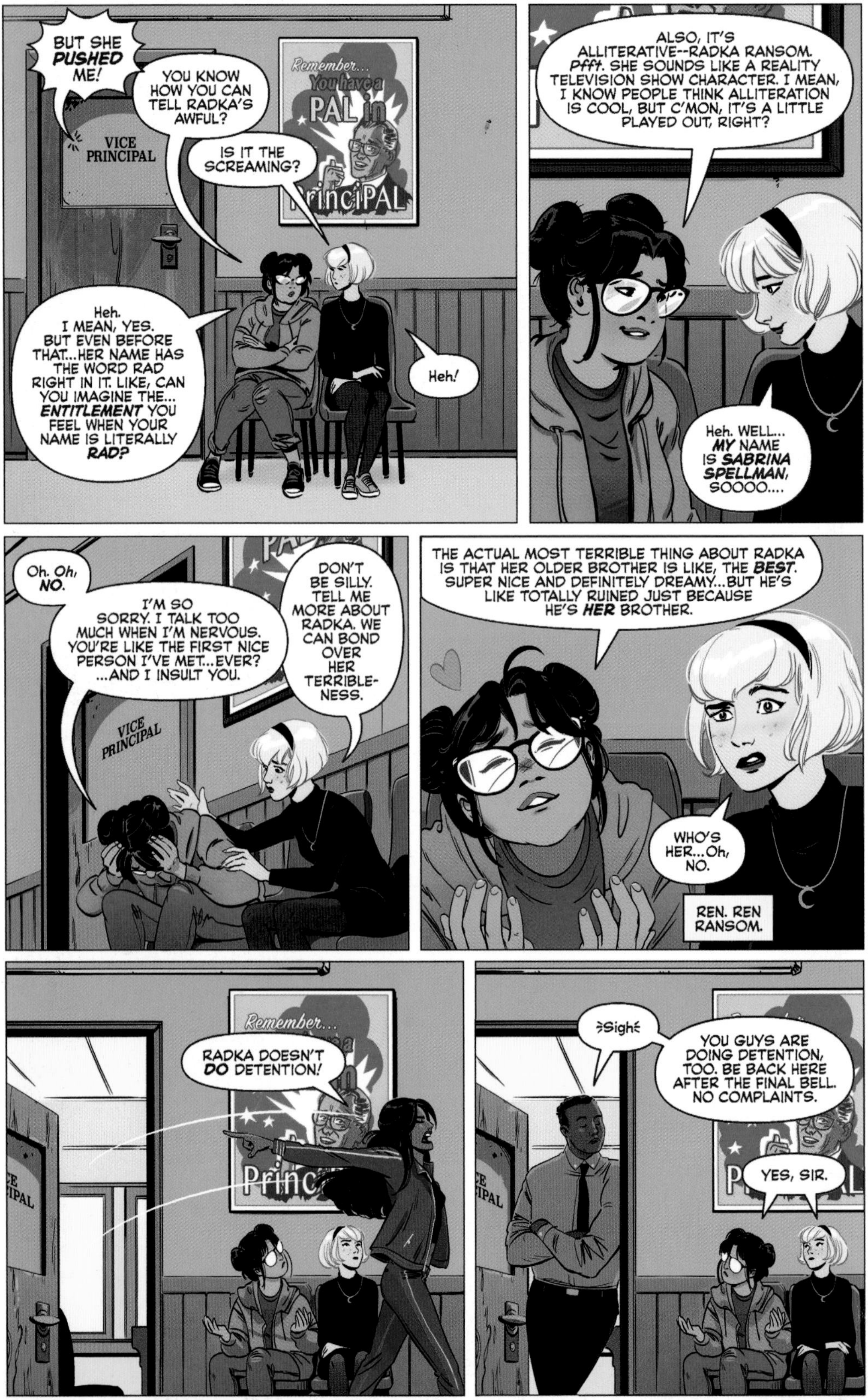
BUT SHE PUSHED ME!
YOU KNOW HOW YOU CAN TELL RADKA'S AWFUL?
IS IT THE SCREAMING?
Heh. I MEAN, YES. BUT EVEN BEFORE THAT...HER NAME HAS THE WORD RAD RIGHT IN IT. LIKE, CAN YOU IMAGINE THE... ENTITLEMENT YOU FEEL WHEN YOUR NAME IS LITERALLY RAD?
Heh!
VICE PRINCIPAL
Remember... You have a PAL in PrinciPAL
ALSO, IT'S ALLITERATIVE--RADKA RANSOM. Pfft. SHE SOUNDS LIKE A REALITY TELEVISION SHOW CHARACTER. I MEAN, I KNOW PEOPLE THINK ALLITERATION IS COOL, BUT C'MON, IT'S A LITTLE PLAYED OUT, RIGHT?
Heh. WELL... MY NAME IS SABRINA SPELLMAN, SOOOO....
Oh. Oh, NO.
I'M SO SORRY. I TALK TOO MUCH WHEN I'M NERVOUS. YOU'RE LIKE THE FIRST NICE PERSON I'VE MET...EVER? ...AND I INSULT YOU.
DON'T BE SILLY. TELL ME MORE ABOUT RADKA. WE CAN BOND OVER HER TERRIBLE-NESS.
VICE PRINCIPAL
THE ACTUAL MOST TERRIBLE THING ABOUT RADKA IS THAT HER OLDER BROTHER IS LIKE, THE BEST. SUPER NICE AND DEFINITELY DREAMY...BUT HE'S LIKE TOTALLY RUINED JUST BECAUSE HE'S HER BROTHER.
WHO'S HER...Oh, NO.
REN. REN RANSOM.
Remember...
RADKA DOESN'T DO DETENTION!
PrinciPAL
Sigh
YOU GUYS ARE DOING DETENTION, TOO. BE BACK HERE AFTER THE FINAL BELL. NO COMPLAINTS.
YES, SIR.

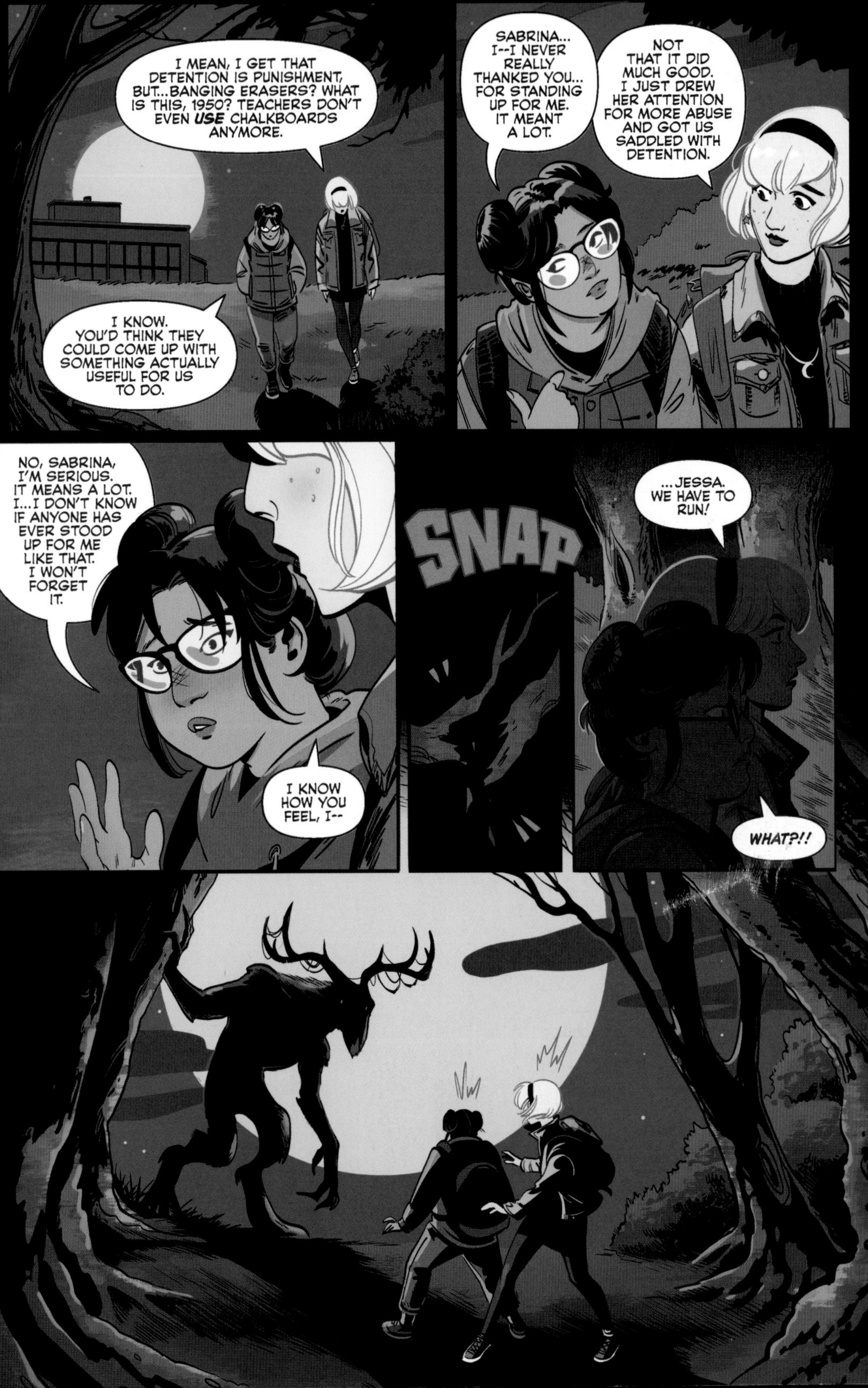
I MEAN, I GET THAT DETENTION IS PUNISHMENT, BUT...BANGING ERASERS? WHAT IS THIS, 1950? TEACHERS DON'T EVEN USE CHALKBOARDS ANYMORE.
I KNOW. YOU'D THINK THEY COULD COME UP WITH SOMETHING ACTUALLY USEFUL FOR US TO DO.
SABRINA... I--I NEVER REALLY THANKED YOU... FOR STANDING UP FOR ME. IT MEANT A LOT.
NOT THAT IT DID MUCH GOOD. I JUST DREW HER ATTENTION FOR MORE ABUSE AND GOT US SADDLED WITH DETENTION.
NO, SABRINA, I'M SERIOUS. IT MEANS A LOT. I...I DON'T KNOW IF ANYONE HAS EVER STOOD UP FOR ME LIKE THAT. I WON'T FORGET IT.
I KNOW HOW YOU FEEL, I--
SNAP
...JESSA. WE HAVE TO RUN!
WHAT?!!

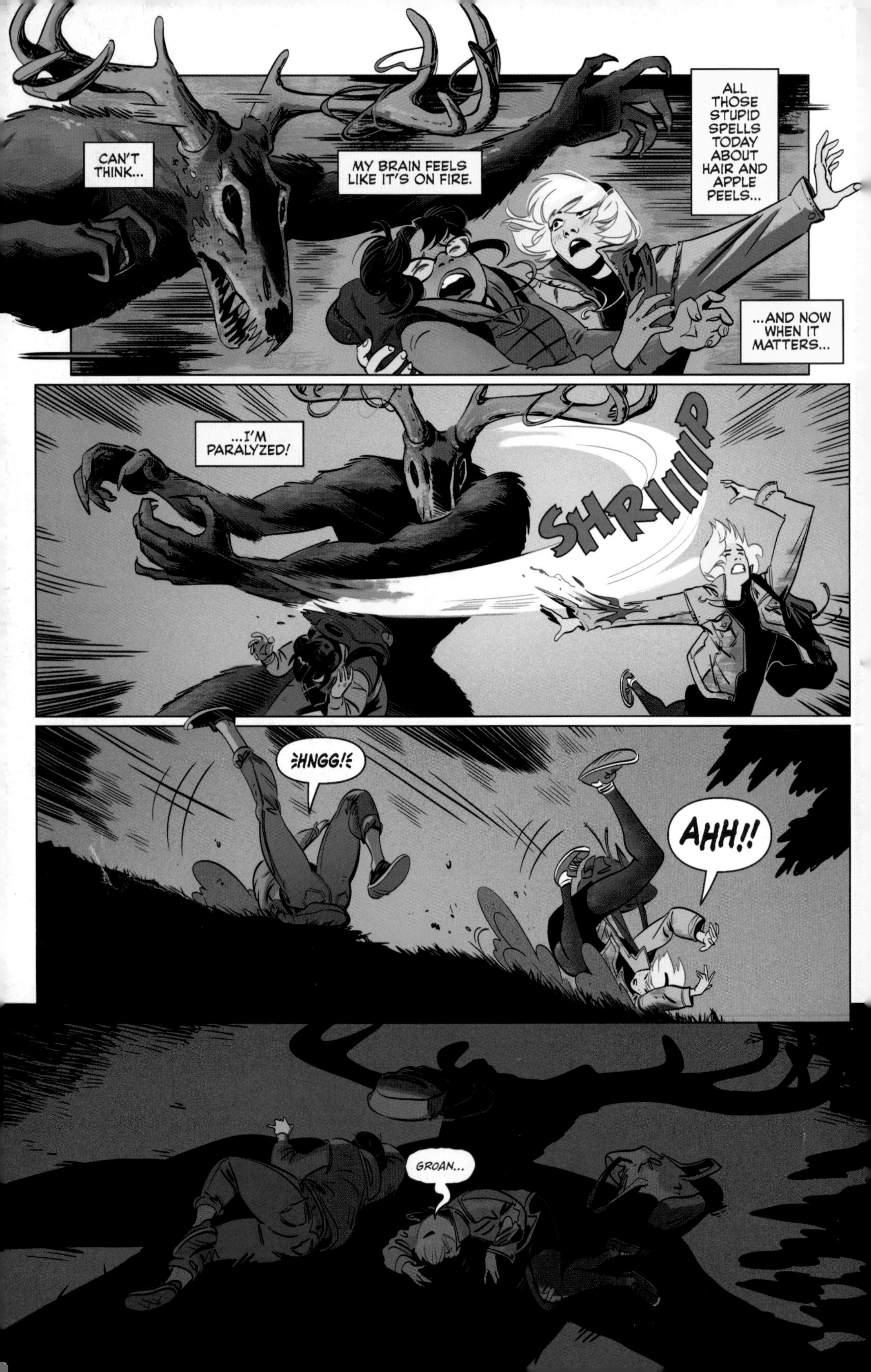
CAN'T THINK...
MY BRAIN FEELS LIKE IT'S ON FIRE.
ALL THOSE STUPID SPELLS TODAY ABOUT HAIR AND APPLE PEELS...
...AND NOW WHEN IT MATTERS...
...I'M PARALYZED!
SHRIIIIP
HNGG!
AHH!!
GROAN...

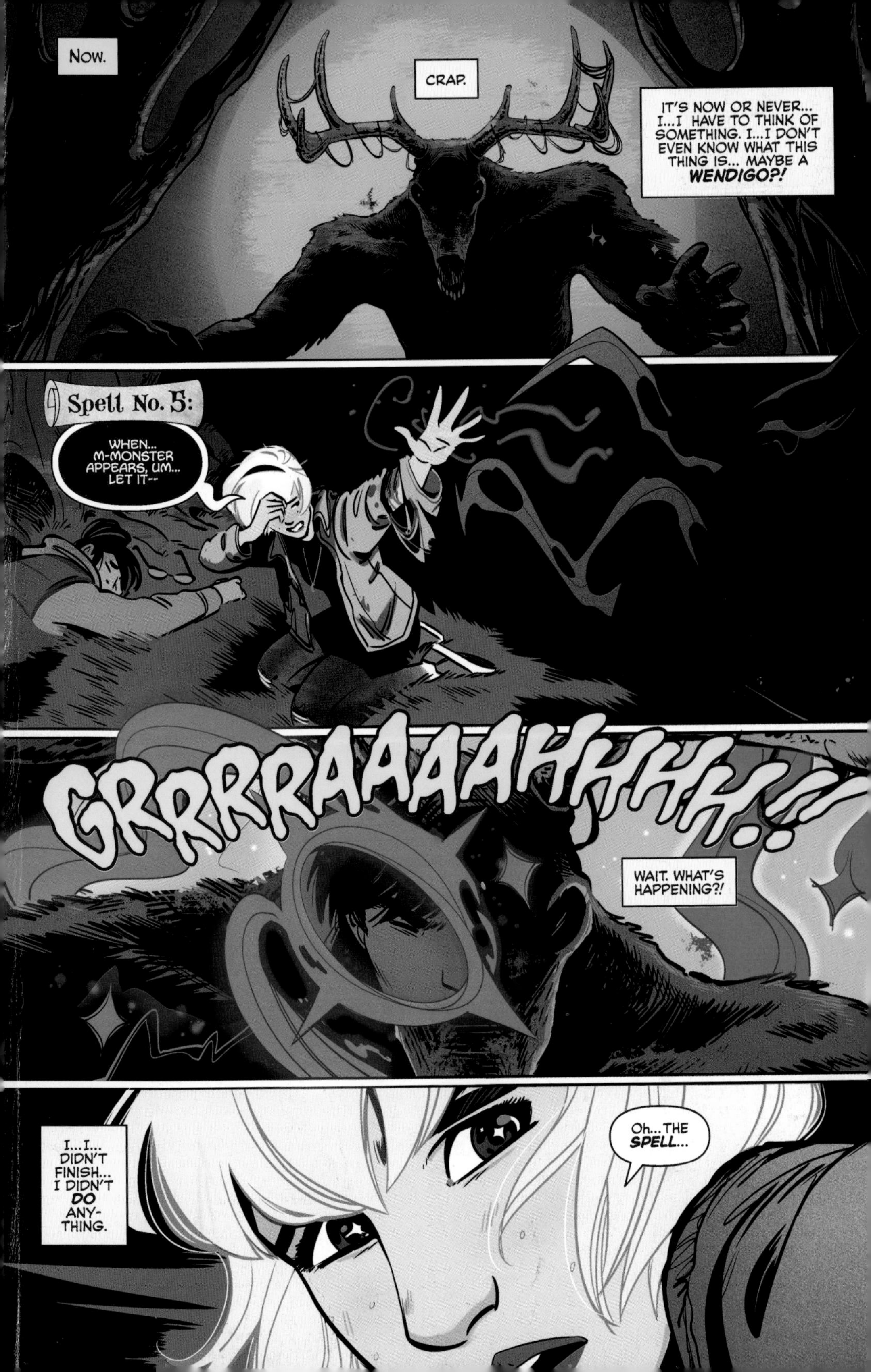
NOW.
CRAP.
IT'S NOW OR NEVER... I...I HAVE TO THINK OF SOMETHING. I...I DON'T EVEN KNOW WHAT THIS THING IS... MAYBE A WENDIGO?!
Spell No. 5:
WHEN... M-MONSTER APPEARS, UM... LET IT--
GRRRRAAAAHHHH!!!
WAIT. WHAT'S HAPPENING?!
I...I... DIDN'T FINISH... I DIDN'T DO ANY-THING.
Oh... THE SPELL...

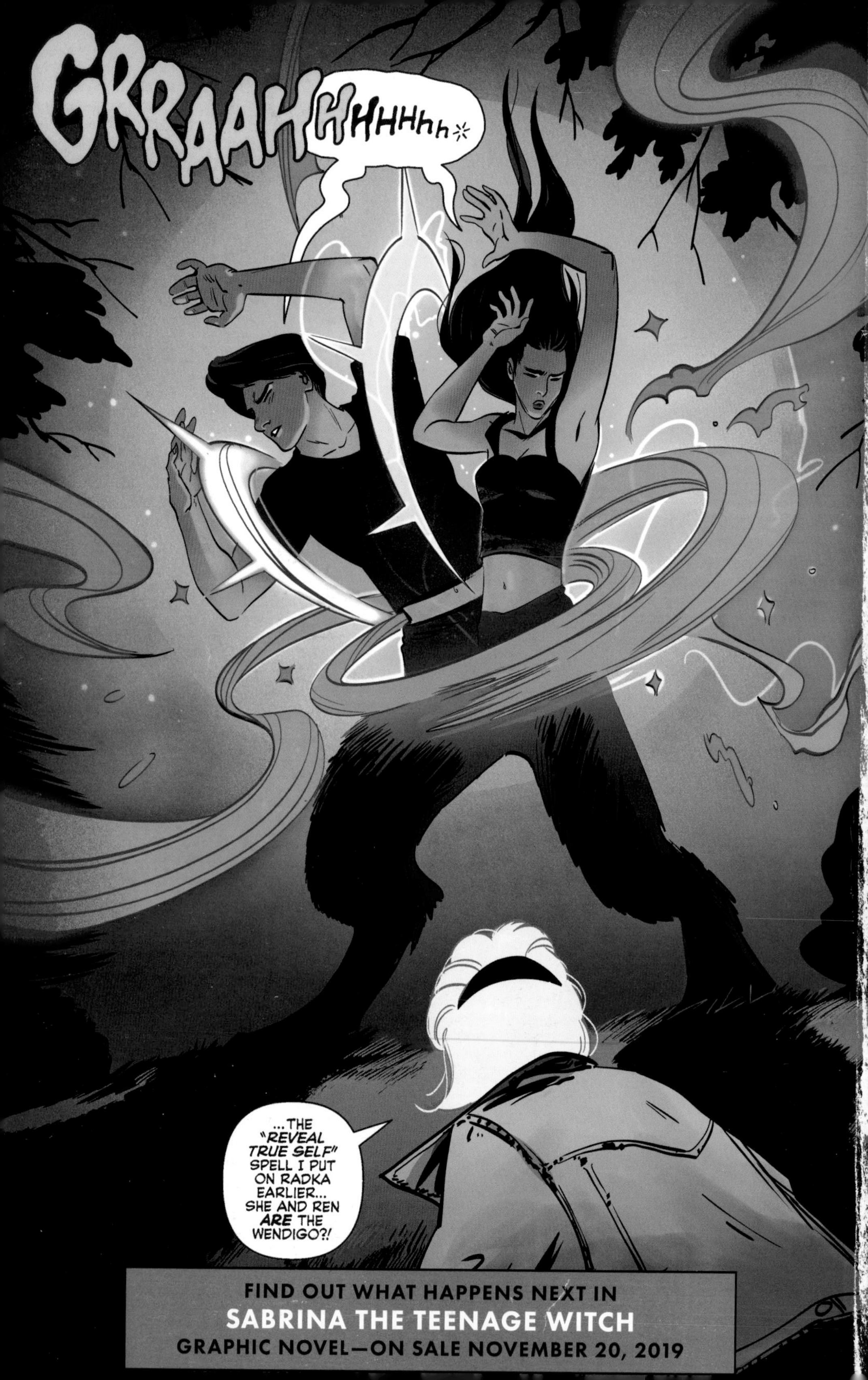
GRRAAHHHHhh
...THE "REVEAL TRUE SELF" SPELL I PUT ON RADKA EARLIER... SHE AND REN ARE THE WENDIGO?!
FIND OUT WHAT HAPPENS NEXT IN
SABRINA THE TEENAGE WITCH
GRAPHIC NOVEL—ON SALE NOVEMBER 20, 2019